PRAISE FOR HER FIRST MISTAKE

"As in any good thriller, the narration, the dialogue, and the action draw us deeper and deeper into the life of the main character."

—Bookreporter

"This will satisfy."

Publishers Weekly

PRAISE FOR THE COLUMBIA RIVER SERIES

"[A] gripping novel of suspense from Elliot . . . Elliot skillfully unravels layers of intersecting stories, each one integral to the overall story of the Mills family and their small-town secrets. Readers will want to see more from this author."

—*Publishers Weekly*

"Elliot succeeds in creating both a thrilling mystery and a fascinating character study of the people inhabiting these pages."

—Bookreporter

"With her riveting, narrative-driven, deftly crafted storytelling style as a novelist, Kendra Elliot's *The Last Sister* will prove to be a welcome and enduringly popular addition to community library Mystery/Suspense/Thriller collections."

—*Midwest Book Review*

"Suspense on top of suspense. This one will keep you guessing until the final page and shows Elliot at her very best."

—*The Real Book Spy*

"Every family has skeletons. Kendra Elliot's tale of the Mills family's dark secrets is first-rate suspense. Dark and gripping, *The Last Sister* crescendos to knock-out, edge-of-your seat tension."

—Robert Dugoni, bestselling author of *My Sister's Grave*

"*The Last Sister* is exciting and suspenseful! Engaging characters and a complex plot kept me on the edge of my seat until the very last page."

—T.R. Ragan, bestselling author of the Jessie Cole series

"Thriller Award finalist Elliot's well-paced sequel to *The Last Sister* opens at the home of fifty-two-year-old Reuben Braswell, a devotee of conspiracy theories, who's lying dead in his bathtub . . . The twist ending will catch most readers by surprise . . . [and] fans will look forward to seeing characters from the author's other series take the lead in future installments."

—*Publishers Weekly*

"Elliot skillfully interweaves the various plot threads, and credible, mostly sympathetic characters match the lovingly described locale. Fans of contemporary regional mysteries will be rewarded."

—*Publishers Weekly*

NO ONE KNEW

ALSO BY KENDRA ELLIOT

Echo Road

NOELLE MARSHALL NOVELS

Her First Mistake

COLUMBIA RIVER NOVELS

The Last Sister
The Silence
In the Pines
The First Death
At the River
The Next Grave

MERCY KILPATRICK NOVELS

A Merciful Death
A Merciful Truth
A Merciful Secret
A Merciful Silence
A Merciful Fate
A Merciful Promise

BONE SECRETS NOVELS

Hidden
Chilled
Buried
Alone
Known

BONE SECRETS NOVELLAS

Veiled

CALLAHAN & MCLANE NOVELS

PART OF THE BONE SECRETS WORLD

Vanished
Bridged
Spiraled
Targeted

ROGUE RIVER NOVELLAS

On Her Father's Grave (Rogue River)
Her Grave Secrets (Rogue River)
Dead in Her Tracks (Rogue Winter)
Death and Her Devotion (Rogue Vows)
Truth Be Told (Rogue Justice)

WIDOW'S ISLAND NOVELLAS

Close to the Bone

Bred in the Bone

Below the Bones

The Lost Bones

Bone Deep

NO ONE KNEW

KENDRA ELLIOT

Published by Montlake, Seattle
www.apub.com

EU product safety contact:
Amazon Media EU S. à r.l.
38, avenue John F. Kennedy, L-1855 Luxembourg
amazonpublishing-gpsr@amazon.com

ISBN-13: 9781662525780 (hardcover)
ISBN-13: 9781662525803 (paperback)
ISBN-13: 9781662525797 (digital)

Cover design by Caroline Teagle Johnson
Cover images: © Rachel Dulson, © mdurson / Getty

Printed in the United States of America

First edition

For my girls

1

Emma Chambers had never seen a dead body.

One of the boys at school had bragged that he'd seen a motorcycle rider hit by a semi. His friends had circled around as he leaned against his locker, three down from Emma's, the boys' mouths hanging open, their eyes wide. "So cool!" Emma had made eye contact with the storyteller. He'd seen she was listening and cranked up the gore in his description. The abrupt mental image had turned her stomach, and she'd dropped her gaze. She'd hoisted her heavy anatomy and physiology textbook into her arms and slammed her locker door, turning away, knowing they watched as she left.

"Loser," one of the boys had whispered.

"Her mother bailed on them," had said another, not bothering to lower his voice.

At one time the comments would have made her face flush and her eyes water.

No more.

Remembering the hateful voices from last year, Emma sighed as she rode her bike along the quiet country road. She shoved the incident out of her mind and sucked in deep breaths of clean air. March in central Oregon was cold and crisp. The air smelled like snow, but the bright-blue sky was clear. Looking to the west, she saw the snowy peaks of the Cascade mountains and inhaled. She was excited because in a few days, heavy snow was forecast.

She loved snow.

Silver flashed off to her right, and she stopped. She laid down her bike and sidestepped down the road bank. Coors Light again. She tipped the can, shook out a few drops, and then tossed it in her plastic bag. Most of the cans in there were Coors Light. Someone—most likely multiple someones—had enjoyed their drive along the winding road, casting cans every hundred yards or so. She hauled herself back up the bank and was about to start pedaling when she realized that just yards away a red car approached, its electric motor rendering it nearly silent.

She recognized the driver.

Shit.

The small car stopped beside her, and the passenger window rolled down. Anita Forkner leaned across from the driver's seat, her silver hair ruthlessly pulled back in a long ponytail. "Emma Chambers! Isn't this a school day?"

"Yes, ma'am. But I'm homeschooled now. I have classes online this afternoon."

A lie.

"Humph." Anita narrowed her eyes at Emma, creating heavy lines between her brows. "Kids should be around other kids. This homeschooling fad is creating a bunch of unsocial pansies who can't carry a decent conversation."

Speechless, Emma nodded.

"Good to see that your parents taught you values." Anita gestured at the bag of cans. "Not sitting around playing those damned video games all day."

Emma nodded again, her face blank.

"Shouldn't you have a driver's license by now?" asked Anita with a frown at the beat-up bike.

"I got my license last year," said Emma, not adding that there was no car for her to drive. She hated this old bike of her father's, but at least she could get around. "Easier to spot cans by bike."

"Say hello to your father for me. Continue." Anita gave a regal wave, rolled up her window, and silently drove off.

Emma exhaled and rode on, keeping her ears tuned to the road behind her, not wanting to encounter any more nosy locals. Especially ones who knew her father.

A minute later, she turned off the pavement and onto a dirt track that led to a teenage party spot in the woods. It often revealed a jackpot of recyclable cans and bottles. She struggled through the deep ruts on her bike, finally dismounting and laying it down. The track threaded among hundreds of lodgepole pines that had grown around the burned remains of old tree trunks. She eventually reached a clearing covered with wide tire tracks and the blackened remains of campfires. She began to pick up cans, shaking out drops of beer and chew spit, wishing she had gloves and cursing the people who'd thrown their cans in the fires, rendering them unreturnable.

Soon her garbage bag was nearly half full. She circled out into the dense, silent woods, finding smaller stashes of empty cans where nearby used condoms suggested that couples had hunkered down, wanting some privacy. A rustling made her spin around, and a jackrabbit raced past.

"Ohhh!" She ran after him, knowing she'd never catch up but wanting another glimpse of the long ears. She was rewarded when the hare scrambled over a fallen black snag. Emma ended her chase at the crumbling burned tree. It'd been stately at one time, the trunk nearly four feet in diameter.

Resigned to the jackrabbit's disappearance, she scanned the forest floor for recyclables. Her gaze locked on a filthy Nike shoe, and she wondered if its owner had walked out of the forest with just one shoe. Enough beer could make it seem like a logical decision.

Then she saw the dark, mottled flesh. A color no living person could have. The body lay on its stomach, nude. She stood frozen as her gaze traveled up the body to its head. It faced away from Emma, dark, matted hair hiding its features.

Emma's hours-old breakfast threatened to climb up her esophagus, and she clamped a dirty hand over her mouth.

Now I've seen a dead person.

2

Deschutes County sheriff's detective Noelle Marshall knew she was in the right place when she spotted the two Eagle's Nest police vehicles on the road's shoulder. There were also two county sheriff SUVs, a county crime scene vehicle, and the medical examiner's black van, but no people in sight. She parked and swapped out her expensive leather boots for the rubber ones she kept in her new county Tahoe and headed up the soft dirt road to find some warm bodies.

And one cold body.

After a few minutes, she spotted yellow crime scene tape and a deputy.

"Detective," he said as Noelle greeted him, and he logged her name. "Everyone's that way." He pointed to the right.

"That your bike?" she joked, pointing at the faded red frame on its side a few yards away.

He grinned. "Belongs to the teenager who found the body," he said. "She was out here collecting cans."

Noelle nodded and wondered if it was the same young woman on a bike with a trash bag over her shoulder whom she'd seen near her new house. Noelle had moved into a home a few miles from the current crime scene less than a month ago. She'd sold her place in Bend—well, it was still on the market. People weren't eager to buy a house where a shooting had taken place. Noelle couldn't live in it anymore since her friend Savannah had nearly lost her life there, and her blood had soaked into the carpet.

Replacing the carpet hadn't changed how she felt about the home.

Noelle had purchased a large house on several acres outside of Eagle's Nest. Her commute to work in Bend was longer and the property was too big, but she'd fallen in love with the place the first time she'd walked inside. It was a few years old, built by a San Francisco CEO who'd planned to escape the big city and telecommute but discovered the town of Eagle's Nest was a little too rustic for him. The home was modern, with high ceilings, big windows, and clean lines. The huge minimalist kitchen looked as if it were from a Scandinavian country; its high-tech appliances had expansive glass, touch screens, and only the absolute essential hardware. The polished cement floors were cold, but she'd bought several fluffy rugs and kept slippers in every room.

The girl on the bike had caught her attention before because the country roads rarely had a shoulder and could be a dangerous place to ride. At least the traffic was always light.

"Where's the girl?" asked Noelle.

"With one of Chief Daly's men," said the deputy. "Nice old guy. He's keeping her company until you could speak with her. Same direction as everyone else. You'll find the remains there too."

Noelle excused herself and headed in the direction he had pointed. Clearly the area was a party spot. Garbage in various states of decay was scattered about, and the twinkle of broken glass was everywhere. She hoped the campfires were kept to a minimum during the dry seasons as she thought of the acres of black snags she'd passed while she drove to the crime scene. Judging by the great heights of the healthy pines around them, the fire that caused them had been decades ago.

But there were plenty of areas in Deschutes County where fires had occurred more recently, leaving fields of black ash and piteous snags where a thriving green forest had once been.

Noelle followed voices and wove through brush and pines, noticing she was no longer on tamped-down dirt, as at the party site. Garbage and glass had given way to clean woods, her boots slightly sinking into the needles on the forest floor. Definitely no cans to pick up.

Why did the girl venture this way?

The teenager came into sight, and Noelle recognized the gray-haired officer next to her. Ben Cooley. A lifer with the Eagle's Nest Police Department who Noelle knew would work as long as the chief let him. Noelle recognized the teen too. It was definitely the girl she'd seen before on the road. The same black rubber boots and oversize orange jacket. A knit hat covered her hair, except for the single long, blonde braid that reached halfway down her back. She turned as Noelle approached.

Thin was Noelle's first thought. The baggy clothes hid the teen's body, but her hollowed cheeks hinted at a poor diet. She had long, black lashes that framed startlingly pale green eyes, the combination giving her an elfin quality. Her clothing was old and faded, and Noelle abruptly understood why she was collecting cans.

"Detective Marshall!" exclaimed Ben with a big grin. He looked at the teenager as he gestured at Noelle. "She's the best. You're in good hands, Emma."

"Thank you, Ben," said Noelle. She turned her attention to the young woman. "Emma? You must live pretty close to me. I just moved to the area, and I've seen you riding your bike a few times."

Emma looked at the ground. "Yes. I bike a lot."

"These narrow roads aren't the safest place to ride," said Noelle.

"I know."

An awkward silence fell. Noelle met Ben's gaze, and he gave a subtle one-shoulder shrug.

"Emma . . . what's your last name?" Noelle asked.

"Chambers."

"I'd like to hear about how you found the body, but I need to check in with the rest of the team first," said Noelle. "Can you stay a bit longer?"

Emma fidgeted, discomfort crossing her face as she looked away. "I guess. But I already told the police chief."

"Good," said Noelle. "I know talking to me will be repetitive, but you'll be asked a few times to recount what happened. It's just the way we do things." She frowned. "How old are you?"

"Eighteen."

"Would you like a parent to be here with you? You're an adult, but maybe you'd be more comfortable with someone at your side."

"No, I'm good. I don't mind," Emma said quickly. "I'll wait."

"Okay." Noelle exchanged another look with Ben. "I'll be back in a few."

He nodded, indicating he'd keep an eye on the teenager.

Eighteen?

Doubtful. Noelle should have asked to see her driver's license. She made her way around some sagebrush, moving toward more sounds of conversation. She recognized Chief Daly's low voice. She'd had dinner with Truman Daly and his wife, Mercy, a week ago with her . . . boyfriend? She winced at the term. She'd only been seeing Max Rhodes for a few weeks; he wasn't her boyfriend.

What is he?

Her skin tingled—in a good way—as she thought of Max. Definitely a good way. He was a special agent at the Bend FBI satellite office and worked with the police chief's wife, Mercy Kilpatrick. The four of them had had a great time at dinner. Noelle had forgotten how good it was to have "couple friends."

Max was extremely attractive. Smart. Funny. Everything she wanted in a man. He'd transferred to the Bend FBI office last month, and it'd never been stated out loud, but she knew she was part of the reason he'd moved. She loved their time together as they navigated the beginning of a relationship. No one had said *exclusive* yet, but it was implied.

That probably should be clarified.

She suspected they were on the same wavelength, but she'd been wrong before.

Will he leave when I tell him my secret?

The question haunted her.

Up ahead, Noelle spotted a crime scene tech photographing the scene and the medical examiner on one knee next to what was obviously the victim. Truman Daly leaned over, his hands on his thighs, his cowboy hat pushed back on his head as he watched over the ME's shoulder. He straightened at Noelle's footsteps.

"Good morning, Noelle," he said, touching the brim of his hat.

The old-fashioned gesture made her smile. The chief had lived in the tiny town of Eagle's Nest less than a decade but had easily adopted its rural mannerisms. He was at ease—and looked good—in the cowboy hat and boots.

"Truman." She nodded and turned her attention to the medical examiner, who was getting to her feet. "Dr. Lockhart."

"I think it's past noon," the petite ME said to Truman before looking at Noelle. "Afternoon, Detective."

Noelle was a big fan of Dr. Natasha Lockhart. The woman was a little younger than Noelle and was one of the smartest people she knew. Especially when it came to dead bodies.

"What do you have, Doctor?" asked Noelle, her gaze going to the swollen, dark body.

Male?

It was hard to tell from the back.

"Deceased male," stated Dr. Lockhart. "He has what appears to be a GSW in his forehead. No exit wound." The doctor frowned. "Unless the exit is this gash under his jaw. Obviously he's been moved since he died. His entire posterior shows livor mortis. He was on his back for several hours after death."

"When did it happen?" asked Noelle, knowing it was too soon to ask the question.

Dr. Lockhart looked back at the body. "Active bloating. Sometime in the last three to five days. But it's been cold. Maybe a little longer. Of course I have no idea how long ago he was moved to this spot. If he'd been indoors, the time frame could be shorter."

"You'll get to his autopsy today?" Noelle asked.

"Tomorrow. Although it could be the next day."

"Any identification on him?" asked Noelle. "Do you recognize him?" She looked at the police chief.

Truman shook his head. "Too hard to tell at the moment. I had Ben take a quick look too. He knows everyone around here."

"No ID," said Dr. Lockhart. "We rolled him to his side to look underneath. Only clothing I've noticed is that shoe." She pointed at a battered Nike several feet away. "Maybe your team will find something."

"He's got a tattoo on his chest," said Truman. "We couldn't get a good look at it when we tipped up the body, but it'll be clear once he's cleaned up."

"Good," said Noelle, her brain starting to speed through the steps to identify the man. First job would be to check for reported missing men in the area. "Age?"

The medical examiner shrugged. "Right now I can't tell from just looking. Not old. Not young. I'll narrow that for you later."

"Of course." Noelle scanned the area. "Anything else for me right now? What about you, Heather?" she asked the crime scene tech who was slowly circling the area, taking pictures.

"Not yet, Detective."

"Okay then." Noelle took one last look at the body. "I'll start with our witness and get a report on local missing men. I look forward to hearing from you, Doctor."

"I'll get you something as soon as I can," said Dr. Lockhart, returning to her kneeling position at the body.

Noelle met Truman's gaze and gave a jerk of her head. He followed as she led him several yards from the scene. "No reports of missing men in your town?" she asked as she came to a stop near a tall snag.

"Nothing. I called Lucas and requested he start a records search and begin asking some questions."

Lucas was Truman's young office manager, who had deep family roots in the community. "Do you know Emma?" she asked. "The girl who found him?"

"Not really," said Truman. "Ben Cooley told me she lives a few miles from here with her dad."

"Just her dad?"

"Yeah. Ben couldn't remember why the mom left. Said it's been at least a decade. Old news, he called it." Truman adjusted his hat. "I haven't met her or her dad before. They're not official Eagle's Nest residents. Live too far out."

"Me too," said Noelle with a smile.

"You're an honorary resident. You spend more than enough money at Kaylie's coffee place."

Mercy's niece made the best baked goods for miles. Noelle had started a bad habit of stopping for coffee on her morning commute and often bought a big box of pastries for the department; it was an excuse to buy an almond croissant for herself.

"I'd appreciate a copy of whatever Lucas finds," Noelle told him. "This will be a county investigation, but I'd like any help you can give."

"It's your jurisdiction," said Truman, holding her gaze. "I just happened to be the closest one to respond."

No argument from him.

She hadn't expected one, but she'd felt the need to say out loud that it would be her case. The Eagle's Nest Police Department didn't have the manpower or equipment to handle what appeared to be a murder investigation. "Thank you, Truman."

He grinned at her. "No ego here. I go with whatever will get the best results. And that's county and you."

"Great." She looked over her shoulder in the direction of Ben Cooley's booming voice. "Something happen?"

"No. That's just Ben. He gets a little loud sometimes."

Noelle smiled and started toward the voice. "I'll take Emma off his hands. What did you think of her?"

Truman strode beside her. "Quiet. Nervous. About how you'd expect a teenager to react after finding a dead body. Seems like a good kid."

My first impression too.

"She was simply searching for cans," added Truman. "Had some bad luck."

Noelle suspected he was right, but she'd reserve judgment until she'd questioned the teen.

Some people weren't who they appeared to be.

3

"Your grandmother is here."

FBI special agent Max Rhodes heard the amusement in Melissa's voice as she spoke through his intercom.

From the other side of his desk, Special Agent Mercy Kilpatrick snorted. "Your grandmother is going to make us all fat."

"I told her that and suggested she bring something else," said Max. He'd worked at the FBI's Bend office for four weeks, and every Monday morning his grandmother Paulette had shown up with doughnuts and usually a friend in tow. She liked showing off her FBI grandson. He sighed and got to his feet. "I'll be right back," he told Mercy.

"I'll start a fresh pot of coffee to go with the doughnuts."

He grinned and headed toward the reception area, nodding at data analyst Darby Cowan as they passed each other.

"Dibs on the maple bar," said Darby.

"You'll have to arm-wrestle Jeff for it."

"Not a problem." She flexed and continued down the hall.

Max knew everyone's name in Bend's small office, and he liked it. No unfamiliar faces here. He'd transferred from the large Sacramento office to be closer to family. His sister Keira and her husband, TJ, lived in town in addition to his grandmother. His mother and other two sisters were in Medford, where he'd grown up, which was a little more than three hours away.

Who am I kidding?

He'd initiated the inquiry to see if the Bend office would be interested in another agent because he'd fallen for Noelle Marshall and hadn't wanted to return to Sacramento. He broke into a wide smile as he thought about her, positive that his blind leap to Oregon had been the right move.

So far, so good.

Better than good. Every day, Max wanted more time with her.

He opened the security door to reception and greeted Paulette. His grandmother was a tall woman, her posture always straight as could be. She'd come alone, and her gray eyes lit up when she saw him. She turned to pick up a tray from the corner table and then held it out with a smile. "Is this better?"

It was a tray of sliced vegetables and fruit.

The office is going to kill me.

"That's terrific," he said, taking the tray. "Thank you."

"Bullshit," she said, her eyes narrowed on him. "This is not better than doughnuts."

"It's hard to beat doughnuts," he agreed. "But this is a good change. For this visit anyway," he said, hoping she got the message that doughnuts were still welcome.

"Hmph." She looked him up and down. "Do you have time for coffee?"

"Not today. I'm in the middle of something."

"What are you working on?"

She always asked; he rarely answered. "Nothing I can share right now. Maybe in a few weeks." It was his standard reply.

"I need something I can tell them about," she said, referring to her group of friends at the retirement community. "I'm tired of hearing about Doris's grandson in the marines."

There was a subtle competition among her friends over whose relative was doing the most important work in the world.

"Maybe next time I'll have something for you." He looked at the tray in his hand. "Are the doughnuts and this a weekly bribe to get me to share about my job?" he said, tongue in cheek.

A shocked expression filled her face. "Of course not. I'm just happy to finally have you in town more."

Paulette was a master of the passive-aggressive comment. And at piling guilt on her grandchildren for not visiting enough.

"You'll be at dinner at Keira's this week?" Max's casual reminder that she *did* see her grandchildren.

"Wouldn't miss it."

He kissed her cheek and thanked her again.

As he went down the hall, Darby stopped him and stared at the tray, her eyes wide. "What did you do?"

"Everyone complained about the calories," said Max, knowing he would be grilled by the entire office.

"Well, yeah. But that doesn't mean we want the doughnuts to stop." She gave him a stern look and then took several slices of red pepper, biting into one with a loud crunch.

Max continued to his office and steeled himself for Mercy's reaction.

Her face showed profound disappointment, but she helped herself to some apple slices. "This is better for us, but I did pack a light lunch since I expected a doughnut this morning."

Max set the tray on his desk and then sat. "Where were we?"

"The letter," said Mercy, taking a carrot stick.

"Right."

Portland FBI counterterrorism had sent a brief about an intercepted piece of mail. It was just one example of an increase in chatter they'd picked up about a possible large terrorism event in Oregon. *Chatter* meaning a number of things that had been intercepted: emails, snail mail, phone calls, and rumors.

"This is your area of expertise," said Max.

"I wouldn't say *expertise*, but I did spend quite a bit of time in counterterrorism. It's like sifting a beach of sand while hunting for a few little rocks. There is an incredible amount of information to go through."

"How do you know what's important?"

"After doing the job for a while, you get a feel for things that aren't right, or you see patterns. It's easier when you're looking for something in particular."

"I had to look up the reference in the letter where the writer said, 'The boogaloo is rising.' I'd never heard of boogaloo. At first I thought it referred to music." Max frowned. "The boogaloo concept isn't very clear. After researching everything, I got the feeling that it's used however someone wants."

"That's accurate," said Mercy. "In general the term *boogaloo* refers to a future civil war in the US. But it's not clear how that is to come about. I've seen extreme boogaloo groups that call for action against the government to provoke the war, other groups that simply preach being prepared for this war, and others that believe the government will create this war by oppressing the people—usually this refers to taking their guns or other rights."

"There doesn't seem to be a centralized network for people who follow the movement."

"There is not. And there's no central ideology. Essentially boogaloo is rather new, starting back in the early 2010s. We've had boogaloo groups espouse white supremacy while other groups demonstrated along with racial justice protesters. Oddly, some have aligned themselves with the BLM movements, speaking out against police brutality, but some suspect this alignment was to have a cover for violence. The common thread seems to be an attraction to areas of high tension. They like chaos and taking advantage of any kind of chaos."

"I assume they spread information and recruit on the internet?"

"Of course," said Mercy. "Their presence has increased since 2020."

"So what's it mean for us?"

"The usual. Keep an ear and eye out. They can be violent, or they can be peaceful. There's no predicting what they're about."

Their boss, Jeff Garrison, appeared in the open doorway. "I heard that your grandmother—" He stared at the tray. "What's that?"

"My grandmother," Max said wearily.

"Huh." Jeff looked at the tray for a long moment and then selected a pea pod. "I've got something else to add to your brief from Portland counterterrorism. One of them met with a CI who claims he heard through the grapevine that maybe *something* was going to happen in central Oregon. It lines up with some of their other vague information."

"Central Oregon or Bend specifically?" asked Mercy.

"He didn't say Bend."

"That's all they got from him?" Max asked.

"Yes."

"And his source?" asked Mercy.

"Said he didn't have a source. Just 'heard' something." Jeff grimaced. "Yeah, I know. It's weak. You should receive an email about it soon. But Portland sees a possibility of something brewing over here, so we sent word to the primary federal buildings to increase their security."

"Better not be about destroying power substations," muttered Mercy. "Not again. But last time that was just a few unorganized locals who shot them up. Portland didn't hear a thing before that happened."

"Any big, organized events happening here soon?" asked Max. "A concert or convention?"

"I'll get Darby on that," said Jeff. "There's the expo center, and a few hotels have convention space. I'm glad it's still too cold for outdoor concerts."

"Reservoirs, dams," said Max. "What else could be a target?"

"Shopping malls, schools, colleges," said Mercy, writing out a list. "Churches, temples, mosques, synagogues."

Max was overwhelmed. "We need more information."

Jeff nodded. "I'll get it to you as soon as I hear anything. Meanwhile, is there someone local who might have heard some rumors?" He looked at Mercy.

Her face lost expression. "I'll ask."

"Thanks, Mercy." Jeff grabbed the rest of the pea pods and left.

Max eyed her for a long moment. She was focused on her list, but he suspected that wasn't what she was thinking about. Jeff had said something that had upset her. "What did Jeff mean, Mercy?"

She sighed. "You know my whole family is in the area, right?"

"You've told me that." He knew a lot of her family were heavily into prepping. Their daily activities focused on being prepared for any disaster.

"At one time my brother got a little too involved with some militia types. My father has had some brushes too." She snorted. "And then there was my dead uncle, who was up to his eyeballs in it. But hardly anyone knew it was him."

"He was killed?" asked Max, feeling she had left something out.

"Well, growing up, we were all told that my uncle had been killed in the Mount Saint Helens eruption in 1980. Turned out he wasn't. He'd used it as an opportunity to change his identity—he was in hot water with the feds at the time—and later became a leader of one of the largest militias in the area. Their activities got him killed just a few years ago."

"That's nuts, but I've heard of people who used 9/11 for the same purpose. Didn't work out."

"We have better tech these days," said Mercy. "Everyone leaves a digital trail. Not so much in 1980. Anyway, Jeff implied that he wants me to ask my brother and father if they've heard anything."

"Wouldn't they have already told you?"

She gave a small smile. "Nope. Heavy distrust of law enforcement is in their blood."

"But you're family."

Mercy shrugged. "They have their own code. They didn't speak to me for a very long time for various reasons. It's much better now, but I keep my expectations low."

"Will they tell you the truth?" asked Max.

"I think they will if I'm very direct." She raised her brows. "Families. Am I right?" she joked.

"You're very right." Max thought about the family history he hadn't shared with Noelle.

I will eventually.

"I might have a better source than my brother or father," Mercy said thoughtfully, looking out the window. "Want to go meet someone?"

"Like a confidential informant?"

"Yes, a CI, but she helps out because she respects me. And because I pay her."

"Why didn't Jeff suggest her?"

Mercy gave him a side-eye. "Because it's confidential."

Max's interest was piqued. "Let's go."

4

Emma locked her gaze on the detective as the woman and the police chief emerged from the woods. She'd heard the police chief was tough but a nice guy, and he'd lived up to that expectation when she met him an hour ago. But the detective . . . a woman detective. Emma didn't know what to make of that.

Detective Marshall was tall, nearly as tall as the police chief, and carried herself with just as much confidence. Her coat and scarf made her look as if she'd just stepped out of a high-end store. Not the Carhartts and Wranglers Emma was used to seeing. Her bright-blonde hair was a shade Emma had never encountered in person, and she'd felt as if someone were shining a spotlight in her face when the detective first spoke to her. She suspected the woman's dark-blue eyes had missed nothing.

Not Emma's hand-me-down coat.

Her boots with holes.

Her baggy sweatpants.

At least the coat hid the big safety pin that tightened the waist of her sweats.

It'd been icy cold when Emma had set out from her house. She'd bundled up with the warmest clothes she could find. She ran a self-conscious hand down her single braid, which she'd pulled over her shoulder. She'd been fiddling with the braid the entire time Officer Cooley talked.

He's nice.

But Emma didn't trust him.

Law enforcement was not to be trusted. Ever. Even the polite police chief.

Emma remembered her father's warning. *"When they want something from you, they'll be as slick as spit, nice as pie. Don't fall for it. You don't have to answer to them. They have no authority over you."*

But I know I did the right thing when I called the police about the body.

She could hear her father now. *"Shoulda minded your own business, girl."*

Emma knew he'd be furious if he found out she'd spoken with the police.

But someone died.

It can't be wrong to let them know.

She needed to get out of there and get home ASAP. She'd been nauseated since she saw the dark body.

The smell.

That was once a person.

Her stomach roiled again.

"You look hungry," said Officer Cooley. "I'll find you something to eat."

"No!" Emma clamped her teeth together.

"Ahhh," said Cooley in an understanding tone. "Yeah, that sight'll turn anyone off their feed. It'll fade."

The woman detective and the police chief came closer. Detective Marshall's direct gaze scanned Emma again. "Emma," she said. "I'd like you to come with me out to the vehicles, so we can talk."

"Okay."

"You're not required to talk to them!" Emma wished she could block out her father's voice in her head. Instead, she picked up her black garbage bag of cans and followed the detective. They passed through the party site and up the dirt path to the road. The two of them were silent, but the cans clanked inside her bag, seeming abnormally loud. Emma stopped at her bike and set down the bag, but the detective motioned her to keep following.

"You can come back to those in a minute," she said. The locks to a big SUV clicked and the detective opened the back passenger door. "Have a seat."

Emma froze.

Where is she taking me? Is she going to cuff me?

"Relax. You just look like you need to sit down," said the detective in a kind voice. "Hang your legs out the side, the door stays open. We're not going anywhere."

Emma studied her face.

I don't think she's lying.

She hoisted herself up to the seat and sat, dangling her legs out as the woman had suggested. Emma hadn't realized how badly she needed to sit down and exhaled, slumping. Letting the stress of the last few hours dissipate.

"Can I see your driver's license, Emma?" asked Detective Marshall. She rested an arm on the open door and crossed one foot over the other as she stood.

Emma stiffened. "I don't have it on me. I'm eighteen, I swear. I do *have* a license, but it's at home. I don't bring my purse when I bike."

"Understandable. Tell me what you were doing and what you saw after you set your bike down." The detective pointed back at Emma's bike in the dirt.

They just want to know what happened. It has nothing to do with me.

Someone is dead.

She told the detective what had happened. The cans. The mess left at the party site. The jackrabbit.

"You didn't see any people?"

"The only person I saw this morning was Anita Forkner. But that was a ways down the road. She stopped her car to talk to me." Emma wrinkled her nose. "She's not the type to party in a place like that."

"Then who does come up here?"

Emma shrugged. "Don't know."

"You described it as a party site. So you must have known about it."

"I think it's pretty obvious what happens there," said Emma.

"You've been here before." Blue eyes met hers. The detective uncrossed her feet and stood up straight.

She's got to be almost six feet tall.

"Not to drink!" Emma clarified. "People at school have bragged about coming here to drink and fool around. Not me."

"Give me some names. Who said they party here?"

Emma pressed her lips together. She'd walked right into that trap. "I don't remember."

The detective rolled her eyes. "Of course you do. I'm not looking to arrest anyone for underage drinking. I want to talk to people who might have seen something, or maybe they can identify that man lying dead in the woods."

Indecision filled Emma's chest.

Don't talk to the police.

But that man's family deserved to know what had happened to him.

Emma looked down, hoping to find an answer in the gravel. There wasn't one. She muttered some names. The detective wrote them down, asking her to spell a few of the last names.

Guilt filled her gut.

I don't owe them anything. Most of them are jerks anyway.

"You won't tell them who gave you the names, right?" she asked hopefully.

"Of course not," promised the detective. Her smile showed perfect teeth.

You can't trust the police.

"Can I go now?" Emma stared over at her bike and cans.

"Tell you what," said the detective. "I'll give you a ride home, and you can show me your driver's license. I don't have room in my vehicle for the bike, so I'll get Ben Cooley to drop it off."

Emma was speechless.

I can't ride in a police vehicle. What if someone sees me?

At least the detective's SUV didn't have DESCHUTES COUNTY SHERIFF emblazoned on the side.

Detective Marshall was silent for a long moment as Emma tried to come up with an answer.

"The bag of cans can come with us," said the woman, studying her intently.

Emma blinked. She'd completely forgotten about the cans. "Okay," she said grudgingly. She slid out of the vehicle to go grab her bag.

My dad will kill me if he finds out about this.

5

Noelle had thought Emma was going to make a run for it when she'd offered to give the girl a ride. The teenager had been hesitant and appeared miserable through their entire talk, and the suggestion of a ride had visually morphed her misery into fear. Making Noelle even more determined to drive her home and find out why she was scared.

Using her peripheral vision, she checked on the girl in the passenger seat. Emma hadn't said a word. She'd turned around twice, trying to reposition the bag of cans on the floor of the back seat to keep them from noisily vibrating. No luck.

Speeding down the country road, they passed the huge black iron gate and long driveway that led to Noelle's new home. She hadn't liked the gate at first; it'd seemed pretentious. No one else on the winding road had a gate. But once she'd been in the isolated house for a week or two, she'd started to appreciate it. It eased her mind a bit, given what had happened at her previous house.

Well, the intruder knew the alarm code.

The iron gate provided an extra layer of defense on top of her extensive home security system, and she also kept multiple handguns stashed around her home. She'd been reluctant to tell her therapist about the guns, concerned she was becoming a paranoid freak.

"Does it make you feel better knowing a gun is in reach?" the therapist had asked.

Noelle had been quiet for a long moment, fighting the immediate denial that had popped into her head. "Yes," she'd finally admitted.

"Do you think I'd tell a child to put away his teddy bear if having it near made him feel better?"

"I think my guns are a little different than a teddy bear."

"You're a trained professional. You understand weapons," the therapist had said. "And you're a responsible person. I think for you, having a few guns in drawers isn't a big deal."

A few weeks later, Noelle had returned most of them to her safe. They'd served their purpose and gotten her over the hump of her emotional recovery after the break-in and violence.

"How much further?" Noelle asked Emma, interrupting the silence.

"A couple miles. You'll turn right at the next road." Emma seemed to shrink into her seat.

"You okay?" Noelle asked.

"Yeah." The teen abruptly straightened. "That was your house we passed, wasn't it?" The words rushed out of her mouth. "The one with the gate."

Noelle hesitated. "Yes."

"Are you rich?"

Startled at the question out of left field, Noelle glanced at Emma. The teen held her gaze for the first time, curiosity in her light-green eyes. "Some people would say I am," Noelle admitted.

Most people.

Noelle had come into a *lot* of money when her second husband died.

"Then why do you work?"

"Because I love my job."

Emma looked doubtful.

"I honestly love what I do. My job is different every day. It's a challenge, and it's important. I truly like helping people." She paused as she thought about the FBI agent who'd steered her toward law enforcement years ago. Alice Patmore continued to be a friend and mentor.

Best guidance I ever received.

"What would I do instead?" asked Noelle with a shrug. "Have my nails done? Spend all day at the gym? Throw fundraisers for charities?" She knew women who were very happy doing all that. She'd tried to live like that because her former husband and his family had expected it of her. She didn't have anything against the life; it simply wasn't for her. "I don't really have any hobbies. I read a bit. I tried gardening and hated it."

"I hate gardening too, but sometimes it's necessary," Emma said softly, now looking straight ahead.

Noelle sucked in a breath and glanced at the girl's heavily worn boots.

She must garden because they need the food.

Noelle didn't know what to say. The silence in the vehicle was deafening.

"Turn there." Emma pointed at an unmarked road Noelle had never noticed before. It was deeply rutted, needing grading and new gravel.

"You ride your bike on this?" Noelle asked.

"I walk it to the road." A hundred yards later, she indicated for Noelle to turn again.

The condition of this road was no better. In fact, *road* was a strong term; it was more of a trail that happened to be wide enough for a vehicle. It wound through scrubby pines and around huge black boulders, the results of a volcanic eruption eons ago. Volcanic rock could be found almost everywhere in the county, including in thousands of acres of lava beds that attracted tourists from around the world.

"It's over there." Emma pointed.

Hidden from the road's view was a single-wide trailer that Noelle suspected was at least forty years old and that made her regret everything she'd mentioned to the teenager about her life. Emma Chambers didn't have much. When Noelle was growing up, her family hadn't had much either. But they had lived in luxury compared to Emma.

Noelle didn't see any vehicles. "Is your dad here?"

"No."

"And your mother doesn't live here, correct?"

The girl whipped her head around to goggle at Noelle. "*Who* told you that?"

"Officer Cooley knows a little bit about everyone around here. He told Chief Daly."

She looks as if she's about to cry.

The pain in Emma's eyes vanished as quickly as it'd come. "That's none of his business."

"I agree," said Noelle. Clearly Emma's mother was a tender spot. Noelle stopped her Tahoe on a semiflat area under a tree. A worn path from the spot to the home told her it was probably where Emma's father parked too. She turned off the vehicle, and Emma was out of the SUV before Noelle could reach for her own seat belt. Then Emma opened the vehicle's back door and grabbed her bag of cans.

"I'll be right back with my license." She ran toward the house and paused to unlock the door before disappearing inside.

Noelle slowly got out of the SUV, scanning the area. It was quiet except for a soft rustling of wind in the tall grasses. A faint clucking told her there were chickens close by. The remote area was peaceful, and if Noelle stretched, she could just see the white tip of a snowy mountain. She felt her spine relax.

Our homes may be vastly different, but we share the same beautiful setting.

She took out her phone to send Emma's list of partiers' names to Detective Evan Bolton.

No service.

Reception had been a problem at her home too, but she'd immediately purchased a system to take care of it. She sighed and slid her phone back in her pocket, not wanting to bother activating satellite service to send the list.

A door squeaked and Emma reappeared. Noelle noticed she deliberately skipped one of the outside steps as she exited the home.

Broken? Rotting?

Emma trudged over and handed Noelle her license. The young woman *was* eighteen. Her birthday had been in December. "Are you a senior?" Noelle asked, studying the photo, where the teenager gave a wide smile that lit up her face.

"I'm homeschooled. But I'll be finished this spring."

"Then you'll take the GED?" Noelle gave back the license.

Emma waited a beat. "Yes."

Noelle already had a cell number for her, so she pulled out a business card and wrote her own personal cell number on the back. "Can you get reception out here?"

"Sometimes I can. It's better out by the road."

"I want you to call me if you think of anything else about this morning. Or if your dad wants to ask me some questions, he can call too." She handed the card to the teenager, who accepted it gingerly.

"Will you need to talk to me again?" Emma asked, eyeing the card.

"Maybe."

"Can you tell me when you identify the body?"

"I can do that once his family is notified." The teenager hadn't looked up, and Noelle sensed she wasn't ready for her to leave.

A few minutes ago, she couldn't wait to get away.

Lonely?

"Are you going back out for more cans now?" Noelle asked.

"I don't feel like looking any more today." She gave a small shudder. "I don't have my bike back yet anyway."

"I'll check with Ben once I get to the road. I'm sure he'll be along shortly."

"Thank you." She finally looked Noelle in the eye.

"You're welcome."

As she drove away, Noelle considered her interaction with the teenager.

Why do I feel like I'm abandoning her?

Noelle scowled. The teenager appeared healthy, if thin. She was well spoken—when she spoke. She'd lost some of her early fear and now just seemed a bit rattled by the morning's discovery, which was understandable. Noelle reached the main road just as Ben Cooley was turning in. She lifted a hand in greeting, and he did the same as he sped by.

If she's lonely, Ben will take care of it.

6

Max drove as Mercy gave directions. She'd texted her CI and asked for a meeting. From listening to Mercy's side of the following phone call, Max had gathered that the woman didn't want to meet today, but Mercy had talked her into it.

Meaning she'd offered more money.

They'd headed north out of Bend and then veered east. The CI had agreed to meet Mercy and Max at her home outside of Prineville, about an hour's drive from Bend.

On a quiet stretch of highway, he finally checked his phone, which had buzzed several times as he drove. Mercy had offered to check it for him, but he'd turned her down.

Sometimes the texts between him and Noelle were . . . suggestive. He didn't need to give Mercy any more ammo with which to tease him about his growing relationship.

Noelle is working a dead body. I doubt she's sending flirty texts.

He was right. The texts were from his sister Keira, who had decided it was a good day to get on his case about seeing his other sisters. He silenced his phone.

"Tell me about the woman we're going to meet," Max said.

"Are you familiar with America's Preserve? Well . . . what used to be called America's Preserve?" Mercy asked. Her tone sounded off, and he glanced at her, but her gaze was locked on the scenery out her window.

"It was a militia compound," said Max after a moment's thought. "Here in Oregon. An ATF operation took it down a few years ago, and at least one federal agent died." He tried to remember more. "It wasn't just men in the compound. There were families living there, and it was being run like a military base—their interpretation of a military base. I remember afterward that the members said it was a brutal dictatorship. They had almost nothing."

"Correct. I was there. *Inside there*," Mercy clarified. "I was undercover in the compound for the ATF."

Max's eyes widened. It'd been a dangerous situation. "Why the ATF?"

"They needed to immediately replace an agent who was scheduled to go inside after months of prep. They came to the FBI to request my help because I resembled their agent, and I had the right background. When things went to hell inside, I was almost killed. A few times." Her voice had grown tight, and she continued to look out her window as she spoke.

"Wow." Max was speechless. There'd been a rumor in the bureau that the FBI had lost someone when the compound was taken down. But the FBI director had publicly stated that was incorrect. Though he hadn't made that statement until weeks after the event.

"This woman and her sister lived in America's Preserve but left before I got there," continued Mercy. "Months after the dust settled, Cory reached out to me with some questions about one of the men who had died in the compound. As we talked, I realized that Cory and her sister still had a finger or two in the scattered remains of that world. People who hated the government and would use violence to express their hate. I fostered our connection, hoping it would be helpful at some point. She became a reluctant informant, but she's shared a couple of names over the years that have been beneficial to our investigations.

"Cory and Rachel thought living in America's Preserve would be a good way to get back to basics. Return to a time when people took care of themselves with no need for government or baseless laws. The women lasted three weeks and then had to sneak out to get away. The militia had essentially used them as slaves." She finally turned to look at Max. "These sisters will like you. I've seen how they respond to tall alpha males," she said with a grin. "Luckily, we're only meeting Cory. Her sister Rachel would tie you up and lock you in her bedroom. I've never met someone like her who has sex on the brain twenty-four seven."

"Thanks for the warning. Sounds like they didn't learn anything from living with a militia?"

"They learned a lot," said Mercy. "Don't underestimate them. I don't think they'll ever let another person tell them what to do."

"Noted."

"Take the next right," she told him.

Max turned off the narrow highway onto a paved one-lane road. They drove for several miles, passing acres of dry land dotted with scrubby bushes, the occasional home or farm appearing in the distance, and then the pavement turned to gravel.

A minute later Mercy pointed. "That's it."

Max spotted the tiny white house in the shadow of a small mesa. The land rose steeply behind the house before it flattened out. He parked several yards from the home, noting an old, faded Suzuki Samurai in front of a small outbuilding.

"That's Cory's car," said Mercy, opening her door.

The two of them walked the packed-dirt path to the front porch. Mercy went up two steps, rang the bell, backed down, and then moved to one side, out of the direct path of the front door. Max did the same in the other direction.

A small woman dressed in faded jeans, hiking boots, and a flannel plaid shirt opened the door. She wore her strawberry-blonde hair in low pigtails, and Max guessed she was in her early thirties. "Hey, Mercy," she said, and then she immediately fastened her light-blue gaze on Max. "Who's the new guy?" She leaned against the doorframe lazily and lifted one eyebrow as she deliberately looked him up and down.

Max hid his amusement at the abrupt change in her demeanor.

"I told you on the phone, Cory. Max is from my office." Mercy tried to hide the annoyance in her tone, but Max heard it.

"Nice to meet you, Cory," said Max.

"Come on in," she said, shooting him a special smile.

This should be interesting.

They followed her into the home. Cory had most of the blinds closed, making it rather dim inside, and Max fought the urge to lift a blind and let in the sun. They joined her at a small, round table next to the kitchen.

"What do you need, Mercy? I don't have a lot of time," Cory said. Her expression was abruptly shuttered, and the flirty looks she'd aimed at Max had vanished. "Usually it's me contacting you. Not the other way around."

"I know, Cory. And my questions are going to be rather vague, but have you heard any rumors of activity going around? Anything surprise you? Catch your attention?" Mercy had a small notebook on the table in front of her, a pen poised over a blank page.

Cory frowned and leaned back in her chair. "Activity?" Her voice had gone up an octave. "You'll have to be more specific than that."

At first Max thought Cory was a good actress, but she couldn't hide that she knew what Mercy meant.

Mercy tried again. "Have you heard anything that made you think you should contact me, maybe send me a heads-up?"

"You're still too vague." Cory slowly shook her head, but Max had spotted a brief flick of her gaze when Mercy said *heads-up*.

She's thought of something.

"Do you work in Prineville?" Max asked, pulling her attention.

"I waitress at the diner. Bartend a little too."

"So you're privy to a lot of conversations," said Max.

Cory's eyes lit up in glee. "Did you just say 'privy'? Who talks like that?"

"Me, I guess. Blame my English-teacher mom."

Cory scooted to the edge of her chair, her arms on the table as she turned all her focus on Max. "Yeah, I hear a lot of talk. Most of it pointless. Nothing ever happens around here."

"What about new faces in town?" asked Mercy. "You know the type I'm talking about. People who look like they'd fit in at America's Preserve."

"Assholes, you mean?" Her face darkened, and Max wondered what exactly had happened to her in the compound.

She's an attractive woman.

He didn't like where his brain shot when he imagined a bunch of disgruntled men locked up with Cory and her sister.

"Yes," Mercy said simply.

A look passed between them that Max couldn't decipher.

Tires crunched on gravel outside.

"Shit," muttered Cory. "It's Rachel. Now we won't get anywhere."

"Then talk fast," said Mercy. "I can tell you've thought of something."

"It was about two weeks ago at the bar," said Cory. "Three men I didn't recognize, although two seemed a little familiar. Exactly the type you'd expect at AP. They'd stop talking every time I approached their table, so I doubled the alcohol in their drinks to get them to loosen up a little." She shrugged. "It's dull around here. When people are trying to hide something, it becomes a challenge for me to figure it out. Booze always solves that problem. You'd be surprised at the shit people say when they're drunk."

"Wait," said Max, surprised at the type of game Cory liked to play with her customers. "They didn't ask for doubles? Did you charge them?"

"No and no," said Cory, patiently. "I use the cheap crap. It usually evens out money-wise because they get loose and spend more on food and order more drinks. Tip better too."

"Any boogaloo talk?" asked Mercy.

Cory rolled her eyes. "Haven't heard that term since America's Preserve. Some of them in there were convinced that a second Civil

War was coming, and they needed to be ready. Which usually meant weapons drills."

"Yeah." Mercy's tone was flat. "I remember."

Boots sounded on the step, and the front door opened. "We got a visitor, Cory?" came a woman's voice. Confident strides moved toward the kitchen. "Well, hello there." The newcomer's gaze locked on Max.

A near duplicate of Cory stopped at the kitchen entrance. But the hair was brighter, the jeans were tighter, and the eyes were heavily lined. Her casual slouch against the doorframe was identical to Cory's, but this woman projected sex instead of flirtation.

"Hi, Rachel," said Mercy, waving a hand to get her attention.

Rachel glanced her way. "The FBI agent, right?" Her focus shot back to Max.

"Yes," said Mercy. "And this is Special Agent Rhodes."

"Mmm. Special Agent," Rachel repeated. "You got a *gun* under that coat, Special Agent Rhodes?" Her eyelids dropped the slightest bit, just enough to emphasize her meaning.

"You're really good at that," Max said evenly. "You could probably turn an enemy agent."

"Damn right."

"As I was about to say," Cory said loudly, pulling everyone's notice. "I got the three guys at the bar loosened up, but someone swept in and held their attention for the rest of the evening." She stared at her sister.

"And I did for the rest of the night too." Rachel winked at Max. "Actually just one of them. Not all three."

Max shot a pleading look at Mercy. The conversation had shot out of his comfort zone.

"Sit down, Rachel," said Mercy, pointing to the only empty chair at the table. "I want to hear about your evening *and* night."

"I don't kiss and tell." Rachel sat.

"That's a bunch of bull," countered Cory. "Nothing you love better than telling."

Mercy held up a hand at Cory. "Rachel, we're here to ask if the two of you have heard any odd rumors around town. Maybe a couple people are angry about something and want to do something about it."

Rachel had gone silent, but she was listening to Mercy.

"Cory told us about these three strangers before you walked in. Would you say these men are people the FBI might be interested in talking to?"

"About what?" asked Rachel. Her expression said she knew exactly what Mercy meant.

Max was tired of the runaround. "Domestic terrorism."

Rachel and Cory exchanged a glance. "There's a lot of people that don't believe—" began Rachel.

"Rachel," Mercy snapped. "You both were in the compound. You know what we're looking for."

Rachel slouched in her chair, resentment simmering in her gaze. "The guy I went with said he hadn't been in the area for several years," she spit out. "He was probably just visiting. I'm sure he's gone back home."

"And his friends?" asked Max.

"Not sure," said Rachel. "I've seen both around a few times. Don't know their names. Don't know what they do or where they hang out."

"Would you recognize them if you saw them again?"

"Definitely."

"Why were the three of them meeting up?" asked Max, watching Rachel's expression.

"I'm not exactly sure." She gave a one-shouldered shrug. "I got the impression that the one I hooked up with was selling something to the other two."

"Like what?" asked Mercy.

Rachel leaned forward, giving Mercy her full attention. "I. Don't. Know." She leaned back, pouting. "He paid for the hotel in cash. He had a lot of money on him." She shifted in her chair and dropped her gaze. "He gave me two hundred."

Cory sucked in her breath. "Jesus, Rachel. We've talked about that!"

"What am I supposed to do when someone hands me cash? Say *no thanks*?" She shot her sister an irate look and crossed her arms. "I didn't tell him he had to pay me something. Not before and not after."

Max looked at Mercy. "A hotel because he's not local or because he didn't want her to know where he lived?" he asked.

"Or he's married," Mercy pointed out. "I don't think we can make assumptions about why he chose a hotel. What was his name?" she asked Rachel.

"He told me Bill, but I doubt that was real."

"Did any of them pay with a card at the bar?" she asked Cory.

"No. Cash."

"And you remember this fact because . . . ?" asked Max.

Cory met his gaze. "Because one left with my sister. I at least try to get a name when she wanders off with someone I don't know."

"Got it." The explanation of sisterly protection had caught him off guard. He turned back to Rachel. "Do you remember what any of them drove?"

"Two were in a dually. Didn't notice what kind. The one with me drove an old Jeep Cherokee. Red."

Max exchanged a look with Mercy. At least they had something.

Maybe. Could all be nothing.

They left their cards with the women with instructions to call if they saw any of the men or recalled anything else.

"What did you think?" Max asked once he and Mercy were in his vehicle.

"I think they're both holding something back, but there's always been a bit of competition between those two. I suspect we'll get a call from one or both later."

Max was surprised. "I guess I was wrong to think that was a waste of time."

"I know it appeared like that from the outside, but I know these two. They've always got an angle. Usually one that will put money in their pockets."

"Think they'll tell one of the men that the FBI is looking for them and ask for cash to not rat them out?"

Mercy laughed. "Cory's done that at least twice that I'm aware of."

"And she seemed like the nice one," muttered Max.

Mercy grinned at him. "I'll bet a hundred dollars that you'll hear from one of them in the next twenty-four hours."

"I'll take that bet," said Max. "I think they've got nothing."

"Don't let Rachel talk you into meeting at a hotel."

He snorted. "I'm not that naive."

It's doubtful we'll hear from them again.

7

Back at the sheriff's department, Noelle scanned the list of local missing men that Detective Evan Bolton had pulled together. Evan looked over her shoulder as she clicked on each one. "The most recent of these vanished two months ago," said Noelle. "Our victim hasn't been dead more than a week."

"That doesn't mean he disappeared a week ago," said Evan.

"True. Would be helpful if I had an age and height for him. All I could confirm was that his hair was dark."

"That bad?"

"That bad," confirmed Noelle. "I asked the ME to send over a height and picture of the tattoo ASAP. I don't know how long it will take her to determine an age range." She clicked on a photo of a gray-haired man with a drooping mustache and jowls. "This guy vanished four years ago."

"We've got records of missing people going back for decades," said Evan. "I narrowed this search to five years."

"Where do people go?" Noelle muttered as she read the gray-haired man's report. He had left behind a wife of forty years and his brand-new Ford truck. "No one even had an idea of what happened to him. Just went for a walk and never came back." She wondered what the wife was doing now. Noelle went back to the man who'd vanished two months ago. His wife had reported him missing, but his vehicle was missing too. "No hits on his credit cards or cell phone or license plate."

"Always makes me wonder how many vehicles and people end up in the bottom of lakes or deep rivers," said Evan. "One wrong turn or sudden health crisis and they're impossible to find. Not that long ago they found a car in the Columbia River that had gone missing in the 1950s. The whole family had vanished except two of the children, who were found in the river a year later."

"I read about that," said Noelle, still looking at the man from two months ago, trying to compare the shape of his head to that of the victim's in the photo she'd taken this morning.

Impossible.

"I don't think we can do much until we hear from the ME," she said.

"A press release went out," said Evan. "That should bring in some tips, but so far it's just people calling with questions, demanding more information. I don't understand why some people believe every fact in a case should immediately be made public."

"Armchair detectives. I think it's gotten worse with the increase in true crime shows and podcasts." Noelle turned away from her screen. "The home closest to my crime scene is a mile away. I sent an officer there, but the owner's camera views are of their house and barn, not the road. Any photos from the forensic tech yet?" Noelle had a few of her own photos for reference, but she wanted to study the tech's images.

"Not yet."

"How'd you do with the student-partier names I got from Emma?"

"I figured out addresses for three," said Evan. "Came up empty for the fourth, but maybe one of the others can tell us." He checked the time on the computer screen. "The high school got out an hour ago. Want to knock on some doors?"

"Absolutely."

◆ ◆ ◆

Noelle frequently partnered with Evan. Together they'd been through some harrowing moments, one of which had nearly cost Evan his life. Noelle was thrilled he'd found happiness with SAR dog handler Rowan Wolff. The two were made for each other. Evan was smart and dedicated, and Noelle admired how his brain put together pieces of their investigative puzzles.

It took a half hour to reach the town of Eagle's Nest, a small, tight-knit community where everyone knew everyone's business. Emma Chambers had given her four names. Noelle suspected that once she and Evan started asking questions, word would spread like wildfire that the sheriff's department was in town investigating the murder.

Evan stopped his vehicle in front of the home of RJ Hampton, the first student on Emma's list. It was a small ranch-style home on a long street of nearly identical structures that all had large lawns and tall trees. This one was older, but the yellow-paint trim looked fresh, and someone had sculpted the front yard's shrubbery into shapes. A teacup, a cat, and a cross. And another that Noelle could only guess was a book.

RJ Hampton was a senior at the high school, and according to what Evan had found online, he was an important part of the football and baseball teams. Noelle and Evan sat in the SUV for a few minutes, scanning local articles on RJ's sports success.

"Ready?" asked Evan.

"I'll send a quick text to the chief to let him know we're in his town talking to some kids."

Noelle sent the text, stepped out of the vehicle, and had barely closed her door when her phone vibrated. She read the text and laughed out loud. "Truman already knew we were in town. Someone texted him our license plate, stating we were suspiciously parked on their street. He'd just figured out it was a sheriff's vehicle a second before he got my text."

"Small towns," muttered Evan.

"I think it's great," said Noelle.

"Probably not great from a teenager's point of view," said Evan. "They can't get into any mischief without a dozen people telling their parents."

"Sounds like a good thing." Noelle grinned. "Also explains that hidden party spot that teenagers frequent."

"I'm sure there's more than one," said Evan. "And I doubt it's just teenagers that use it."

He followed Noelle up the stepstones to the concrete porch. She rang the doorbell and fought the urge to make a weird face for its camera. A woman in faded jeans and a thick green sweater answered the door and eyed them suspiciously from behind her long bangs.

"Chief Daly says you're with the sheriff's office," said the woman before they could say a word. She looked Noelle up and down with a frown. Evan got a faster study, and her gaze returned to Noelle. She narrowed her eyes, her distrust apparent.

"That's correct," said Noelle. "He told me someone was concerned with our unfamiliar—"

"You sat there for four minutes," said the woman, pointing at Evan's SUV. "Doing nothing. It didn't make sense. And I don't know why you're at my door."

A guardian at the threshold.

Noelle quickly introduced herself and Evan and asked, "Are you Mrs. Hampton?"

"I am." She raised a brow at Noelle. "Why?"

"We'd like to talk to RJ," said Evan. "Is he here?"

Evan sees that she doesn't like me.

Noelle was used to that. She struggled to connect with some women. She'd blamed her height for many years, but Savannah had a different opinion. "Besides your stunning looks, you've got loads of confidence. It oozes from you," her best friend had told her bluntly. "Women are defensive because they instinctively know they can't compete."

"I'm not competing with anyone!" Noelle had argued. "I'm just me!"

"And that's why I love you," Savannah had told her. "Wouldn't take you any other way."

"You're not intimidated by me."

"Hell no. I'm way more confident than you."

It was true. Nothing sparkled and filled a room like Savannah's confidence and personality.

Noelle silently sighed, resigning herself to taking a step back from the interview. Evan knew to pick up the reins.

"Why do you want to talk to RJ?" Mrs. Hampton's mother bear emerged. She seemed to grow two inches as she stared at Evan.

"We have some questions for him," Evan said politely.

"Why." It wasn't a question this time.

"I assume you've heard about the body discovered—"

"Yes," she cut him off. "Everyone knows about it, and RJ has nothing to do with it. That happened miles from here."

"We're talking to people who've been in that area in the past."

"RJ doesn't go there! He's not involved!"

"Mom?"

RJ walked up and looked over his mother's shoulder, his shaggy red hair confirming his identity. "What's going on?"

"Nothing. Go back to the kitchen," she ordered.

"You were yelling. And I heard my name." RJ looked from Evan to Noelle.

"We're with the sheriff's department and would like to talk to you for a minute," Noelle said quickly before his mother tried to send him away again. "We're hoping you can shine some light on a situation. We'll ask some quick questions and then be on our way."

"Mom, ask them in. It's freezing out there."

Guilt flashed on Mrs. Hampton's face, and she reluctantly stepped back. "Just for a minute," she said grudgingly.

"We appreciate that," said Evan.

Noelle stepped past the mother and felt the woman's gaze centered on her back. The inside of the home was neat and clean, but Noelle caught a subtle hint of cat box. On her left was a large living room with an uncomfortable-looking orange sofa and matching chairs. Two cats eyed her from their cushy resting places on a cat tree in front of the large window. One was black, one tabby.

"Have a seat," said RJ's mother. "Can I get you some coffee?"

Noelle started to decline, but Evan spoke first. "That'd be great. Black works for both of us."

Surprise and then annoyance flashed on the woman's face. She glanced at her son and back at the two detectives and then gave a small huff and went to make the coffee.

If you offer coffee, be prepared to deliver.

Evan pointed at one of the chairs and looked at RJ. "Let's talk." Noelle sat on the sofa and Evan joined her. The teenager stiffly sat on the edge of the chair. He wore navy sweatpants and mismatched socks along with an oversize sweatshirt with the high school's mascot on the front.

"What's going on?" RJ asked.

"What can you tell us about that party spot a few hundred yards off the Old Mill Highway?" asked Noelle.

RJ looked from Noelle to Evan. "I heard they found a body there this morning. It was all over school. Is it true?"

"Yes," said Noelle. "When were you last there?"

The teen leaned back as shock filled his face. "You think I killed someone?" His voice was high, and it cracked on the last word.

"We didn't say that," said Evan. "We're trying to get a current picture of what goes on there. Who hangs out. We were told you've been there before."

"Everybody's gone there. Not just me," said RJ. "Who said my name?" Anger sparked from his eyes.

"Doesn't matter," said Noelle. "We've got a list of names. When were you last there?" she repeated.

He slumped and looked at the cats. One had decided to sleep, but the other was intently watching the exchange. "I was there Saturday night," he muttered. "There were probably twenty-five or thirty people there."

"It had to be nearly freezing," said Noelle, recalling how she'd cranked up her gas fireplace and used a heated throw that evening.

RJ shrugged. "That's why we build a few fires."

"Anything unusual happen?"

The teen sat up straight. "Was that guy already dead?" He paled, which made his freckles stand out. "We were partying near a dead guy?" His voice cracked again.

His mother entered with two mugs of coffee. "You shouldn't be questioning him without me in the room," she snapped as she thrust the mugs at Noelle and Evan. Evan's mug was a solid blue; Noelle's read COFFEE MAKES ME POOP.

Noelle looked at the phrase. "That's hilarious," she said with a fake grin. She wasn't about to give the mother any satisfaction over her attempt to embarrass her. Then she took a long sip.

Ugh. Lukewarm.

"Are you eighteen?" Evan asked RJ.

"Yes."

Evan looked at his mother. "He doesn't require an adult. Unless you feel you really need one?" He glanced at RJ.

Noelle appreciated the play on the teen's ego.

"I'm good." RJ cleared his throat. "I don't remember anything weird happening. Some people were drinking beer. Others just standing around talking. I saw a few couples making out and one that went off into the woods, but they came right back. It was fucking cold."

"Robert James!"

"Sorry," he muttered to his mother.

"Did you know everyone there?" asked Noelle.

"Pretty much everyone was from my school. There were a couple of guys from a Bend high school. Don't know their names, but I think I recognized them from baseball."

"Any adults?" asked Evan.

"Nah." RJ's expression cleared. "I heard it was Emma Chambers who found the body this morning. That true?"

"You know Emma?" asked Noelle.

He shrugged. "It's a small school. I know who she is, but I don't hang around with her. Can't think of who does."

"You can't think of who she's friends with?" asked Noelle. No doubt RJ's friends were a different group. Athletes. Middle-class kids. Emma was . . . not.

"Always a loner," he said. His brows came together. "I don't think I've seen her around lately. Maybe not since before winter break. Her locker is near mine," he quickly added.

"She's homeschooled," said Noelle.

"Well, that's new." RJ snorted. "Not sure who'd teach her. Her mom took off years ago."

Ire burned in Noelle's throat. "She has a father. And she's old enough to study on her own."

"Father," echoed RJ's mother. "He's useless. I guarantee he didn't create a homeschooling curriculum for that girl."

Evan shifted his weight on the sofa, and Noelle knew the tones and attitudes of the Hamptons toward Emma were bothering him too.

Snobs.

"What other gossip have you heard about the body?" asked Noelle, including the mother in her question.

Neither spoke.

"No one is questioning who it is or what happened?" asked Evan skeptically. "No one is worrying about community safety?"

He has a point. Someone was killed near their town. But I don't see any concern for the victim or that a killer could be nearby.

"We always lock our doors at night," said Mrs. Hampton.

Noelle waited for her to say more, but that was the extent of her statement. Noelle dug a small notebook out of her bag and handed it to RJ along with a pen. "We need names of people you saw there on Saturday."

The room was quiet as RJ worked. He included some information from his phone and occasionally wrinkled his nose in concentration.

Noelle continued to drink the bad coffee. The black cat got to its feet, did a Halloween-cat stretch, and then promptly lay back down.

RJ handed over his list and indicated the last name. "I remembered an older guy who shows up sometimes. I think he graduated about five years ago. He's brought hard alcohol a few times."

"Was he there Saturday?" asked Noelle, looking at the list. The last name was Trevor Baylor.

RJ's handwriting is atrocious.

"I think so."

She set the poop mug on the coffee table and stood. Evan did the same.

They said a polite goodbye and were out the door. As they bundled themselves into the SUV, Evan turned to Noelle. "I almost died when I saw your mug. That took some balls on her part," he said with a big grin. "I need to get a mug like that for the lieutenant."

"Tell me if you do, so I can be there to see his reaction," said Noelle. There was a running joke in the office about how much time the lieutenant spent in the bathroom. "What did you think of RJ?"

"I suspect he's a teenager who probably doesn't think about anyone but himself. Which I feel is pretty normal. What was the deal with their attitude toward Emma Chambers?"

"Her family is poor." Noelle's words were clipped.

"They were so dismissive." Evan glared as he started the engine. "And I still don't know what to think about their lack of concern for the victim or that a killer could be walking around."

"I don't either." Noelle thought back over the interview. "At least we have a few more names. But which do we visit next?"

"Let's stop and talk to Chief Daly. I bet he could prioritize our list." Evan put the SUV in gear and pulled away from the curb.

"Good idea." Noelle looked at the list and thought about the Hampton interview.

Neither asked who died.

Weird.

8

Evan parked in front of the Eagle's Nest Police Department. It was a small building from the previous century, its name on the glass door along with TRUMAN DALY, CHIEF OF POLICE. The department was on the main street along with most of the other small businesses in town. Café, general store, post office. Noelle spotted green Saint Patrick's Day banners in the department windows, and a few large four-leaf clovers dotted the door.

"Why doesn't our department have sparkly green decor?" asked Evan as he stepped out.

"Go for it," answered Noelle. "I won't complain."

She pulled open the door and was instantly greeted by Lucas Ingram, who sat behind the reception desk. The big man had been a high school football star but had found his true calling when he took over the front desk after his grandmother retired. There was nothing he enjoyed more than keeping the department organized and interacting with the locals.

"I told the chief you were on your way over," said Lucas. "But right now he's talking to a guy Royce arrested this morning. A domestic violence call." He rolled his eyes. "Dude is a piece of work. I wouldn't have believed it if I hadn't heard it myself, but the guy actually said his girlfriend shouldn't have been disrespecting him."

Noelle grimaced. "Victim blaming. She okay?"

"She's at urgent care. He slapped her *and* choked her."

"Jesus," muttered Evan.

"'I found her sleeping under a bridge in Texas,'" Lucas said in a country drawl, apparently imitating the man. "'I gave her a house and *two* big-screen TVs. But she fucked her boyfriend under the bridge a lot more than she does me. That's not right.'"

Noelle stared. "He did not say that."

"He did. Several times. He's pretty indignant about the whole situation."

"He bought her a house?" asked Evan.

"Nah. She moved in with him. He does have the two TVs, though."

A door slammed, and Truman strode down the hall toward them, fury on his face. Lucas took one look at him, grabbed a cookie from a pink bakery box on his desk, and held it out.

"I need the whole box," said Truman, taking the cookie and then the box. He tipped his head at Noelle and Evan. "Follow me."

He led them down the hall to his office, where he closed the door and handed the box of cookies to Noelle. "They're from Kaylie's. Have a seat."

Noelle sat, opened the box, and immediately recognized the chunky peanut butter chocolate cookies from the Coffee Café. She took one and passed it to Evan.

Truman sat down in his chair, leaned back, and took a bite. Crumbs fell on his shirt. He neatly plucked them off and popped them in his mouth. The earlier anger on his face had subsided into a look of disappointment. "I never know what will happen on this job day to day."

"That's one of the benefits," Noelle said around a mouthful of cookie.

Truman sighed. "How did it go at the Hamptons'?"

Noelle and Evan exchanged a look. "Fine," said Evan. "RJ said he didn't notice anything odd when he was there on Saturday night. He gave us a few more names of people who were there."

"Think your victim had been dumped by then?" asked Truman. He started a second cookie.

"I hate to think that a bunch of partying teenagers wouldn't notice a body nearby, but I guess I shouldn't be surprised," said Noelle. She slid a piece of paper across the chief's desk. "Here's RJ's list of names, and we added the ones we got from Emma Chambers. We were hoping you could prioritize one or two for us?"

Truman picked up the list. "Put this kid at the bottom," he said immediately. "He'll catch hell from his father if he talks to you, and he knows it. You won't get anything out of him. It'll be a big waste of time."

"Sounds like some good parenting going on there," said Evan, sarcasm heavy in his voice.

"Yes." Truman scanned the rest of the list. "Don't know who Trevor Baylor is."

"RJ said he's older. Graduated a few years ago."

"And still hangs around with high schoolers?" Truman made a face. "I'd try the Linville kid first. He's the type of teenager that knows everyone and what they're up to." He handed back the paper. "I saw the press release from county. I assume you don't have any good leads yet if you're interviewing teenagers."

Noelle's phone vibrated, and she glanced at the screen. "Text from Dr. Lockhart." She tapped her phone and found herself looking at a closeup of a tattoo. "Victim's chest tattoo. That should help. Looks like a thin tree towering over a brick wall." She handed her phone to Evan. "She also said his height is five ten."

"No age?" asked Evan, studying the tattoo and then passing it to Truman.

"I guess she can't offer a range at the moment. She also said she can't get to the autopsy until tomorrow but wanted us to have this information to help with our identification."

"I couldn't guess at his age this morning," said Truman, looking at the tattoo. He gave a shake of his head. "It looks like a flower, not a tree," he said. "But that would be a big-ass flower if that's a stone wall."

There was a sharp rap on the door, and it swung open. Ben Cooley peered in. "Oh good. Lucas said you were back here, Detective Marshall. Hey, Detective Bolton. Good to see you."

"Come in, Ben," said Truman.

The older officer stepped inside, his cowboy hat in both hands and his gaze locked on the pink box. He swallowed and then looked at Noelle. "Did you go inside Emma Chambers's home when you dropped her off?" he asked.

"No." Noelle's attention homed in on Ben's cautious expression. "Why? Did you?"

"Yeah, I talked my way in. I can do that pretty much anywhere."

A faint snort came from Truman.

"You didn't like something you saw." Noelle turned in her chair to get a better look at the officer.

Ben scratched his head. "Her daddy is Gage Chambers. You met him?" he asked Truman.

"Never have. Was he there?"

"He wasn't there," said Ben. "I chatted with Emma as I unloaded her bike and then asked if I could get a glass of water. She'd been nervous and flighty, so I wanted a look inside."

Noelle mentally kicked herself for not going in the home.

"I waited outside on the porch but first nearly broke my neck on a rotten step. She said her dad's been meaning to fix it. Anyway, I held the door open while she went inside, and I swear the air that came out was almost colder than outdoors. She put something inside the fridge first, and I got a good glimpse. Those were some bare shelves in there."

"She's so thin," muttered Noelle. "What the fuck does her dad do?"

"Last I heard he worked at the lumberyard, so after I left, I called Nick Walker, who said Gage hasn't worked there since before Thanksgiving. He showed up late too many times, and Walker fired him. He told me he kept him around a lot longer than he wanted to because he knew he had a daughter, but he'd had enough the day

Gage strolled in two hours late with the smell of tequila coming out his pores."

"Where is he now?" asked Truman.

"Walker said he didn't know and didn't care. I didn't ask Emma about him before I left. I was already making her uncomfortable by being on her front porch."

"Was the home clean?" asked Noelle.

"Oh, yeah. Spick-and-span. Just cold and empty feeling." He looked at Truman. "Thought we could do something for her out of the private fund. Maybe some groceries."

Truman nodded. "Of course. Tell Lucas I said so. Was there a fireplace?"

"I saw a woodstove. But maybe it doesn't work."

"Maybe pack up some firewood just in case."

The officer disappeared, and Noelle studied the police chief. "Private fund?"

He shrugged. "Lucas's grandmother started it years ago, when she worked the front desk here. Wanted to help the locals that came up a little short on money for necessities."

Noelle thought she understood. "But there really isn't a private fund. Let me guess: No one knew the money came out of her pocket, and now the money comes from yours. And lets people who need help keep their dignity."

"Something like that. I've had plenty of folks insist on repaying what they were given, so a lot of it comes back around."

"Do your officers know?" asked Evan.

"Just Lucas. I think he figured it out when he was ten." He shifted in his chair. "People know they can come here for help, and it doesn't end up on the gossip train."

Noelle looked at Evan. "Small towns," she said softly.

"I think you mean *good people* in small towns," said Evan. "Not all of them have someone like Truman."

Truman waved a hand. "I didn't start it. I just keep it going."

Noelle dug her wallet out of her bag. She counted out ten hundred-dollar bills and handed them to Truman. "Add this to your fund. And get Emma and her father whatever they need. Let me know if you need more."

"Christ, Noelle," exclaimed Evan. "Do you always carry that much cash?"

"Depends on the day." Actually she rarely did, but that morning she'd grabbed a bag she had last used on a shopping trip to Seattle with Savannah. An expensive shopping trip. She'd forgotten about the money until she went to buy her coffee this morning and was greeted with a wallet full of green.

She suddenly wished she could take Emma on a shopping trip. Maybe then people like RJ and his mother wouldn't look down on her so much.

That teenager needs more than just new clothes.

She stood, ready to say goodbye to Truman, which prompted Evan to do the same.

"I appreciate your donation," said Truman, shaking her hand. "Keep me in the loop. I'll send Ben back to check on Emma and her dad later to see what they need." He frowned. "Maybe best if we avoid Gage Chambers. Don't want to bruise his pride, but he still won't be happy to come home and find out someone bought a bunch of stuff for them."

"What about a woman?" asked Noelle. "Would he handle it better if the donations seemed focused on Emma and were started by a woman? Maybe one of her former schoolteachers?"

Truman rubbed his chin, his expression thoughtful. "Don't want to imply he can't take care of his daughter."

"He *isn't* taking care of her," said Noelle, a sharp note in her tone. "Screw his pride. His daughter needs to eat better. And have a warm place to live."

"I'll run it by Ina," said Truman. "She's a master at getting people to do what she wants and making them think it was their idea."

"That's Lucas's grandmother," Evan told Noelle before she could ask. "The one who originally started the fund. She's a force. She'll get it done." He looked at Truman. "Ina doing okay?"

"Her hip replacement made a world of difference," said Truman. "I think she was hiding a lot of pain. It didn't dull her razor-sharp tongue, but her overall health seems to have improved."

"Can't imagine her without a cane," said Evan.

"Oh, she still carries the cane," said Truman. "I don't think she really needs it, but she likes to wield it to convince people she knows best."

Noelle grinned. "Sounds like the type of person Emma needs."

I suspect the girl needs all the help she can get.

9

Emma lifted the lid of the big plastic bin on her front porch. She'd cut a hole in one end, lined the sides with some insulation, and then put in a thick layer of straw. She grinned when she saw a round, cat-size indentation in the center of the straw. The orange cat had finally used the shelter.

He had shown up a week ago.

I think it's a he.

Something about the large, fluffy cat with white socks and a white belly had made her guess that he was a boy. She'd tried to coax him inside her house, but he ran away every time she went near him—another reason she wasn't certain of its sex. He would eat from the little bowl of food she left out and then sit and watch her from the far side of the yard while she refilled it. The nights were cold, but getting him to come indoors clearly wasn't going to happen. So she'd emptied a bunch of her dad's tools out of the bin and cut the hole.

I assume the cat used the bed. Maybe I provided a warm night for a raccoon.

But in her gut, she knew it was him.

She was making progress. The orange cat ran a shorter way each time she opened the door and had even taken a few steps in her direction yesterday as she noisily filled his bowl with kibble. The first two days she'd seen him, she'd put leftover mac and cheese in the bowl and then spied on him from a window as he hungrily wolfed it down. Then she'd biked several miles to town and bought the cat a small bag of cat food.

He needs a real name.

Pumpkin, Cheeto, Garfield.

But for some reason nothing seemed to fit. She'd been mulling it over for two days. She'd never had a cat around before, not even other strays. She wondered where he'd come from. He clearly wasn't comfortable around people.

Dorito, Mango, Ginger.

He was a mystery, but she hoped one day she'd get to pet that soft-looking fur. It was a little matted in spots, and when she'd bought the cat food, she'd stared at cat brushes in the store for a long time but couldn't justify the cost. The cat food was already outside her budget, but she worried that human food wasn't good for him. He seemed a little thin under all that fur, and she wanted to do the best she could for him. He deserved a chance. She filled his bowl and looked around in the waning light, hoping to spot him spying on her. But she didn't see him.

Her heart sank as she hoped he was okay.

She'd grown used to his presence.

Emma went back inside and drained the pasta for her mac and cheese. She wished she had some ground hamburger to mix in, but she'd used the last of it two days ago. She poured the sauce she'd made from flour, milk, and cheese over the pasta and added a dash of pepper.

Her dad hated pepper.

She added more pepper and then spooned some into a bowl and sat down at the little dining table.

Mac. Cheese. Kraft?

She snorted, amused at the orange food names on her brain.

Cornbread.

She froze with a bite of food halfway to her mouth, caught up in a memory of her mother dumping a yellow, powdery mix into a mixing bowl and the anticipation she'd felt as a child, knowing that warm cornbread and butter were minutes away.

Cornbread.

I anticipate his visits every day.

She chewed her food, confident in her name for the cat.

After several more bites, she heard an engine approach. Her appetite vanished. She moved to the window and stood where she could peer out but no one could see her.

Not Dad. I don't know that truck.

She exhaled and continued to watch, conscious of the handgun in a drawer two feet away. It was rare for strangers to come to the house. If they did, they were usually up to no good.

The dark truck stopped a few yards away. A big man jumped out of the driver's side and then jogged around to the passenger side, where a white-haired woman sat. Emma smothered a giggle as the man actually lifted the older woman out of the seat and set her on her feet. Emma couldn't make out the words, but clearly the woman was voicing strong opinions on how the man should help her. The woman straightened her coat and took out the cane she had tucked under one arm. She pointed the cane at the man and then at the truck and then made a sweeping motion toward the house.

What do they want?

Not sensing any danger, Emma was driven by curiosity to open the door, and she stepped out onto the porch. "Can I help you?" she asked the older woman, who'd stopped at the bottom of the stairs and now eyed her. Instead of answering, the woman gripped the handrail and carefully took the first step.

Emma was down the stairs in a flash. "Don't step on the next one. It's rotten."

"Well, that's not good," said the woman. "Help me over it," she ordered. She held out her arm and Emma took it with both hands. The older woman easily stepped over the rotten board. "That wasn't as bad as I expected." She went up the rest of the steps without Emma's help. "Now." She turned and looked Emma up and down. "You must be Emma Chambers."

"Yes. Can I help you?" Emma asked again, glancing at the man, who had loaded up his arms with grocery bags and was headed their way. "What's going on?"

"I'm Ina Smythe," the woman announced. "I'm Eagle's Nest's official representative."

Emma didn't know what to say.

"Invite me inside," Ina directed, pointing her cane at the door.

"Please come in," Emma said automatically, and opened the door.

Ina glanced at the cat's bin and food bowl. "You have a cat?"

"Not really. It's for a stray. He comes around a lot but won't let me touch him."

"Sounds to me like you have a cat. Lucas!" Ina turned toward the man. "After you unload those groceries and firewood, go get some bags of cat food." She looked at Emma. "Does the cat have a favorite food?"

"No." Emma blinked, feeling a little lightheaded.

What is going on?

"Yes, ma'am," answered Lucas, and he brought the groceries up the stairs. He brushed by Emma and Ina and then set the bags on the dining table next to Emma's bowl of mac and cheese. He winked at Emma as he passed, headed back out to the truck. He looked familiar, and she tried to think of where she had met him before.

"And then take a look at that step!" Ina hollered after him as she moved into the house. "I don't want you breaking your neck."

Emma looked at the woman, who now was opening and peering into all her cupboards. "Excuse me," Emma said. "This is *my* house."

Ina turned around and clucked her tongue. "I'd hoped you had a backbone, and there it is. We brought you some groceries. Courtesy of the Eagle's Nest community fund. When Ben was here earlier, he noticed you had an empty fridge." Ina opened the fridge, and Emma wanted to vanish through the floor.

Besides condiments, milk, and cheese, it was empty.

"He said it was cold inside too, and he's damn right. You shouldn't have to wear a coat while eating your dinner." Ina's gaze stalled on Emma's bowl, and her lips twisted. “Humph.” She continued to look around the room. “At least someone installed a woodstove. Does it work?”

“Yes.”

The woman strode over and rapped on the wall behind it with her cane. “Cement board?”

“I think so.”

She tapped on the metal chimney and studied where it went through the roof. “Clearly an amateur job, but looks all right. I’ll have Lucas inspect it from the roof. Had any problems with it?”

“No.”

“Then why isn’t there a fire?” Eagle-sharp eyes focused on Emma. “No wood, right?”

“Right,” she whispered.

“Don’t you know there’s snow coming this week? Lots of it. Sit down.” Ina pointed at the chair where Emma had been eating her dinner. Emma obediently sat, and Ina took the chair next to her. There was a lot of thumping on the porch. “That’s Lucas unloading some firewood. We didn’t bring enough. Lucas!” she shouted toward the window.

“Yes, Grandma?” he answered.

“Get extra firewood when you get the cat food.”

“Yes, ma’am.”

Emma had had enough of Ina Smythe’s orders. “Look. You can’t—”

Ina cut her off. “You need a hand. Eagle’s Nest has a private fund for its residents who need a little extra to get by. Ben nominated you, so here I am.” She slapped a hand on the table to emphasize her point.

“I don’t need charity,” Emma snapped.

Ina held her gaze. “Your fridge is empty. Your woodpile is gone. There’s more food outside in that cat bowl than is in yours.” She pointed at the mac and cheese. “You know the saying *Don’t cut off your nose to spite your face*?”

“Yes,” Emma choked out, looking away from those eyes that saw right through her.

"Good. That's exactly what you're doing, so get over it. I wanted to check in on you anyway after the goings-on this morning. Finding a dead body would turn anybody upside down and inside out. Even if that millionaire Christian Lake had stumbled across a body, I'd be at his house to check on him."

"You'd take food to a millionaire?" Emma bit out.

"He's probably got plenty of food." Ina rubbed her chin in thought. "I'd probably bring him some homemade cookies. Everyone has different needs."

Emma looked at the half dozen bags of groceries in front of her and stopped fighting her pride. Relief immediately swept over her. Groceries were exhausting. She had to bike several miles to and from and figure out the smallest amount to spend, all while considering how much she could pack home on the bike.

"Thank you," she whispered. Tears smarted.

Ina set a hand on her arm. "Where's your daddy?" she asked in a kind voice.

Emma shook her head, not wanting to speak of him.

The woman waited a long moment and then sat back. "Okay. I'll listen when you're ready. So for now, if you can bring in some wood, I'll start the fire with that bit of kindling over there while you finish your dinner."

Emma nodded silently and headed out the door to where she'd heard the wood being stacked on the porch. She froze as the cat lifted his head from the food bowl and stared at her, his gaze full of suspicion. "Hi, Cornbread," she whispered, trying out the name. "Please don't run away." She slowly inched in the opposite direction, toward the wood, not looking away. He watched her for a long moment, then turned back to his food.

He didn't run!

She stacked as much wood in her arms as she could, trying to make sense of what had happened in the last ten minutes. The old cop had reported her.

But she wasn't in trouble; he'd sent help.

Her eyes smarted again, and she blinked hard to get rid of the tears. She didn't want to go back inside, where that pushy woman would take one look and know she'd been crying.

Her father had always refused any sort of help, saying they were just fine on their own. *Charity* was a four-letter word to him. And assistance from the government? Forget it. He could take care of his own.

But he's not taking care of me.

I'm an adult.

She lifted her chin and took the load of wood inside. Cornbread ignored her, focused on eating.

Ina had already made a little pile of paper and kindling in the woodstove. Emma silently set down the armload of firewood and then handed the pieces one by one to Ina, who expertly placed them.

"Matches?" Ina asked.

Emma grabbed the box, but the woman wouldn't take it.

"Light your fire," Ina ordered.

Emma lit her fire. Once she was certain it'd taken hold, she closed the iron door and adjusted a dial to make sure plenty of oxygen was getting inside. She held her hands near the door, soaking in the heat that was barely starting. Beside her, Ina was silent for once.

"Can I get you some coffee?" asked Emma, feeling gratitude toward the woman. And Ben, the old cop.

"Got decaf?"

"I don't think so." She didn't drink coffee, but there was a jar of instant that her father used.

"No, thank you, then. I'll never get to sleep tonight." She braced her cane against the low hearth and awkwardly pushed to her feet with a groan. "I'll help you put away the groceries."

"No," said Emma, deciding she could be pushy too. "Sit at the table, and I'll make some tea. No caffeine. Then I'll do the groceries."

Ina eyed her. "There's that backbone again," she said softly. "I won't pass up that offer," she said in a normal voice.

A few minutes later, Emma had put away the groceries and joined Ina at the table. "I feel like I've seen that man before . . . Lucas?" said Emma.

"He works at the city police department. Last name is Ingram."

"I haven't been to the police—" Emma began, and then the name clicked. "He went to my high school!" she said. "He graduated before I started there, but there is a picture of him in the trophy case with a football. I knew he looked familiar."

"That's him," said Ina with a proud smile. "He was a star at Eagle's Nest High School. Still is, apparently."

"That's cool." Emma went silent, not wanting to talk about school.

"Is this going to be a problem with your father?" Ina gestured at the woodstove and fridge.

"No. I'll explain. He'll understand." She squirmed in her seat.

"Doesn't look like you think he'll understand," said Ina.

Emma clenched her teeth, fighting to not say more.

Ina took a sip of her tea, her sharp eyes watching Emma over the rim. She set the cup down with a clang and gave a loud sigh. "I can't put a face to your daddy's name, which is unusual, considering I sat behind the front desk at the police department for decades. Ben knows a bit about him, but that's beside the point. The man isn't doing his duty by you."

"I'm eighteen," Emma said. "He doesn't have to take care of me."

"Is that what he told you?"

"No." Emma looked at her tea.

"Humph." Ina took a sip from her cup. "Well, you let me know if we've caused any problems. You got a cell phone?"

"An old one. But I have to go to the road to get steady service."

"You can call me anytime. I'll leave my number." Ina fixed her gaze on Emma's. "I'll be checking on you in a week."

Emma fought to hold eye contact. The woman was surprisingly intimidating. "You don't have to do that."

"I know. But I want to." Ina snorted and lifted her cup. "Like you, I got a soft spot for strays. Once you're in with me, you're in for life."

I'm her Cornbread.

10

It was nearly seven when Max punched in the security code and watched Noelle's black iron gate slowly glide to one side, disappearing behind the brick wall. He wondered how much the huge gate weighed. It was a solid slab of iron; there were no elaborate designs with iron bars to see through.

He'd been to her house at least a dozen times and still wasn't used to some of the [illegible]

He searched for the right word.

Not grandeur. *Not* ostentatiousness.

Gravity *sounds accurate.*

The home and grounds had quality and strength, but not in a flashy way. It wasn't in your face; it was understated like the gate. The entire property was stately and minimalist at the same time. The acreage had two guest homes, an empty stable and covered arena, and a swimming pool. With a pool house, of course.

He drove up the long drive and parked in front of the garage. Garages. Noelle had two oversize two-car garages and a double RV garage. She'd laughed as his jaw dropped when she showed him the inside. The giant space was completely empty except for her Toyota 4Runner.

"Maybe I could put in a small running track," she'd joked.

Max had envisioned a personal showroom of motorcycles.

But kept that thought to himself.

When he was based at the Sacramento FBI office, Max and another agent had spent weeks digging into the more-than-a-decade-old murder of Noelle's husband. The cold case of the California assemblyman's death had landed on Max's desk for review, needing fresh sets of eyes. Part of that review was reinterviewing all involved parties.

The spouse always drew heavy scrutiny.

Noelle Marshall had impressed him on the first day, when she'd walked into the Bend FBI conference room and found a surprise FBI interview and their camera pointing her way.

She'd raised her chin and coolly answered their questions in an all-day marathon interview.

As Max had prepared his research, he'd followed Noelle's journey from Sacramento bartender to assemblyman's wife and socialite to police officer and then Deschutes County detective. As he'd worked, in the back of his mind he'd constantly wondered if Noelle had murdered her husband. She'd been present when it happened and become very rich after his death.

Then Max met her during that interview last January.

Now he passed under the portico to Noelle's front door. Another giant work of black iron, elegant and simple. Noelle had told him several times in the past to just walk in, but he wasn't ready for that and rang the doorbell. Three seconds later he heard her voice over the speaker. "I said you don't need to ring the bell. And the door's unlocked."

"I know. Just feels weird to stroll on in. Plus I know better than to surprise armed law enforcement." She snorted at that, and he opened the door.

The scent of Italian spices enveloped him, and he was instantly hungry. He headed toward the large kitchen, but she came around a corner first, a glass of red wine in her hand. And he got lost in her dark-blue eyes.

She takes my breath away.

Noelle had spent her morning at a murder scene, but the woman in front of him looked relaxed and happy. She wore soft yoga pants and a long-sleeved tee along with thick slippers, her platinum hair in a messy bun. She gave him a quick kiss and long hug.

"Did I ever tell you how I felt when I first saw you at that espresso bar?" he asked as he followed her to the kitchen, his hand in hers. Before the FBI's surprise interview in January, the two of them had bought coffee at the same espresso place.

She poured him a glass of wine, and her brows came together as she thought. "At the interview you said you didn't realize I was in line behind you when you paid for my latte. You were just continuing the pay-it-forward chain."

"That's true," Max said, taking a sip. "But when I turned away from the cash register, we made eye contact ever so briefly as I passed."

"I remember."

"During my next ten steps, all I could see was your eyes." He studied her face, enjoying the disbelief and then acceptance in her gaze. "It's true. It wasn't until I was in my car that I matched your face with the file I'd been studying for weeks."

"You didn't recognize me."

"I did." He slipped an arm around her waist, set down his glass, and pulled her close. "But it was a delayed response. Your photos didn't do you justice." He gave her a long kiss and then looked up at a faint sound. "Your sauce is about to boil over."

She pulled away and turned down the gas as she gave the red sauce a stir. Then she checked the pasta, and then she opened the oven and frowned at a loaf of warming bread.

This feels homey.

He craved homeyness. While he'd been in town for Noelle's interview, he'd realized how much he missed family time with his grandmother and his sister Keira, who was married to his college friend TJ Siddell. Deep in his soul, he wanted something, and he'd felt it as he'd joked with his sister and her husband.

That camaraderie. The shared history.

That acceptance that comes with family.

Most of the time.

He set down his wineglass. One of his goals in moving back to Oregon had been to make peace with his mother and his other two sisters. They *knew* he was back in the state because he'd texted each of them with the news. But all he'd received back was a "that's nice" from his mother, a thumbs-up from Amber, and silence from Brittany.

Essentially that was silence from all three.

I have to get through to them.

I had to do it.

"Had to do what?" asked Noelle as she dumped the pasta into a strainer over the sink and leaned away from the hot steam.

"Talking to myself," said Max, surprised to learn he'd spoken out loud.

Noelle glanced at him, a knowing look in her eyes. "A case?"

"Yeah. The ones from the past pop up occasionally," he hedged.

"Want to talk about it?"

"Not at the moment."

But he did. He'd stopped himself from bringing the incident up with Noelle several times. They weren't at the point in their relationship to talk about ghosts from the past. They were at the willing-to-drive-each-other-to-the-airport stage.

Max wanted to move forward to the other stage. But Noelle had emphasized that she wanted things to go slowly, and he'd agreed to her pace. Even though she'd been single for about thirteen years, she'd been married twice before that, and both marriages had ended roughly. She'd admitted she kept people at arm's length, so he held back, afraid to scare her off.

As if she'd scare.

She was one of the most confident and bravest people he'd ever met. He'd watched her walk into a house where she knew an armed murderer was holding hostages. He'd seen her hold it together after her best friend had been shot in her home. And he'd seen how hard she worked to combat sporadic memory loss and head pain, lingering effects of the attack when her husband was murdered, determined not to let them affect her job.

But relationships were the place where she moved tentatively.

Except when it came to family. She was tight with her sisters, Eve and Lucia, who lived nearby. Max knew Noelle would walk into fire for either of them. Both women had been through hell the past year. Lucia had recently finished an inpatient drug addiction program and was trying to get back on her feet. Eve was mourning the betrayal and loss of her husband. Noelle's great-aunt Daisy—who lived in the same complex as his grandmother Paulette—was another she would battle to the death to protect.

Noelle sliced into the bread, and the scent made his mouth water. "Ready?" She pointed at the end of her huge island, where she'd set two places. They always ate in her kitchen. The formal dining room had a huge table for twelve and the oddest light fixture he'd ever seen. It looked like a manifestation of a child's scribble. The kitchen was warm and welcoming, and sitting next to her made him happy.

"It's been a rough day," she said, dipping her bread in olive oil.

"Leads?"

"Some things to follow up on. Dr. Lockhart had to push the autopsy to tomorrow, and I haven't spoken with anyone who saw anything helpful near the crime scene."

"You'll figure it out."

"I plan on it," she said with a tired smile. "I feel for the teenager who found him. She was collecting cans and bottles. Finding a murder victim was not on her list for the day."

"That's a hard way to make money. Poor kid," said Max between bites. The pasta was excellent.

"She *is* poor," said Noelle. "Broke my heart when I saw where she lives with her dad, but he wasn't around today to give her any support. I hope he did so this evening. Truman Daly is aware of her situation and said he'd send someone out to check on her." She poured more wine but hadn't touched her pasta.

Work can be hard on the appetite.

"How was your day?" she asked, clearly done talking about her own.

"Good. Took a ride with Mercy to a home out near Prineville, where we met one of her CIs and the CI's sister." He shook his head, remembering how assertively Rachel had flirted. "Interesting women." He told Noelle what he'd learned about the past implosion of America's Preserve and Mercy's role there.

Noelle nodded emphatically. "Evan told me about that. His girlfriend Rowan's search and rescue dog is the one who tracked Mercy. She'd gone missing for like a week after the compound was raided." She slowly spun the stem of her glass, her gaze on the wine. "It was a bad situation."

"Sounded like it," said Max. "We went to see her informant today because there is chatter about a possible domestic terrorism event around here. Have you heard anything?"

Noelle thought. "I saw a memo from the FBI about that; basically it said nothing specific but told us to keep ears and eyes open. So business as usual. It's hard to *not* encounter someone who's angry with law enforcement or another government entity. Threats are pretty common but usually amount to nothing."

"Are you going to eat?" Max asked, reaching for a second piece of bread.

"Yes." Noelle focused on her food, taking several bites. "I guess I'm not as hungry as I thought." She took a sip of wine, holding his gaze across the rim of her glass. "Maybe I need something else."

Heat ripped through Max's body.

I can provide that.

He set down his bread and took her hand, pulling her from her seat. "Dinner can wait."

Damn, I'm a lucky man.

11

Emma jerked awake and lay unmoving in the pitch dark. She'd decided to sleep on the sofa, which was in the warmest room of the house due to the woodstove. But she could tell the fire was out because now there was a chill in the air. She looked toward the window, trying to guess the time. Then she heard scratching near the front door.

That's what woke me.

Then came the howl.

She lurched upright, holding the blanket against her chest. The sound came again, low and angry.

Cornbread.

Emma lurched to her feet and stumbled to the front door, where the sound seemed to come from. The cat sounded as if he was dying. The sound morphed into a pleading cry, making her heart break.

Is he hurt? Did something attack him?

She pressed her nose against the window, trying to see the cat and what had attacked it in the dark. A bobcat or even a black bear could be on the porch. Instead, she saw Cornbread dart down the stairs and dash into the woods, a faint ghost moving at ground level. Nothing followed him.

He's not running like he's hurt.

She shifted her view to check the rest of the porch but didn't see any predators. The chickens were silent, not throwing fits like when a fox or worse was near. Emma strained her eyes trying to see where

Cornbread had vanished into the woods. Her heart pounded, his cries still reverberating in her head. "He must be okay," she muttered. "I doubt—"

She froze and then slowly sank until she could just see over the windowsill.

A light had moved in the woods. And then cut out.

Her gaze fixed on the location, and her heartbeat continued to speed. She waited.

I'm seeing things. I was staring too hard to spot Cornbread.

The light appeared again, and she stopped breathing. It was faint with an almost pinkish-peach tone.

As if someone has their fingers over the lens of a flashlight.

Confirming her suspicions, the light became clear and then abruptly went pink again. And it moved, bobbing as if someone was walking.

Walking toward the house.

Shit! Move!

She grabbed her blanket and pillow from the sofa and thrust them over the back, not wanting anyone to see the couch had been slept on. She touched the top of the woodstove; it was warm. The house was cold, but anyone who touched the stove would know it'd been used recently.

There was nothing she could do about it now.

If they came in the house and checked her bed or her dad's, they would feel cold. And maybe they'd believe no one had been home.

Emma thrust her feet in her boots and grabbed a heavy coat and knit cap. She'd slept in her clothes as usual. A habit from always being cold. She spun in the dark, wondering what else she should grab. The gun.

Darting back to the kitchen, she took the gun out of the drawer and shoved it into her raggedy backpack along with her cell phone. She silently tore down the hall into her father's bedroom and dropped to her knees by his bed, shoving her hands between the mattress and box spring until she felt the plastic bag. She tucked the bag of cash into her backpack next to the gun and crawled to the window on her hands and knees. She silently slid open the window a little and listened, her ears straining for sounds in the night.

There was no back door in the old mobile home. Her father had always said it was a death trap in case of fire, and so, when she was six, he'd shown Emma how to get out through her bedroom window in case of an emergency.

A kick to the screen.

Then a drop to the dirt.

She'd landed on her knees the first time she'd tried it, which had made her cry. He'd made her do it two more times.

But this time she was at her father's window at the front of the house, his screen long gone. A better place to spy and listen. She peeked over the windowsill. The dim light had moved closer, and she swore she saw two figures. She questioned her decision to not automatically go out her own window at the back of the house. But if someone circled the house, they'd see she'd had to leave the screen on the ground.

Besides, this would be the fastest route to the woods.

She was counting on them coming to the front door. This window was the best place to keep tabs on where they went. If they came in, she'd go out her father's window and get to the trees.

". . . bike's not here." A male whisper.

"Check around back for it." Second male whisper.

They want to steal my bike?

Emma closed her eyes and listened hard, thankful she'd not gone out her bedroom window. Soft crunching told her someone was right outside the window, heading around the house. A muffled sigh from the direction of the porch indicated the second person was waiting. She realized she was holding her breath and forced herself to breathe in and out.

I'm so loud.

Jogging footsteps came back around to the front of the home. "No bike. Think she's here?"

"Gotta check."

"What do we do with the girl?"

"What I already told you. We need her."

Emma held her breath.

Need me for what?

The freshly repaired board on the steps gave a loud creak and then, a second later, creaked again.

They're coming in.

She slowly slid her father's window fully open, praying it didn't make a sound, her ears still trained on the front porch.

"Where's the key?"

"Here."

Something rustled like dried leaves.

They knew the key was tucked in the door's wreath.

They've been here before. Or someone told them.

She heard the characteristic squeak of the opening door and mentally counted to five, allowing time for both men to move into the house. The door squeaked again as it closed, and she stuck her head out the window to check the porch. Empty. She lifted her backpack out and dropped it as silently as she could and then climbed out, lowering herself to the dirt. She slid the window closed, grabbed her pack, and ran for the woods.

12

The next morning, Max had just entered the parking lot at the FBI office when his phone rang and Keira's name popped up on his screen. He cursed. He'd forgotten to reply to her texts yesterday about his other two sisters.

I didn't forget.

He'd ignored them. Amber and Brittany were a sore spot for him. And usually talking with Keira about it only made it worse. But he knew she'd keep poking at him until she got a response. He parked and bit the bullet.

"Hey, Keira, what's up?"

"You didn't return my texts yesterday." Keira was direct as usual.

"Sorry, busy day."

"Have you talked to Amber recently?"

"Is that a trick question?" He'd tried for more than ten years to establish a relationship with his other two sisters. The refusal was on their end. And his mother had sided with them.

"I hate that you don't get along." Keira's relationship with the other women in the family was solid.

He bristled. "Not for lack of trying on my part. Why are you calling? I'm about to go into the office."

"The girls are coming up next weekend, so they'll be at our usual dinner."

He and Keira still referred to their younger siblings as "the girls" even though they were now twenty-eight and thirty.

"They're going to stay with you?" Their sisters lived three hours away.

"Yes. I told them that you would be at dinner, and that was fine with them."

I seriously doubt that.

Either Keira hadn't said anything to them, or she didn't want to repeat their replies to him.

I did nothing wrong.

But his sister Brittany had been emotionally hurt by Max's actions during his worst day ever on the Medford police force.

Actually, it had been the worst day of his *life*.

Amber and his mother had also blamed him, making the rift between him and his younger sisters even wider.

Amber and Brittany were much younger than Max because they had been born after his mother remarried. His stepfather had raised him and Keira all through their teen years, which had not been pleasant. He and Keira had essentially been the home's staff. All the cleaning, babysitting, yard work, and errands had fallen to them. Not only had he and Keira lost a relationship with their father when their parents split up, but they'd later lost their connection to their mother because of her new husband.

Max had hated the way his stepfather, Oscar Forkner, treated their mother and had told him so when Max had moved out of the house. Oscar had thrown the first punch, and by the end of the pummeling, eighteen-year-old Max had had two black eyes and a split lip. He hadn't landed a blow on the older man.

His mother had screamed for Max to leave her husband alone, and his younger sisters had bawled as the two men fought. Keira, who was sixteen, tried to pull them apart, earning a shove from her stepfather that threw her against the fireplace. She still had the scar on her forehead.

Max never set foot in the home again. He finished college and joined the Medford PD, where he learned that Oscar Forkner was well known to the police force. He'd had numerous drunk and disorderly citations and three domestic violence incidents. His mother had refused to press charges each time.

When Max had tried to talk to her about the abuse, she wouldn't discuss her husband, claiming that her marriage was the most important thing in her life.

"What about your kids?" he'd asked. "Brittany and Amber deserve to grow up in a better home."

"They're the most important thing *after* my husband."

She hadn't mentioned Max or Keira, and he never forgot how abandoned he'd felt at her words.

Oscar had died while driving drunk three years ago and had been lucky he hadn't killed anyone else. After his death, Max thought he could heal the rift with his family. He was wrong. If anything, it was worse. His mother was bitter and resentful. She never said it out loud, but Max suspected she was angry that he'd been right about the man she'd married.

Will she ever get over that?

Brittany carries Mom's gene for being unforgiving.

"Check with me later this week," Max told Keira.

"Which means no."

"It's a maybe."

"There's something else . . ."

Her voice trailed off, which surprised him because Keira wasn't hesitant about saying anything. Some would call it having no fear; others would call it having no filter.

"What?" he asked.

"I got a flower delivery last evening. They weren't from TJ."

"You have an admirer?" TJ would have strong words with anyone who hit on his wife. After Keira had even stronger words with them.

"I don't think so."

The odd tone of her voice put him on edge. "What happened?"

"Max, the note with them reads, 'Congratulations on having a murderer for a brother.'"

Max froze.

Murderer.

"You should have called me right away," he finally said.

"I'm telling you now. By the time I got home from work and opened the note, the florist was closed. And I wanted to talk it over with TJ before you."

"TJ's name's not in the message!"

"It feels like some sort of mean prank, Max. I didn't know if it was worth telling you. Clearly it was just meant to upset you. And me."

"Did you ask Brittany about it?"

"Jesus, Max! And no, I didn't. She wouldn't do this."

Max didn't know what Brittany would do. He hadn't seen her in years. Oscar—and their mother—had effectively made Max and Keira feel like unwanted strangers in their own home.

"Which florist?"

She told him. Max wanted to turn his vehicle back on and drive directly to the florist, but he needed to work. "Are they black roses?" The joke went sour in his mouth.

"White. I looked it up. They're appropriate for weddings and funerals."

Max hadn't gone to the funeral they were both thinking about, but he'd gone to the interment and watched from afar, knowing his presence could be upsetting.

"I'll check with the florist later," he told her. "I need to go." He wanted off the phone.

"Max, you did nothing wrong."

"I know."

But it never felt that way.

"Don't let this upset you," said Keira.

"Same with you."

They ended the call, and Max headed into the office wishing he'd bought an apple fritter with his coffee that morning. Maybe two.

Who would send those flowers to Keira?

Anger shot through him. If someone had a problem with his past actions, they needed to come to him. Not disturb his family.

He didn't know if he could stomach a dinner with his sisters. Especially after hearing about the flowers.

He hadn't told Noelle why the relationship with his younger sisters and mother was so bad. She only knew they were estranged.

I haven't told her a lot of things.

Maybe it was time.

◆ ◆ ◆

The man watched Max stride across the parking lot. He'd kept an eye on the FBI agent for a few weeks, learning his habits and mulling over what he wanted to do.

He knew messing with the FBI was a dangerous thing, but he believed that Max Rhodes moving to the Bend area had been a sign. It was almost as if Max were being handed to him on a platter. Max was in his territory, his world.

He would have never known if he hadn't seen the man in a newspaper photo weeks ago and learned that he was a local FBI agent.

All the old hatred had flooded back.

The bitterness had faded over the years, so he'd been surprised at his boiling reaction to the photo. And now he couldn't get the man out of his head.

But what if I get caught?

He didn't want to spend the rest of his life in a federal prison for murder.

The man put away his binoculars, feeling the anger surge through him as it did every time he spied on the agent. He closed his eyes and exhaled slowly, willing the anger to dissipate.

There was no reason to rush.

I'll take my time.

13

Noelle had been reading whatever she could find on Trevor Baylor, the man who'd partied with the high school kids Saturday night. Most of it was high school sports articles. Trevor had been a star basketball player for Eagle's Nest High School. But something had gone wrong after that and he'd developed a record of stupid shit: vandalism, underage drinking—which continued into DUI as he got older—reckless driving, and an assault case from a protest in Portland.

Evan drove as she read out loud on their way to an early morning pop-in at Baylor's home. He pulled into the pitted parking lot of a small run-down apartment building and parked next to an old Dodge pickup with a flat tire. Noelle eyed the thick coat of dust on the windshield and hood. The vehicle registered to Baylor was a Subaru, which she didn't see in the lot. Trevor Baylor's home address wasn't that far from the Deschutes County sheriff's office, so they were still in Bend.

"There's apartment four," said Evan. "Can't read half of the other door numbers."

Noelle had noticed that too. The building was in desperate need of new paint, and someone had given up the pretense of trying to maintain the grounds. The beds were full of weeds. She pressed the doorbell for apartment four.

"I didn't hear a bell," said Evan.

"Me neither." She rapped hard on the door with her knuckles and listened. "Someone's moving inside." The door had a peephole, and Noelle put on a pleasant expression, trying not to look like a cop. Evan stood out of view, knowing that seeing just Noelle would lower people's defenses.

The door opened, and she recognized Trevor Baylor from his driver's license photo. She had to look up, which was unusual for her. She had read he was six foot five, but it was still a surprise. His thick canvas coat and large boots told her he had just been about to leave.

He looked her over, a small smile starting on his face. "Can I help you?" Then Trevor scowled as he noticed Evan.

Noelle and Evan held out their identification and introduced themselves.

"Police? Why? What do you want?"

"Just to talk about something you might have seen," Noelle said in a reassuring voice. "Can we come in?"

"I was just leaving."

"Can you give us five minutes?" She gave her warmest smile.

Trevor blinked as if slightly blinded and stepped back. "Is this about those shoplifters?" He'd worked at a Bend grocery store since he graduated high school.

"It's not," said Noelle, moving into the dim apartment. She spotted a light switch and flipped it on, lighting up a harsh single bulb in the living room ceiling. A worn-out imitation leather couch covered with laundry faced a large TV, which sat on a rickety cabinet whose top sagged under the weight. Noelle stepped closer to read the framed diploma hanging prominently on the wall and was surprised to see it was from high school. Next to it was an eight-by-ten photo of Trevor shooting a basketball. He was in the air, his feet far above the gym floor, concentration on his face, the ball just leaving his fingertips. Next to that, thumbtacked onto the wall, was the jersey that Trevor wore in the photo.

Noelle pointed at the photo as she turned to Trevor. "Did you make that shot?"

"No," he said with a sheepish grin. "But it's an awesome picture." He took off his heavy coat and set it on the back of the couch.

"It is," she agreed.

He was extremely thin. She'd wondered about the low weight on his driver's license, but now saw it wasn't an error. On his sweatshirt was the high school's mascot.

He's twenty-five.

She wondered if the high school items represented unfulfilled dreams or if he was clinging to an identity once central in his life.

"What do you want to talk to me about?" asked Trevor. He quickly shoved aside the clothing on the couch and sat down, his knees akimbo, making her think of a giant grasshopper. She and Evan took seats in chairs that appeared to have once belonged to a dining room set.

"We're talking to people who were out off Old Mill Highway on Saturday night," said Evan.

Trevor tore his eyes away from Noelle to look at Evan. "What?" There was a small quiver in his voice.

"We've been told you were there," said Noelle. Trevor was instantly nervous, triggering her Spidey-sense.

"Nah, wasn't there. Somebody's lying."

Yeah. You.

"We know you were there, Trevor," said Noelle in her best bored-cop voice. "You're not in trouble. We just want to know if you saw anything unusual. Any fights or altercations."

"Unusual? Like what? I didn't see any fights. Everyone was in a good mood."

Sweat beaded on his temples, and he wiped at his upper lip.

"Trevor, we're not here because you might have bought alcohol for minors or maybe some other things that are illegal for anyone under twenty-one."

"I didn't see anyone fight," he said quickly. "And I wasn't in charge of bringing alcohol this time."

This time.

It appeared Trevor didn't know that a murdered man had been found nearby, which Noelle found odd, considering that the discovery had been in the news. And had ricocheted up the gossip chains.

Evan brought Trevor up to speed about the murdered man found near the location.

He jerked up straight on the couch, his anxiety skyrocketing. "I don't know anything about that. I didn't see nothing there on Saturday. Who was killed?"

"We don't know yet," said Noelle, watching him closely. "Are you aware of anyone who is missing? Or any rumors?"

"Nah, don't know anyone who's missing. Only rumors I hear about is work stuff."

"Trevor, why do you hang out with kids who are still in high school?" Noelle asked. "Shouldn't you be down at the local bar shooting pool with adults?"

There was no point to her question except curiosity.

Trevor straightened, instantly defensive. "I don't. I mean, sure, sometimes I do. I just happen to have some friends that age. It's no big deal. I go to bars too," he said emphatically, his nervousness returning.

This wasn't the man Noelle had expected to meet. She'd thought he'd be some lazy jerk who was making money by buying alcohol and pot for kids. Instead, he appeared to be someone who genuinely missed high school life. Hanging with the younger crowd could be an effort to hold on to the past. His glory days.

She'd heard of people who peaked during high school. Trevor Baylor appeared to be one of them.

"Can you write down some names of people you saw Saturday night?" asked Noelle.

He jumped up, opened a drawer in the TV cabinet, and took out a pencil and notebook paper.

Are those old school supplies?

Noelle couldn't remember the last time she'd bought notebook paper. College, probably.

She and Evan were quiet as he wrote for a bit, amusing Noelle by scrunching up his face and staring at the ceiling as he concentrated.

A few minutes later they were out the door, three more names in their hands.

"What did you think of him?" Noelle asked Evan.

"I think he needs to find something to focus on besides high school."

"I thought so too." The encounter had left her a bit depressed.

Hopefully he'll find something else.

14

"Jus' sit up real slow and stick your hands out so I can see them, or I'll shoot your head off!"

Emma jerked awake at the threatening voice and froze.

"I've got a double barrel pointed at your brains. You're trespassing, so I've got no qualms about pulling the trigger."

She tried to speak, but her dry tongue was hung up in her extra-dry mouth. A weak squawk was all she could do.

"I'm gonna count to five. No, make that three. One—"

"Uncle Tommy!" Emma forced out from underneath the horse blanket. "It's me!"

The moment of silence was heavy in the barn. "Emma?" he asked.

"Yes!"

"For Christ's sake, girl! What the hell you doin' here?"

Emma exhaled and shakily shoved off the blanket. She pushed up her knit cap, which had covered her eyes, and blinked at him in the morning light.

"Holy crap, Emma! Couldn't tell it was you under all that shit. *What if I'd blown your head off?*" Shock filled the old man's face.

"Sorry," she muttered, sitting up. Her feet and hands were numb from the cold, and her brain and tongue still weren't functioning correctly since the rude awakening had scared her to death.

I knew this might happen.

After the two men had invaded her home the night before, Uncle Tommy's farm had been the only place she could think of that offered safety. She'd run and walked for nearly an hour, cutting through fields and tripping over rough rocks that left stinging lacerations on her palms and shins. When she finally reached his property, she didn't dare wake him in the middle of the night. Uncle Tommy had a reputation for shooting first and asking questions later. So she'd curled up in the barn with the ancient horse blankets to wait until morning.

"Get up. It's freezing out here." He tucked the shotgun under one arm, shoved a hand under her armpit, and lifted her to her feet. Her cold legs didn't want to participate, and she struggled to get her balance. "Your daddy know you're here?"

"I don't think so," she hedged.

"Well, let's get inside the house, and you can tell me what's going on while I make you a hot breakfast."

Tears smarted. "Thank you."

"Don't thank me just yet. Something tells me I'm not going to be happy after we talk."

She followed him out of the barn and headed toward the old farmhouse, slowing her pace to match his limping one. Uncle Tommy wasn't really her uncle. Just a friend of her dad's. But he'd been in her life for as long as she could remember. He bought the best presents for her birthday and never forgot to send her some cash on Christmas. She'd loved going to his farm as a kid because he'd had a few old horses that hadn't minded if she climbed on and rode bareback, guiding them with her legs and tugs on their manes. Only one was left now.

Uncle Tommy had been an old man since she'd first met him. He was missing a few fingers, he always limped, and because he'd heavily favored one leg and hip for decades, his back was crooked and his shoulders bent. Emma had never known him without his white, thick beard and wiry eyebrows that seemed to grow longer every year. He frequently wore tropical shirts that made him look like Santa Claus on vacation. She'd worried about him living alone, but her dad had laughed, saying Tommy was too ornery to die.

A few minutes later, Emma was in a warm kitchen with a hot mug of coffee while he fried ten eggs in a ton of butter. He'd thrown two pieces of bread in the toaster and buttered them with a spatula and had them on the table in front of her within moments of her sitting down. His missing fingers never slowed him down in the kitchen. He continuously refilled the toaster as the eggs bubbled in the fat, and he stacked a plate high with the butter-laden slices.

Emma's bones finally started to defrost during her third piece of toast. Uncle Tommy slid six eggs onto a plate and cooked the other four eggs a minute longer. Then he transferred them onto her plate and sat down. He ripped a piece of toast in half, jabbed it in a yolk, making it run, ate the piece in two bites, and then repeated the process several times. Emma cut into her firm eggs with a fork, already full but pleased that he'd remembered she didn't like runny yolks.

"Start talking," he said with his mouth full of eggy toast.

Emma set down her fork, her stomach churning, and told him what had happened last night.

The bushy eyebrows shot up his forehead. "You recognize them?"

"I couldn't really see faces. The voices weren't familiar." She paused. "One of them asked what to do about me and the other said to do what they were told." Her voice cracked. "I don't know what that meant, but it can't be good." Her brain had played the conversation over and over as she'd tried to fall asleep in Tommy's barn.

They were going to kidnap me. Or kill me.

Tommy stabbed at his eggs, his heavy brows coming together, and swore under his breath. "I doubt they'd been told to take you out for coffee."

She made a choking laugh-snort sound.

"And you think a stray cat purposefully warned you that these men were coming?" Doubt filled his tone.

"I do," she said emphatically. "He's never acted like that before." She'd worried for Cornbread as she'd made her way to Tommy's, but figured he was smart enough to stay away from the house until the men left and would then bed down in the straw-filled bin.

"Huh." Tommy scooped an entire fried egg into his mouth and chewed, a thoughtful look on his face. "You don't know where your daddy was last night?"

Emma shook her head, her gaze on her plate, feeling him study her.

"How long's he been gone?" he asked softly.

She swallowed hard. "I'm not sure."

"It's not a hard question," said Tommy, his eyes narrowing.

Tell him.

"I haven't seen him since November," Emma whispered, staring at her cooling eggs.

Silence filled the room. And then he roared, *"Your daddy's been gone for four months?"*

She nodded and dared to look up.

His face was bright red, making his white hair and eyebrows pop. "You call the police?" he asked, and then he answered his question before she could. "Of course you didn't, otherwise I would have heard about it." He pushed back from the table and crossed his arms on his chest. "Dammit, Emma," he muttered. The anger faded as quickly as it had come as he studied the ceiling of his kitchen. "Do you know where he is?"

"No," she whispered.

"He got a new girlfriend?"

"Dunno."

"What about his truck?"

"He took it." She took a deep breath. "I came home from school one day and he wasn't there." She hadn't worried. Her father would occasionally head out of town or bunk with a new girlfriend for several days at a time without telling her. But by the fifth day, Emma had known something wasn't right.

And she'd done nothing.

"I get it. I understand why you didn't tell me," Tommy said slowly, holding her gaze. "He was an asshole to you. About the worst a daddy could be. I got on his case several times about how he treated you. Even suggested you come live with me, but he wasn't having it."

Emma didn't realize she was crying until a tear tickled her lips, and she wiped it away with her sleeve. She'd long hated her father. Not only did he physically beat her, but he beat her with his words. She was dumb, stupid, retarded, ugly, useless, a whore, clumsy, and not worth spending money on. He expected her to put meals on the table and keep the house perfectly clean. Any slowness or mistakes meant no food for her or that he would burn her clothes.

I was just a slave to him.

The only time she could breathe was when he was gone. When he hadn't come back in November, she'd told no one. Wanting him to stay gone forever.

She'd had peace. No fear.

Her quality of life had dramatically improved with him gone. She was no longer forced to go to school, where the other kids harassed her. She'd always known her dad kept some money under his mattress, so when the landlord came by for the rent each month, she paid it. But the bag of cash was getting low. She'd collected cans and bottles to buy her food because she knew that if her father came back and more money than the rent was gone, there'd be hell to pay.

"You should have come to me," Tommy said firmly.

She'd considered it a hundred times, but she had been too scared he would find her father and then her life would be miserable again.

"And school?" he asked carefully.

"I'm working on my GED. I use the computer at the library. I don't want to go back to that school."

He sighed. "Can't blame you there." He slapped his hands on the table. "Finish eating, and we'll make a run to your house. Get your stuff and then you can stay here."

Relief swamped her. She'd regretted leaving behind all the groceries that Ina Smythe had bought. Now she could stock Tommy's fridge as a thank-you.

Ten minutes later they were in his ancient pickup, which smelled of motor oil, horses, and old-man sweat. Then she realized she hadn't told him about finding the body yesterday. Her thoughts had been caught up with the invaders last night and almost being shot in the head that morning.

She shared the story, trying not to let the images of the body stick in her head as she talked.

"That was you that found him?" Tommy asked with a shocked stare. "I heard about that. I knew it was a teenager who discovered the body. Did they identify it yet?"

"I don't know. The detective said she'd let me know when they did, but I'm sure she's very busy."

"You good?" he asked, scowling at the road.

"Yeah. Last night was worse than that." She dug her fingernails into the fabric seat.

How can anything be worse than finding a dead body?

And it happened on the same day.

Tommy sighed. "You'll be safe with me." He patted the revolver at his side. "We'll figure out where your daddy is."

"You don't know where he might be?" Emma finally asked. Tommy hadn't speculated out loud, but she knew he was thinking about it.

"I've got some places to check." He glanced at her. "I'll find him. You shouldn't be on your own."

"I'm eighteen."

"Really? No shit." Tommy shook his head. "Guess it's stuck in my brain that you're still around twelve."

"I don't want him to come back," she whispered.

Tommy kept his eyes on the road. "I know. We'll cross that road when we come to it."

I'll run away if he comes back.

The old truck bounced down her road, and Emma gasped in happiness when she spotted Cornbread on her porch, waiting by his empty food dish. "The cat's okay!"

"Don't know about bringing a cat with you," said Tommy. "They make me itch. Sneeze too."

"He won't let me touch him," said Emma. "But I can come back and feed him along with the chickens each day." She slid off the truck's high seat and slammed the door. Cornbread's amber eyes held her gaze as she slowly approached, and the tip of his tail twitched in annoyance.

"Good boy," she said softly as she went up the stairs. "Oh, shit!" The front door was wide open.

"Hang on, Emma," Tommy said sharply. "Let me check it out first."

Emma didn't think Cornbread would be sitting calmly on the porch if strangers were in the house, but Tommy pulled his big revolver from his holster and went inside.

Emma knelt and slowly reached a hand toward the cat. Cornbread glared but allowed her to touch his back. She gave a few gentle strokes, and his glare seemed to fade a bit.

He let me pet him!

Tommy was back a moment later. "All clear. But watch your step inside." He looked at Cornbread, who had backed away as Tommy appeared. "Thought you said you couldn't get near him."

"First time." Emma stood, still delighted. "I'll pack up some groceries and get my stuff." She stepped inside and gasped at the broken glass strewn across the floor. It was dark green, clearly some of the drinking glasses from the cupboard. She was sad for only a brief second; she'd always thought the glasses were ugly. Careful where she placed her feet, she pulled out the plastic grocery bags she'd unpacked yesterday and started loading them back up.

"Ohhh!" She stared in one cupboard.

Tommy stepped inside. "What happened?"

"They took the cookies." Now she was definitely sad. The package of chocolate chip cookies from the grocery store bakery had been a luxury and special treat. She'd eaten one and tucked away the box to ration them. She stopped packing, quickly checked the other cupboards, and then wandered the house, wondering if they'd taken anything else, but nothing else seemed to be missing.

We had little of value to take.

Apparently cookies were the only item worth stealing from the house.

She packed up the rest of the groceries, filled Cornbread's bowl—he watched carefully from a close six feet away—and climbed back in the truck.

"You sure you don't want to take the cat?" asked Tommy as he started the old truck.

Emma was touched that the allergic man had asked. "This is his home. I don't want to take him away from that."

"You can take the truck to feed him anytime."

"Thank you." She'd been determined to feed him each day and had planned to ride her bike back to her house. Tears started at his simple offer, which would save her so much time and energy.

She watched the home fade away in her side-view mirror, and her anxiety started to rise.

What will happen when Dad comes back?

15

Max hung up the phone.

The florist who'd delivered Keira's flowers said a man had paid for them with cash and written and sealed the enclosed note himself. Their floral shop didn't have cameras, she'd told him. Why would they need cameras? She'd said the man had been polite but in a hurry. He'd worn a baseball cap and a blue jacket. The florist guessed he was in his thirties. Maybe late twenties.

Max sat at his desk, tapping his fingers, trying to think who could have sent the flowers.

Why harass Keira?

Either they couldn't get to Max or they wanted him worried about his sister's safety.

They'd achieved that goal.

A brief conversation with TJ hadn't provided any answers. He'd told Max that Keira had been angry about the note and hadn't wanted to tell him, but TJ had convinced her to do so. "She didn't want to stir anything up for you. Bad memories and shit. Especially since your sisters are coming to town."

Memories had definitely been stirred.

All that blood.

He slammed his palms on the desk, wanting the brief sting of pain to pull him out of the past. His fingers tingling, he clicked to his work email.

Focus.

He opened the latest memo on domestic terrorism from Portland and read every word out loud to stay on topic. "They really think something is going to happen in Central Oregon," he muttered to himself. "Why can't we find anything over here that indicates that?"

Central Oregon was separated from the west side of the state by the Cascade mountain range. The largest cities were on the west side, where it was often wet or gray from October to June, so Max preferred Bend's high desert climate. It could be twenty degrees outside, but the odds would be in his favor that it was also sunny. He also liked that he only had to drive fifteen minutes in almost any direction to find himself in the country. In one direction were the Cascade foothills, with towering pines and lots of privacy, and in other directions the land changed and ranches took over, interspersed with some amazing rock and hill formations that had happened when the earth was young.

As the largest city east of the mountain range, Bend had suffered growing pains. Everyone had rushed to live there over the last few decades. It'd brought heavy traffic, strained infrastructure, and high home prices. And of course a massive number of tourists came to hike and whitewater raft during the summer and ski in the winter. Many of them decided to stay permanently.

When he'd moved to Bend, Max had worried that he'd miss the bigger-city feel of Sacramento. He couldn't have been more wrong. In this city and the surrounding areas, he could *breathe*. He felt it in his lungs and head and heart. Open spaces, clean air, and blue sky. People thrived here.

He was in the right place.

Now he needed to figure out who was planning to do some damage in this beautiful area. He picked up the phone and was abruptly aware of a disturbance in the office. He set the phone back down, jumped to his feet, and opened his door to see Mercy running his way. "Let's go, let's go, let's go!" she hollered at him.

"What's happened?" he yelled back as he grabbed his coat.

"Explosion at the courthouse!"

Shit. There it is.

"It could have been worse," Max kept mumbling under his breath as he surveyed the scene. He and Mercy had seen the black smoke from their parking lot and reached the crime scene in minutes. So had a dozen city and county vehicles and three fire trucks. The area was taped off, and they had checked in with the Deschutes County sheriff's sergeant, who'd taken charge of the scene.

A single car in the courthouse lot had been the source of the explosion. It'd caused damage to the cars around it, but no one was hurt except a tourist who'd been on the sidewalk and had a heart attack. With so many fast first responders, he'd received care immediately.

The smoking car was a large Mercedes-Benz sedan, and the stink of burning rubber and fuel was heavy in the air. Max breathed through his mouth to avoid the smell but stopped as he tasted burned tire on his tongue.

"The sergeant said the car belonged to Judge Holtz," said Mercy. "Do you think someone was sending a message?"

"If they were, their message got my attention," said Max.

Mercy nodded. "My thoughts exactly."

"Hey," came a voice behind them. "Look who beat us here." Max turned to see Noelle striding his way, her gaze locked on his. Her partner, Evan, had been the speaker, but she snagged his attention. Noelle was bundled up against the cold, her eyes matching the dark-blue knit scarf at her neck. She looked as if she'd just stepped out of an ad for pricey winter wear and should be walking into a snowy mountain resort instead of investigating a car bombing.

The four of them greeted each other. Acutely aware of the public watching, Max gave Noelle's hand a quick squeeze.

"You've been assigned to this case?" he asked Noelle.

"Evan and me," she said.

"Maybe you shouldn't be here," he said softly. "It hasn't been that long." Noelle and her sisters had nearly been killed when someone set off a car bomb in her vehicle.

Noelle looked at the smoking Mercedes. "I admit I felt sick to my stomach on the way over here. Still do."

"They can assign someone else," said Max. "Your lieutenant knows—"

"Max. I can do this." Her tone clearly stated she didn't want to discuss it.

He'd stepped over a line. Noelle was an experienced detective. She didn't need him telling her what to do. "I'm sorry. I was out of my lane."

"Yes, you were." Her blue gaze held his for a long moment. "I assume you and Mercy are here because of a possible terrorism angle?" she asked in a normal, back-to-business voice. "Is there any issue if you and I are on the same case?" Her forehead wrinkled with concern.

"Correct. Terrorism," said Max. "And I don't think there is an issue with us?" he asked while looking at Mercy for her opinion. He'd never worked on a case with someone he was dating.

"Should be okay," said Mercy. "Just keep your lieutenant informed."

"I've got a forensics crew on their way," said Noelle. "They're not far behind." She frowned at the firefighters still soaking the smoking vehicle. "They're washing away evidence."

"I'm pretty sure they teach that skill at the fire academy," Max said wryly, acknowledging that the firefighters and investigators often had different priorities. "Can't be helped."

"Is this explosion related to the terrorism chatter we heard about?" asked Evan.

"That's what we're here to find out," said Max. "Has anyone claimed responsibility?"

"Nothing's come in to us," said Noelle.

Mercy eyed the vehicle. "I was expecting something bigger than a single car if this is what we've been warned about," she said quietly to the other three.

"Me too," said Max.

Maybe this is someone angry about their court case.

"I'll talk to the sergeant about getting video from the courthouse cameras," said Evan.

Max turned in a circle, spotting several cameras outside the courthouse. "Should have plenty of video available. Ask him about local business video too."

Evan nodded and headed toward the sergeant.

"We're ready, boss." Two women and a tall man wearing Tyvek jumpsuits approached Noelle. The forensics team.

"Take your time," Noelle told them. She gestured for Max and Mercy to move back, and the tall man immediately started taking photos of the surrounding area, working his way in a circle toward the smoking sedan. "We'll need a state fire investigator too."

Max nodded and scanned the growing crowd outside the yellow tape. He pulled out his phone and covertly filmed the watchers. Fire setters often returned to see the reactions to their work. Most of the people appeared to be courthouse employees who'd evacuated after the explosion.

Doesn't mean it couldn't be one of them.

"We've got an explosives canine coming," said Noelle. "No one is to go back in the courthouse until it's completely cleared. Especially if they worked near Judge Holtz's rooms." Her attention turned to a man speaking loudly with one of the patrol officers manning the caution tape to keep the crowds back.

"Speak of the devil," said Noelle.

"That's the judge?" asked Mercy. "Let him in."

Noelle strode to the judge, gesturing for him to duck under as she lifted the tape. He followed her to Max and Mercy, and Noelle made quick introductions.

Judge Howard Holtz was young—in his late thirties, Max guessed. He wasn't very tall and was extremely pale with tightly cropped blond hair. He carried himself with authority, and the fury in his gaze grew every time he looked at his smoking vehicle. "I've had that vehicle for six months," he said after meeting the group. "What if I'd been in it?"

"Have you had any recent threats?" asked Max. "Phone calls or emails?"

"Threats are an everyday part of my job," said the judge. "Sometimes they occur right inside the courtroom."

"Anyone come immediately to mind?" asked Noelle.

Judge Holtz was quiet for a long moment, clearly weighing his options. "I don't want to point at any one person. Sometimes the most violent threats are just hot air or keyboard warriors who feel safe behind their screens, but I can make you a list." Frustration filled his gaze. "What if they know where I live? I've got two kids."

"The Marshals Service will increase your security," said Max, sympathizing with the man. He understood what it was like to work in a government job where half of the people you dealt with were angry at you.

"Detective!" The tall crime scene technician approached Noelle, urgency in his voice. "You need to see this," he said in a hushed tone.

His words made the hairs on Max's arms stand up.

What did he find?

Noelle took a step to follow the tall tech and then turned and held her hand up to the rest of the group. "Wait here. I don't want too many people in the scene."

"It's *my* car," said the judge.

"It's evidence now," said Max. "And we want it handled right." His gaze hadn't left Noelle as he spoke. She joined the tech at the car, where he pointed at something in the sedan's open trunk. Noelle's hand rose to cover her mouth and nose.

That wasn't open when we got here.

And it's bad.

Noelle glanced back at the group, meeting Max's gaze and then looking at the judge.

"What'd they find?" asked the judge.

Max said nothing. Neither did Mercy.

We all know that look.

Noelle snapped a few photos of the trunk and then strode back to the group, her expression stormy. "I'm sorry, Judge Holtz," she said flatly. "But there's an adult male body in your trunk."

"*What?*" The judge stumbled back a step. "A dead body?"

"Yes," said Noelle. "Any idea how it came to be there?"

"For God's sake, no! I have no idea!" He slapped a hand to his forehead, his eyes full of disbelief. "Are you sure?"

"Positive," Noelle said grimly.

"Do . . . do I know him?" The judge looked past her to the car.

"It'd be helpful if you could identify him," said Noelle. "But he's hard to look at right now, and his face isn't visible. I'll leave that decision up to you. Maybe later would be best."

Max shifted his feet, impatience rising. The sooner the body was identified, the faster the investigation could go.

"I'll take a look," said the judge.

Noelle opened her phone and showed him the screen. The judge stared and then quickly looked away, his throat visibly moving. She swiped to another photo. The judge sucked in a breath and glanced at it. His gaze shot away again.

"I can't tell who that is," he said. "*Excuse me.*" He darted to the side of the parking lot and vomited in the bushes.

"I'll get him some water from my car," said Mercy. She ducked under the police tape and jogged away.

Max stayed Noelle's hand so he could see the photos. The man in the trunk lay on his side, his legs folded up, ankles tied together, and his face turned toward the floor with his hands tied behind his back. He was nude and covered with soggy soot. His hair was short and either dark brown or black. Max wasn't sure due to the fire debris. He wasn't surprised the judge couldn't tell who it was.

"Could you tell an age?" he asked Noelle. "Anything?"

"No."

Max straightened his back and checked on the judge. The man was sitting on the curb with his head on his knees as Mercy approached him, a water bottle and napkins in her hands.

Either the judge was a very good actor, or he'd had no idea there was a body in his trunk.

Max's gut told him the judge hadn't known.

"My second dead body in two days," muttered Noelle.

"FBI will take the lead on this one," said Max. "It could be domestic terrorism."

"I have absolutely no problem with that," said Noelle. "Let me know what you need."

Max nodded and studied the car. All three techs were huddled around the back of the car, taking photos and making notes. One turned around and waved Noelle back over. Max followed.

The tech had turned the naked man's head.

There was a bullet hole in his forehead.

Noelle looked at Max, and he read her thought.

Just like the man in the woods.

16

The phone call came just as Max arrived at his office that evening. He'd been officially assigned to lead the car bomb investigation for the FBI, and working on it had taken most of his day. He'd finally been able to return to the office to look through all the incoming information flooding his email. Camera views, interviews, collected evidence. He and Noelle had agreed to not see each other that night. Both of their work plates were full from the explosion. And the dead body.

There had been no ID with the deceased. When the medical examiner had arrived, she'd looked the victim over and then requested the entire burned vehicle be towed with the body inside. She wanted to examine it still in the vehicle and supervise the removal in a protected environment.

Figuring out how to move the vehicle without destroying more evidence had taken hours. But it was now safely in a garage at the medical examiner's building. She hoped to get to it tomorrow. Her office was backed up, and she still had Noelle's first gunshot victim to autopsy tomorrow.

Max glanced at the call on his work cell. No name. "Rhodes," he answered as he set down his laptop bag.

"Special Agent Max?" asked the woman, her voice low and full, dripping dark honey. "It's Rachel Johnson."

The sister from yesterday.

Max closed his eyes, wishing the forward woman had called Mercy instead. "What can I do for you, Rachel?"

"Anything you want," she purred.

"Rachel," he said firmly. "It's been a long day, and I don't have time for this. Do you have something important to tell me?"

"You're no fun."

From her tone, Max could easily picture the pout on her face. "I'm about to be a lot less fun and hang up."

She gave a loud exhalation, clearly exasperated and disappointed with his answer. "You told me to call."

"To call if you had relevant information. You've got five seconds." It was more time than she deserved.

"I saw the guy again."

Now he was listening. "Which guy?"

"The third one," she said. "The one I spent the most time with."

He appreciated her PG answer. "Where and when?"

"Eagle's Nest hardware store today. It was around noon."

"And you waited until now to tell me?"

"I couldn't exactly run and call you. He was happy to see me."

In other words, she's been with him.

"Did you get a name?"

"He wouldn't tell me more than Bill. We spent the afternoon at the little motel north of town."

"Is he still there?" Max touched the key fob in his pocket, ready to race to Eagle's Nest. He knew exactly where the motel was.

"No. He left before I woke up."

"You fell asleep in the middle of the day?"

"Pot does that to me."

Max couldn't speak. Rachel had known he and Mercy wanted to hear from her if she saw this man, but she'd decided to sleep with him and smoke pot before she called. "Do you have anything helpful for me?"

"He was laughing about that car bomb today. He said it was just a small test."

Max's blood ran cold. "A small test for what?"

"That's what I asked. He wouldn't expand on it."

"Tell me everything he said about it."

"Ummm." She was quiet for a long moment. "He said the bomb was just the beginning. And that people were starting to rise and fight back. And seeing this bombing would make more people fight back."

"Why should more people do something like that?" he asked.

"I have no idea. I told him that sounded like boogaloo crap, and I think I startled him. He didn't expect me to know the term."

"He didn't deny it?"

"He sorta ignored it. He was smug, joking around about how the police were distracted by something so trivial. A car bomb didn't sound trivial to me."

"It wasn't," said Max, wondering if she'd mention the body in the trunk. "The judge was lucky he wasn't in the car."

"Yeah."

"It could have killed some bystanders. It nearly did," he said, thinking of the man who'd had a heart attack.

"His cocky attitude pissed me off," said Rachel. "I told him blowing up shit wasn't funny."

Definitely not funny.

"He got pissed and gave me one in the lip."

"He hit you?" He was floored by her casual tone.

"Yeah. It's nothing."

"Was this at the beginning or end of your meeting with him?"

"A meeting." She chuckled. "You're so formal."

"Rachel." He infused her name with as much impatience as he could.

"Toward the beginning." She sounded a bit uncomfortable admitting the fact.

He hit her, but she spent the day with him.

"What else happened? Which of you rented the room?" Maybe he could get a name from the motel.

"I did. He told me to rent it and that he'd join me in about an hour. He came much quicker than that." She cackled at her pun.

"Where are you now?"

"Still here," she said. "I've got it for the whole night, so no way am I leaving. You busy?"

Max closed his eyes. "Where did he go? You said he wasn't local. Do you still believe that?"

"I'm not so sure now," said Rachel. "He seemed to know a lot about the area." She paused. "You didn't answer my question." Her voice lowered, sending chills up Max's spine—the wrong kind of chills.

"Rachel. Any chance you have something he might have touched? A beer bottle? Or a glass that we could lift his prints off of?" If Bill had been arrested before, he should turn up in a database.

"How about a beer can?"

"That'll work. Don't touch it, and I'll come get it right now."

"I knew I could get you over here."

He glared at the ceiling. "*Rachel*, is there really a beer can?"

"Yeah," she said reluctantly. "There's a lot of them."

"Don't touch any of them, and I'll be there in thirty minutes. Be fully clothed, please."

"Can't wait," she purred.

17

Max knocked on the motel room door again and wondered if Rachel was being passive-aggressive because he was late.

It was only ten minutes later than he'd told her he'd arrive. Impatient and standing in the cold outside her door, he tried her cell phone again, but it went straight to voicemail, so he left *another* brief message and then pounded loudly on the door. The door to the next room opened, and a dark-haired man wearing a cowboy hat and jeans but no shirt stepped out.

"Do you mind?" asked the man. "Tryin' to hear the TV."

"Sorry," said Max, looking away from the clumsy tattoo of a woman's face on the man's right pec and wondering if the woman represented there truly resembled a female Seth Rogen. He kept his eyes on the door and knocked politely.

"You here earlier?" asked the cowboy.

"Uh, no. Why?"

The man grinned. "Just wanted to shake the feller's hand." He touched the brim of his hat.

Max briefly closed his eyes. "Wasn't me." He tried the doorknob. Locked.

"Hey! If she's not letting you in, she's got a good reason." The cowboy took a protective barefoot step closer.

"I'll check at the motel office." Max strode away before the cowboy could say any more. He shouldn't have tried the doorknob, but at that moment he'd wanted to escape the nosy neighbor.

The motel was an L-shaped one-story building. Four cars were parked along the long part of the L, each most likely in front of its owner's rented room. The space in front of Rachel's door was empty, but a small white Toyota pickup was two spots down, and he suspected it was the same one he'd seen at her and Cory's home yesterday when he left. As he passed, Max spotted several crystals dangling from the rearview mirror.

He pulled open the weathered door next to the hand-painted OFFICE sign. Somewhere behind the reception counter, a buzzer sounded as he stepped in, and the door creaked loudly as he yanked it closed. The lobby smelled of popcorn, old coffee, and cigarette smoke. The black-and-white-checked floor looked as if it belonged in an old diner and was dingy with layers of grime. He waited for several seconds, noting there were at least a dozen different little odd bells lined up on the reception counter to choose from. If no one came out soon, he decided he'd ring the one that looked like a turtle with a ringer button on top of its shell. No . . . the goose one with the long neck and a clapper between its feet.

A plastic accordion door slid open behind the desk.

"Help you?" a teenager asked, her hands on her hips.

"Can you open room twelve for me?" Max held out his identification.

The girl stepped forward and peered at the ID. She had the most elaborate and skillful eye makeup he'd ever seen. The swirls of blue and black looked as if an artist had applied them. Her dark hair was up in what Max thought looked like animal ears, but his sister had said they were called space buns.

"Uh-huh. Right. How do I know that's real?" She rolled her eyes and reached for the energy drink next to the computer.

Max didn't have a good answer. "It's real."

"Heard that before."

"Rachel Johnson. Room twelve. I've knocked several times, and she's not answering. She's expecting me, and I'm concerned."

The girl tapped on the keyboard with one hand. "Maybe she doesn't want to see you. Or she's *busy*." Her tone suggestive. "Besides. No Rachel Johnson registered here."

"She's in room twelve. Don't know what name she's using, but that's her real name."

The teen looked at him and shrugged. "Dude. I can't let you in there."

"Call her room."

She considered it for a moment and then picked up the desk phone and dialed. She held his gaze as she waited. "She's not answering."

"Give it a little longer."

Eye roll. She hung up after another ten seconds. "Not there—well, not answering."

"I'm concerned," he repeated. "You could open the door—"

"Not opening the door," she snapped. "I'm going to call the police if you don't leave now."

Good idea!

"Do you know Chief Daly?" Max asked.

"Of course. He or one of his guys has been out here dozens of times. And dropping his name doesn't impress me at all."

Max held back his comment about how the dozens of police visits reflected on the hotel. "How about this?" He scrolled through photos on his phone until he found one of the four of them from their recent dinner and held it out to her. "I work with his wife. She's also FBI."

The teen took the phone from his hand and enlarged the photo. "I've heard about her." She swiped through a few of his photos.

"Hey!" He grabbed for the phone, but she stepped out of reach.

"Is that your wife?" She'd gone back to the dinner photo and held it up with Noelle's face filling the frame.

"Girlfriend," he said.

"Pretty." She smirked as she handed him back the phone. "I'll open the room."

"Thank you." He quickly checked his photos, wondering what else the desk clerk could have seen. Most were nothing unusual, but he had taken several dozen photos and videos of the car bomb crime scene that day.

The teen grabbed a key off a numbered board and stepped around the desk into the lobby.

Max stared at the board of room keys. "That doesn't seem very safe."

"I've told the owner that dozens of times," she said as she passed him. "He doesn't want to pay for a card system."

"How about just move the board out of sight?" He followed her out the door.

"Brilliant." She gave him a side-eye. "I'm sure no one's suggested that."

Max decided to stop talking. She led the way to number 12 and rapped on the door. "Ms. Johnson?" she hollered. "You in there?"

Silence.

She knocked again, and the cowboy opened his door. "Really, Oakleigh?" He had on boots now, but still no shirt.

"Shut your door, Mr. Mumford! You're not supposed to be within a hundred yards of me!"

He slammed his door.

"Asshole," whispered Oakleigh.

"You have a restraining order against him?" Max managed to ask.

"Nah. I should, though."

Max was about to ask why, but she slipped the key in the lock and pushed the door open two inches. "Ms. Johnson?" the teen said into the room. She didn't get an answer.

"Step out of the way," Max said. The girl willingly did so, and he pushed the door fully open.

Rachel Johnson was on the floor, blood pooled around her head.

"Get back," Max snapped at Oakleigh, who had stepped closer to get a look over his shoulder.

"Holy shit! Is she dead?"

The cowboy's door opened, and his boots sounded on the concrete walkway. "What's going on?"

"Get back. Both of you!" Max wanted to shut the door, but the room was almost pitch black. He spotted a light switch and flipped it with his elbow and then let the motel room door swing closed behind him. He'd drawn his weapon without even realizing it.

"She was all bloody!" he heard Oakleigh say outside.

"Was she naked?" asked the cowboy.

Max swore under his breath. He did a quick check of the bathroom, the closet, and the space under the bed. All clear. He holstered his weapon and squatted next to Rachel. He felt for a pulse even though he knew it was too late.

Her lifeless eyes and the bullet hole in her forehead had told him that.

18

Noelle stared at Max, Mercy, and Chief Daly, trying to understand.

"This is *your* informant?" she asked Mercy, gesturing at the body on the motel floor, where two crime scene techs were working.

"No, her sister is," said Mercy. "But Rachel always inserts herself into whatever is going on."

"Clearly." Noelle looked down at the dead woman. "Did you notify the sister?"

"Not yet." Mercy looked uncomfortable. "I want to have some answers for her first."

Noelle turned her attention to the police chief. "This is the second body in as many days in *your* area. Both shot in the head. And that doesn't include the body from this afternoon in the judge's trunk because that was in Bend."

"I'm well aware," said Truman, frustration on his face. "I appreciate county stepping up to help when you have so much going on."

"Not a problem," said Noelle with a sigh. Truman's tiny police force didn't have the manpower or resources to investigate murders. Especially multiple murders.

Are the murders related?

Max caught her eye, and she suspected he was wondering the same thing. "You saw both sisters yesterday," she said to the FBI agents. "What was the reason?"

"The domestic terrorism chatter," said Mercy. "Both Cory and Rachel rub shoulders with people who dabble in that area."

"And?"

"They'd seen some new faces in town but didn't have anything concrete."

"Rachel called me because she spent time with one of them today," Max said. "I've already told Mercy about this, but Rachel said he claimed the car bombing was just a taste of what was to come."

Noelle stared at him. "This murder *is* tied to the judge's car bombing? Did he mention the body in the trunk to her?" Connections were appearing among the three deaths, starting a spirograph pattern.

"I didn't want to lead her there by asking about the body," said Max. "So I didn't bring it up. I think she would have told me if he had."

"Then maybe it's not related," said Noelle. "Maybe he was just an asshole commenting on a car bomb and trying to sound important."

But which is it?

"Could be. I'm sure everyone was talking about it today." Max glowered around the hotel room. "Rachel told me she had beer cans the man had handled, and I was coming to collect that evidence when I found her like this. And as you can see, there isn't a can in sight. Her phone is missing too."

"Maybe she lied to you about the cans," suggested Truman.

"I don't think so." Max looked positive. "I think he cleaned house. Including Rachel," he added in a quiet voice.

"Could he have known you were coming?" Noelle asked.

"I guess it's possible, but honestly I don't think she would've told him. I suspect he already had a goal in mind when he came back."

"You're assuming it was the same man who returned," Noelle said.

"Good point," said Max. "But if he wasn't related to the earlier man, why would he take the beer cans?"

"You're also assuming it's a he," added Truman.

"That too," agreed Noelle. It was easy to get tunnel vision on a case and miss things. "What about the other sister? Could she be involved?"

Mercy grimaced. "I hate to think she'd do this, but I can't say it's impossible."

"I think it's time for a notification and a discussion with the sister," said Noelle.

"Ben's talking with the other motel guests to see if they heard or saw someone," said Truman.

"I'll check in with him," said Noelle, and she stepped out of the room and spotted the older cop at a motel room door several rooms down. She headed his way, needing to get away from the sight of the dead woman on the floor. Her brain needed some air. She'd seen three dead bodies in two days, and it was three bodies too many.

Ben touched the brim of his hat and stepped away from the door as it closed. He was about to write something on his notepad when he saw Noelle coming toward him. "Busy day, Detective," he said. He looked as strained as she felt.

"Too busy. What have you found, Ben?"

He pointed at the door that had just closed. "Family of six in there. None of them heard a gunshot or saw anything unusual today."

"Six?" asked Noelle. "How big is that room?"

"Two queen beds," he said. "Saw two of those playpen cribs in there too. Not much room to move around. I don't think any of the kids were older than five. Nice young couple. Horrified to hear what happened. Said they're packing up. Not going to stay here another night."

"Can't blame them," Noelle said. "What else?"

"Most of the rooms are empty," said Ben. "There's a young couple two more doors down. They said the only thing they heard today was one or two of the babies crying from this room. And that was when they were checking in to their room. Haven't heard anything since. I took identification from everyone except for the guy in that room. Tom Mumford." He pointed at the room next to Rachel's. "Gave me a name and address, but he said his wallet was stolen."

"Uh-huh."

"Also said he spoke with Rachel a few hours ago." Ben stared at the closed room door. "Something about the guy bugged me."

"On it," said Noelle. "Thanks, Ben." She strode back toward the scene and rapped on the man's door. After a long moment it opened a few inches, the chain clearly latched, and a brown eye came into sight.

Stupidest security device ever. I could bust that with one kick. Even in heels.

"Mr. Mumford?" Noelle showed him her ID. "Can I speak with you for a few minutes?"

"I already answered the cop's questions," he said.

"I know," said Noelle. "And now I have a few more." She gave her most winning smile.

He blinked several times and then closed the door. The chain quietly clanked as he removed it. When it reopened, she saw he'd put on a beige cowboy hat. She estimated that he was in his early forties.

"Officer Cooley said you saw the woman from next door not too long ago. What was she doing at that time?"

"She was getting ice." He pointed down the building. "Headed that way with her ice bucket."

"When did you speak with her?"

"At the ice machine. I needed ice too."

You mean you grabbed your bucket and followed.

"What did you two talk about?"

"Well, not much. I was trying to be nice, but she didn't have much to say."

Noelle spotted the small alcove holding the ice machine. If Rachel was getting ice and Mr. Mumford was waiting his turn, he'd essentially pinned her in the area.

"All I asked was how long she was staying at the motel," he said. "A simple question, but she didn't answer. Just nodded and finished filling her bucket. I told her polite people replied when someone talked to them." He crossed his arms and nodded emphatically.

"Did you tell her to smile?" Noelle asked with her own wide smile.

"What?" Confusion flashed on his face. "No, she had a split lip."

"Maybe she didn't feel like talking since she had a split lip. Probably why she needed ice."

"Yeah."

"Did you see her with anyone today?"

"Nope. Just heard the two of them," he said with a faint leer.

Noelle tapped the hotel's wall. "You heard them through cinder block walls?"

"Yep. What's that tell you?" His smile was smug.

"Officer Cooley said you didn't have your wallet."

"Pretty sure my wallet was stolen," he said. "Left it on my dashboard when I was at a rest stop. Didn't notice it was gone until later."

"Good thing you had cash for the hotel."

"I'm a big believer in carrying cash," he said. "Credit cards are just a way for businesses to make money and track you."

"What's your address?" Noelle asked, her pen ready at her notepad.

"I told the other guy."

"Well, now you can tell me."

He rattled off an Idaho address, which she planned to compare to the one he had given Ben.

She looked at the vehicles in the lot. "Which vehicle's yours?" Her gaze locked on a big Dodge truck nearby with Idaho plates and a yellow bumper sticker of a snake.

He pointed at it, and she squinted in the dim light as she wrote down his plate number, noticing the registration stickers were old. "You know your tags are expired? They expired almost a year ago."

He gave a shocked expression. "Damn state didn't inform me. They're always screwing up."

"Wait here a moment," Noelle told him. "Officer Cooley has one more thing for you." She heard the motel room door close as she went back to Ben. "Can you give him a citation for expired tags?"

Ben peered at the truck she pointed at. "Gladly. Frankly, I'm surprised he even has plates."

Noelle nodded as Ben confirmed what she'd suspected during the interview. "You think Mr. Mumford is a sovereign citizen?"

"Yep. Although some of them are calling themselves something else . . . American States Assembly or American States Nationals or something like that. Mumford probably has a wallet with one of those made-up licenses in it. Didn't want to show it to me."

Many sovereign citizens believed they were not under the jurisdiction of many levels of government and therefore that they were exempt from the laws.

"So a citation for expired tags will probably be pointless. The plates probably aren't even his to begin with."

"That'd be correct," said Ben. "I could run the plates and see if they're reported stolen."

Frustrated, Noelle glared at Tom Mumford's motel room door.

Probably not his real name either.

"You've got other things to deal with," Ben said kindly. "I'll keep an eye on him as long as he's at the motel. See if I can figure out where he actually lives. Maybe he's just passing through the state. Let him be someone else's problem. He's not your priority today."

"Thank you, Ben." He was right. Bigger things were going on.

Noelle went back to where Max and Mercy were speaking, a few yards from Rachel Johnson's room, giving the crime scene team space to do their job.

"What did you get out of the front desk clerk?" she asked Max.

"She said that Rachel paid in cash, and she didn't see a man with her or near her room today. Rachel gave her name as Lana Turner."

"That's an old one," said Noelle.

"Yeah. It didn't raise a flag with Oakleigh. Not that she cares what name a guest gives. And I asked her about motel cameras," said Max. "She laughed as if it was the funniest joke she'd ever heard. There aren't any cameras on the property. Never have been. From what I've seen, I can't say I'm surprised that the owner of this old place didn't invest in cameras."

"Did she say anything about the man in the next room?"

"Not this time," said Max. "But right before she opened Rachel's door for me, she yelled at him to get back in his room. Told me she should get a restraining order against him. I didn't have time to ask her why."

Apparently Mr. Mumford likes to harass women.

"Ben is going to dig into his background a bit," said Noelle. "Can you ask the desk clerk what he did that made her comment about the restraining order?"

"On it."

"Thanks, Max," said Noelle. "Ready to go see Rachel's sister?" she asked Mercy.

"Yes, but no."

Noelle understood that answer; it perfectly summed up family notifications.

She and Mercy started to head across the parking lot. A crime scene tech had set up several bright spotlights on Rachel's little pickup and was taking photos in the cab.

Multiple shootings.

I need to compare the bullets.

19

Noelle steeled herself as they parked at Cory Johnson's house.

It'd been after ten o'clock when Mercy had called Cory from the car and woken her up, telling her they needed to stop by and talk. Cory had asked why, but Mercy had been vague with her answer.

"She knows something's up," said Mercy, getting out of Noelle's vehicle.

"Anyone would, considering the time," said Noelle. "This is always so hard," she muttered. "But it's important, and I know that we'll do it right." Empathy swamped her when she talked to a deceased's loved ones.

She didn't like to imagine someone showing up on her doorstep to inform her that one of her sisters, Eve or Lucia, had died. But she put herself in the victim's family member's shoes when she had to deliver crushing news, saying what she would want to hear if it'd been one of her sisters.

It was one of the most difficult aspects of her job.

Mercy exhaled loudly as they headed toward the door. Cory had opened it the moment the SUV's engine had turned off.

"What's going on?" Cory's voice was shrill.

"Cory, this is Detective Noelle Marshall with the sheriff's office," said Mercy. "Let's go inside and sit down."

"No! Tell me now!" Her terrified gaze flew between Mercy and Noelle.

"Cory, can we sit? It's been a hell of a long day for us." Noelle's tone was weary.

Cory clamped her jaw shut. She motioned the women in and led them to the table, where they each took a seat. She stared expectantly at them, her fingers twisting a chunk of hair over and over. "It's Rachel, isn't it? What did she do?"

"Did you talk to her today?" asked Mercy.

"No. I haven't seen her either. She was asleep when I left for work and gone when I got home. Pretty typical for us."

She was calmer than at the door, but the fear in her eyes made Noelle's heart hurt.

"I'm sorry, Cory," Mercy said softly. "But Rachel was killed today." She reached for Cory's hand, which rested on the table.

Cory yanked it away. "*Killed how?* What happened?" Her voice had shot up an octave.

"She was found in a motel room near Eagle's Nest," said Mercy. "I'm so sorry."

Freckles stood out on Cory's face as she went white. "No," she said firmly. "It can't be her." Her gaze shot to Noelle's, begging her to back her up.

Noelle couldn't speak. Her throat was tight at the fear on Cory's face.

"Cory," said Mercy. "I identified her. It's true."

"Someone murdered her?" Cory whispered.

"Yes."

Cory shot out of her chair, knocking it over backward. *"This is your fault!"* she shrieked at Mercy. "You did this! You and your stupid FBI! I told you to leave us alone!" She slammed her hands on the table and then pointed her finger at Mercy.

Mercy jerked back, stricken. "Cory—"

"Don't talk to me! Do not talk to me!" She whirled around and ran down a hallway. A door slammed seconds later, and her wailing echoed through the house.

Noelle's heart pounded in her chest as she looked at Mercy. The FBI agent stared at the ceiling, blinking hard, her rapid pulse visible at her neck. "Mercy—"

"Wait." Mercy held up a hand, her face still turned upward, but she had closed her eyes. "Give me a minute."

It's not your fault.

Noelle held in the words. Mercy wasn't ready to hear them.

Cory's wails continued.

Noelle sat silently, recalling the time she'd caused someone's death while on the job.

No. His actions caused his death. He gave me no choice.

He'd had a gun at a woman's head, a split second away from firing.

Noelle had fired first.

That decision still haunted her. She didn't regret it, but the emotional aftermath of taking a life hadn't gone away.

"This wasn't your fault, Mercy," Noelle whispered. "She's just looking for someone to blame, and you're the closest. The person who pulled the trigger is the only one at fault."

"I know." Mercy now stared toward the hallway. "Did you know my brother was murdered?" she asked quietly. "I was there. I held him as he died."

Noelle was stunned, and it took her a few seconds to answer. "I didn't know."

Mercy turned toward her, her eyes sad. "A piece of me is still missing. I completely understand Cory's reaction."

"What do we do now?" asked Noelle. "We can't leave."

"We can search Rachel's room while we're waiting."

"Jesus, Mercy. We need to at least first tell Cory what we're doing and why." Noelle knew the agent was right. They needed to move fast to find Rachel's killer. But searching through personal belongings felt incredibly inappropriate at the moment.

"I'll talk to her." Mercy rose and followed the wails. Noelle jumped to her feet.

"Cory." Mercy knocked on the door where the crying was the loudest.

"Fuck off!" The pain in her voice made Noelle's stomach churn.

"Cory," said Mercy again. "I understand how you're feeling. But because we've got to find her killer, we need to search Rachel's room."

"No! Don't touch *anything*!"

"The house is rented in Rachel's name," Mercy said in a low voice to Noelle. "We can search." She stepped into the next bedroom, flipping on the light switch.

The room looked like it belonged to someone much younger than Rachel's thirty-five years. There were a lot of faded pink tones, leopard print, and concert posters on the wall. One of the pink throw pillows on the double bed had RACHEL spelled out in a tiny checked print.

We're in the right room.

Noelle had worried that Cory might be in Rachel's room.

The door to the next room flew open. "Get out of her room! Get out of my house!" Cory screamed at them. Her face was red and wet with tears.

"Cory!" Mercy snapped. "Your sister was murdered! We need to look through her things! There could be a lead to finding her killer in there."

Cory froze at the word *killer*.

Noelle touched her arm. "We need to do our jobs to find out who hurt her."

Cory looked at Noelle, blinking as if she couldn't focus.

"Did Rachel tell you she was seeing anyone?" Noelle asked, remembering that Cory had claimed she hadn't heard from Rachel today and that, according to Max's conversation with Rachel, she'd just happened to run into a man around noon.

But maybe she didn't tell Max the truth.

"I don't know," Cory said in a shaking voice. "She was always seeing various men. I stopped paying attention years ago."

"Did she say anything more about the three men after Max and I left yesterday?" asked Mercy, watching Cory closely.

Cory wiped her face with her sleeve, her arm shaking. "I can't think. Give me a minute."

Mercy moved in close and hugged the woman. "I'm so sorry, Cory. I really am. And we'll find the bastard who did this." Cory froze for a split second and then returned the hug, burying her face in Mercy's shoulder.

"It's okay," Cory whispered, her voice soft.

"No. It's not okay," said Noelle. "Nothing about any of this is okay."

After a long moment, Cory stepped out of the hug, wiping her eyes. "Go ahead and look in her room. I need a glass of water." She turned and headed toward the kitchen, trailing one hand along the wall for balance.

Noelle eyed Mercy, who was wiping her own eyes. "Better?"

"Yeah. She's not hating me right now, but I'm sure that will come and go." Mercy pulled a pair of gloves from her coat pocket and handed them to Noelle. "Let's get looking." She dug out another pair for herself.

Noelle started on one side of the room, and Mercy took the other. "Laptop," muttered Noelle. "It's charging." The computer was old and battered.

"Don't touch it," said Mercy, on her knees, looking under the bed. "Let forensics handle that. We can mess things up by simply unplugging it."

Noelle nodded and moved on, yanking open dresser drawers and quickly digging through them, running her hands along the sides and bottoms to check for hiding spots.

She's got more lingerie than Victoria's Secret.

The drawers turned up nothing of interest, and Noelle slid the dresser out a few inches to check its back. Nothing. She moved on to the desk. It reminded her of the small one she'd had in high school. It only had three drawers, and Noelle repeated the actions she'd used on the dresser.

“Look at this photo album,” said Mercy. She had a three-ring binder and was examining elaborate pages full of cutouts, borders, and stickers.

“That reminds me of when everyone was into creating memory albums, which took an insane amount of money and hours,” said Noelle. She’d never been interested in the trend.

“This stuff is a decade old,” said Mercy. “Concert ticket stubs. Photos. Looks like she wrote poetry.”

“She did,” Cory said quietly from the door. “She always wanted to get it published.” She sucked in a nervous breath. “Guess that will never happen now.”

“You could collect her poems and do it,” said Noelle. “Even if you just wanted to make one book for you to keep. There are companies that do that.”

Cory met her gaze and slowly nodded. “I might.” She looked at Mercy, who was on the floor by the nightstand. “What exactly are you looking for? Wait. You didn’t tell me what happened to Rachel. How did she . . . die?”

Mercy got to her feet and moved closer to the woman, placing a hand on her shoulder. “She was shot, Cory. And I strongly suspect the medical examiner will say that she died immediately. I don’t believe there was any suffering.”

“Medical examiner?” Cory’s chin quivered. “They’re going to cut her up,” she whispered.

“It has to be done,” said Mercy softly. “It’ll help our investigation to find who did that to her.” She squeezed Cory’s shoulder.

“I don’t want to see it.”

“Of course not. I’ll make sure it goes okay,” said Mercy.

“You’ll be there?”

“Yes.”

“She liked you, Agent Kilpatrick,” Cory said slowly. “She wouldn’t ever say it to your face, but she was impressed with you and your job. Said she wished she’d gotten into a profession like that.”

“Thank you for telling me,” Mercy said. “I appreciate it.”

Cory nodded and more tears started. "Did you find anything in here?"

"Not yet," said Noelle. "Why don't we talk some more? We can come back to this later." She wanted to speak with Cory while she was calm. "Do you have some tea?"

"I have some wine," she said. "I have tea too, but wine sounds much better at the moment."

Noelle agreed but said, "We'd join you, but we're working. Tea works for us."

"I'll start it." Cory left.

"Thoughts on the bedroom?" Mercy asked Noelle.

"I want to go through her closet." She opened the folding doors. "Jesus." Every square inch of the closet was stuffed. Clothes, shoes, boxes, books, purses, stuffed animals. There was less pink in the closet but more animal print. Especially leopard. Noelle plucked a stuffed raccoon off a crowded shelf. It was missing an eye. "How does she find anything?"

"You have sisters," said Mercy. "Didn't at least one of them have a closet like this? Kaylie's looks this packed all the time. I can't bear to go in her room when the closet door is open. Don't get me started on the stuff all over the floor."

"My sisters and I didn't have this much stuff," said Noelle. She pictured her walk-in closet at the huge house she'd shared with her second husband. It was the size of most homes' primary suites. She'd had more clothes and shoes and bags than she could ever wear. She'd donated 80 percent of it when she sold the house. Many items had still had the tags. Her lips twitched at the memory of her mother-in-law's shock when she learned Noelle had given away thousands of dollars' worth of clothing. Her mother-in-law had been the one who insisted that Noelle purchase most of it.

That was a different world. A different life.

The memory surprised her. She rarely thought about those previous years.

She'd spent hours and hours volunteering and serving on charity boards during that time, but she'd never felt that she truly helped anyone until she joined the Sacramento police force. It'd given her a purpose in life.

Noelle touched the back of her head, surprised that thinking about that period hadn't caused the little spikes of head pain that it usually did.

"Your head hurt?" Mercy asked. She knew about Noelle's old head injury.

"Actually, it doesn't. I expected it to, but it's good."

"Nice!"

Noelle returned the raccoon and closed the closet doors. "We can do this later. Interviewing Cory is the priority."

"Agreed." Mercy disappeared out the bedroom door, her boots making confident sounds as she strode down the hallway to join Cory.

Noelle took a last look at the silent room, seeing Rachel in every element. Every photo, glittery pillow, and sparkling crystal. The woman had made it her space, and now she'd never enter it again.

It almost feels as if it's waiting for her.

Noelle pressed her lips together. Rachel wouldn't be back, but Noelle could find her killer and get justice for her death.

Justice for the man left in the woods.

Justice for the man in the trunk.

Everyone deserves justice.

20

Max glanced through the conference room door's window and saw Noelle was already seated at the long table in the Deschutes County Sheriff's Department, the yellow pad in front of her already full of notes. She always wrote down or recorded everything, her insurance against her occasional memory loss from the brain injury she'd gotten when her husband was murdered.

It was 7:00 a.m., and Max knew she'd been at Cory Johnson's house until nearly three that morning. He walked in and set a latte in front of her. A latte of the same flavor from the same coffee shop where they'd seen each other for the very first time. The latte was their *thing*. He surprised her with one occasionally, and it always made her face light up.

Like right now.

The exhaustion he'd seen on her face melted away. "Thank you," she whispered. He bent over and kissed her since they were the only ones in the room.

"You had a long night," he said as he rolled out the chair beside her and sat.

"Both Mercy and I did." Noelle checked the time. "She should be here any minute."

"Is Evan going to make it?" asked Max.

"No. He got called out to a robbery an hour ago, but Mercy said Truman will be here."

The FBI and the Deschutes County sheriff were pooling their resources to form a task force and examining the three recent murders that Max was nearly certain were tied together. This morning was their first joint meeting. Voices sounded in the hall, and Mercy and Truman came in, both carrying large coffee tumblers.

Max foresaw a lot more coffee in everyone's future.

He stood and shook hands, but Noelle stayed in her seat; the exhaustion had returned to her face. Mercy looked similar. Both women had faint purplish hues below their eyes. She took the seat next to Noelle with Truman beside her.

Max had a small déjà vu moment, remembering how recently the four of them had sat down to dinner together. That had been fun and relaxing; today was not.

Many more law enforcement personnel were involved in the three cases, but Max wanted to start with this core group of the new task force and establish a plan. He walked up to one of the huge whiteboards on the wall and wrote across the top: *John Doe 1*, *John Doe 2*, *car bomb*, and *Rachel Johnson*. He spaced the headings far apart and put a thick line below each. He turned to his audience. "John Doe One. The man Emma Chambers found in the woods the day before yesterday. Where are we at?"

"The autopsy will be late this morning," said Noelle. "I plan to go. I hope the medical examiner can get an ID, because we need it to get this case moving. The people I spoke with so far didn't know anything about a body near their party site and didn't see anything odd happen. There won't be an official age range until the autopsy, but Dr. Lockhart told me he's not a teenager and not over sixty."

"Not real helpful," said Mercy.

"I've combed missing persons databases with his height and hair color. I've made a short list of the recent missing persons that fit that description—which isn't many, but I need more physical information on our John Doe," said Noelle. "I've checked all West Coast states and Idaho. I can expand the searches, but I want to wait until after the autopsy, when I'll have a better idea of age and hopefully some other identifiers."

"What about the tattoo?" asked Truman.

"I sent a picture of it to the gang teams at the FBI and at the Portland Police Bureau. You might be right that it's a flower," Noelle said to Truman. "Still looks more like a tree to me."

"Any other witnesses from the scene to talk to?" asked Max.

"I have a few more high school kids on my list," said Noelle. "But I'm not optimistic that they can tell me anything, so first I'll see where the autopsy leads and then decide if I want to interview more. We'll at least have the bullet when the medical examiner is done."

"Kids talk," said Mercy. "Trust me that the message is out that we're looking for anything or anyone unusual from that party area. I suspect we'll hear if someone has something to report."

"And if they're trying to hide something?" asked Truman.

"Rumors spread. We'll hear about it," said Mercy.

"Forensics report from the crime scene?" asked Max. "What about the shoe that was there? It was the only clothing object, right?"

"Forensics found beer cans and other scattered garbage," said Noelle. "As for the Nike shoe, they believe it was there much longer than the body. It was a man's shoe, but there were pine needles and even some packed dirt inside that were consistent with the surroundings. I doubt it came with the body."

Max wrote *autopsy*, *bullet*, *tattoo*, and *interviews* with a question mark under *John Doe 1*. "What do we have on the car bomb and the body in the trunk from yesterday?" he asked.

"I know the medical examiner has removed the body from the trunk," said Mercy. "She said he also has a gunshot wound in the forehead and no exit wound, so if the bullets from both men are in good shape, we'll be able to tell if they were fired from the same weapon."

"Rachel was shot in the head too," said Max. "But I'm getting ahead of myself. When will John Doe Two's autopsy be done?"

"Possibly this afternoon, but most likely tomorrow," said Mercy. "Dr. Lockhart told me that he wasn't shot in the trunk. There was very little blood on the carpet, and like our first victim, the lividity didn't match up with the position we found him in."

Max wrote *autopsy* and *bullet* under *John Doe 2*. "The media reported that there was a body in the trunk. Has that brought in any solid leads on his identity? I know two deputies were assigned to handle calls."

"It's brought out the wackos and the desperate," said Noelle. "I was told the calls have been everything from it's Elvis in the trunk to accusations that we're covering up that it was actually the judge's wife, even though both she and the judge have been on camera since then. One person swore the woman on camera wasn't really his wife and that she had been murdered."

"I have faith that Dr. Lockhart can verify the victim's sex as male," said Max.

"I saw him," said Noelle. "I have no doubt he was male and that he was not Elvis. The deputies have a few leads that could be legitimate. We'll rule them out after the autopsy."

"Check the leads against both John Does," said Max.

"Callers were also asked if their missing person had tattoos," said Noelle.

"Good," said Max. He tapped the *car bomb* entry on the board. "Cameras at the courthouse showed Judge Holtz parking his vehicle in the morning. The Mercedes was in view until the bomb went off. The trunk was never opened, and no one stopped near the car."

"The judge drove in with the body?" asked Truman.

"It's looking that way. At home he parks his car outside. He sent over video from his own cameras for us to review, but he said he already fast-forwarded through forty-eight hours' worth and no one had tampered with his vehicle."

"So it was done somewhere else," said Mercy. "Did he tell you where he's driven the car recently?"

"He's putting together a list of locations." Max noticed Noelle shifting in her seat and tapping her pen. She met his gaze and gave a brief reassuring smile.

Talking about the car bomb has got to be hard on her.

He'd seen the video from when her SUV had exploded. Watching it shook him up every time, even though he knew that she'd been okay.

"When I get it, I'll send deputies to check for video at each place the judge has been the last few days," Max continued. He wrote *videos* under the *car bomb* heading.

"Dr. Lockhart said the victim hadn't been dead very long when the car blew up," said Noelle. "Again, we'll have a better time frame after his autopsy."

"We don't have a report on the device that caused the explosion yet," said Max. "Both the FBI's fire investigators and the state fire marshal's office will examine the vehicle and device. They'll bring in the explosives experts they feel are needed." He added *explosive device* and *fire reports* to the same column. "Most likely the device was activated with a cell phone. I feel a timer is unlikely because I think he wanted the bomb to go off at the courthouse. There was no guarantee that the judge would be there at that time yesterday. It was likely, but not definite."

"It seems like the bomber didn't want to hurt the judge," said Mercy. "Just scare him. And everyone else. Possibly his primary goal was to shock us with the body in the trunk."

"Showing off?" Max asked.

"Any bomb is showing off in my book," said Mercy with a shrug. "Someone wants attention."

"And according to what Rachel told me, it's possible something bigger is planned," Max said. "Or else the guy with her was showing off too. Acting as if he knew what was going on."

"The judge will get me a list of people who expressed anger with him in the courtroom. He plans to take a closer look at his records today for more. I'm not sure how far back he should look. Someone could have been holding a grudge for a decade."

"I'll pull the judge's financials," said Mercy. "I want to know if he's having any money problems. And I want to know how his marriage is. This could be an angry ex-lover of his or his wife."

"The wife's movements for the last few days should be looked at too," said Truman.

"The wife put a dead body in her husband's car?" asked Mercy, looking at her own husband.

"Great way to point suspicion at the husband," Truman said. "Maybe she has *Gone Girl* aspirations. What do we know about her?"

"She has a law degree but never practiced," said Noelle. "Two young kids. Essentially a stay-at-home mom." She looked at Max. "We need to know if she ever drives his vehicle."

Max wrote *wife's movements* under the *car bomb* entry. "What else?"

The room was silent, so he went on to the next item. "Rachel Johnson. Did you learn anything from her sister last night?" He directed the question to Noelle and Mercy.

"Cory didn't take it well," said Mercy. "As expected. She pointed a lot of blame at me and the FBI. She seems to think our questions the other day are what triggered this."

"Do you believe that?" asked Max. Mercy was staying composed, but he could see behind her straight face. The idea that Rachel had died because of their interview with the sisters was very upsetting.

He understood. He'd had several nauseating moments when he'd wondered about something similar.

"It's very possible," said Mercy, staring at her hands. Truman reached over and gently took one, and she gave him a weak smile. "I know Rachel didn't mention it to you, Max, but she may have told the man in her room that she'd been questioned by the FBI."

"What else happened at their home last night? And this morning?" he asked.

"We went through most of Rachel's room," said Noelle. "We really didn't find anything of interest except a laptop. I had a tech come pick it up before we left."

"At three in the morning?" asked Max.

"Yep. We wanted to go home at some point, and I didn't want to leave it there. Maybe something will turn up on it. Perhaps she emailed our killer for some reason."

"What about the rest of the house?" asked Max.

"Just a general walk-through," said Mercy. "Noelle checked the outbuilding while I kept Cory occupied in the kitchen. And Cory didn't know anything about the car bomb. She'd heard it happened but pretty much ignored the story.

"I also asked her if there was anyone who'd want to hurt Rachel." Mercy exhaled. "Cory looked miserable when I asked. Said Rachel's sleeping around often got people angry with her. Both men and women."

"Anyone lately?"

"She wasn't sure. She and Rachel had an informal don't-ask, don't-tell rule about that. Cory said she hadn't been aware of any incidents since last summer."

"Define *incidents*," said Max.

"A woman actually came out to their house to tell Rachel to stay away from her husband. Cory was there too. Said the woman and Rachel screamed at each other for fifteen minutes, and then she left. As far as Cory knew, that was the end of the affair." Mercy frowned. "That doesn't feel like the right word."

"*Dalliance*?" suggested Noelle.

"That's a little better," agreed Mercy. "We did learn that Rachel had been cleaning houses. Cory said her jobs weren't very regular, and Rachel spent everything she earned."

"Got any client names?" asked Max.

"Yes. I'll forward them."

Max wrote *cleaning houses* and *affairs* under Rachel's name. "Any other surprises about Rachel?"

"We're making her seem like a bad person," said Noelle. "She wasn't. Cory said she regularly volunteered at the animal shelter and even did free housekeeping for a few senior citizens in Eagle's Nest."

"That was her?" asked Truman. "A few months ago someone in town told me that a woman was cleaning her grandmother's home and a few of her neighbors' at no charge."

"Cory said Rachel didn't like sitting around," said Noelle. "So if she didn't have any paying jobs, she'd do some for free. I guess this led to a few referrals for paying customers. And yes, I also got her free-client information, which I'll send to you."

"Thank you." Max added *free housekeeping jobs* and *animal shelter* under Rachel's name. A small swirl of guilt spread up his throat. He hadn't been aware of how harshly he'd judged Rachel Johnson until that moment. "When's her autopsy?" he asked gruffly.

"Same as John Doe Two," said Mercy. "Should be today or tomorrow. I told Cory I'll be there."

"I'll attend John Doe One," said Noelle.

"A bit off topic, but what about Emma Chambers?" asked Truman. "Someone should check in with her today. Ina had the impression that Emma's father hadn't been around much lately."

"I'll stop by," said Noelle.

"I've got clothes you can take," said Mercy. "Kaylie cleaned out her closet yesterday when I told her about Emma."

"Will that be okay with Emma?" asked Truman. "We don't want to offend her."

"I'll make it work," said Noelle.

"Let's divide up these," said Max, tapping the board. "Deschutes County has promised more manpower. And Truman has too." He nodded at the police chief.

Mercy turned to her husband. "You can't spare anyone."

"I told Max I'd cover anything that came up within the town limits." He paused. "So far that's nothing," he added wryly. "Well, that's not quite true. Ben is keeping an eye on Tom Mumford from the hotel—turns out he didn't lie about his name. His address in Idaho checked out too. I also have my ear to the ground for any rumors from town or the high school. Don't know if that will help with the car bombing, though."

"I asked Oakleigh why she said she should get a restraining order against Tom Mumford," said Max. "She said he'd been at the hotel for three days and would always hang out in the lobby during her shift. Said he'd follow her to her car when she finished working."

"Jesus," said Noelle.

"The night before Rachel was shot, Tom tailed her to her car again. She grabbed a revolver from under her seat and pointed it at his crotch. Told him she'd shoot off his balls if he came near her again. He hightailed it back to his room." Max shook his head. "She didn't seem scared of him. Claimed he was just a pain in the ass."

"I'm not so sure about that," said Noelle. "Sounds like he has a problem to me. He admitted he cornered Rachel near the ice machine. He's going to step over a line sooner or later."

"I'd say he's stepped over several lines already," said Truman. "Have we eliminated him as a suspect for Rachel's murder?"

"We haven't," said Max. "That's pretty cocky if he shot her, then stepped into his own room next door and stuck around. Or else stupid."

"His prints are in the system," said Truman. "He got in some trouble back home. If they turn up in Rachel's room, we'll know it."

"Find out if he has any weapons registered," said Max.

"Already did," said Truman. "Four handguns and eight long guns."

"That's an arsenal," said Noelle.

"Not around here," said Truman. "I know lots of citizens who have upwards of twenty guns. They have different reasons for buying each of them. Some collect, some will buy a different one depending on what they're hunting or even skeet shooting. Some are sentimental purchases. Like they learned to shoot on a particular type of gun when they were a kid, or they might have inherited the weapons."

"He's right," said Mercy.

Max still didn't understand the need for so many weapons, but he knew Mercy and Truman had better insight into the local population. Max looked at his whiteboard. "I think these deaths are all tied together," he said. "We don't have proof yet, but my gut tells me they are. Did Tom Mumford seem like the type of person who could rig a car bomb?"

No one answered.

Max had his doubts.

Mumford could have paid someone to do it.

"Let me know if he gets ready to leave town," he said to Truman, who nodded. "Once we have all three bullets from the murders, hopefully that'll let us know if I'm right about the connection between the deaths."

It was a big *if.* The bullets might be from three different weapons.

One step at a time.

21

Emma learned that not all vehicles have power steering when she discovered it took all her muscles to turn the steering wheel on Uncle Tommy's truck. He'd made her drive it around his property and given her a brief tutorial. She hadn't driven any vehicle that much. Her only opportunities had come when her father needed something from the store and told Emma to go get it. His pickup was old too, but it wasn't exhausting to drive like this one.

She bounced down her road in Tommy's old truck, not caring that the ride was rough. She felt free. Something about driving a vehicle by herself and realizing she had the ability to go anywhere she wished was incredibly empowering.

Emma wasn't about to drive anywhere but her house, but just the thought of the freedom lifted her spirits.

Oh shit.

Those lifted spirits vanished as she neared her home. She recognized the dark SUV parked at the house and the woman on her porch.

Detective Marshall.

What does she want?

Emma slowed the truck to a jerking stop next to the SUV. She pushed open its creaking door, jumped down, and then slammed it as Tommy had shown her—otherwise it didn't latch. She slowly walked to the house, unease building, as the detective came down the steps. Emma didn't understand it, but the detective looked as if she'd just stepped out of a high-end store even though she wore just black pants and a black jacket. Her presence made Emma's home look ancient and run-down.

"Hi, Emma," said the woman, taking a sharp look at Tommy's truck.

"Hi, Detective Marshall. Is something wrong?" Emma added a smile, hoping the detective couldn't see how nervous she was.

"I dropped by to check on you," said the detective. "How's it going?"

"Everything's great." Another forced smile.

The woman's gaze was intense, and Emma felt as if her own skin were transparent, revealing her lie to the detective. "Can I get a glass of water?" asked the detective.

"Of course." Emma walked up the stairs and noted Cornbread's bowl was empty. She paused, wanting to fill it right that moment in case the cat was hungrily watching her from some hidden place.

"Whose truck are you driving?" asked the detective as Emma unlocked the door.

"It belongs to my uncle Tommy."

"Is that your father's brother?"

"Not exactly." She explained who Tommy was as she led the woman into the house.

She's police. I shouldn't lie to her.

"That's nice of him to loan you his truck," said the detective. "Where's your father?"

"Out of town." Emma kept her face turned away from the woman and grabbed a glass out of the cupboard. Something crunched under her boot, and she realized she'd missed a piece of glass while cleaning up the mess the two men had made in the house.

"Is that glass?" asked the detective. "Be careful—there's some more. What happened?" She turned on a light and scanned the floor.

"I dropped a glass the other day," said Emma, focusing on filling the detective's glass with water, not wanting to tell her about the break-in.

So much for not lying.

The detective was silent for a long moment and then took two steps to the fridge and pulled it open.

Emma whirled around, clasping the water glass with both hands and holding her breath.

The woman looked from the nearly empty fridge to Emma. “Where’d the food go? I know some was delivered.”

“I took it to Tommy’s house.” She clung to the glass in a death grip as the detective’s blue gaze looked her up and down.

“Why?”

Emma’s mind went blank, and she couldn’t think of a reason except the truth. “I’m staying there, so I took the food over.”

Detective Marshall closed the fridge and looked around the home. “That’s why it’s so cold in here.” She frowned. “Is Tommy married?”

“No.” A split second later she understood why the detective had asked. “He’s old! It’s not like that. He’s practically family!”

“Does he know where your father is?” the woman asked quietly.

She knows that I lied about my dad.

Emma looked down at the glass of water and realized some had splashed over her hands and she hadn’t even noticed. “No,” she said quietly.

A loud meow made them both look toward the door, which the detective had left ajar. Cornbread had shoved his head through the space. He looked at Emma and meowed again.

Is he checking on me or just hungry?

“Just a minute,” she told Detective Marshall. Emma set down the glass and grabbed a bag of cat food from another cupboard and stepped outside. She poured the food into his bowl and stepped back to watch him for a few seconds, knowing she was avoiding the detective. Cornbread started to eat, ignoring Emma.

He’s no longer scared to be near me.

“Nice cat.” The detective stood at the door.

“He’s a stray,” said Emma. “He’s only been here a little while, and I don’t know if he’s ever been around people.”

“Well, someone took care of him at some point,” said the detective.

Emma frowned. “How do you know?”

"His ear. It's tipped. The vet does that when they neuter or spay a stray."

Emma squatted down to get a better look at Cornbread's ear, and he lifted his head from his bowl, meeting her gaze. She'd noticed his ear was blunt but had assumed it was from a catfight. His other ear had a small, old tear, which had left an odd flap.

"So he might be a girl," said Emma, knowing the cat wouldn't let her peek under his tail.

"With that wide face and thick cheeks?" asked Detective Marshall. "That says *boy* to me. He was probably fixed later in life. Are there other stray cats around here?"

"No," said Emma.

"Then he must have been dumped nearby. He's lucky he found you. Did you name him?"

"Cornbread." The cat looked at Emma again.

Does he know his name already?

"That's adorable," said the woman. "I love it when pets are named for food."

"He's a good cat," said Emma. "He—" She stopped talking as she realized she was about to say that he'd warned her about intruders.

"He what?"

"He's a good cat," she repeated, her brain spinning.

The detective sighed. "I'll take that water now." She stepped back inside the cold house and Emma followed. "Sit down, Emma." Detective Marshall grabbed her water glass off the counter and sat at the table, waiting for Emma to take a chair.

Emma sat.

The detective set her elbows on the table and leaned forward. "I get the impression that you're a good kid who's had some bad luck come your way."

"But—"

Detective Marshall raised a hand for Emma to be quiet. "Where's your father?" she asked quietly.

Emma stayed silent, staring at the fake wood pattern on the table.

"Why are you staying at your uncle's house instead of here?" She pointed at the door. "Something's up when you won't stay with a cat that you clearly adore." The detective rapped her knuckles on the table. "Is your uncle threatening you?"

Emma's gaze flew up as she jerked in her chair. "No! He's the best! I'm staying there because . . ." She squirmed, and the story of the intruders spilled out of her mouth.

"Jesus," muttered the detective when she was done. "Why didn't you call the police?"

"I don't know."

Because my dad taught me to never call them.

"Do you know what they meant by 'What I already told you. We need her'?"

"Probably nothing good." Emma fought back tears.

"Why would someone come looking for you?"

Emma shrugged. "I have no idea."

The woman thought for a moment. "And this Uncle Tommy didn't call the police either?"

"No." Emma met the detective's blue gaze. "We don't call the police," she said softly.

The woman nodded and sat back in her chair. "Got it." She crossed her arms on her chest and blew out a breath as she considered Emma. "Back to your dad. Do you know where he is?"

"Why do you keep asking about him? He's an adult. He can do what he wants."

"True. But you get very squirrelly every time I bring him up. Makes me wonder what's up."

"Nothing."

"You were almost attacked in your home. That's not nothing. Emma, could those men be the reason your dad isn't here? Are other people looking for him?"

"I don't know." She'd wondered the same thing several times.

"That body you found in the woods." The detective softened her voice. "Did you get a good enough look to know that wasn't your father?"

"Oh my God!" Emma was instantly nauseated as the image popped up in her mind. "That wasn't him! I know it wasn't! Not even close. My dad is super skinny and not very tall."

"Okay. I had to ask. I didn't mean to upset you."

Emma's stomach continued to swirl, and she tried to put the memory out of her head. "Tommy'll find him. He knows everybody," she said stoutly.

But I don't want him to come back.

"Is there anything else you should tell me?" asked the detective. Her gaze said she believed Emma was holding back.

I am.

"No. Everything's fine."

"You're awfully calm for someone who might have been killed the other night."

"Nothing happened." She wanted to cry.

"Emma, it's okay to trust me. The only thing I want to do is help you and make sure you're safe."

I want to believe her.

But she knew law enforcement wasn't to be trusted. Just look at all her questions about Tommy and her dad. She was fishing for something to get them in trouble.

"What's Tommy's full name?"

Emma blinked. She had no idea. He'd been simply Uncle Tommy forever, and she couldn't think of ever hearing her father say his last name. "I'm not sure."

"Do you have an address for him?"

"Yeah." She rattled off his address, and the detective wrote it down. "You're not going to bother him, are you?"

"I don't plan to. I just want to know where to find you if I have more questions. I'm also going to send a deputy here to see if your intruders left some fingerprints. Can you stick around for a few hours until one comes?"

"Yes." She was pleasantly surprised that the detective would bother. "When will you know the name of the man who died?"

The detective grimaced. "I'm meeting the medical examiner next. Hopefully we'll have some answers after that."

"You'll let me know?"

"When it's okay with his relatives." She put her little notebook in a jacket pocket. "Are you going anywhere else today?"

"No. I just came to check on Cornbread and get some more clothes."

"That reminds me," said Detective Marshall. "I've been carrying around bags to drop off at the donation center. I keep forgetting to stop. I'll let you look through the clothes first. I noticed my friend's niece added some good things that look about your size."

Emma wanted to disappear. She knew the woman was lying and thought Emma needed charity for clothing. Emma touched a hole in the thigh of her baggy joggers. She couldn't remember the last time she'd had anything new—or at least new to her.

"I can take a look," she said casually.

"Great! Two less bags in my vehicle." The detective stood and headed for the door.

Emma followed.

Maybe Detective Marshall isn't so bad.

22

At the medical examiner's, Noelle grabbed two masks. She didn't know if it would help block the smell of death, but it was worth a try. She was tempted to wad up tissues and shove them in her nose but didn't want Evan to see her do it. It was bad enough that his probing gaze hadn't left her since they entered the medical examiner's building.

He expects me to pass out. Or make a run for it.

Evan had met her at the building after she'd watched Emma go through two bags of clothes. The teen had kept everything Kaylie had sent. They'd been mostly practical clothes. Sweaters, jeans, coats. The things looked a little big but not too bad. Kaylie had also included a few sparkly things, which had made Emma's eyes light up.

If anyone deserved something pretty, it was Emma.

Noelle was determined to find out what was going on in that girl's life, why two men had shown up and spoken as if they had orders to kill her.

She also wanted to know exactly who Uncle Tommy was.

After the autopsy.

Evan eyed her two masks, but Noelle refused to meet his gaze, focusing on tying her gown behind her back and adjusting her face shield. She followed Evan into the autopsy suite while trying to get her gloves on. "These're too small." She turned and went out the door. He followed a split second later.

"Are you okay?" His voice was full of concern.

"Jesus, Evan." Noelle threw the gloves in a bin. "I'm getting bigger gloves. I'm not about to fall on my face." She snatched two out of the box of mediums and deliberately yanked on the first one, finally meeting his gaze. "Go," she ordered.

From behind his shield, he studied her eyes, the only part of her face he could see. He must have believed her because he turned and went back in the suite. Noelle followed, feeling sweat form on her upper lip. It was already growing hot behind the two masks. She breathed through her mouth and tried not to focus on how stuffy the air felt.

Am I getting enough oxygen?

I don't want to end up on the floor.

She should have let Evan attend the autopsy alone. They'd cover more ground if they split up. But she'd been the one at the crime scene in the woods and felt an obligation to see it through.

I can't back out now.

Nearly five years ago, new to the sheriff's office, Noelle had gone weak kneed during the autopsy of a child in this very suite. The deputy next to her had grabbed her arm just in time, as her face had been a foot from hitting the floor. Noelle had known fainting was a possibility but had been trying to prove herself in the department and had hoped she could muscle through it under Dr. Lockhart's careful gaze.

Nope.

The deputy had jokingly called her Crash, and for two years the nickname had followed her around the department.

Since then she'd interacted with Dr. Lockhart at several crime scenes and during postautopsy phone calls. But she hadn't attended another autopsy until today.

Inside the bright suite, Dr. Natasha Lockhart was speaking to her assistant. She stood on a custom platform that made a large U around the stainless steel table where their victim silently lay, his torso splayed open. Dr. Lockhart was petite and looked very young; she could easily pass for a college student. It took Noelle a moment to realize the music playing over the speakers was Taylor Swift's "Shake It Off."

The doctor glanced over as Noelle and Evan entered, her eyes widening slightly as she identified Noelle under the mask and shield.

She hasn't forgotten.

"Detective Marshall. Did you see my email?" asked Dr. Lockhart.

"No. From when?" She hadn't checked her email since the earlier conference room meeting.

"I sent one this morning." The medical examiner's eyes twinkled. "We got an ID off his fingerprints."

"That's great!" Noelle started to grab her phone out of her pocket, under her gown, and hesitated.

I shouldn't touch things with my gloves.

Dr. Lockhart guessed at her hesitation. "Don't worry about your gloves. You won't be touching the patient."

"Good point." Noelle looked at her phone. "Michael Munoz. Age twenty-eight."

Emma was right that it wasn't her father.

Why wouldn't she tell me what is going on with him?

"I'll get someone going on a current address and family," said Evan, pulling out his own phone.

Noelle finally looked squarely at the body on the stainless steel table but couldn't bring herself to look at his face. Knowing his identity didn't make her feel any better. In fact it personalized the tragedy before her. She tried to slow her pounding heart with calm breaths under the double masks.

It sort of worked.

"What can you tell us, Doctor?" Noelle asked in what she hoped was a normal voice. It appeared the medical examiner had finished with the organs in the torso. She had moved to the head.

"Mr. Munoz was a healthy man. He has an old, healed break in his radius and a few faded scars here and there, but he has recent contusions around his wrists and ankles."

"He was tied up," said Evan.

Like the man in the judge's trunk.

"And not fed," said Dr. Lockhart. "His digestive system was empty, and somebody beat on him close to his death. There are more recent contusions on his face, and his jaw was recently fractured."

Noelle flinched, thinking of the blow it would take to break a jaw. "Maybe it happened after he died."

"No," Dr. Lockhart said in a flat voice. "I guarantee it didn't."

"Maybe that's why he hadn't eaten," murmured Evan. "He couldn't."

Dr. Lockhart nodded. "A good theory. At the crime scene, I determined that he'd been moved after death, remember?"

"The livor mortis," said Noelle, recalling the dark shade of his back, which indicated Mr. Munoz hadn't died on his stomach, as they'd found him. "Do you have a time of death?"

"Not yet," said Dr. Lockhart. "I'm waiting on labs. But I haven't seen anything that contradicts the three-to-five-day timeline I said the other day."

"And the gunshot wound?" asked Evan.

"The entry wound is actually from two bullets. Someone fired twice without moving the weapon," said Dr. Lockhart. "There is heavy stippling in the skin around the entry, telling me the gun was very close to his forehead when it was fired. One of the bullets exited under the jaw, but X-rays show one is still inside. My next step is to find it."

Noelle finally looked Michael Munoz in the face. He didn't look twenty-eight. He was grossly swollen, and his skin was mottled, but the hole in his forehead was apparent.

Two bullets. Someone wanted to be certain he was dead.

Dr. Lockhart's last words sank in, and Noelle glanced at her. The doctor was hesitating near Mr. Munoz's head, a scalpel in her hand, her gaze on Noelle.

She's waiting to see if I want to leave.

Because the need to find the bullet meant the medical examiner was about to slice his scalp, peel part of it over his face, and then cut into the skull with her bone saw. Noelle hadn't watched—or listened—to it in person before, but she was well aware of the next steps. She tried to take more deep breaths, but this time the double masks worked against her. She grabbed at them and yanked them under her chin to suck in air. And then the smells hit her.

"I'll be outside," she barely managed to say before spinning and making a beeline for the exit. Outside the suite door, she ripped off all her PPE, wadded it up, and crammed it in the bin.

I won't faint.

I need fresh air.

She headed down the hall toward the reception area and heard the suite door swing open behind her.

"Noelle!" Evan's voice was muffled behind his mask. "Wait up."

"I'm okay, Evan," Noelle said, not looking over her shoulder. "I'm not going to pass out."

He caught up with her halfway through the reception area, stripped of his PPE. "Hang on."

Noelle stopped and made herself look him in the eye. "What?"

Evan touched her arm, sympathy in his gaze. "I don't like what she was about to do either."

Frustration boiled through her. "Mentally I know I can tough it out, but my body betrays me. It has other plans."

He shrugged. "Fine. You gave it another shot. We'll go back to me attending the autopsies like we've done for the past several years. Not a big deal."

"I *should* be able to do this!" She rarely encountered a situation she couldn't power through.

"I get it," said Evan. "This is your thing. For me it's heights." He grimaced. "As soon as I look down, I'm completely frozen. It's ridiculous. Going up I'm fine as long as I focus on where I'm going. But damn, one look down, and I have no control anymore."

"I didn't know that." She tried to recall if they'd ever been in that type of situation together.

"It's not something I brag about." He sighed. "Dr. Lockhart will let us know what she finds. Neither of us needs to be there."

"But it's important because—" started Noelle.

"I know," said Evan. "So it's a good thing we can divide up duties. Autopsies for me, and you can be in charge of anything that involves standing on a cliff." He held up his phone. "Lori got back to me with a last known address for Munoz. Feel up to that?"

Another death notification.

Still preferable to an autopsy.

"Yes, let's go." Her stomach growled, reminding her she hadn't eaten lunch. "But we need to grab some food on the way."

Evan grinned. "If you can eat after being in there, you're fine."

"I can always eat."

23

The address for Michael Munoz was that of an older home on the outskirts of Bend. It was hard to read the house numbers because several were blocked by bushes and trees, but Noelle managed to spot the right home. Evan parked on the road, and Noelle eyed the small bike in the bark dust next to an old Toyota Tercel in the driveway.

He has a child?

"This is the address on his driver's license renewal from two years ago," said Evan, leaning forward to look out the window past Noelle. "But the name on the home is Roger Jones. I'll have someone run the Toyota's plates." He sent a text.

Noelle gestured at the bike. "He might have kids."

Evan nodded grimly. "Always makes this part of the job even tougher. I prefer to talk to the spouse alone." His phone buzzed. "Toyota comes back to a Louisa Munoz. We're in the right spot. Maybe they're renting."

They got out of the SUV and headed up the driveway. Noelle swore it was getting colder as the day went on. She glanced at the gray sky.

Snow. Soon.

The concrete driveway was cracked in several spots, stubborn grass growing in the crevices. Noelle rang the doorbell and heard it jangle inside, setting off loud barking from multiple dogs. A moment later a small woman with long, dark hair opened the door. Two white, fluffy dogs flanked her as she stood behind the screen door. The barking stopped, and two tails wagged at lightning speed.

"Mrs. Munoz?" asked Noelle, holding out her ID as the woman nodded. "We're with the Deschutes County Sheriff's Department. Can we speak with you for a moment?"

Louisa Munoz looked from one of them to the other, concern growing in her eyes. "What's this about? Is it Michael?"

"Is he your husband?" asked Noelle.

"My brother. Is he okay?"

"He's not okay," said Noelle gently. "Do your dogs mind strangers? Can we come in?"

Louisa gave a jerky nod. "They'll be good." She grabbed the collar of one and opened the screen, stepping back to let in Noelle and Evan. She gestured for them to enter the living room, and Noelle was relieved to not see any kids close by.

"What happened to Michael?" Louisa crossed her arms, an "I'm prepared for the worst" expression on her face. She didn't sit down, and neither did Noelle and Evan. One of the dogs hopped up on the sofa, its black gaze never leaving the new people. The other sniffed at Evan's shoes.

"I'm very sorry, but your brother has passed. His body was found the day before yesterday," said Noelle.

Louisa flinched and tightened her arms across her chest. "*What?* Was it a car accident?" She blinked rapidly.

"No. He was shot." Noelle hated to be so blunt but knew there was no way to soften that fact. "I'm so sorry."

"Are you sure it was him?" she pleaded.

"Yes. I'm so sorry," Noelle repeated, hating the brief look of hope in the woman's eyes. "He didn't have ID on him, so he wasn't identified until the medical examiner took his prints today."

Louisa looked away for a long moment, her hands covering her mouth, the news sinking in. Suddenly her gaze flew back to Noelle, her eyes wet. "Was he the one found near Old Mill Highway?" she asked in a hoarse voice.

"Yes," said Evan. "You didn't realize he was missing?"

"I don't see him much," she whispered. "I'd heard that a body was found. I didn't think for a second that it could be Michael." She wiped her eyes, her posture softening. *"Oh, Michael."* The dog on the sofa hopped down and circled Louisa's legs.

"Can we sit?" Noelle asked.

"Please." With shaking legs, Louisa moved to the sofa and seemed to melt into the cushions. Noelle sat beside her as Evan took a seat in an easy chair. The other dog continued to sniff at his shoes and then his legs.

"He smells Thor," Evan said quietly. "My fiancée's dog," he explained to Louisa.

She blinked, looking lost, and then nodded at his explanation. The woman blew out a lungful of air, and shock slowly faded from her face as she pulled herself together. "Who did this to him?" she asked, her voice low.

"We don't know yet, but we'll find out," said Noelle. "When did you see Michael last?"

Louisa thought. "It was the weekend before last. He used to live here, but I made him move out just after Christmas. He's stopped by a few times since then to pick up more of his belongings." She smiled sadly. "The garage is still packed with his car stuff and tools, even after several trips."

"Where did he live?" asked Noelle, not missing that Louisa had made him move out.

"I don't *know.*" Frustration filled her face. "I didn't ask, and he didn't say where. I was angry with him, and he was mad that I made him leave. I gave him several chances," she said earnestly. "But things kept happening."

"What sort of things?" asked Evan.

"I have an eight-year-old son," said Louisa. "He's into everything; he's so curious. Michael had several guns, which I don't have a problem with, but it's not a good situation in a house with my son, especially when Michael forgets to lock them up. He has a safe, but he'd often lay a weapon on top of it instead of putting it away. That's not good enough. Austin was fascinated with them." She held up her hands. "What could I do? I told him to move out. I wasn't taking any more chances. I know Michael loved my son, but I couldn't handle the pressure that something bad could happen because Michael got lazy." She rubbed her forehead. "Austin was in tears for weeks because he missed his uncle. So we made an agreement that he could see Austin here for an hour or two, and he wasn't to bring any guns. Not even if he left them in his truck. *No guns.*"

"He respected that?" asked Evan.

"He did. I insisted on looking in his truck before I'd let him see Austin. Then I'd let him hang out at the house while I ran some errands. Very *short* errands. Most of the time I was close by. Usually they just played video games." Louisa was very emphatic about protecting her son. Noelle had no doubt she only let Michael see Austin in a regulated environment.

"You can't guess where Michael moved to?" asked Noelle.

"To a friend's, I supposed. He hadn't worked in several months, so he didn't have much money for rent, and I doubt anyone would rent to him if he didn't have a job."

"Where did he used to work?"

"Post office in Bend. He told me he quit, but I know he was fired. My friend whose husband works there said he missed too many shifts. It had gone on for months."

"What about your parents?" asked Noelle. "Are they nearby?"

"My father died several years ago," said Louisa. "My mother lives in Arizona with my other brother and his wife." She paused for a long moment. "They need to hear about Michael from me. Michael wasn't close to our brother, and I don't know the last time he talked to our mother," she said slowly. "It's best that I'm the one who tells them today." She turned imploring eyes to Noelle. "I'll get their numbers for you, but could you wait until tomorrow to contact them? Give them overnight to process this?"

"We can wait," said Noelle, knowing it was news best heard from Louisa. "Do you know of anyone that Michael had a dispute with? Or of anyone who would hurt him?"

A dog hopped up on the sofa and laid its head on Louisa's thigh. She absentmindedly stroked its fur as she stared at the wall across the room. "I don't know," she said slowly. "He's never talked about something like that to me."

"Can you tell us who his friends are? Maybe they would have some ideas."

A dark look flashed on her face. "He didn't have many friends. Never has. But he started hanging out with some people about the same time as he got fired. That's when he started buying more guns too."

"You don't seem to like these people," said Evan. "How come?"

"His behavior changed, and I'm sure it was from their influence. Michael started staying out half the night, and he was rude when I pointed out he was upsetting the routine of the house. So disrespectful. He'd wake up Austin, and then the boy can't get back to sleep, so he's a mess the next day. He acts out in school and can't focus.

"I tried to talk to Michael about it, but he said that his schedule was none of my business and that's how things were going to be now. His attitude was dark, and he acted angry with the world. When I caught Austin alone in his room with a rifle in his hands, that was the last straw. I told Michael to leave that day." She slumped on the sofa, her fingers burrowing into the dog's white fur. "I shouldn't have done that. Maybe he'd still be alive."

"Or maybe we'd be sharing this news about your son instead," Noelle pointed out. "You did what was best for your family. Why the late hours for Michael? You said he didn't have a job. Could it have been a girlfriend?"

"Not a girlfriend." Her forehead wrinkled in concentration. "I asked that too, and he brushed me off." She exhaled and looked at Evan. "I'm worried he was involved with a gang," she said quietly.

Noelle was surprised. "Does he have a motorcycle?" Most of the gang activity she was aware of in the area involved motorcycle gangs. Other activity was mostly young adults trying to imitate gang behavior.

A gang hit?

The two bullets in the forehead does seem like an execution.

"No." Louisa slumped again. "But I don't know what else it could be. What could change him so dramatically?"

"Did he seem to carry more cash?" asked Evan. "Any evidence of drug use?"

Louisa shook her head as he spoke. "None of that. When I started to suspect it was a gang, I searched his room several times. I never found either of those things." She grimaced. "He never had money. I gave him money here and there. Mainly to get him off my back. I'd hoped he'd go look for a job."

"How could we find out who his new friends were? Would some of his old ones know?" asked Noelle.

"You could talk to Carson Vohland at the post office. He and Michael used to go out sometimes. I've met him, but he hasn't been around since at least last fall."

Noelle wrote down the name, and an idea occurred to her. "Does the name Rachel Johnson mean anything to you?"

Evan met her gaze and gave a tiny nod, acknowledging it was a good question.

Louisa thought. "No. I never met anyone he dated, and I can't think of any female friends he had. Why do you ask?" She shifted on the sofa. "Did she hurt him?" she asked hoarsely.

"No," said Noelle before she realized she didn't know that for a fact. "Just a woman we came across in another case recently," she added, not wanting to mention Rachel had also been shot in the head. "Can *you* think of anyone who'd want to hurt your brother?"

"No. I rarely knew what was going on with him."

"There's a Chevy pickup registered in Michael's name," said Evan, looking at his phone. "I assume you don't know where it is?"

"I don't," said Louisa. "He loves—loved that truck even though it was almost twenty years old. Always kept it sparkling clean and was very proud of its custom wheels and huge tires. It wasn't with him?"

"It wasn't," said Noelle. "We'll put out a BOLO for it." She exchanged a look with Evan and lifted an eyebrow.

Anything else?

He shook his head and stood. Noelle followed suit. She handed Louisa her business card. "You can pass on my number to your brother and mother in case they want to speak to me before I call them tomorrow. And please contact me if you think of anything that can help us," she said. "Anything, no matter how small you think it is. We're determined to find who did this to your brother."

"I will." Louisa took the card and got to her feet. "I appreciate you coming in person. This can't be an easy part of your job."

Noelle was touched. It was rare that someone who'd just learned a family member had died would express sympathy for the messenger. "It's not. But it's nothing compared to a family's pain. They become victims too. A death is like dropping a stone in a pond. The ripples spread out and impact the circle of people who loved him."

"I agree." Louisa walked them to the front door, and they said their goodbyes.

Inside the SUV, Evan and Noelle sat in silence until they were several miles from the home.

"You did really well," said Evan. "People can tell that your sympathy is genuine."

"It's not hard to be sympathetic," said Noelle. "I can easily slip into their position. I know how it feels to abruptly lose someone." Her grandfather's face flashed in her memory.

Because I've been there.

A wave of emptiness washed over her, and she suddenly craved Max's touch, aching to relax into his arms, where she didn't have to think about anything else. It'd been a difficult day with first the autopsy and then this. Who knew what else would happen today?

She sent him a text.

Rough day so far. Can you come over this evening?

A moment later she had his reply.

Absolutely. I can't wait

She settled back in her seat, relieved that she'd get to see his face and hear his warm voice that evening.

A few days ago they'd had a fantastic dinner with his sister Keira and her husband, TJ, at their home. Lots of good conversation and embarrassing stories about Max when he was younger. After dinner Keira had pulled out more wine and a version of the card game Uno called No Mercy. Noelle had never heard of it. The game was brutal. Draw ten cards. Mandatory hand swaps. Keira, TJ, and Max fiercely attacked one another, laughter filling the house. She suspected his family took it easy on her, but there was definitely no mercy for each other.

But the love among the three of them was apparent.

Noelle had thoroughly enjoyed the evening. Several times Max had caught her gaze, his full of joy and happiness, making her smile and warming her heart. The serious FBI agent was a different person with his family.

There had been almost no mention of his other two sisters and mother. Too little, Noelle had noticed. It felt deliberate. Keira had started to mention something about one of her sisters, and then Max had changed the subject, and TJ had exchanged a look with Keira. Noelle thought back over their other dates and realized he hadn't told her much about the rest of the family.

Something is up there.

Noelle took a long second to evaluate how she felt at this very moment in their relationship.

Happy. Not pressured. Ready for more.

That's pleasantly surprising.

Max Rhodes was a good man. She'd been lucky to have him appear in her life.

She hadn't asked him for this kind of support before, where she'd had a bad day and needed his presence to get past it. In the past she would have picked up a pint of ice cream or a bottle of wine or both and wallowed alone. It'd been years since she'd trusted a man enough to get this close, and she was taking the relationship very slowly with small, tentative steps. So far, so good. She almost worried it was too good to be true.

She still had a secret to tell him. It sent chills through her when she tried to picture his reaction. She worried that the longer she put it off, the bigger it would seem in his eyes. Because it indirectly involved him, and he'd realize she'd held back something important.

And he'll wonder what else I haven't told him.

But I had no way of knowing we'd be looking at a future together.

"Future?" she said out loud.

Is that what's happening?

24

Max turned off his engine and studied Judge Holtz's large house.

A county deputy had closely examined Max's ID before he'd let him drive onto the property. Max had parked next to two black SUVs with government plates that he suspected belonged to the US Marshals Service. Since the car bomb, the judge's security had been bumped up to a high alert.

The judge's home's style was what Max thought of as high desert modern. It was a long, single-story house with an exterior of earth-tone tiles, rough stones, and vertical wood panels with huge windows. The dark wood front door was twice his height. The home had been created with the colors and elements of the surrounding nature in mind. An architect had clearly enjoyed the project.

Max paused inside his vehicle, taking a brief mental break and closing his eyes for a long moment. The amount of information pouring in from the car bomb investigation was overwhelming. He'd intended to start going through it last night, but Rachel's murder had put a stop to his plans. This morning he'd realized that her death had thrown him for a bigger emotional loop than he'd expected; the guilt was overwhelming.

Did I miss something?

He couldn't help but feel that if he'd driven faster to her motel or been a little nicer to her on the phone or suggested that she leave the motel, maybe, *just maybe*, she'd still be alive. He'd told himself a dozen times that she had been an adult and responsible for her own actions. Rachel Johnson had played with fire and been badly burned.

Surely I could have done something. Said something.

But Rachel's sexpot act had annoyed the fuck out of him, and his patience with her had been short. Then suddenly she was dead.

He would find her killer; that was his only path to peace.

But the car bombing at the courthouse was the FBI's priority at the moment. The investigation of Rachel's murder had been officially assigned to the sheriff's department, with the FBI providing supportive resources.

I know the crimes are tied together.

He was convinced that the person who'd killed Rachel knew something about the bombing.

He was at Judge Holtz's home to interview him again. Yesterday Max had only talked with the man for about a half hour after the body was discovered in his trunk. This time the interview would include the judge's wife, Tamara.

Max had taken a quick look at the judge's financial statements, and his wife's, an hour ago. He'd skimmed them, not sure what he was looking for, hoping something would jump out at him. Not seeing anything unusual, Max had left the statements with Darby, the office's data analyst, and asked her to study them. And to assemble a background for Tamara Holtz.

They were considering everything and everyone at the moment.

Max strode up the wide concrete steps to the giant door, which a marshal opened before he reached it. The marshal was in casual clothing and wore an earpiece, a holstered gun, and a Kevlar vest with US Marshal emblazoned on the front. He nodded at Max and let him in.

"The judge is this way." Max followed the marshal through a long glass hallway between two landscaped courtyards to a great room at the back of the home, where the judge and Tamara Holtz were seated at a huge table adjacent to the kitchen. The wood slab table had raw edges, and a blue epoxy strip ran down the center of the table like a river. They stood as Max approached. The judge shook his hand and introduced his wife.

Tamara was a small woman with blonde hair and a lovely smile, but stress and fear were evident in her eyes. The three of them sat, the tension in the room rising, and the marshal silently vanished. Max fought back the urge to touch the smooth blue wave in the table.

"Have you identified the man in the trunk?" asked the judge. He'd taken his wife's hand, and Max noticed her knuckles were white.

"Not yet. The medical examiner started the autopsy about a half hour ago. She'll email me with any immediate findings," Max said, including Tamara with his gaze. "The state fire investigator and the ATF confirmed the bomb was a type controlled by cell phone. I know your cameras here at your home didn't show anyone approaching your car for more than a week, so we need to look elsewhere to figure out when the body was put in your trunk. Did you pull together a list of locations you've been at?"

"I did." The judge slid a piece of paper across the table. "I golfed on Saturday morning and opened my trunk. So it happened after that. I haven't opened it since then."

Max scanned the short list, which included locations, dates, and times where the judge's car had been elsewhere. Two restaurants. Gas station. Gym. He took a photo and sent the list to Darby so she could request camera footage from the businesses. He looked at Tamara. "Do you ever drive the vehicle?"

"I drove it Sunday," she said, looking at her husband. "Your car had blocked mine in the garage, so I took it to Trader Joe's."

The judge paled. "That's right. I forgot. That's not on the list." He gripped his wife's hand tighter, and Max knew he was picturing her coming in close contact with the killer. He texted the name of the grocery store to Darby.

"Anywhere else?" Max asked.

Both shook their heads.

"My clerk and I went through my cases and pulled together a list of people who've been . . . *outspoken* about their treatment in my court." He gave Max another list. "It includes threats made in person and made by email or online."

"How far back did you go?" asked Max.

"Two years. Plus a few older ones that have always stuck in my head. A lot of people flow through my courtroom," said the judge. "Sometimes it's someone in the family who is the outspoken one. I've included them too."

Max nodded, reading the list. There were at least two dozen names. Assault. Robbery. Domestic violence. "Any of these people out of prison?"

"The last three were released recently," said the judge. "The rest are still serving, but I gave you their names because it could be an angry friend or family member."

Max took a photo of the list and sent it to Darby with a text telling her to start investigating with the last three names. He figured a sentenced person was more likely than their family to retaliate against the judge.

"Mom!" Little running footsteps sounded on the wood floors, and two identical blond boys tore into the room. "Jett won't leave me alone!" The first boy flung himself at his mother, wrapping his arms around her and crawling halfway into her lap. The other boy hit the brakes and looked at Max with big eyes. Max estimated he was about five years old.

Twins.

"Chase, get off your mother," said the judge. He turned to the other boy. "You picking on your brother?"

"No, sir." Innocent blue eyes met his father's gaze. "I'm Spider-Man! He's the Green Goblin."

The other twin twisted in his mother's lap. *"I'm Spider-Man!"* he shouted at his brother. "It's my turn!"

Max stifled a grin.

Kids.

The marshal who'd let Max in the door reappeared and looked over everyone in the room. He said something into his mic and left.

A sudden pain hit Max in his stomach as he imagined the parents' escalated fear about their boys' safety. He noticed dark areas under Tamara's eyes and wondered if she'd slept last night.

She must be worried sick.

"I got this." Tamara slid Chase off her lap, holding his hand, and then took Jett's. She led them away in the direction the marshal had gone. Chase glared at Jett behind their mother's back as they left. "We'll flip a coin," Max heard her say.

"Always flipping a coin," muttered the judge. "Only way to settle anything with those two. Or else we set timers to give equal time. Heaven forbid one boy get a minute longer with a toy than the other. Although usually we buy two of everything just to avoid the fighting."

"Cute kids," said Max. Worry about the boys still gripped him.

Their parents must feel it a hundred times worse.

"What does your gut tell you about who could be behind the car bomb?" Max asked. The large room felt very empty without the energy of the boys and their mother's presence.

The judge mulled over the question as he rubbed his chin. "I honestly don't have an answer for you. Every time I consider one, someone else's name replaces it."

"Who popped into your head first?"

The judge reached for the list and tapped the bottom name, a rueful look in his eyes.

Mark Bourdon. Age forty-three. Domestic violence. Released eight months ago.

"Why him?" asked Max.

"He was furious when he was sentenced. Had beaten the crap out of his girlfriend a number of times. Absolute hate and anger in his eyes. The sight still sticks with me. When they notified me he'd been released, I actually shuddered." The judge ran a finger along the table's rough edge, avoiding Max's eyes.

"Does your wife know this?"

"No. I won't add to her worry. She has enough."

"Tell me about him." But Max's phone rang, showing a call from the medical examiner's office. "Excuse me," he told the judge as he stood. "I'm going to take this outside." The judge pointed at a sliding glass door to the backyard, and Max stepped out.

"Rhodes," he said into the phone.

"It's Dr. Lockhart. Do you have a moment?"

"Always when you call," said Max. "I'm not flirting," he quickly added.

She snorted. "I know. We have an identification on the burned body from the car bomb yesterday. His name is Eli Chisholm. Age thirty-one. We were able to get fingerprints since his hands weren't burned that badly. He has multiple convictions for assault."

"Was he local?"

"Pretty much. Redmond is his last address."

"Do you have a cause of death?" asked Max. "And when?"

"The two gunshots in the head are what killed him," said Dr. Lockhart. "And I believe he'd been dead for approximately forty-eight hours when he was discovered."

"So he was killed on Sunday?"

"Most likely. And the restraints on his wrists and ankles left the same pattern in his flesh that I saw on this morning's victim, Michael Munoz. Chisholm was tied up with a half-inch white nylon rope. The type you could find at any hardware or home store. I found a few small pieces of white nylon fiber on Munoz's ankles. Visually it's a match to the rope from Chisholm, but I'll wait for the lab to confirm."

"I wonder why Munoz had the ropes removed before they dumped the body," mused Max.

"I don't have an answer for you," said the medical examiner. "Possibly it was easier for them to quickly move Chisholm's body with the extremities bound?"

Max tried to imagine moving the dead body to the judge's trunk without being seen.

It had to be more than one person.

Where did they do that?

"Do you have the bullets?"

"One of them. The other exited the skull, so it's possibly still at the murder site. Almost the exact same thing happened with Mr. Munoz. I only recovered one of those bullets too. I sent both bullets to the state lab for comparison and asked for a rush."

"Both men received two shots to the skull? At close range?" Max was more and more convinced that the killings were related. Even if the bullets hadn't been fired from the same gun, the methods had been identical, along with the ankle and wrist restraints.

"That's correct. The primary difference between the two men's injuries so far is that Mr. Chisholm wasn't beaten before his death. Mr. Munoz was battered severely."

"I'll call the state lab and emphasize your rush," Max told her. "Everyone asks for a rush, but maybe coming from the FBI, it'll get pushed to the top."

"These two men were executed in the same manner," said Dr. Lockhart. "Bullets from the same weapon would be the final nail in the coffin—so to speak."

"Have you looked at Rachel Johnson yet?" asked Max.

"I haven't started, but I'm aware she has a similar head injury." She paused. "You think these three deaths are related."

"It's possible."

"I'll call you as soon as I finish," said Dr. Lockhart.

Max ended the call, texted Chisholm's name to Darby, and then stood for a long moment, looking at the giant play structure in the judge's backyard, easily picturing the twins climbing all over it, each pretending to be Spider-Man.

Is this family in danger?

Two bullets at close range in each man's head. Dr. Lockhart was correct to call the killings executions.

Do these deaths tie into the domestic terrorism chatter?

He'd suspected the car bombing was related to the terrorism threats, but now he wasn't so certain. Something felt very personal about the killings.

He needed to find a common thread in the victims' backgrounds or activities.

Max went back inside the house, where the judge hadn't moved from his seat. He appeared drained. More so than when Max had first arrived. "Does the name Eli Chisholm mean anything to you?" Max asked him.

He thought for a long moment. "No. Why?"

"That's who was in your trunk. He had a record. I need to know if he went through your courtroom."

"Give me a minute." The judge stood and grabbed a laptop that had been sitting on the kitchen island. He set it on the table and started typing, intently focused on the screen.

Tamara returned, her footsteps nearly silent. "The twins should be occupied for at least the next twenty minutes," she said. "Then hopefully there is a smooth transition to Jett being Spider-Man for the next twenty. Marshal Simpson offered to supervise." She smiled at Max, but the smile didn't reach her eyes. "I admit it's odd to have strangers in the house, but I do feel safer."

Her husband put his arm around her shoulders as she sat next to him and pressed a kiss against her temple. "We'll be okay," he told her.

"I'm definitely rattled," she told Max. "And I'm terrified for Howard. I'm glad he won't be going back to work for a while. Possibly never again, if I have my way."

She's serious.

"Once they figure out who did this, I'll be safe," her husband said.

"Until the next asshole," snapped Tamara. "You don't need to keep doing this job. Any private practice would hire you."

"Tamara." The judge shook his head, and Max sensed this was a conversation that had frequently taken place during the last twenty-four hours.

"We've got boys. Young boys," she whispered.

"We'll be getting out of town for a bit," the judge told Max. "That will help."

"Three days is not enough, and that place is too close to town," said Tamara. "We need to take a few weeks out of state."

Max didn't disagree. "Where will you be?"

"Ferrandis's cabin. Huge place about an hour outside of town. Nothing to see but pines and the river. No internet."

Max knew the name but couldn't place it. "Friend of yours?"

"That's right. You're new to the area," said the judge. "Julie Ferrandis is the DA, and she invited us and some other friends up there for a few days. It's good timing." He looked at Tamara for support.

She didn't give it. "I don't feel like being social at the moment." She looked at Max. "And frankly, the lack of internet just puts more on me to entertain the kids."

"Might be a good distraction," he suggested.

"Maybe." She clearly didn't agree. "Two weeks in Cancún with internet sounds more relaxing."

"Do you know a man named Eli Chisholm?" Max asked her.

"Is that who set off the bomb?"

"No. He was in the trunk."

She looked away, fighting a small shudder that made her chin quiver. "I don't know the name."

"The man was never in my courtroom," said the judge, looking back at his computer screen. "I don't have anyone with that last name." He glanced up. "Now what?"

"We're already digging into his background," said Max. He picked up the judge's list of names, wondering if Eli Chisholm was tied to any of them. He didn't need to ask Darby to check. He knew enough about the data analyst's habits to know she was already trying to find a connection between them and Chisholm.

"Do either of you have anything more for me?" asked Max. He looked at Tamara. "I didn't ask if you've had threats or problems with anyone."

Her eyes widened slightly. "This can't be about me. They targeted his car."

"True. But you're part of his family. Anything odd happen lately? Like an unusual encounter in a store? Maybe a restaurant? Something that simply felt off to you."

She looked down as she thought, tilting her head to one side, running one finger along the rough edge of the table. "Not that I can think of."

Max set his card on the table. "Call me if you do. I hope your time out of town is helpful." He made his way down the long glass hallway. No one was at the door, so he let himself out.

As he drove away from the house, he raised a hand at the deputy at the end of the long driveway before heading back to his office.

Eli Chisholm. Michael Munoz. Rachel Johnson.

Time to find a connection.

25

Noelle and Evan stopped in front of Carson Vohland's home and stared at the vehicle in the driveway. They'd driven straight there after interviewing Michael Munoz's sister.

"I'll be damned," said Noelle. "I didn't think it'd be that easy."

An older-model Chevy truck with big tires was in the driveway, and Evan quickly checked the plates. "Yep. That's Munoz's truck. I'll cancel the BOLO."

Noelle got out and paused next to the truck. "Look at the pollen on the windshield. It hasn't been driven for a while."

"I don't know," said Evan. "I swear I find that much on my vehicle every morning. Especially with the giant trees near us."

Noelle looked at the small gray house. It seemed quiet and subdued, set back from the road and its neighbors a good hundred feet on each side. It felt lonely. "What do you think?" she asked, knowing Evan would understand her question.

"I think that if Carson Vohland killed Michael Munoz, he's probably smart enough not to leave Michael's truck sitting in his driveway." Evan shrugged. "But nothing surprises me these days."

"True. Let's see what we've got." She followed the flagstones to the front door and rang the bell, stepping to one side while Evan moved to the other. A man cautiously opened the door, and Noelle immediately recognized Carson from the driver's license photo she'd pulled up after leaving Louisa's home.

"Can I help you?" The man blinked several times as he looked from Evan to Noelle.

Carson Vohland was in his early forties, with fuzzy tufts of hair that resembled steel wool and stuck out at odd angles. Round, too-small glasses perched on his nose, making his eyes oddly large.

Noelle showed her ID. "Are you Carson Vohland?"

"Yes. Why?" Blink, blink.

"We'd like to talk to you about Michael Munoz," she said, watching him closely, wondering if the blinking was a sign of nervousness or just a habit.

He suddenly scowled. "He didn't go postal, did he?"

Postal? Like on a murderous spree?

"No," exclaimed Evan. "Why would you ask that?"

"'Cause the dude's got a screw loose. Always angry about everything." Blink, blink.

"Don't you work for the post office?" asked Noelle, surprised he'd so easily used the negative phrase.

"I do. Twenty-one years now. I think it's fine for me to use *postal* to describe someone with his attitude."

"Can we come in?" Evan asked. "We'd like to ask you some questions about him."

Blink, blink. "He in trouble?"

"No." Noelle decided to jump in with both feet. "Michael was murdered."

Carson froze, and his eyes stayed open for so long that Noelle wanted to tell him to blink.

"What—what happened?"

"Can we come in?" Evan repeated.

The blinking returned, and he gestured for them to enter. He led them to a breakfast nook adjacent to a spotless but dated kitchen. "Can I get you something to drink?" he asked as they took chairs.

"Water," she said at the same time as Evan. She didn't plan to drink it, but she wanted to observe Carson some more before he sat. The man was twitchy. It wasn't just his rapid blinking; he walked with short, jerky movements.

As the man got two glasses out of the cupboard, where the cups were in perfect rows, Noelle asked, "How well did you know Michael?"

"I met him a couple years ago. We both worked at the downtown post office. He was a decent guy then, and we got along. Discovered we both liked playing darts, so we'd often meet up in a pub or bar for a game or two." He took a bottle of water out of the fridge and poured. "He lived with his sister until a few months ago, but she threw him out. Even though his attitude sucked, I told him he could stay here until he got back on his feet."

"Why did she throw him out?" asked Noelle, curious if the story would match Louisa's.

"She's got a young boy," said Carson. "Michael forgot to lock up his gun safe a few times, and she'd had enough. Can't blame her. Kids get into anything. Michael understood but was seriously crushed that he couldn't see the kid as much. Really liked his nephew."

Noelle thanked him as he set down the glasses of water. "Was he a good roommate?"

"Yes. No issues. Although he could be a little neater," Carson sat heavily in a chair. "Does his sister know he's dead?" He ran a hand through his wiry hair.

"We just came from there," said Evan. "She gave us your name. She didn't know he was staying with you, though."

"It doesn't surprise me that he didn't tell her," said Carson. "He was really secretive and moody recently. What happened to him?"

"Someone shot him and left his body not too far from Eagle's Nest."

Again the eyes stayed open too long. "Shot him?" he finally asked, leaning heavily on his forearms on the table.

"Yes. What can you tell us about his activities lately?" asked Evan.

"Wait a second," said Noelle. "Michael lived here, but you didn't report him missing?"

"I didn't think he was missing," said Carson, lifting one shoulder. "He'd take off for days at a time since he moved in. I mean, usually he'd tell me he would be gone for a while, but not every time." He slumped. "Someone picks him up and drops him off. I never thought to report him missing."

That's why his truck is still here.

"*Who* picks him up, and where does he go?" asked Evan.

"Don't know the guys," said Carson. "His new friends. He tried to get me to come to one of their meetings, but I wasn't interested."

"Meetings?" Noelle's mind raced.

"Yeah. Crazy shit. He started hanging out with them last fall. Dudes worship their guns and run around practicing what to do if there's a crisis of some kind. Like a *big* crisis. Like if the government lost electricity for the entire country or martial law was declared. Michael tried to explain it to me, but he's always been a big talker, and I can't take things he says too seriously, so it sort of went in one ear and out the other."

Noelle exchanged a look with Evan.

A militia?

"What happened at the post office?" asked Noelle. "He was fired, correct?"

"Yeah. Missed too many shifts. I think that's when he started hanging out with these odd guys. He'd miss days of work. I told him he needed to shape up if he wanted to keep his job, but he'd laugh. Said government work is for losers and that we're all just empty-headed slaves, paying taxes simply because we are told to. Said he was never going to pay taxes again."

Shades of sovereign citizen philosophy.

"How'd he plan to avoid taxes?" asked Evan.

Blink, blink. "That's what I asked. He said he'd find a place that paid under the table. Construction or maybe ranching. Never met a guy more unsuited to work on a ranch. Physical labor was not his thing. Especially outdoors."

"Do you know of anyone who would want to hurt him?" asked Noelle.

"Well, if he was shot, I'd guess it could be one of the new people he hung around with. They were into guns. I think Michael bought five more since he moved in here."

"Was he scared of anyone? Or worried about making anyone angry?" asked Noelle.

"Not that I was aware of."

"Did you ever meet any of his friends? Or see their vehicles?" asked Evan.

"Didn't meet anyone. As for vehicles, I remember a Jeep. I think it was black. And there was a big pickup too. Maybe silver."

"Know what town Michael would be in when he left for a few days?"

"Dunno. Sorry, but I try not to be nosy, so I don't ask many questions. If Michael wanted me to know, he'd tell me."

"You're one of the first people I've met who's not nosy," said Noelle as she stood up. "Can we see his room?"

Carson paused, looking up at her, and Noelle gave him a patient smile.

Act as if it's what he's expected to do.

"I guess that's okay." Carson slid his chair back and led them through an immaculate living room and then stopped at the first bedroom off a short hallway. "He's sort of a slob," he said in a concerned voice, blinking at the piles of clothing on the bedroom floor.

"Is this his furniture?" Noelle asked. The room had a twin bed, a small dresser, and a desk. It looked like furniture for a twelve-year-old. Except for the tall gun safe in one corner.

"No, the furniture's mine. This was a guest room."

Evan checked the safe. "Locked." He glanced at Carson. "Any chance you know how to get in?"

"Nah. I never asked about it. I did joke that he'd soon need another if he kept buying guns."

"Do you recall what type of guns he had?" Noelle had checked, and only three weapons had been registered for Michael Munoz.

Carson looked thoughtful as he blinked several times. "Not sure. I think only one was a handgun, but I could be wrong. He liked the long guns best."

"How many?"

"At least eight. Maybe ten altogether."

Noelle put on a pair of vinyl gloves and opened the desk drawers. They were all completely bare. Not even dust remained.

Cleaned out? Or never used?

"Have you cleaned in here recently?" she asked Carson.

"No." He shoved his hands in his pockets as he watched them search.

"Where's his computer?"

"He doesn't have one," said Carson. "He got rid of a laptop last fall. Said the government could see and track everything he did on it, so he used the computer at the library sometimes."

Noelle tried to imagine life without her laptop; she couldn't. "What about his cell phone?"

"Threw out his phone for the same reason. He's only used a dumbphone since he moved in here."

"I can't imagine not having the internet at my fingertips," said Evan as he opened the closet. "I'm not sure if that's a positive quality for me or not." He'd done a quick check of the small dresser, which had only held clothes. He pushed aside the hanging clothes and checked the back and sides of the closet. Then he started going through each piece of clothing.

"Wow," said Noelle, taking in all the bright print shirts hanging in the closet. She glanced at Carson, who wore a gray sweatshirt and faded jeans. "He wasn't afraid of some color in his wardrobe." She moved to the other end of the closet to search each item, checking pockets and squeezing hems. She stopped on one bright shirt, its trees reminding her of Michael's tattoo. "Carson, you've seen Michael's tattoo on his chest, right?"

"Yeah."

The tone of his voice made her turn around. Her gaze met his blinking one. "You don't like it?"

"It's stupid," said Carson. "If you're gonna permanently mark your body, pick something that'll still be important to you in sixty years. Not something to make you look cool with your friends."

"What exactly is the tattoo?" she asked. "No one was sure."

Carson scowled. "It's an igloo and a palm tree. Stupid, right? That doesn't make sense."

"I thought the igloo was a stone wall," said Noelle, now understanding what she'd seen. "And it was suggested the palm tree might be a flower."

"The quality sucked," said Carson in a sour voice. "Another rule for getting a tattoo: Go to someone who knows what they're doing."

"He got it because of the new people he was hanging around with?" asked Evan.

"Yes. I guess a lot of them have something similar."

An igloo and a palm tree!

Evan pulled out his phone and started typing, and Noelle knew he was searching for information on the tattoo. She turned back to the closet and quickly finished the rest of the colorful shirts. Evan slid his phone back in his pocket but first gave Noelle a *look.*

He'll tell me what he found later.

"You mentioned that Michael talked about a big crisis," Evan said nonchalantly as he ran his hands under the mattress. "Was he ever more specific about a location? Like something that could actually happen here?"

Evan's odd tone made the hair rise on Noelle's arms.

What on earth did he discover about that tattoo?

"Well, he told me I should be prepared if like our water system got poisoned or if the power grid went down here," said Carson. "That seemed sort of logical, so I've got lots of bottled water stored in the garage and bought those tablets for treating dirty water. Bought a generator too."

"What kind of generator?" asked Noelle.

"Propane. Haven't bought any of that yet, though. Guess I should get on it, but it's expensive to buy a big tank."

Evan stood up from checking under the bed. "Anything else you can tell us about Michael's new group of friends?"

"You think one of them did it?" Carson asked slowly, blinking from one of them to the other.

"Need to eliminate the possibility," said Noelle. "I'm going to send a forensics team over here to go through Michael's room again. Try to not touch anything before that. Is it okay if I give his sister your number? She might like to have some of Michael's things once they're done."

"That's fine." Carson looked around the room. "Are they going to leave black fingerprint dust everywhere? I've heard that's hard to clean up."

"I assume they will," said Noelle. "You can ask the team what cleans it up. They would know best." She handed Carson her card. "Call me if you think of anything else." Carson led them to the front door, and they left the house.

Noelle breathed deep of the icy-smelling fresh air as they strode to the vehicle. The home had had a strong smell of cleaners and bleach. She yanked her car door closed and twisted in the seat to face Evan. "What did you find on that tattoo?"

"It's a boogaloo symbol."

"What the fuck is that?" Noelle stared at him.

"Something we need to talk to Mercy about," said Evan. "We're supposed to keep an eye out for domestic terrorism signs, and according to what I found about that tattoo, it's one. Boogaloo has roots in white nationalism and antigovernment movements. The people who use the term want to shake up society, bring about change by creating chaos. Chaos through destruction. Somehow the terms *big igloo* and *big luau* have evolved from the word *boogaloo*, and putting together an igloo and a palm tree represents the movement."

"What do you mean by *change*? Change what through chaos?"

"It was a bit unclear, but I got the impression it was government and societal norms. More-power-in-the-hands-of-the-people-and-less-government sort of stuff."

"Shit." Noelle thought hard. "Was Michael's death part of that?"

"We need to figure out who his 'friends' were." Evan did air quotes.

Her phone rang, and she didn't recognize the number. "Detective Marshall."

"Detective, it's Louisa, Michael Munoz's sister."

"Hang on, Louisa, I'm putting you on speaker so Detective Bolton can hear too."

"I wanted to tell you about something odd that happened yesterday," said Louisa. "I don't know how it could be related, but it stuck with me. The news was on TV as I made dinner, and the station was covering that car bombing at the courthouse. My son, Austin, was in the room. He listened for a minute, and then he told me that Michael had said that he shouldn't be scared if a bomb went off because he would be safe."

"Austin would be safe?" asked Evan. His gaze met Noelle's.

"Yes," said Louisa. "It was creepy watching Austin listen to that news story and then say something like that. He didn't sound like an eight-year-old. The violence didn't bother him one bit because of what Michael had said to him one time." She paused. "Do you think Michael knew that explosion was going to happen?"

"I don't know, Louisa," said Noelle slowly, her mind trying to process the odd incident. "Michael passed away several days before that happened, but maybe he'd heard something about it before that. Say, Louisa, did you know Michael had a tattoo on his chest?"

"No! He never told me that. Hey, Austin." Her voice quieted as she turned away from the phone. "Did Michael ever show you a tattoo?"

Noelle heard the boy speak in the background but couldn't make out the words.

"Austin knew," said Louisa into the phone, irritation in her tone. "Michael showed it to him and said it hurt when he had it done. I'm surprised that Austin didn't tell me."

"Louisa, does the word *boogaloo* mean anything to you?" asked Evan.

"Isn't that a type of music?"

"That's one definition," said Evan. He gave her the same explanation he'd given Noelle.

"I don't understand," Louisa said softly.

"I think Michael may have been involved with a group with those intentions," said Evan. "We spoke with Carson Vohland. He said Michael's new friends had influenced him in that direction. And by the way, Michael was living at Carson's for the last few months. His truck is still there."

"I'm glad he had someone he could count on," said Louisa softly. "I was worried he was on the street."

"Don't feel bad that you asked Michael to leave," said Noelle. "You did the right thing for your son. Michael was an adult and made his own choices."

"My head knows that, but my heart is having a tough time with it."

"That's understandable," said Noelle, hurting for the woman. "He was your brother."

She hung up after another minute of reassuring Louisa. She leaned back in her seat and exhaled loudly. "This has been a hell of a day."

"Look what we've learned, though," said Evan. "Michael has been identified. And some things indicate that he might be a part of the domestic terrorism that the FBI was looking for."

"We need to figure out who he was associating with," said Noelle.

"We will," said Evan. He awkwardly stretched in his seat. "Now where?"

"Back to the office."

26

Emma grabbed a currycomb and thick brush and let herself into Harley's stall.

"Hey, boy." She stroked the big horse's neck as he sniffed at her pockets, looking for a treat. "Sorry, I didn't bring you anything. Next time." She ran a hand along his back, noticing his visible and bumpy spine. Harley had already been an old horse when Emma was younger and first rode him, so now he was very old.

She massaged circles on his neck with the currycomb and then ran the thick brush over the area to remove the loosened hair and dust. He was already shedding his winter coat, even though it'd been less than thirty degrees today. On her way to the barn, Emma had seen her breath hang in the air, and outside it smelled of snow, that crisp, cold, clean scent. There was no snow to be seen, but Emma knew it would come soon.

Finished with his neck, she moved on to his shoulder. Harley stood perfectly still, his eyes half closed in pleasure from the grooming. Emma relaxed, enjoying the mindless repetition of the motions. Spending time with the horse always brought a calm to her heart and head. Harley was a good listener too. She could tell him anything. He knew all about the kids who'd bullied her at school, how much she missed her mom, and how she hoped her dad would never return.

Is he dead?

Half of her hoped he was; the other half was racked with guilt because of that hope.

Tommy had promised to ask around about her father but so far had no updates for her. He hadn't seemed overly concerned once he'd calmed down after hearing he'd been gone for four months, so Emma simply went on as she had been. Waiting and hoping and feeling guilty.

Telling someone else that he was missing had made her feel a bit better. A very tiny bit.

At the front of the barn, the door creaked and then was shoved to the side with a long, low scraping sound. She couldn't see who'd entered because of the high walls in Harley's stall, but she expected to hear Tommy's voice.

"You're reckless," Tommy said loudly from the back of the barn. "Completely out of control!"

Emma froze, listening hard.

"Fuck you, old man. You don't know what you're talking about. It's a new world."

Emma bent over and inched into a front corner of Harley's stall, where no one could see her unless they stuck their head over the stall's half door. She didn't want Tommy to know she was overhearing an angry conversation.

"Sloppy," hissed Tommy. "You're going to blow it up before you even get started."

"It's already started, thanks to me. All you do is talk. We needed action."

"Your *action* is raising questions with law enforcement. They're going to look long and hard at everyone."

"So what? Cops can't prove nothing."

"I think you've gotten too personal," said Tommy. "You've made it all about you and what you want."

"Nothing wrong with that. It'll all come together soon."

Their footsteps came closer, and Emma huddled into a tight ball, trying to disappear into the shadows. Harley shuffled forward and thrust his head over his stall door.

Good boy.

"How you doin', Harley?" Tommy asked.

The footsteps stopped, and Emma sensed that Tommy was scratching the horse's head.

Don't look in the stall.

"Fucking horses, man," said the other voice. "All they do is eat and shit."

"You don't do anything different," snapped Tommy.

The footsteps started again, moving past the stall. "You need to slow the fuck down," said Tommy. "I don't know what the hell you were thinking with the judge's car."

"I killed two birds with one stone." The other man laughed. "Catch that? Didn't plan to say it that way. Just came out." He snorted. "The judge deserved the fear of God put in him."

"And Chisholm?"

"He was a liability. Talked too much. Same with the other one."

"[illegible]." Tommy drew out the word. "No one knew you were gonna do that."

"Someone had to do something."

"This isn't for you to carry out some personal vendetta," said Tommy, his voice growing fainter as they neared the other end of the barn.

"I know what I'm doing," said the other man. "There's been some cleanup along the way."

A door slammed, and Emma knew they'd gone out the back door on the west end. Somehow Tommy hadn't noticed her bike leaned up against the wall as they came in. She stayed in her ball for several more minutes, still listening. Harley turned her way and lipped her hair, blowing air—and other gunk—out of his nostrils.

"Ugh." Emma gently pushed his nose away and got to her feet. Then returned to working on his winter coat.

What judge? Who was a liability?

She ran through the conversation in her head, wondering who had been talking with Tommy. She suspected Tommy didn't know she had already returned from collecting cans. She'd ridden her bike and gone straight to the barn when she got back.

"You're the best boy, Harley," she murmured to the horse, hoping he hadn't been insulted by the man's comment about horses. "I'd rather hang out with you any day than some jerk like that."

Her face flushed slightly as she remembered the jerks she'd had to avoid at school. She didn't miss school—or the people—one bit. Emma glanced at her feet. She was wearing a pair of leather boots with heavy soles from the clothing the detective had dropped off. They were a little big for her feet, but they were warmer and much nicer than her old rubber boots.

She also wore a new thick wool sweater, which was a shade of pink that made her feel as if she glowed. She'd looked in the mirror and noticed it made her cheeks pink. In a good way. Then she'd put her old orange coat over it, and the color in her cheeks had vanished. She'd stood in front of the mirror for a few moments longer, opening and closing her coat, watching the color of her cheeks change each time.

Silly. They're just clothes.

The far-off sound of an engine and tires on gravel told her the visitor had left. A moment later the noises repeated, and she realized Tommy had left too. After giving Harley one last hug and a swipe of the brush down his blaze, she stepped out of the stall and put the brushes on a small shelf.

The men's conversation continued to repeat in her head. Tommy's tone had been harsh. Nothing she hadn't heard before. He tended to freely espouse all his opinions, and several times she'd heard him argue with her father. But her father usually kowtowed to Tommy. The man today had not.

Killed two birds with one stone.

She wondered what he'd done to get law enforcement attention. And who was Chisholm? And "the other one"? She left the barn, still trying to understand the conversation, and was halfway back to the house when a memory made her nearly trip.

I know that voice.

The other man had broken into her house.

"'What I already told you. We need her,'" she whispered, remembering this voice from that night, when she'd been convinced that the two men were there to harm her.

Tommy knows him.

She covered her face with her hands. "No. Not possible. That can't be right." Emma sucked in a deep breath, convinced she was wrong about the voices, that her brain had made a mistake. How could she compare a man's whispers to the voice she'd just heard?

I'm wrong.

She shook her head and continued to the house.

What if I'm right?

A little voice in her brain ordered her to pay attention, to follow her gut. "But this doesn't mean Tommy knows he was at my house," she muttered. "Why would the other man tell him? Besides, it didn't sound as if the men were on the best of terms."

Emma went inside and washed her hands at the kitchen sink, watching Harley's brown dust and grime vanish down the drain.

I'm safe here.

She wished she had seen the other man or heard his name. Perhaps she'd met him before. If he was friends with Tommy, he might even know her dad.

That night, they knew where we hide the house key.

She let the warm water run over her fingers, chasing away the chill from outside. Tommy knew everyone in the area. Her father had often said that nothing happened in the county without Tommy knowing about it. She shook her head, still watching the water.

Tommy doesn't know what that man tried to do.

But she didn't know if she could tell him. What if she was wrong about the voice?

Maybe I should call Detective Marshall.

27

Max nodded at two county deputies as he made his way toward the conference room where he'd met with the task force that morning. There was a hum and hustle in the department. A lot of energy and manpower were being focused on the murders and the bomb. Max looked through the conference room door's window, where two more county detectives and several support staff worked on connecting the incidents. Mercy was scowling at her laptop at the far end of the room but got to her feet as Max set down his bag.

"I'm going over Darby's notes," she said. "What she's found so far on the list of names from the judge."

"Good." Max turned to look at the whiteboard, disappointed that it hadn't changed since he'd written on it that morning.

What did I expect? That someone would have solved things while I was out?

He erased *John Doe 1* and *John Doe 2* and wrote in the names of Michael Munoz and Eli Chisholm.

"Here." Mercy handed him large headshots of each man and of Rachel, which he attached with round magnets next to their names.

He stepped back and studied the faces, feeling that uncomfortable awareness he always got from looking at photos of people who had died. How could someone who was so alive in the picture no longer exist? Simply snuffed from existence.

Max's gaze lingered on Rachel. She'd had a strong energy and wasn't the type of person to allow herself to go unnoticed. But now she was gone. He checked the time, wondering when he'd hear about her autopsy results.

He added an *s* to the word *bullet* under Munoz's and Chisholm's names. Two bullets fired at close range.

Executions.

"Did you read what Noelle and Evan discovered about Munoz's tattoo?" Max asked Mercy.

"I did. I dug up more information on the boogaloo movement and let domestic terrorism in Portland know that's who we might be dealing with over here. The good part is that if it's boogaloo followers, they are not an organized national group. I suspect it's a small local bunch that has found a common enemy or gripe. They're not going to draw support from some big coalition. It's grassroots."

"Would you say that the judge's car bomb is an example of what they'd do?" he asked.

"Possibly. Violence targeting a federal official or branch isn't unheard of. If we could find out more about Eli Chisholm—the man in the trunk—it might confirm that it was."

Max opened his laptop. "Chisholm was thirty-one with a number of assault arrests. Never married. Work history is sporadic. He worked for several construction companies and car dealerships. No family in the area." He stood and wrote *interviews* under Chisholm's name. "We need to talk to his most recent work associates. Neighbors. Let's find out what he was up to."

The room's door swung open, and Noelle strode in with Evan right behind her. Her gaze locked on Max, and she smiled, creating happy butterflies in his stomach. "Good work on Michael Munoz," he told them. He'd read the summary of their interview with Carson Vohland. "The information from the tattoo might crack this whole thing open."

"Good," said Noelle, setting her bag next to a chair. "And I realized on the way here that the dozen bright Hawaiian-style shirts in Michael

Munoz's closets could indicate his focus too. The shirts are a known thing with Boogaloo followers. The connection is a play on the name into *big luau*. I guess Hawaiian shirts go well with tactical gear," she said sarcastically as she rolled her eyes. "I've found photos of them at protests and demonstrations. They wear camouflage gear, tactical vests, multiple weapons, and loud Hawaiian shirts. Why did these guys have to ruin the good reputation of the Hawaiian shirt? They've replaced its longtime association with Tom Selleck in my brain."

"I was just saying we need to start interviews for Eli Chisholm," said Max, wondering if Noelle would have a problem if he wore one of his Hawaiian shirts that summer. "Let's see if we can connect him to the other victims or boogaloo. So far it appears he hasn't crossed paths with the judge."

"I'll start interviews tomorrow," said Noelle, making a note. "Anything from his autopsy?"

"A double tap that matches Munoz's," said Max. His phone rang. "Speaking of autopsies." He answered the phone and put it on speaker. "Dr. Lockhart? You're on speaker. Agent Kilpatrick and Detectives Bolton and Marshall are here."

"You've kept me busy today," came the medical examiner's voice.

"Sorry about that," said Noelle. "Hopefully that's the extent of it."

"I finished Rachel Johnson," said Dr. Lockhart. "She has the same close double bullet hole in the head. But for her, both bullets exited the skull, and forensics dug them out of the motel room floor. Some differences are that she didn't have the contusions on the wrists and ankles like your others, and she was clothed."

He didn't have time. He shot her and ran.

"Johnson had an alcohol level of point one," the doctor continued. "There was evidence she'd been sexually active recently. She had vaginal tears, but there was no semen present. Condom use was most likely why."

"She'd been raped?" asked Noelle. "By someone who wore protection?"

"Based on what Agent Rhodes told me about their phone call, it sounded like the sex had been consensual that day. So most likely it was rough sex and possibly not rape."

Noelle didn't look convinced.

"She was also approximately eight weeks pregnant. She may not have even been aware of it."

Mercy looked stunned. "Neither she or her sister mentioned it," she told the ME. "That's awful." She looked at Noelle. "I don't know if I should tell Cory or not."

Max didn't know either.

"Anything else we need to hear, Doctor?" he asked.

"Bullets went to the lab, but they were deformed from hitting the concrete floor. I don't think they'll be much help."

"Thank you, Doctor." Max ended the call.

The room was silent.

"That's so horrible about the baby," murmured Mercy. She took a deep breath and looked to Max. "What's next?"

He struggled to mentally shift gears. "I have someone—"

A loud knock sounded at the door, and Janice, one of the support staff working with the task force, stuck her head in. "Max! Did you drop this in the parking lot?" She held out a manila envelope.

He took the envelope, frowning at his name, which was written in the upper left-hand corner. Not his handwriting. "I didn't." He opened the unsealed flap and pulled out several photos.

Keira.

One photo had been taken in front of his sister's home, her purse over her shoulder as she walked to her car. He flipped through the other three photos. All were of Keira doing normal everyday things, but she appeared unaware she was being photographed. "Shit!"

He grabbed his cell phone and called her, his hands shaking.

Answer. Answer. Answer.

Acid in his stomach burned up to the back of his throat.

Please be safe.

Noelle had pushed back her chair as he looked through the photos. "Max! What's wrong?" She moved next to him, took in the pictures, and sucked in a breath. "When are these from?"

The phone continued to ring at his ear.

Answer. Answer. Answer.

"Max. What's up?" Keira said.

He dropped into his chair, his hand over his eyes as he leaned heavily on the table. "Keira. Are you okay?" His voice shook.

She was silent for a long moment. "Yes. Why? What's going on?"

"Okay," he said. "Hang on."

How do I ask without scaring her?

"Bear with me for a minute. Can you tell me what you're wearing right now? Or what you wore when you left the house today?" His hand tightened on the phone, and he stared at the photos.

"Jeans. White sweater and white jacket. Black boots."

Exactly what she wore in the photos.

Someone is stalking her and wanted me to know it.

Just like with the flower delivery she received.

"Congratulations on having a murderer for a brother."

It's all aimed at me.

"Is TJ home?"

"Yes. Why? *Max.* What is going on? You're freaking me out."

"You know the flowers you got?"

"Yes."

"Someone just sent me photos of you, and you're wearing exactly what you just told me. One photo was taken in front of the house. One is you getting out of your car somewhere. Another is of you through a restaurant window, and another is you gassing up your car."

Noelle gripped his shoulder, her eyes wide with concern. He moved his mouth away from the phone. "Get Janice back here. I want to know where she found these." Noelle nodded and left.

"Someone is stalking me," Keira said slowly. "But they let you know. Like with the flowers. Who's doing this, Max?"

"I don't know, hon. But I want you and TJ out of that house. Now. Get a hotel somewhere. Use his truck and try to pay with cash. Can you get into his truck without being seen?"

"Yes," she whispered.

Max heard TJ's voice in the background. "Let me talk to him."

"What the fuck did you say to Keira?" asked an angry TJ. "She's shaking."

Max gave him a quick rundown. "Go now, TJ. Get her out of there. Leave her phone in the house in case it's being monitored somehow. Do not take her car. And exchange yours for a rental or try to swap with a friend in case you're being followed too. Pick up some burner phones and send me the numbers."

"Got it." TJ was all business. "I'll let you know where we end up."

"Thanks, brother. Stay safe."

Max ended the call. And looked up to find four sets of worried eyes staring at him. "Janice," he said to the woman Noelle had brought back to the room. "Where exactly did you find the envelope?"

"At the east edge of the parking lot. I was heading out to my car and saw what looked like an office envelope behind Jessica's minivan, so I went to check." She looked at the photographs. "What are those?"

"It's my sister," he said quietly. He looked at Evan and Noelle. "Camera view of that part of the parking lot?"

"If it's where I'm thinking," said Evan, "there isn't coverage. It's just out of view, and if Jessica's minivan was there, it was probably used for more cover."

"The envelope might never have been picked up," Max said. "The sender had no way of knowing that I'd actually get the photos." He slid the photos around, studying each one. They were photocopies of photos. Completely untraceable.

But maybe the envelope.

Evan had put on gloves and was already reaching for the envelope. "I'll take it to the lab."

"Thanks."

Who would do this?

He looked at his whiteboard with three murders and a car bombing to solve. "Shit." He had to focus on the cases. Not Keira.

Noelle touched his arm. "She's safe, Max. TJ can watch out for her. And she's very capable of taking care of herself now that she knows. You've got a tough sister."

"I do," he agreed. He was suddenly exhausted. "Why, though? Why harass Keira when it's clear that they're trying to get under my skin?"

"Did something else happen?" asked Mercy.

He told her and Noelle about the roses Keira had received. And the note that called him a murderer. Both women had big questions in their eyes.

"Why would they say that, Max?" Noelle asked gently.

He took her hand and held it tight in his.

What will she think?

My family still shuns me.

"There's something I haven't told you."

28

Twelve years ago

Max grabbed the sniper rifle and duffel bag out of his trunk, slammed it shut, and ran toward the other Medford SWAT team members. So far all he knew was that this was a callout for an armed and barricaded man with a hostage. When his pager had gone off, Max had been painting the bathroom. He'd hammered the lid back on the paint can, thrown on his tactical gear, and reached the site within twenty minutes.

The team commander nodded at Max as he joined the group and continued his briefing. A teenager had stabbed his mother during a fight and then locked himself in a bedroom with a younger cousin, threatening to kill the girl. Officers had been called out and tried unsuccessfully to convince the teen to leave the house or let the cousin go. The teen had turned off his cell phone, and there were no landlines in the home.

As Max listened, an officer thrust a sketch of the property's layout at him. He immediately committed the two-story home's details to memory and studied the surrounding area for the best location for him to get eyes on the subject. It was one of his jobs as a sniper to relay visual intel to the team. With his high-powered scope and binoculars, the command center and the entry team relied on his observations, sometimes the only information available about what was occurring in the home. Finding a good vantage point was vital for the operation's success.

It was only 10:00 a.m., but Max saw waves of heat rising off the home's roof. The forecast stated the temperature would reach 107 degrees that day, and Max was already sweating in his dark, heavy gear.

"We broke a window and put a throw phone through on the second floor," said the commander. "Negotiators have been calling it for the last five minutes. The teen is believed to have the hostage in the second-floor southwest bedroom, which belongs to his parents."

"What's this?" Max asked the officer next to him, pointing at a square on the property sketch.

"Shed in the backyard. Like for a lawn mower and such."

Strong enough to hold me?

Ideally Max wanted a slightly elevated position where he could watch the suspect. Another option besides the shed roof could be one of the homes next door. Either a roof or one of their windows.

"Suspect is highly agitated," said the commander. "His name is Jacob and he's eighteen. His parents said they believe he stopped taking his medication. He threw an empty vodka bottle at his father before police arrived, and the father said the bottle previously had several inches of alcohol in it, so he may also be intoxicated. The hostage is his cousin Eleanor. She's twelve."

"Other weapons?" asked one of the officers.

"Parents own two handguns and one long gun. The weapons are locked in a safe in the parents' bedroom, but Jacob knows the combination and has taken several gun use classes. The knife used on the mother was from the kitchen. She's on her way to the ER. He aggressively slashed her in the face and neck."

"Jesus," muttered someone.

Anything could happen.

That was why the Medford SWAT team trained every month. Why Max and the other team members left thousands and thousands of shells on the practice range every year. Why he and other snipers spent hours on advanced training until their rifles were extensions of their limbs. Why he'd developed the ability to put a round in a single square inch.

When the shit hit the fan, they had to be ready to protect lives.

The commander was assigning perimeter positions in the home and outside. The original responding officers had cleared the house except where the teen was barricaded in the parents' bedroom, which had an attached bath and walk-in closet. The teen had refused their pleas for him to come out and then threatened to kill the cousin if they came through the bedroom door.

The SWAT team had then been activated.

The commander looked at Max. "Pick your spot," he told him. "There are two windows to the parents' bedroom on the second level. One was broken for the negotiators to throw in the phone."

Several yards away, a burst of conversation and energy came from the mobile command unit, pulling the team's attention. "The negotiators made contact," said the commander, a sliver of hope in his voice. "In positions. Now." Three of the SWAT officers went inside the house, and the other five, including Max, headed for the back of the home. The Medford SWAT team had a total of seventeen officers, including the two negotiators in the van and the commander. If they were available, more team members would show up. But Max was pleased with the number who had been able to respond to the callout so far.

Max ran to check the shed in the backyard and then swore as it came into sight. It was a rickety affair, guaranteed to collapse if he tried to climb on top. He scouted for another option and decided on the neighboring home to the west. The house had a second-story deck with stairs. One side of the deck appeared to have a good view of both of the parents' bedroom windows. A six-foot fence divided the properties, so Max jogged back out front to find the gate, knowing the surrounding homes had already been evacuated.

He relayed his plan into his mic, receiving a "Copy" through his earpiece from the team leader. He found the gate to the neighbor's yard and then ran along the side of the house to the stairs, quickly moving up to the deck.

He shoved an outdoor table against the deck's railing, pulled up a cushioned deck chair, and set up his rifle, thankful there was an awning that blocked the sun. But he couldn't ignore the heat in the air; it radiated from the house's siding and deck boards. Max opened his duffel and set out two water bottles, several PowerBars, and his binoculars, estimating that the windows to the bedroom next door were a comfortable fifty yards away. He wasn't a military sniper who had trained at a thousand yards or more, but Max was confident at two hundred yards and under.

He settled into the chair and put the butt of the rifle into the perfect spot in front of his shoulder, his cheek on the stock and his eye at the scope.

There he is.

The rest of the world faded away as he locked his gaze on the teen through the broken window.

"This is Red-one," said Max. "I'm on the second-story deck of the home to the west. Suspect is in view. Teen is pacing in the bedroom. Has phone at his ear. I don't currently see a weapon."

"Copy, Red-one," said the commander. "Negotiations are in progress. Can you see the hostage?"

Max moved the rifle a fraction to check the other window. "Negative."

Shit. Where is she?

He scanned what he could see of the floor and bed, looking for blood or anything that could indicate the hostage's location. Max returned to the window with the view of the teen. He was barefoot, wearing baggy shorts and an oversize tee.

"Red-one. Suspect has blood on his shirt," said Max, his voice tight.

"Copy, Red-one. Officers said blood was already on his shirt when they responded. Most likely from the mother."

"His right hand is bloody, and he keeps wiping it on a towel," said Max, following the teen's movements. "May have injured himself during that attack."

"Copy."

Everything receded except for the occasional voices in his earpiece and the view through his scope. Max sat motionless, watching the teen yell at the negotiators. He could faintly hear him but couldn't make out the exact words. He lip-read a lot of *fuck offs* and *no ways*.

Where's the cousin?

"A nightstand has been dragged in front of the bedroom door," Max relayed through his mic. "But it doesn't look too heavy. It's more of a small table, maybe two feet by eighteen inches, with shelves below. The bed is directly across from the door. Walk-in closet on the east side of the room, and attached bath is north of the room along the home's west wall. There is privacy glass on the window to the bathroom."

Through the broken window, Max could see the bedroom's door to the hall, the moved nightstand, and part of the bed. Through the other window, he saw an open sliding barn door to the walk-in closet with clothes hanging in the background. The teen was walking in circles, primarily visible through the first window. He'd occasionally appear in the second window and pause in front of the closet, looking inside.

That's got to be where the cousin is.

Did he already hurt her?

The teen wiped his hand with the towel on the bed, and this time Max spotted a knife next to it. "Red-one. Knife is on the bed. No other weapons visible."

"Copy."

"Red-one," said Max. "Where is the location of the gun safe?"

There was a long moment of silence. "Gun safe is in the walk-in closet," the commander finally replied. Then he added, "Suspect's mother is in surgery. Prognosis is guarded."

Shit. His mother may die.

Does he know that?

The teen stopped and threw the phone down on the bed, rage in his face.

Max relayed the location of the phone. "Was he told about his mother?"

"Negative," said the commander. "Negotiations have stalled. Suspect refuses to release his cousin."

Max continued to watch the teen. He was tall and lanky in his baggy clothes with a mop of blond hair that he frequently brushed out of his eyes, leaving a smear of darkening blood in his hair. Max's crosshairs centered on the suspect's forehead over and over as he waited and watched.

The suspect was eighteen, but in Max's mind he was still a child.

He didn't want to shoot a child.

Ideally, the negotiators would convince the teen to give up his hostage. But that meant he needed to answer the phone again.

The suspect grabbed his knife and stomped out of sight. Max switched to the other window and watched him move into the closet. "Red-one. Suspect has picked up knife and moved out of sight into closet."

Max waited, his scope trained on the open closet door.

"Get out of there," he murmured. "Let me see what you're doing."

Don't hurt the girl.

The teen reappeared.

"Red-one," Max said rapidly. "Suspect has a pistol and has pulled the hostage out of the closet, making her sit on the bed. I don't know where the knife is now."

The hostage looked younger than her twelve years, her face blotchy and wet with tears. She was in shorts and a tank top, her blonde hair loose around her face. "Hostage appears unharmed," said Max. He scrambled to remember her name.

Eleanor.

A deep calm had settled over Max when he'd first looked through his scope, and his heart rate and breathing were as steady now as if he were reading a book. This was his job. He was the sole pair of eyes on the suspect, but he knew a team of officers was right outside that bedroom door, ready to burst in if the situation escalated or to step back if the teen surrendered.

Eleanor stood and defiantly headed to the door. She grabbed the nightstand to move it out of the way, but the teen pointed the gun at her head, his index finger not on the trigger, but lined up along the frame.

He's indexing.

The girl stopped and slowly inched back onto the bed as the suspect lowered the weapon.

"Suspect drew on the hostage," said Max, and he relayed the rest of what he'd just seen.

He didn't believe the teen had intended to shoot the girl. At least, not at that moment. Max knew that the suspect had been trained on gun use, and the position of his index finger had made Max pause.

"Next time, you are cleared to act," said the commander.

Max inhaled deeply. "Copy."

The decision is in my hands.

Max could have taken the shot when the suspect pointed the gun at his cousin. It would have been considered a good shoot in the eyes of law enforcement, but he'd watched Jacob's facial expression and the placement of his finger. And made a split-second decision not to fire.

What if someone dies because I waited?

It was the catch-22 of his job. By waiting to fire, he'd preserved the suspect's life. But had preserving the suspect condemned someone else? Sweat ran from his temples, and he was damp everywhere under his clothing. He wiped his upper lip and checked the time. He'd been in place for forty-five minutes, watching the suspect rant as he paced in the room.

The teen finally picked up the negotiator's phone again and answered, never taking his gaze from his cousin, the pistol still in his hand, his index finger positioned along the frame.

"C'mon," Max whispered. "Listen to the negotiators." He knew the officers were telling the suspect that he hadn't done anything bad yet and that hurting his cousin would be an action he couldn't reverse. If the teen stopped now and came out, everything could be worked out.

He knew the negotiators wouldn't bring up the possibly fatal attack on his mother.

The suspect handed the phone to his cousin, who spoke into the receiver.

"The girl says that Jacob has sworn to kill her," said the commander.

Max watched Jacob's lips move.

"And that he'll shoot any officer that he sees after that."

Fucking A. That poor girl.

The suspect twitched and quickly spun toward the bedroom door. Max suspected the officers outside the door had made some sort of noise or demand.

The teen grabbed the phone away from Eleanor and hurled it out the broken window. She lunged from the bed after the phone but halted at the window, watching the phone hit the grass.

Behind her, Jacob froze, the pistol hanging at his side, his gaze locked on Max.

Through his scope, Max saw Jacob's eyes widen as he took in the large rifle pointed directly at him.

The teen grabbed his cousin and yanked her in front of him as a human shield, clamping his arm across her chest and pinning her arms.

Fuck. Did I wait too long again?

Eleanor also spotted Max and started to scream, the teen yelling in her ear to shut up. Jacob made lurching, rough movements, keeping Eleanor between himself and Max as he backed away from the window. The officers outside the door must have reacted to her screams because he abruptly pointed his gun at the bedroom door.

"Weapon is aimed at the bedroom door!" said Max. "He threw the phone out the window and spotted me. He's using Eleanor as a shield. He's escalating."

The negotiators can no longer help.

Max stayed calm as the tension rose in the bedroom. Jacob waved his gun and shouted toward the door. Eleanor couldn't peel her cousin's arms off her chest, so she scratched him, infuriating and distracting him. Max's aim stayed on the suspect, but Eleanor's blonde hair and face kept moving through his crosshairs.

Her eyes were green.

Jacob kept his head behind hers as he yanked her from one side to the other, trying to watch Max and the door. He swung the gun from the door to his cousin's temple and then back and forth several times. "I'll kill her! I'll kill her!"

Max watched it play out through his scope, feeling time slow down and sensing a tipping point approaching. The point where the teen would finally act. Where he would decide he had no other choice. Jacob's eyes were full of anger, his teeth bared as he shouted over Eleanor's screams.

Jacob whirled his cousin toward Max, her green gaze aimed straight into his scope. The teen raised the weapon and ground it into the girl's cheek, and she jerked her head away from the gun, leaving Jacob in the crosshairs.

His finger's on the trigger.

Max took his shot.

Jacob dropped to the floor, taking Eleanor with him. Blood poured from his eye.

"Red-one. Suspect is down," Max said into his mic as he watched the girl roll away and stare at her cousin in horror. The back of Jacob's head had exploded from the power of Max's rifle.

Eleanor's okay.

The bedroom door flew open, knocking the nightstand table onto its side, and helmeted officers flowed in, weapons leading, clearing all corners. One grabbed Eleanor and hustled her out the door as the others cleared the closet and bathroom.

Jacob lay motionless.

Two officers knelt next to him and started CPR.

Max knew there was no point.

29

Noelle didn't know how to react.

Her heart was breaking as she listened to Max's story, watching the emotions on his face and hearing them in his voice. She'd pulled up a chair next to him, gripping his hand as he told her and Mercy what had happened.

"It was a good shoot," Max said, staring at their clasped hands. "I knew it and the review confirmed it."

"That doesn't take away the pain of ending someone's life," said Noelle, recalling how she'd emotionally struggled after shooting a killer, even though her decision had saved several lives.

"No, it doesn't," said Mercy softly. "It will always be with you. Popping up when you least expect it." She took a breath. "I've been there too. It's a club no one wants to join."

"Besides Jacob's family condemning me," continued Max, "the media tried and sentenced me in public. There were maybe seventy-five thousand people in town back then. It sounds like a lot, but it was a tight community. Everyone knew everyone else's business. And they'd decided my business was theirs." He looked away. "There was a petition to get me fired. Lawsuits were filed."

"Oh, Max." Noelle hated the distant look in his eyes.

"In the media they said I shot a child," said Max. "I considered him a child too, and not that it matters, but he was eighteen and a legal adult. Other people claimed that he'd never hurt his cousin—how could

Jacob hurt someone in his family? I guess they forgot he nearly killed his mother first. Which told me he'd probably kill a cousin too. Other people complained that he hadn't fired the gun, so I had no right to fire when I did. I was hounded for months."

"That's not how it works," said Noelle. "You can't wait until they fire; by then it's too late. The public simply doesn't understand that concept. It's the same people who ask, Why didn't we shoot him in the leg? Or they claim it wasn't a 'fair fight' because we used a gun when the suspect had a knife."

Mercy nodded emphatically.

"I know all this," said Max. "I know how invalid their reasons are, but they still ripped me apart inside."

At least he said it in the past tense.

"When it was revealed that Jacob's gun hadn't been loaded, the uproar got worse. As if I should have been able to tell it was empty. There was a magazine in it." He waved a hand, as if brushing the words away. "Once again that is irrelevant because he had a gun at her head. But it felt as if the entire city hated me." He snorted. "Those were fun times. But do you know what was the worst part?" He looked from Noelle to Mercy. "Well, it wasn't the worst part, but it was definitely a horrible twist . . . my sixteen-year-old sister was Jacob's girlfriend."

Noelle sucked in a breath.

"Right?" he asked. "I had no idea Brittany was even dating. We're twelve years apart and hadn't lived under the same roof in a decade." He shook his head. "You can imagine how distraught she was. And she hated me too."

"I'm sure she didn't—" Noelle began.

"She's never forgiven me," Max told her. "She told me I was wrong to shoot and that Jacob would never hurt anyone. She still doesn't speak to me."

Noelle remembered how Max had always given minimal answers when she asked about his two sisters who lived in Medford. When she spoke of meeting them, he'd just nod and say, "When they come to town." Now she understood why he was so quiet about that part of his family.

"It's been more than a decade," said Mercy. "How can she still hate you?"

"We have a strong stubborn streak in my family," said Max. "And for some reason it's even worse in my two younger sisters. Amber goes along with whatever Brittany wants and vice versa. They're very tight, and I suspect they'll take this grudge to the grave. Keira has played mediator for a long time, and she hates it. She's tried several times in the past to repair the rift with no results."

"What about your mother?" asked Noelle.

"She sided with Brittany. My mother taught English at the high school. She knew Jacob and said she couldn't believe that he'd do such a thing. That I must have screwed up. It had to be my fault."

Noelle was speechless.

"It's not healthy to be angry that long," said Mercy. "It festers."

"My sisters are good people," said Max. "My mother too. But they're blind about that one incident and won't let it go."

"Jacob's death is the murder mentioned in the note with Keira's flowers?" asked Noelle.

"I haven't taken anyone else's life." His eyes were calm. "That has to be what it refers to."

"So you think whoever sent the flowers and photos is still angry about the shooting," said Mercy.

"That makes the most sense to me."

"But why now?" asked Noelle. "What's changed? It's been more than a decade. I assume you haven't had this level of harassment in a long time?"

"I haven't," admitted Max. "This is abruptly coming out of left field."

"Could it be your sister Brittany?" asked Mercy.

"Absolutely not. She wouldn't want to scare Keira. This is someone who is trying to threaten me. This is solely about me," he muttered.

"I've had enough experience in the past with people who were angry about the shooting. This feels the same."

"But who?" asked Noelle. "Someone in Jacob's family?"

"Or perhaps the harasser is totally unrelated to that incident, but they're using your past to get in your head," said Mercy, looking up from her phone. "The shooting in Medford is easy enough to find online by searching your name."

"I never thought to Google you, Max," said Noelle. "I always dug for information on anyone I went out with in the past, but I never did it with you." She forced a weak smile. "I believed the FBI had already done the work for me."

Noelle had tried online dating. The profile information in the apps was supposed to be minimal to protect people's identities, but she found that men always revealed some sliver of information that allowed her to find out who they were. They'd post photos she could image search, talk about when and where they went to college, or even give a phone number. All these things helped her figure out their last names, and then she'd learn they had prison sentences, wives, assault charges. The list went on.

But she'd never Googled Max.

"The harassment doesn't matter at the moment," said Max. "TJ and Keira can take care of themselves—I'm ninety-nine percent certain it has nothing to do with them anyway. We need to concentrate on these people." He pointed at the whiteboard. "That's what's important."

Noelle didn't completely agree. "Give me the names of people who hassled you the most after the shooting. I'll have someone look into them. See where they are and what they're doing these days." He started to refuse, and she held up a hand. "It will let you focus on our cases."

He held her gaze for a long moment, and she knew he was devising a way to refuse. "Tomorrow," he finally said.

He's trying the procrastinate-and-hope-she-forgets method.

"Okay, tomorrow," she agreed.

She might have a crappy memory, but she wasn't going to forget this.

Her phone rang with an unknown number, and she sent it to voicemail. "What do we have left to address tonight?" It was late and she wanted to catch up on some sleep so she could start early tomorrow.

"As expected in a hotel, forensics lifted dozens of fingerprints from Rachel Johnson's room," said Mercy. "They'll run what they can through our database. They also collected a lot of hair from the shower drain. I'm hoping our suspect showered after sex with Rachel, but who knows. When we find a suspect, hopefully we can match him to hair and fingerprints to place him in the room."

"And if he isn't a match to any of those?" asked Noelle.

"Doesn't mean he didn't do it," said Mercy. "The right evidence could still turn up." She looked at Max. "We need to call it a night. I'm about to fall asleep in my chair. Noelle and I didn't get much sleep last night."

"Agreed." Max stood and started to pick up his area.

Noelle watched him for a long moment, glad he'd agreed to come to her place that night. His emotional story made her want to burrow her head into his neck while under the covers and just hold him.

She checked her phone and saw the earlier call had left a voicemail. The transcript was jumbled and confusing, so she hit play and listened.

"Detective Marshall? It's Emma Chambers."

Why is she whispering?

"I might've figured out one of the men who was at my house that night. I heard him talking to Tommy today, but I didn't see him. I'm almost positive it's him. Can you call me back right away?"

"Shit." Noelle hit the call button on the voicemail. Emma's phone rang and rang. "Doesn't she have voicemail set up?" she muttered as she dialed the young woman again.

"Who doesn't have voicemail?" asked Max.

"Emma Chambers. She left a message saying she might know who was at her house that night, and now she's not answering." She met Max's gaze. "She was whispering, so I wonder who she didn't want to overhear." Noelle ended the unanswered call. "She said she heard this man talking to Tommy."

"Who is Tommy?" asked Mercy.

"Good question," said Noelle. "Emma said he's her uncle but not really her uncle. She was staying with him at his home after the break-in. I have his address somewhere. I made her give it to me so I'd know where to find her."

"It's probably an address but not his address," said Mercy. "Did you check it?"

"Looking right now." Noelle opened her laptop as Mercy and Max watched over her shoulder. "Looks like it's a real address and not too far from Emma's home. She sounded super nervous in her voicemail, so I'll go check on her. If she's not at this home, I'll check her house."

"I'll follow you," said Max. He looked at Mercy. "Go home."

"Gladly. Let me know if you run into any problems." She headed out the conference room door. Then returned ten seconds later. "Just letting you know the snow has started. There's already an inch."

"Thanks, Mercy." Noelle looked at Max. "Ready?"

"What do you want to do after you talk to Emma?" His gaze held hers, a subtle message in its depths.

Noelle paused, caught up in that look. "I want you to come over like you agreed," she whispered.

"Good answer."

Max's smile warmed her to the tips of her toes. He followed her out the conference room door and then locked it.

Find Emma first.

I hope nothing has happened to the girl.

30

Noelle strained her eyes to see in the dark ahead of her vehicle.

As she and Max drove out of Bend, the snow turned into a heavy downfall of big flakes that blocked her view on the unlit country roads and reflected her headlights back into her eyes. The snow had filled the tracks of any cars that had gone before her, leaving a smooth white surface where she couldn't be certain of the edge of the road's shoulder.

She was thankful that Max was following and that her county Tahoe had heavy snow tires. She also had chains but hoped she wouldn't have to put them on in the cold and dark.

Their drive to Tommy's house had taken them past the gate to her home, so she'd known the roads until that point. Now, several miles beyond, every turn and hill was unfamiliar. She continued to dial Emma's phone and had sent a text asking her to call, but all she'd gotten back was silence.

A text from Max popped up on her dashboard screen. He wanted to know if she could see well enough in the snow. Noelle hit the reply button. No, but I don't have much choice. She slowed to a crawl, studying the side of the road for a driveway that her GPS said was imminent. And drove right past it.

She was about to text Max to turn around but saw in her rearview mirror that he had stopped in time and was waiting for her return. She did a cautious K maneuver, hoping the snow on the side of the road wasn't hiding a deep ditch. She got her vehicle facing the right direction and then turned up the driveway. Max followed.

The gravel driveway was in good shape and lined with small pines that helped guide her along the invisible road under the snow. The pines thinned out, and she drove into a clearing, her headlights picking up nearby buildings. Suddenly, from high above a barn door, a bright floodlight came on, illuminating the entire clearing.

Motion sensor.

She stopped her Tahoe in front of the small house, and Max parked beside her. No other vehicles were present, and she didn't see a garage. If someone was home, perhaps they'd put their vehicle in the barn.

Before they'd left the city, she'd learned the property belonged to Thomas Hammaker, so she knew they were in the right place to find Emma's uncle Tommy. She stepped out of her Tahoe, leaving the headlights on, lighting the front of the home. She lifted her coat's hood against the snow that tried to float down her neck and noticed that Max's hair was already white. They approached the porch and went up the stairs, where Noelle pounded on the door. "Mr. Hammaker?" she hollered.

There were no lights on in the home.

Maybe he's gone to bed.

She pounded again. "Emma?" she shouted. "Are you here? I've been trying to call you!"

"Check the barn?" asked Max.

"Might as well."

Hopefully Mr. Hammaker isn't a shoot-first, ask-questions-later type of guy.

They crossed the wide clearing, and Max rapped loudly on the barn door with a flashlight, calling out the man's name again. He looked at Noelle and shrugged. Not ready to give up so easily, she grabbed the huge door and slid it open.

"Hello! Mr. Hammaker! We're looking for Emma Chambers!"

There was a rustle down the wide dirt aisle, and a horse stuck his head over a stall door, his ears turned in their direction.

"Emma?" Noelle called again.

Silence.

"Let's take a look," she said to Max. Something about the empty property was getting under her skin. He switched on his flashlight, and she followed as he cast his light in every corner and stall. She stopped to pet the horse, and he nibbled at her sleeve. "Hungry?" She looked and saw he had part of a flake of alfalfa hay in his manger. "Somebody fed him not too long ago."

Did we just miss Emma or her uncle?

"Noelle." Max had stopped near the end of the barn, his light shining on something. "Is this her bike?"

Noelle gave the horse one last pat and joined Max. "That's hers," she said, recalling it from the first time she'd met Emma. "But I know she's borrowed one of Mr. Hammaker's vehicles before. Or he could have driven her somewhere. She wouldn't try to ride the bike somewhere in the snow. Let's check her house."

"Anything more on her father?" asked Max as he slid the barn door closed.

"I never got a clear answer from her," said Noelle, thinking of her conversation that morning with the girl. "I got the impression that he'd been gone awhile—but I didn't know if that meant days or weeks. She did say that this Uncle Tommy would find him."

He frowned. "That implies that Emma *can't* find him. Doesn't that strike you as odd?"

"Very." Noelle wondered if she should have pressed harder on the issue. "She didn't seem to want any help from me regarding her father. Honestly, she didn't seem worried—just didn't like answering questions about him. Maybe we're making a bigger deal out of it than it is?"

"Maybe." He gave her a quick kiss and got in his vehicle.

A kiss in falling snow.

Noelle followed their tire tracks down the driveway, trying to remember if she'd ever been kissed in the snow before. Out on the road, she resumed her snail's pace as she drove toward Emma's. They met no other vehicles on the road.

Because smart people are at home. Not driving in near-whiteout conditions.

She turned up the unmarked road she'd driven twice before and compared the rutted, rough ride to Tommy's smooth lane. The next turn appeared, and after a few moments of Noelle weaving among the huge volcanic rocks and pines, Emma's house came into sight. Next to the front door, a dim porch light was on. But there'd been no tire tracks leading to the home, and again there were no parked vehicles.

I don't think she's here either.

Noelle exchanged a look with Max as they went up the snowy porch steps. And then she grabbed the railing to avoid a fall as an orange mass rocketed past her feet. "Holy shit!"

"It's a cat," said Max, who'd turned to watch the creature vanish in the snow.

"His name's Cornbread," said Noelle. She pointed at his covered tub near the door. "We must have disturbed him." The cat had left little blurry prints in the white fluff, and Noelle avoided stepping on the cute tracks before knocking on the door. "Emma? Are you home?" She waited a moment and tried the door. Locked.

There were no lights on inside, and Noelle knew they'd struck out again. She checked her phone. No reception. Emma had told her the home was in a cellular dead zone. Noelle turned away from the house and paused on the bottom step, staring into the heavy falling snow.

I don't feel good about this.

"Where else could she be?" Max stopped beside her.

"I don't know. I don't think she had many friends. She must be with 'Tommy.'"

"You had the impression she felt safe with him?"

"I did. She was very emphatic about that. Perhaps when I didn't return her call, she told him about the man she suspects was at her home that night. I feel horrible that I wasn't there for her when she called."

Max took her hand, and they stood together in silence for a long moment, watching the snow fall. But Noelle's thoughts were anything but silent. She was concerned for Emma, and Max's revelation about the past shooting was still spinning in her head.

He must have hated sharing that.

She sucked in an icy breath. Max had shared. And now she needed to do the same. It'd been on her mind for weeks, but the right moment had never come.

That's a lie. I've been scared to tell him.

An FBI investigation into her second husband's years-old unsolved murder had brought Max to Bend and face-to-face with Noelle a few months ago. The murderer had been found and then shot by police when he took a family hostage. The investigation was now closed.

Max—and everyone else—believed that Derrick's murderer was dead.

The killer had beaten her husband with a crowbar.

But no one knew that Derrick was already dead.

Before the suspect beat her husband, he hit Noelle in the head with the crowbar, knocking her unconscious and leaving her with no memory of the attack. And with years of headaches and struggles with her short-term memory.

"Max," she whispered. "I need to tell you something." She kept her gaze on the falling snow, blinking as wayward flakes found their way under her hood and onto her eyelashes.

"Is it about Derrick?" he asked.

Surprised he'd guessed, she searched his calm gaze. "It is."

"You remembered something."

"I remembered that I hit Derrick in the head with the heavy figurine that the medical examiner said caused his death. The crowbar attack came after. I'm the one who killed him."

Max said nothing and just studied her face.

He doesn't seem surprised.

"I didn't recall until after you closed the case, and I struggled with whether to tell the FBI. I had no idea back then that you and I would . . . become involved." She pulled her hand out of his and covered her face. "Knowing that I was the one who did it has been a huge weight on me. I've wanted to tell you for a long time."

He turned and lifted her hands away from her eyes. She struggled to hold eye contact. The absolute calm in his features was terrifying her.

Scream at me or something. Call me a liar. Tell me you'll have me prosecuted.

"I suspected that might have happened, Noelle. I knew what a monster Derrick had been to you."

"I defended myself," she whispered, gripping his hands. "He was attacking me."

"I believe you."

"I didn't want any secrets between us." Her gaze pleaded with his.

"I don't want secrets either, and I'm glad you told me. I know that wasn't easy." Understanding was in his eyes. "I'm proud of you."

Noelle couldn't speak. The moment she'd been dreading for months had finally happened. "Are you going to dump me?" she blurted out.

Shock resonated in his face. "Dump you? Is that what you thought? Fuck no, Noelle. I'm in love with you." He gripped her hands. "Who do you think I am?"

He loves me?

"I love you too." The words spilled out before she could think, and his face lit up.

I didn't think I'd ever say that to another man.

But this feels right. Oh so right.

He pulled her close and pushed her hood off. And then kissed her. It wasn't the quick peck from twenty minutes ago. It was long and slow and deep and took her breath away.

Now this *is a kiss in the snow to remember.*

He pulled back and took her face in both hands, his gaze searching hers. "I think I fell in love with you that first day you walked into our interview and gave us so much attitude. You were like some sort of amazing Greek goddess who wanted to rain fire on our heads."

She shook with laughter. "I was pissed. With good reason."

"True." He moved in closer, and she sank into his arms, resting her cheek against his.

"Emma's not here. Let's go home," she whispered.

"Best idea of the day."

31

The next morning, Max glanced at Noelle as she sat in his passenger seat. Worry and concern hovered around her like a cloud. She still hadn't heard from Emma.

He was worried too. But he couldn't stop thinking about what had happened between them last night. They'd taken a big step. Both of them. He'd been holding in those three little words for several weeks, concerned he'd send her running if he spilled them too soon.

Apparently, in the middle of a crisis was the right time to tell her.

"Emma's phone could have died or broken," he said, fully aware he wasn't saying anything she hadn't thought of a dozen times. "She could be in another dead zone."

"I know," said Noelle, looking out the window at the white fields of snow-covered sagebrush as they drove to Redmond. "But it doesn't feel right."

They'd done a quick stop at Emma's and "Uncle Tommy's" homes again that morning. Both had appeared undisturbed since last night, so they'd tossed another flake of alfalfa in the horse's manger. At Emma's she'd filled Cornbread's bowl with a bag of food they'd bought on the way, and then she'd checked the chickens, who still had plenty of feed.

But now they needed to maintain the forward momentum on their murder cases. Their focus today was to go through the home of Eli Chisholm. The victim from Judge Holtz's vehicle explosion.

The skies were clear at the moment, but the storm yesterday had left six inches of snow in Bend, and they'd get another eight inches that night. Approximately half of their yearly snowfall was occurring within two days. Not taking into account the snowfall in the Cascades.

"I can have someone check her phone's location," said Max. Typically a warrant would be needed, but he knew someone who could work around that. He tried not to abuse the shortcut, but he wanted to alleviate Noelle's stress.

And his. He'd never met the teenager, but he knew she needed help.

"You can?" Noelle sounded skeptical.

He picked up his phone and opened his texts. "What's her number?" He typed it in as Noelle read it off and sent it in a text to his friend.

"You feds get all the perks," said Noelle.

"This one's a favor," said Max. He glanced at his GPS. They were close to Chisholm's house. "Is that it?" Up a long, steep driveway to his left were two small homes. A set of tracks on the hill had already broken the snow. Max switched to 4WD and easily climbed the long driveway. A small Honda was at the end of the tracks in front of the house on the left. The home on the right had an unbroken layer of snow.

"That must be the owner," said Noelle. A tall man with a cigarette and no coat stood on the home's porch, his shoulders hunched against the cold.

Eli Chisholm had rented the little house for six years. The owner had agreed to let them into the property.

Max parked in front of the garage and sized up the owner as they got out. The man reminded him of Lurch from the Addams Family but was not nearly as tall. "You must be Will Tomac," he said as he approached and held out his hand. Tomac's cigarette dangled from his lips as he shook their hands.

"Mind if I see some ID?" Tomac asked. He appeared to be in his late fifties, and his long-sleeved T-shirt had a dark stain near his belly. Noelle already had her ID out, and Tomac studied it carefully as Max dug for his. Tomac eyed Noelle. "Heard of you."

Noelle tensed. "Some people have," she replied. Her shooting of a killer last year had been in the local news for weeks.

"You did good. Bad business, that," Tomac told her with a solemn nod, and then he studied Max's ID. He handed it back without comment. "I haven't been in the house for three years," he told them. "Not sure what we'll find." He took out a key, unlocked the front door, and waved them inside with a flourish.

"Do you own that house too?" Noelle asked, pointing at the other home that shared the steep driveway.

"Yep. Both renters up here are good tenants. Pay on time for the most part. Don't break much stuff."

"Did you know Eli that well?" asked Max as they stepped inside. He put on a pair of gloves and turned on the light. "Please don't touch anything while we're here," he added.

"Just know him enough to collect the rent," said Tomac. "Seems okay. So, he's missing?" He blew out a long stream of smoke.

Law enforcement had managed to keep Eli Chisholm's identity as the body in the trunk out of the media so far. Locating family to inform of the death was proving difficult.

"Something like that," said Max. "Like I said on the phone, we can't talk about it yet." The home was dark, and the furnace rattled in the background. He'd sniffed cautiously when they entered, on edge from the thought that they might find another body inside. Instead, he'd smelled a home that needed to be dusted and have its bathrooms scrubbed. He and Noelle quickly checked all the rooms and closets while Tomac impatiently smoked in the entryway.

Max entered the garage and flipped on the light, wincing at the disorganization and clutter. Chisholm had stacked boxes, all sorts of yard tools, and various paper supplies haphazardly around the garage. He could have opened a small convenience store that sold toilet paper, laundry detergent, and paper towels. In the center was a Chevy pickup that had seen better days. The smell of spray paint was strong in the garage, and Max spotted several cans of gray spray paint on large sheets of stained cardboard near one tire. He realized Chisholm had done his own paint job on the Chevy. It looked like crap.

Max took out his phone and sent the plate number to Darby back at the office. She replied almost instantly that the plates had been stolen off a Dodge Durango three months ago in Bend.

Not surprised.

He moved next to the driver's door and snorted. Chisholm had sprayed just enough paint on the windshield to hide the VIN. "Idiot," Max muttered, realizing the truck was most likely stolen too. He opened the driver's door and took a picture of the frame's sticker with the VIN and sent it to Darby. If Chisholm had also covered that VIN with paint, he would have simply popped the hood and checked the engine block or firewall. VINs were all over the place on newer vehicles.

Not an experienced car thief.

His phone rang. Darby.

"Rhodes."

"Max, that vehicle belongs to Gage Chambers. Isn't that the dad of the teenager you told me about?"

Emma's father.

"Dammit." Ideas ricocheted through his brain, unable to form a complete thought.

How . . . why . . .

The plates were stolen three months ago.

"Is the truck reported stolen?"

"No."

"Dig up whatever you can find on Gage Chambers," said Max. "Noelle couldn't get Emma to talk about her dad that much but suspected he'd been gone for a while. See if you can access any banking or credit card information. I want to know where he's been."

"On it." Darby ended the call.

Max was still trying to wrap his head around what he'd found when Noelle spoke from the doorway. "It reeks of paint out here."

"That's because Chisholm—or someone—spray-painted Gage Chambers's truck. And attached stolen plates." He watched her face and saw the same confusion that he felt.

"Chambers? I don't get it . . . What the *hell*?"

"That's what I thought too," he said. "What's the connection between Chisholm and Emma's dad?"

"I don't know. But now Emma—well, a Chambers—has popped up twice in this investigation. First *she* found Michael Munoz, and now her father's truck is in the garage of our second murdered man." Noelle spoke slowly, trying to find the link. She pulled out her phone, and he knew she was checking for a reply from Emma. "Still nothing. How long do you think that truck has been here?"

"Plates were stolen three months ago, but they could have been on a dozen different vehicles since then." He ran a finger over the ridiculous paint. "Dusty. It was painted a while ago."

"Did you look inside?"

"No." Max turned back to the open driver's door and did a quick scan under the seats using the light from his phone. He leaned over and popped open the glove box. It'd been cleaned out. "No one has an empty glove box," he said. He opened the cab's rear driver's-side door and did the same quick search with his light. Something dark caught his eye, and he leaned closer to the bench seat, studying the seams. They were stained in several spots.

That could be anything.

Then he caught a faint whiff of bleach and a citrus-scented cleanser. "Noelle. I smell bleach."

She opened the door on the opposite side and nodded as he pointed at the stained seams in the rear seat. "I smell it too. We need a forensics team to go over the truck. *Shit.* I hope nothing has happened to her dad."

"When you hear from her, we need to pin down exactly how long he's been gone."

"If she ever gets back to me," said Noelle grimly. "Emma is definitely a skittish one."

"She'll turn up," Max said with a confidence he didn't feel. "Anything in the house?"

"I didn't see anything unusual," said Noelle. "Other than Chisholm probably hasn't changed his sheets in six months or cleaned the shower since he moved in."

"So he's not likely the type of guy to bother thoroughly cleaning something with bleach if there's a spill in his truck."

"Definitely not. Although it's not his truck."

"True."

"There's no sign of a struggle anywhere in the house. His toothbrush is in the bathroom, and there's a suitcase in the crowded closet. The food in the fridge hasn't expired, and there's even a big T-bone that has a use-by date through today," Noelle told him. "So he hasn't been gone that long, which likely means he wasn't held for much time, if at all, before his death."

"Let's talk to Tomac." Max slammed the truck doors shut and headed back inside the house. Tomac was still smoking near the front door.

"Anything helpful?" he asked.

"We're not sure," said Noelle. "When did you last see Eli?"

"Jeez. It's probably been more than a year. Made him drop off his rent check in person that time because it was two weeks late. Seems like that was around the Christmas before last."

"Do you ever talk to him? Text?" she asked.

"No. Sorry. He's not my buddy." He inhaled deeply on the cigarette. "If you want to know about what he's been up to, you should talk to Ricky Dowd next door. He knew Eli before he moved in. He's the one who suggested he rent this house."

"Thank you, Mr. Tomac. We'll do that." Noelle raised a brow at Max, who nodded.

"Let's see if he's home." Max told Tomac that more investigators were coming and asked if he could keep the key, promising him he'd see to it personally that Tomac got it back. The man reluctantly handed it over.

"You think something bad's happened to him," said Tomac. His concern seemed genuine.

"Possibly," said Max as they all headed out the door.

Tomac got in the little Honda and drove off as Max and Noelle went next door.

The houses were identical except that Chisholm's was a pale gray and this one was dark. Max knocked on the door, which still had a Christmas wreath, and Noelle stomped the snow off her boots. "I really love snow," she said. "I get excited when it's in the forecast. Last winter in town we only got about an inch twice. We were cheated."

He grinned at her, enjoying the animation in her face as she gazed at the snow. It was a pleasure to see the confident detective he'd learned was a perfectionist show glee in her eyes and smile.

The door was opened by a thirtysomething man holding the hand of a small boy. His gaze was suspicious. "Can I help you?"

"Are you Ricky Dowd?" asked Max, "We just met with your home's owner, Will Tomac—"

"Yeah, I saw all of you over there. What's going on?" The boy yanked on his father's arm, and Ricky hoisted him onto his hip.

Max and Noelle presented their IDs and introduced themselves.

"You're from the FBI? Is Eli okay?" Ricky asked, his forehead wrinkling in worry.

"Can we come in and talk?" asked Noelle, her breath hanging in the cold air.

"Umm. Yeah, sure."

The boy stuck his thumb in his mouth, his gaze locked on Max.

"Who's this?" Max asked, nodding at the boy as they entered the house.

"Trey. He's almost three."

Ricky moved some toys off a dated sofa, and they all sat, he with Trey on his lap in an easy chair that seemed to have had its sides ripped up by a cat.

"Is anyone else home?" asked Max.

"No. Just us. This is my weekend with Trey." He shifted the boy to his other leg. "Now. What's up with Eli?" He frowned as he looked from Max to Noelle. "What happened?"

Max debated telling the man the truth. His concern felt legitimate. "He's a person of interest in a case we're working on. He may have witnessed something."

Ricky pulled his son's thumb out of his mouth and distracted him with a stuffed elephant. "You're being vague. I get it. But I suspect Eli's associations might have caught up with him."

Max exchanged a look with Noelle. "Explain."

"How much do you know about Eli?" asked Ricky. "Because I've known him for about ten years. Not much goes on with him that he doesn't tell me about." His tone was matter-of-fact, and Max suspected that Ricky had guessed that something bad had happened to Eli.

"We don't know much about him at all. When did you see him last?" asked Noelle.

"Probably last week sometime. Haven't had a sit-down-and-talk discussion for a while, but we always say hello when we cross paths." He sighed and set Trey down as the boy tried to squirm off his lap, his attention locked on some brightly colored cardboard bricks. "We were of the same mindset for a long time. But a few years ago, we took different directions.

"There's a lot about this country that needs changing," said Ricky, his gaze on his son. "But Eli and I have different opinions on how that should be done. At one time I'd go with him to the meetings and such. Everyone was on the same side, and we wanted to make our voices heard. But it started going too far for me. I could see some of these people were ready to cross lines that I didn't think we should."

And he thought I was being vague.

"Impatience grew over the years. The legal channels were too slow. They wanted to burn everything down and start over. Get rid of taxes and laws and build everything from the ground up. Eli was fully on board." Ricky shook his head. "I'd say to Eli, 'Well, what about regulations that keep our meat safe? Does that need to be burned down? What about the regulations for baby food and keeping chemicals out of their toys?'

"Eli'd say, 'We won't touch that.' So then I'd ask, 'Will there be programs that help the people who can't afford to heat their homes during the winter?' His reply was that they should rely on family and friends. So I'd say, 'Eli, which of your friends or family will buy you heat?'" Ricky chuckled. "That shut him up because he's had to get government assistance for that before. I don't think he had any real friends but me, and I've never heard a word about his family. He knows I ain't buying his heat *and* mine. So he said, 'We'll keep that program.' Drove me crazy how he'd berry-pick what to keep and what to get rid of based on his personal decisions. It was like he didn't understand that different people had different needs. Then I'd ask, 'If no one has to pay taxes anymore, who's going to pay the firemen when your house catches on fire?'" Ricky grinned, his gaze still on his son. "It took the wind out of his sails every time."

"Do you think you changed his mind?" asked Noelle.

"I *know* I didn't change his mind. He wouldn't talk to me for a week or two after we had one of those discussions, and then he'd try to avoid the topic for a couple months. But lately he's seemed convinced that we're in for a big shake-up, but that it won't affect the average American. Claims it'll be good for everyone."

Max struggled to sit still. Ricky's description lined up with what the FBI had been hearing. "What's the shake-up?" he asked in a neutral voice.

"Don't know. He wouldn't tell me outright," said Ricky. "But I have some ideas after listening to him. He said it's going to get people's attention and create a vacuum at the top."

"Top of what?" Noelle asked sharply. "Is he going to assassinate the president?"

"I asked the same. He laughed at me and claimed it wasn't anything close to that. That this would be only a beginning."

"What are they going to do?" asked Max, a stir of panic rising in his gut. "This isn't the time to be vague, Ricky."

"I could say the same to you," said Ricky, his voice rising. "Eli's dead, isn't he?"

Max counted to five and made a decision. "Yes. He is, and we're trying to find who did it. And there's a good chance the murderer could be from this group that you keep alluding to but not giving any details about." He held Ricky's gaze. The air in the room was suddenly thick with tension.

Trey squealed as his brick wall fell over, and the tension evaporated.

"Ricky, what do you know about this group?" asked Noelle.

Ricky blew out a breath and rubbed a hand down his face. "If that's so, then it's my fault he's dead. I introduced Eli to them back when we first met. But a few years ago, I wasn't comfortable there anymore and stopped going. I'd gotten married and had different priorities." He stared at his son. "But the group . . ." He shook his head. "They started suggesting riskier things. Like damaging substations or having a public gathering where we all open carry."

"Open carry's legal here," said Noelle.

"Yeah, they said that was the point. They just wanted to get people's attention. They hoped someone would react with force and then they'd have reason to 'exert their rights.'"

"They wanted to shoot people?" she asked.

Ricky shrugged.

Max felt sick to his stomach.

"They talked about it a lot. Any government official they were angry with at the moment was always a topic of discussion. How to pinpoint public attention on that bureaucrat or their family. Publish their address and phone number. Pressure the official enough to step down."

"You mean scare and threaten them enough to step down," said Max.

Ricky simply nodded. "They started weapons training a couple years ago, after I left. Militia-type shit, you know. I was glad I was out by the time they started that. Eli loved it. Bought paramilitary gear. Practiced shooting as a group all the time."

"Ricky, were these people part of America's Preserve?" Noelle asked, referring to the militia group that Mercy had infiltrated a couple of years before.

"I know some left our group and went with them, but Mac—he's the guy who led us—had always hated their leader. Hodges, I think his name was. Mac said he was an asshole who didn't know what he was doing. Apparently he was right, because America's Preserve pretty much imploded a while back, and a lotta people died.

"It wasn't long after I left that Mac stepped down. Talk about leaving a vacuum in leadership. No one else could inspire and keep men focused the way Mac could. Eli told me about all the infighting. Everyone had a different opinion of who should lead. That bickering went on for years. I thought Eli would finally give up, but he kept going back, hoping someone who could actually lead would appear."

"But you weren't involved anymore," Max clarified.

"Nope. I'd gotten married. Had a kid on the way. Joanne—my wife—ex-wife now—tried to convince Eli to leave the group, but he refused. I think it's the only place he felt like he belonged somewhere. He didn't get along with many people. Had a hard time keeping a job. Probably because of his temper."

"What did Eli most recently talk about?" asked Noelle.

"He sorta kept things to himself. He stopped telling me particulars and who was involved. Said it was for my safety and his." Ricky paused, regret filling his face. "I guess his safety didn't last." He looked Max and then Noelle in the eye. "Mac must have come back, because last fall Eli was pumped and excited about the group again. Said their leadership was back in good hands and things were finally happening."

"Like what?"

"I don't know. That's when Joanne and I started our divorce. I didn't have time for long talks with Eli. I told him I was glad they'd gotten their shit together and left it at that."

"What do you think was happening?" asked Max.

"Mac was back," Ricky said simply. "Couldn't stay away, I guess."

"I thought Eli wouldn't tell you who was involved," said Noelle.

"True. But Mac is the only person who held everyone's respect. He's the only one every man would listen to. If it was suddenly smooth sailing there, it was because Mac came back. I even considered going to a meeting once I heard how good things were."

"What can you tell us about Mac?" asked Noelle. "What's his full name?"

"Mac is a nickname," said Ricky. "Had it forever. His real name is Tom. Last name—"

"Hammaker," Max and Noelle said at the same time.

Ricky's brows shot up. "Sounds like you already know him. He goes by Tommy Mac too."

And Uncle Tommy.

"Not really," said Noelle. "We just know of him. What else can you tell us about him?"

"He's a whiz with weapons. You name it, he's got it. He's also good with explosives. If you had a question about that sort of thing, he was the guy to see. Although he lost a few fingers during an explosion. But that was probably twenty years ago."

"What did he blow up?" asked Max.

"Nothing like you're thinking of," Ricky said quickly. "He'd demonstrate on stumps or even rocks. Always out in the middle of nowhere."

"Could he blow up a car?" Noelle had shifted to the edge of her seat.

"Sure. I've seen him do that to ones he got from the junkyard."

Max didn't know how to tell Ricky that this leader he admired might have killed his buddy Eli.

If he did, there's a strong possibility he killed Michael Munoz and Rachel Johnson.

"Do you know Gage Chambers?" asked Noelle.

"Sure. He was with the group before I was."

"There's a gray truck in Eli's garage," said Max. "You familiar with it?"

"Yeah, it's new. Well, new to him. I told him he needed to get that gray color repainted. Looks like a teenager did it with spray paint."

"How long has he had it?" asked Max.

Ricky twisted his lips as he thought. "First time I saw it, Joanne was dropping off Trey. It was early in the divorce. So maybe Thanksgiving?" He looked at both of them. "You gonna tell me what happened to Eli?"

"We're still trying to find family to notify," said Noelle. "Do you know Michael Munoz?"

Ricky shook his head. "Don't know the name."

Max wasn't surprised since Munoz's sister had said he'd gotten involved with the group more recently.

"Ricky," said Max. "You mentioned that Eli said something big was going to happen, but he wouldn't tell you exactly what. I assume this 'big shake-up' could involve explosives? Or weapons?"

"I know what you're getting at. You want to know why I haven't told anyone," said Ricky, earnestly. "But what was I going to report? No one would take me seriously if I said that there's rumors *something* might happen, but I don't know what or where or when. How helpful is that?"

"You could have suggested they question Eli," said Noelle.

"He's my friend. And I doubt he knew details."

"He knew something," said Max.

"Too late to question him now." Ricky shrugged.

"Let's look at it in a different way," said Max, his mind scrambling to figure out how to get more information out of Ricky. "You say you don't know where *something* is going to happen, but maybe you know enough to stop it *before* it happens. Where would the supplies come from to make that unknown thing happen? That unknown thing possibly being an explosion."

"Tommy Mac's place," Ricky said firmly. "He's got storage bunkers on his property. I've seen them. Enough weapons and explosives for a small war and even a place to live—not that I'd want to live in such a small space. Said he had the supplies to stay in there for six months. He encouraged all of us to build bunkers if we had the property. He always warned that shit could hit the fan, you know. Maybe our country could be attacked or—"

"We've been to his home," interrupted Noelle. "We didn't see anything like that."

But it was nighttime.

"The bunkers are beyond the barn," said Ricky. "Probably two or three hundred yards away. Easy to miss. They blend into the scenery pretty well, covered with dirt and bushes. There are two of them about five yards apart. Not really underground, they form large mounds and are taller at one end, where there is a vertical door hidden by more trees and stuff." He frowned. "There were two when I was there. Could be more by now."

Max looked at Noelle, who had excitement in her eyes.

We've got a solid lead.

32

Max banged on the conference room door with an elbow, and it was immediately opened from the inside. His arms were full of serving containers of rice, beans, tortillas, and a dozen fillings and toppings. The sight of the food caused a chorus of happy exclamations. The task force was working nonstop with the information he and Noelle had gathered that morning, and most of them had missed lunch.

He'd volunteered to pick up the huge takeout order from the Tex-Mex place downtown, wanting a break from all the questions and bustle in the office. He'd needed to get away to clear his head. Noelle had suggested someone else could go, but he'd insisted. Concern had filled her face until he'd told her in a low voice that he just needed some silence for a few minutes.

And the inside of his SUV had been completely silent during the drive to and from the restaurant. Unless you counted the ruckus of thoughts still spinning on inside his brain. The team was close to solving the murders and car bomb. He could almost taste it.

He and Noelle had grilled Ricky on everything he could recall about the bunkers on Thomas Hammaker's property. Max had made some calls, and a team from the ATF and the Portland FBI office were headed to Bend. They would be in charge of breaching the bunkers, where they hoped to find Uncle Tommy, explosives, and weapons earmarked for . . . something.

Noelle had wondered if Emma was in one of the bunkers.

Max's source had said that Emma's cell phone had last pinged near Hammaker's place yesterday. Her last phone call had been to Noelle.

When they'd stopped by Emma's home that morning, Noelle had been upset to see the cat's empty food dish. The cat was unhappy too. He'd sat at the far end of the porch and glared at them. "I don't think he'd come this close to us if he'd already been fed," Noelle had said. They'd made a quick detour to buy a bag of cat food, and she'd filled his dish. "Emma would never let him go unfed," she'd said quietly. "Something has happened to her."

Max was afraid she was correct.

Darby had called as he and Noelle drove back to Bend to inform them that Gage Chambers hadn't used any credit or debit cards since Thanksgiving. She'd filed a warrant to locate his phone, but Max doubted it would turn up. Most likely it hadn't been used since November either. He'd thanked her and then looked at Noelle, whose eyes were wide with disbelief.

"Do you think Emma's been alone since November?"

"Sounds like it," he'd said.

Gage Chambers is likely dead.

"No wonder she's been collecting cans and bottles." Guilt had filled her tone. "I should have done more for her."

Noelle had put together a bulletin alerting local law enforcement agencies to keep an eye out for Emma Chambers, and Max had studied the driver's license photo. Emma had a thin face with sharp cheekbones and a strong chin. There was a spark of stubbornness in the girl's expression that matched Noelle's description of her personality. From the little he knew about her homelife, she was strong and independent out of necessity.

That strength made him cross his fingers and hope she was hanging on somewhere.

Maybe in a bunker with her uncle Tommy.

And not in the woods with two gunshots to the forehead.

Max set the armload of food on a side table in the conference room. New faces had arrived and joined the group since he'd left to pick it up.

"Max." Noelle pulled his attention. "This is Special Agent Jasmine Keyes from the Portland FBI office and Special Agent Chad Reed from Portland ATF."

Max shook their hands. "We've talked on the phone," he said to Keyes. "Glad to have the two of you here."

"Our SWAT team will handle the entry and seizure. Several ATF agents will be on-site to deal with any weapons and explosives we find," said Keyes. "I expect all of my team members to be in the area within the hour." She frowned. "Roads were a little dicey coming over the pass."

"It's not going to get any better," said Max.

Keyes nodded. "Unless something comes up, I'd like to plan on being in position around eight p.m."

"You know we've got more snow coming this evening, right?" asked Max.

"We can work in snow." The agent was confident.

"Good to know." Max looked at the rest of his team, now focused diligently on their tacos, and noticed someone had added a large headshot of Hammaker to the whiteboard. It showed an old man with a white beard and fierce eyebrows. "What do we have on Thomas Hammaker so far?"

Mercy wiped her mouth with a napkin and went to the whiteboard, writing as she spoke. "He's been off the radar for several years. Before that is a list of arrests but no prison or real jail time. Charges included DUI, driving while suspended, reckless driving, original trespass, and false information given to police. He must have turned over a new leaf a few years ago for some reason because he's stayed out of trouble."

"But now he's back," Max heard Noelle say under her breath.

"He had an FFL license that expired several years ago," said the ATF agent.

Federal firearms license.

"He bought and sold firearms?" Max asked.

"Yes. He had a small storefront in Prineville. Closed up shop about a decade ago."

"He must have made a lot of contacts during that time," said Mercy. "No doubt he's still in communication with some of them."

"Maybe," said Agent Reed. "He's sort of faded into the woodwork with the ATF. We considered him washed up and too old. He was injured at some point. Lost some fingers, I believe. Like with Agent Kilpatrick, he hasn't shown up in any of our reports for a long time either."

"Agent Reed," said Noelle. "Agent Rhodes and I were at Hammaker's last night and early this morning looking for a young woman who was temporarily staying with him. The house was dark and locked, but we went through the barn, calling for her. If he has cameras—and he's sounding more and more like a person who would—he's going to be on edge about seeing us on his property. I have no doubt that he suspected we were law enforcement."

"Another reason we need to act tonight," said Reed, looking at Agent Keyes. "He may feel he's been forewarned, but we'll be ready for anything."

"Possibly he believed we were just there to find Emma," said Max. "Which we were. And won't connect our presence to anything else."

"Doesn't change our plans," said Keyes. "We assume he knows we're coming."

Mercy attached several satellite photos of the Hammaker property to the board with magnets. "This one was taken within the last few months," she said. "And I've added others from a few years back." Several people, including Max, stepped closer to the board to get a look.

He recognized Hammaker's home and barn in each photo. In some photos, the landscape was green, and in others it was the dry light brown of late summer. "Where are the bunkers?" he asked.

"They're hard to see," said Mercy. "If your witness hadn't been very specific, they would've never caught my eye." She indicated a point some distance from the barn. "You can see here that it's green on these two patches of land. But the green shade is different from the surrounding area. He must have planted some things on the top after the bunkers were dug out and built. But they don't match the other flora quite right. Too structured and symmetrical, unlike the surrounding areas. Supposedly they're mostly aboveground but have been well disguised." She indicated an irregular patch of green that was clearly a grove of trees. "There is also a very faint path that runs from the barn to the bunker area."

Max had to take another step closer to verify the pale line. "What about here for a staging area?" He indicated a clearing approximately a half mile from the bunkers and glanced at Agent Keyes.

The woman eyed the photo for a long moment and then nodded. "I'll have someone check it out first. See if we can get a drone up while there is a break in the weather. Can I borrow that?" Max handed her the photo, and the agent stepped out of the office. The staging area would soon be under a foot of snow no matter where they set up.

"What else?" asked Max.

"Simple Google searches turned up these photos," said Special Agent Reed. He added a few photos next to Mercy's satellite imagery. "They're a little old. But this one was taken during a Fourth of July parade in Prineville. According to the caption, Thomas Hammaker is the third man from the left."

The photo showed a group of men wearing old-time buckskin pants and shirts and Davy Crockett hats marching with ancient muskets against their shoulders. Two were in the act of loading their muskets. "I went to a few parades as a kid where they had that sort of thing," said Mercy. "They'd fire those muskets as they marched. They were incredibly loud. I'd always cover my ears when I saw them coming."

The face on the third man was younger, but it was definitely their subject's. One of the other photos had been taken in front of the courthouse, which gave Max pause, as he recalled being there after the car bombing. Hammaker was part of a large group casually standing around and chatting with rifles slung over their backs. Again it was an older photo; Hammaker's beard was brown.

Agent Keyes returned to the room. "We're still going to aim for staging at eight p.m. I'd like your county SWAT team to clear the rest of the property before we surround the bunkers by ten. We'll have constant eyes on the bunkers and the other buildings starting in about an hour."

Max noticed Mercy had taken her seat, her face slightly pale, and she pushed her food around on her plate. He glanced at Agent Keyes. Her gaze was on Mercy too, a small frown on her lips.

The raid on America's Preserve didn't go well for Mercy.

Agent Keyes is aware of it.

In the two months he'd known Mercy, she'd proved to be a hell of an agent. Fear wasn't something he associated with her. She might be uncomfortable with the memories this operation was bringing back, but he knew they could count on her in the field.

Max picked up a plate and dished up some rice, realizing there wouldn't be any food left if he waited much longer.

"Here are some old aliases for Thomas Hammaker," said Agent Reed as he stepped to the whiteboard. "Let's get research going on these too. Perhaps he's been using one of them more recently." He started a list of names under *A.K.A.* next to Hammaker's license photo.

Max loaded some shredded pork onto a few small tortillas and sprinkled them with red onions, a little cabbage, and cilantro. He munched as he watched Reed write on the board.

Tobias Hammaker

Tobias McHale

Thomas Navarro

Max's gaze locked on the name Tobias McHale, and his mouth went dry.

Coincidence.

He forced himself to swallow the bite of taco and grabbed a water to wash it down and then moved to where Noelle was working on her laptop. "Noelle," he said quietly. "Can you see if Tobias McHale is linked to either a Robert McHale, Jacob McHale, or Lorelei McHale?" He swallowed and added, "In the Medford area."

She held his gaze; she knew one of the names. "No problem."

The three names were burned into his brain. But Tobias McHale was a new one.

He looked away from her screen, not wanting to see what she found. Everyone else in the room was focused on their work or in conversation with a colleague.

Noelle gave a slight gasp.

I was right.

"Max, did you know about this?"

He looked over her shoulder and saw the name Tobias McHale grouped with the three names he'd given her, along with several more relatives. Jacob's was at the top. Max dropped into the chair next to her, his palms suddenly sweaty. "I didn't. Can I use your computer for a minute?"

She silently slid it to him, and he ran a quick search for a specific press conference from twelve years ago. It was the one in which the large McHale family had gathered behind their lawyer to condemn Max and the Medford PD for killing their son, Jacob.

He found the video and played it with no sound, studying the emotionless faces behind the lawyer, who wore a righteous mask and whose mouth wouldn't stop silently moving as he berated the police department.

There.

Max paused the video and zoomed in.

In the very back of the family group stood Thomas Hammaker, a.k.a. Tobias McHale. His round face and graying beard were very clear in the video. Anger emanated from his stiff shoulders and neck.

"What's the relationship to Jacob?" he asked softly.

Noelle switched tabs. "Not his grandfather. Looks like paternal great-uncle."

"I know both Jacob's grandfathers have passed since the shooting," said Max. He occasionally Googled Jacob's family, but he'd never paid attention to a relative named Tobias McHale. Possibly because the man didn't live in Medford and hadn't spoken publicly about the shooting.

Max sat back in his seat and stared at Hammaker's photo on the board as memories of Jacob's death slithered through his brain.

Is Thomas Hammaker the person harassing Keira and me?

And who killed our three victims?

33

Emma's skull pounded with pain.

She was cold and tired and thirsty as she sat on the dirt floor with her head on her knees, a heavy blanket wrapped tight around her shoulders.

Who did this to me?

Someone had locked her up. But first they'd hit her on the back of the head, where she could feel a huge lump, and there was dried blood in her hair. She had no memory of being hit or left in this little room. She believed the attack had happened as she walked from Tommy's barn toward his house because she remembered feeding Harley after dinner, but she didn't remember making it back inside Tommy's home.

Now she was stuck in some sort of weird room.

Or cell.

It wasn't much larger than Harley's stall. The floor was dirt and the walls were plywood, making her feel as if it was part of a barn. But she felt she might be underground because she'd yelled and banged on the walls, and they didn't sound right. There was something behind the plywood. As if another thick layer of wood or dirt insulated and kept the noises inside her room (*cell*).

There was a dim light bulb in the ceiling behind a layer of thick plastic. She'd unsuccessfully tried to stand on a bucket to see if she could move the plastic and twist the bulb to turn it off. She'd always only been able to sleep in a completely darkened room, and she suspected a night had passed because she'd been so tired and slept on and off for a long time. It was disorienting to not know the time or see outdoors. Her exhaustion had kept making her vision blur, and the crappy light had interrupted her sleep, waking her over and over.

And the cold. So much cold.

At least she still had her orange coat. The snow had been falling hard after she'd fed Harley. She recalled being outside the barn, wearing the coat and trying to catch a flake on her tongue like a kid. It'd made her cough, the falling snow was so thick.

I remember coughing. And then nothing.

She wondered if her attacker had watched her stick out her tongue.

Emma wiped her eyes, still shaken that someone had actually hit her and locked her up. The only people she could think of were the two who'd broken into her home that night. Clearly they'd had a goal in mind.

I think that was the same man who talked to Tommy.

Or was she completely wrong? Making connections where none existed. Perhaps she so badly wanted to learn who'd been there that she was making up things in her head.

Do I have a concussion?

"Maybe I've been here for three days," she said to the light bulb. "Or a week." But she suspected she would be hungrier. A few weird protein bars had been left in her room (*cell*), and she'd eaten one a while ago, finding it tasteless and dry. Three bottles of water had also been left. She'd drunk one. And then wished she hadn't.

When she'd first woken and explored the room (*cell*), she'd looked in the bucket in a corner, hoping to find more food. It was empty, and she immediately understood what it was for and that she wouldn't have access to a real bathroom. She'd waited until she thought her bladder would burst and then finally used the bucket.

Now when she was thirsty, she didn't want to drink because she didn't want to use the bucket. But she knew better than to get dehydrated, so she drank.

And used the bucket.

It wasn't as if anyone was watching.

I hope.

The door to her room (*cell*) had no knob or window or visible hinges. Everything was on the outside. She'd crammed her fingers into every slight groove she could find in the door and the walls and pulled and yanked to no avail. Nothing would move.

It was a prison.

So she'd sat on the dirt floor and wrapped the blanket around her shoulders. She'd leaned against a wall for a while but discovered it was even colder than the floor.

She waited for someone to come. Surely they would bring more water and food and empty her bucket. If they'd wanted her to die, there would have been no supplies. They had a purpose for keeping her, but she couldn't think of what it could be.

Perhaps this was God's punishment for wishing her father would never return. She'd known those were bad thoughts, practically evil ones, because deep down she'd hoped he was dead. She deserved to be punished.

Maybe he's in a cell too.

She hadn't missed him. Not one bit.

Not like she'd missed her mother. Emma closed her eyes and tried to remember what her mother had looked like. Emma had been eight when she left, and her father had burned every single photo of her mother.

He'd told Emma her mother had left because she was a bad girl. Emma had cried and cried, convinced it was because she'd broken her mother's Christmas charm bracelet. The bracelet she'd been told to never touch, but it was so beautiful that Emma couldn't resist putting it on. She'd sneak into her parents' room and look in the little box of jewelry. Emma didn't care about the other bracelets and necklaces. She only had eyes for the charm bracelet.

But she'd dropped it, and the candy cane and golden star had broken off. The two charms had skittered under the bed after it hit the hard tile floor, and Emma had scrambled on her hands and knees to find the charms, terrified that she'd hear a parent coming down the hall any second. With shaking hands she'd set everything back in the box, ridiculously hoping her mother would believe it had broken inside the box.

My mother wasn't stupid.

Instead, her mother had left without saying goodbye. She'd even left the bracelet behind instead of taking the constant reminder of what a bad daughter Emma had been. It'd taken weeks after her mother left for Emma to gather the courage to look in the box. The bracelet was right where she'd left it. She stared at it for a long time and then snatched up all the pieces. She scurried to her room with the bracelet gripped tightly against her chest and hid it deep inside a rip in her mattress.

A few years later she'd managed to reattach the charms. But the bracelet always stayed hidden, pulled out to look at only when her father was asleep. Or gone.

After that she'd tried hard to be a good girl for her father. She did his laundry and changed his sheets. She tried to cook but only knew how to open a can or put something in the microwave. As she got older, she tried to make a few recipes, but her father never noticed. He just assumed she'd heated a frozen meal. She stopped trying.

One time the microwaved meatloaf had still been icy in spots while cooked to rubber in others, and he'd been furious. After shouting at her, he'd shoved her against the stove, and she'd slipped and fallen, landing on her hand and pinkie finger wrong. The finger turned red and swelled and hurt horribly, but she didn't tell him, terrified he'd get angry again. She knew it was broken. The finger eventually stopped hurting, but it was always crooked, a constant reminder that she was a bad daughter.

A few years ago, when Uncle Tommy had been there for dinner, Emma had accidentally knocked over her water glass and it had soaked her dad's lap. He'd reached over and slapped her hard, nearly making her fall off her chair. Uncle Tommy had roared and punched her father in the face, making his lips bleed and knocking a tooth loose. He'd made her father swear to never slap her again. But that night he'd spanked her and spanked her because she'd made him look bad in front of Uncle Tommy.

The stupid daughter.

Uncle Tommy didn't come to dinner for two years after that. But every time Emma saw him, he always studied her, a small scowl on his face, and she knew he was looking for bruises. But her father was smart, and after that dinner he'd only left bruises that were hidden by her clothes.

Emma learned to fade into the background and stay under the radar in her own home, never calling attention to herself. A talent she also used in school. She anticipated her father's needs so he wouldn't have to speak to her. The home was spotless. A ragged but clean towel always within reach. His coffee brewed before he woke. A supply of sandwiches in the refrigerator, easy for him to grab so he wouldn't yell that there was never anything to eat. She made herself scarce, so he would never have to think about her.

In her cold little room (*cell*), Emma adjusted her blanket and wished she had a heavier coat.

She decided to make a deal with God that if he got her out of this horrible place where she had to pee in a bucket, she'd never hate or complain about her father when he came home. She would be a good daughter.

Her fingers twinged as she tightened her grip on the blanket, and she stared at her crooked pinkie, remembering the long nights when it'd hurt so bad she'd believed it would turn black and fall off.

Sorry, God. No deal.

She'd rather stay in the cold cell than see her father again.

34

Noelle trudged through the deepening snow toward Hammaker's house, thankful the flakes had taken a brief break.

Ten minutes ago the county SWAT team had sneaked onto the Hammaker property in the dark and silently cleared the house and barn. Noelle had watched from the Deschutes County sheriff's command center in a nearby RV. Monitors showed eight different views of falling snow and trees as the SWAT team worked their way from a wide perimeter to the farm. Simultaneously the home's front door was breached with a small battering ram as other team members slid aside the big barn door.

No one was in either the house or barn.

Knowing Hammaker was an explosives expert, the SWAT team had worried about booby traps and had checked thoroughly before breaching the doors. Noelle was thankful none had been found.

What if Max and I had triggered one when we entered the barn last night?

Noelle wiped sweat off her forehead, aware they could have died. She wasn't accustomed to checking for explosives before entering a property, and the thought hadn't even crossed her mind.

Meanwhile, three hundred yards away, the FBI's SWAT team out of Portland had established a perimeter around the two bunkers. They were waiting in the dark, their night vision locked on the bunkers and surrounding area to see if the raid on Hammaker's home would drive him out.

Noelle knew the FBI would silently wait one hour before breaching the bunkers, hoping he'd come out. They preferred to take him outside the units instead of going inside, where they had no idea of who or what they would encounter.

During the wait, Noelle was to search Tommy's home and barn, looking for anything that would help the FBI know what to expect in the bunkers. She carefully stepped up the snow-covered porch stairs and winced at the sight of the broken front door.

We had no choice.

"Detective." One of the entry team, bulky in his heavy SWAT gear, greeted her with a nod. His night vision equipment was flipped up on his helmet, his weapon still at the ready. His team had turned on every light in the house.

"Anything I should know?" Noelle asked.

"Well-hidden cameras." He pointed at a corner of the porch overhang. "Two more inside and another covering the back." He gave a cheerful wave and grin at the porch one.

Noelle glanced up, and it took her several seconds to spot the camera. Not surprised she and Max hadn't noticed it the day before, she wondered if they were being viewed that very second from inside the bunkers. "What did you find inside?"

"Follow me."

In the home she heard more team members' voices down a hall. The man leading her pointed out the other two indoor cameras, one in the kitchen and one covering the living area. She put on gloves and yanked open a few drawers in the kitchen, finding the usual kitchen junk. She followed him down the hall, passing a bathroom with open cabinet doors and an olive-green shower curtain pushed to one side.

In the largest bedroom—which wasn't very large—two SWAT members stood in front of a large gun safe in the corner. "Locked?" she asked.

"Yes," said the man she recognized as a lieutenant. "But if this guy is as active—or was as active—in the gun community as you believe, there should be several more safes. This one doesn't hold much."

"Could mean that he keeps them in one of the bunkers," said Noelle, checking the time. She poked around in Hammaker's closet a bit. His clothing gave off scents of horse and engine oil as she pushed items aside.

"Detective? You need to take a look at these."

His tone made her stomach clench, and she turned to see the lieutenant scowling at several pieces of printer paper he was shuffling through his hands. "What is it?"

He handed them to her. They were several poor-quality photos of Keira. Exactly like the ones Max had received, but there were more. Several photos were of Max. Outside his home, getting in his vehicle at work, and punching in the code at Noelle's gate.

He followed Max to my home.

But there were also photocopies of old newspaper articles that covered Jacob McHale's shooting. An official police department photo of a much younger Max accompanied two of the articles.

More confirmation that Hammaker is still bitter about the shooting.

"They were on top of the safe," said the lieutenant. "Why does he have photos of Agent Rhodes?"

"It's a long story. But we were aware of this."

The lieutenant frowned, his gaze questioning hers. But he didn't press further.

"Is there a computer?" Noelle asked. She hung on to the papers.

"Other room."

She followed the lieutenant back down the hall into a very small bedroom with a twin bed and a desk with an ancient computer on top. The keyboard had a thick layer of dust. "Doubtful he monitors his cameras from here."

"Probably on his phone," said one of the team.

Noelle looked in the open closet and caught her breath. All the clothing she'd given Emma was neatly hung up and arranged by color. Noelle ran a hand over the clothes. Every button was buttoned and every zipper zipped. "She felt safe here," Noelle said too quietly for anyone to hear.

How long was she planning to stay?

"This is green team leader," said one of the men. He listened to his earpiece for a moment. "Copy." He looked at Noelle. "There's been no activity at the bunkers."

I still have time before they start.

She wanted to be back in the sheriff's command center to watch the FBI's feeds from its SWAT team when the team breached the bunkers.

"I'd like to see the barn," she told him.

Noelle followed the lieutenant out of the little house and across the yard, tucking the photos and articles about Max in her coat. The snow had picked up again and looked like a blizzard as it blew across the bright light above the barn door. She shivered in her heavy coat, on edge after looking at the papers.

Proof of Hammaker's anger.

"There's a camera built into that light fixture," said the lieutenant, pointing at the motion sensor light. "And another inside that must pick up the entire length of the aisle." He slid the door open, and they entered. "We didn't find anything else of interest in here. No weapons. No locked storage."

The horse nickered in her direction. Noelle strode down the aisle, scanning to her right and left. It appeared nothing had changed since she and Max had been there that morning. "Remember me?" she said softly to the horse as she stroked his cheek.

"Detective, you should get going," said the lieutenant. "They're counting down."

It's almost time.

"Thank you." Noelle patted the horse and made a mental note to have the county check on him tomorrow. Regardless of what happened tonight, his living situation was going to change. She went out of the barn and tightened her collar as she pushed through the snowfall, which blew sideways with the wind.

She'd know soon if Emma was in the bunker with Hammaker. Noelle didn't know where else to look for the teenager.

Emma's uncle Tommy wasn't who the teen had thought he was.

Please be safe.

35

Max and Special Agents Keyes and Reed watched over the shoulders of the agents sitting at the monitors in the FBI's mobile command center. The big RV had driven slowly over the snowy Cascade mountains from Portland and had arrived only within the hour. The team had had it set up and running almost immediately.

Currently Max watched a dozen green tinted views from the FBI SWAT team's cams. The men were motionless, lying in wait in a wide perimeter around the bunkers, giving the command center boring views of falling snow. Occasionally the commander in the RV would tell one of the team to clear his camera because snow had covered it.

"Never seen that before," said Commander Stevens. "Snow's not supposed to stick to them."

"It's falling and blowing in every direction possible," said the woman sitting next to him. "It's bound to build up."

"Any more information from the county team?" asked Max. He knew Noelle was checking the property, but he wouldn't hear from her directly.

"Was just told that it appears no one had fed the horse since this morning," said the woman, touching her headset. "Poor guy. Indicates that no one has been on the property since you and Detective Marshall were there."

Max pressed his lips together and checked the SWAT member view that showed the metal doors of one of the bunkers. His biggest fear was that they were too late. That Hammaker had cleaned out his cache and was out somewhere preparing for the big thing Ricky Dowd had heard about.

But if he saw us at his home last night, he may have decided to leave his weapons and explosives behind and hit the road.

Max preferred that option.

Option three was that Hammaker was inside, convinced that law enforcement didn't know about the bunkers.

Or he's inside, somehow watching us like we're watching him.

The drone reconnaissance had been a failure due to the snow and wind. It hadn't even launched. Instead, the FBI had done its recon on foot, which had proved to be a challenge in the dark with the deepening snow and rough terrain. The leaders had discussed the possibility of a bolt-hole in one of the bunkers, an underground tunnel that would allow Hammaker to escape unseen. The SWAT team members had taken their positions and begun waiting to see if Hammaker would react to the invasion of his home and barn nearly an hour ago, watching the bunkers and the surrounding area in case he took a tunnel.

Nothing in the area had moved.

According to Ricky Dowd, who'd been to the bunkers once, each one was a lengthy, skinny space with shelving and storage lining both long walls, leaving a narrow aisle. One was full of explosives and weapons. The other one was the same but had a bit of room at the far end for living with bunk beds, food, and water.

The plan was to breach the doors of both simultaneously with two teams. Two ATF explosives experts would first make a quick check of the doors and surrounding area for booby traps. Then they would set the explosives and blow the doors. After that the team would enter the bunkers. They wouldn't use flash-bangs inside due to the presumed explosives.

The entry would be the most dangerous part of the mission. The teams would essentially move in through a funnel, only able to protect themselves with their shields and gear. Max had been on

Medford's SWAT entry team a few times. Going into the unknown had brought some of the highest anxiety he'd ever experienced, but he'd compartmentalized it and focused on the job; his team had deserved his best.

Tension was heavy in the RV. The team had talked through the plan from every angle, trying to maximize the chances of success. But the weather and inability to see inside the bunkers drove up the risk. Blowing the doors and going in before Hammaker had time to react was their best plan.

Commander Stevens asked for a check from each team member, and all responded.

It was time.

"Alpha-one and -two, go!"

Max held his breath as two of the helmet-cam views started to move in toward the bunker doors. The ATF explosives specialists had the high-pressure job of rapidly checking the entries for motion sensors, pressure plates, and booby traps, then setting their own explosives to blow the doors. The two men quickly cleared the fluffy snow from around the doors.

"Alpha one, entry is clear."

"Alpha two, second bunker entry is clear."

"Copy one and two. Proceed."

The specialists attached their own devices and moved a safe distance from the doors, their camera views jolting as they jogged away.

"Alpha one in position."

"Alpha two in position."

Time to blow the doors.

"Copy one and two. Detonate on my count. Three, two, one, go!"

Snow exploded and filled the monitors. The RV was several hundred yards from the bunkers but gently jerked as the detonation waves hit it. Three seconds later the flying snow had settled, leaving them with views of crooked metal doors, fully detached from the bunkers.

"Blue entry teams A and B, GO!" said Stevens. Several more camera views jolted around as the men dashed toward the doors. The two explosives specialists stayed in position, their camera views steady on the doors.

Light shone out of each bunker, but Max couldn't make out anything inside. The door views were suddenly crowded with the green ghost shapes of the two entry teams as they approached. The entry team's cameras showed jostling views of their teammates' shoulders and helmets as they funneled in.

Shouts of *clear, clear, clear!* came through the RV's speakers. Max leaned closer, trying to make out what he was seeing on the cameras as the men covered the inside. Empty shelves. Empty frames. Some boxes and plastic bins.

No Thomas Hammaker.

Or Emma.

Max was suddenly exhausted. The tightly wound energy his tension had been building had vanished.

"Blue team A. Bunker one's clear."

"Blue team B. Bunker two is clear. No one's here."

It's empty. Hammaker cleaned it out.

"Fuck," stated the commander, tossing down his headset. "Let's go take a look. Jensen and Mendez, stay here." The woman and other man at the monitors nodded.

Max stepped out of the RV with Commander Stevens and Agents Keyes and Reed.

"God damn it," said Reed, stomping through the snow. "Do we know where he's gone?"

"If we knew that, we'd be there," said Keyes.

Max said nothing, his thoughts wound up as he considered Reed's question.

Where did Hammaker go?

We're back where we started: trying to figure out where and if a domestic terrorism act is about to take place.

He mashed his lips together to hold back a string of curses. Ahead, Reed was swearing enough for the whole group.

The commander dropped back to join Max at the rear of the group. "Thoughts?" he asked Max.

"Special Agent Reed has a colorful vocabulary," said Max, trudging through the snow.

"Were we given bad intel?" the commander asked in a low voice. "Or was this a distraction?"

I hadn't considered that.

Max thought back to their interview with Ricky Dowd, wondering if he'd deliberately misled them. Max hadn't thought he was lying to them. Usually his bullshit meter was pretty accurate.

"I don't know," he said. "I don't think the intel was bad. He could have cleaned out after seeing me and Noelle on his property."

Stevens touched his earpiece. "They report no tunnel found in either bunker. We've been idiots, watching and waiting for absolutely nothing. Hammaker's probably laughing from a hundred miles away."

They finally reached the bunkers. The SWAT teams had spread out, creating a perimeter a few yards outside the bunkers in case someone decided to surprise them. Reed and Keyes ducked their heads and went through one of the blown entries. Max and Commander Stevens headed toward the second bunker.

A blast of white-hot air blew Max to the side as the first bunker exploded.

I'm hit!

He landed in the snow, his breath knocked out of him, and rolled over, sucking air, his ears ringing. He held up a hand to block a bright light and realized the first bunker was on fire. Screams and shouts filled the air.

Where are Keyes and Reed?

36

What the fuck happened?

Noelle had been watching the FBI camera feeds in the sheriff's mobile command center, listening to the disappointment about finding empty bunkers. Then a bomb had gone off. Monitors flashed and they lost most of the feeds. A fire raged on the views that remained, unintelligible shouting from the site filling the RV.

"Holy fuck," whispered the county SWAT team leader, frozen as he stared at the monitors. Abruptly jumping into action, he'd yelled for the green team to get in the BearCat and dashed out of the RV. Noelle followed, running for her SUV.

It was a trap.

Where is Max?

She didn't have a headset or earpiece to listen with, and her arms shook as she drove behind the BearCat. She didn't know what was going on. After the longest silent minutes of her life, the armored transport stopped, and the sheriff's SWAT team swarmed out, racing toward the dying glow of the bunkers.

Where is he?

She parked and ran after them. Most of the flames were gone, but her lungs burned as she got closer. Heavy, acrid smoke hung in the air, snowflakes floating through it.

Or is that ash?

The area lit up as two portable lights switched on, dragged through the snow from the FBI's mobile command unit. Several SWAT agents maintained a perimeter. Three groups of agents huddled around people down in the snow. Orders were yelled. Agents tore back and forth. Two fire extinguishers were cast aside near the smoking bunker.

It was chaos.

Where is Max?

Noelle darted to the closest group working on an injured agent spread out in the snow. It took Noelle a few seconds to realize it was Agent Keyes, her face and scalp severely burned, her hair mostly gone. Agents bustled around her, desperate to help. She was wrapped in several emergency blankets. One agent pumped her chest while another hovered at her mouth. An agent lifted away part of a blanket to start an IV, and Noelle saw Keyes's clothes were burned away, her skin black and bloody.

She can't survive that.

The faces of the men doing CPR were grim.

Noelle stumbled away, her stomach threatening to empty itself into the snow. Snow battered her face, and she rubbed the icy cold into her cheeks, seeking its distraction. A similar group worked on another person nearby.

I can't see that again.

What if it's Max?

She swallowed the bile that crept up her throat and cautiously approached the other group. Another severely burned victim. Again covered in the silver blankets. But there was no energy around this group, and she watched someone pull the blanket over the victim's black and bloody head. She touched an agent's arm, startling him. "Who is that?"

"Reed. From the ATF."

Her heart cracked in pain as relief simultaneously poured through her that it wasn't Max.

"Do you know where Agent Rhodes is?" she asked.

The man looked over at the third group bustling around a victim. "Not sure."

Noelle followed his gaze to the group. At least they were still trying to help the victim. There had to be hope.

She made her legs move, taking her to the other group.

Please. If that's him, let him be okay.

Noelle scanned the area, the SWAT members easily identifiable from their heavy gear and helmets. The sheriff's SWAT team moved around the FBI members, checking for burns and injuries, taking over the perimeter and sending the wounded SWAT agents to their command center. "Don't put snow on your burn," she heard one say. "You'll make it worse."

Two agents stepped away from the third victim before Noelle reached him. She stopped them with a hand to one's chest.

"Who is that?" she asked, her heart in her throat.

"SAC Stevens," said the agent. "Our commander. He's gonna be okay. Concussion. Some contusions. He wasn't in the bunker when it went up."

"Do you know where Agent Rhodes is?"

One shook his head, but the other said, "Check the RV. He was injured."

"How badly?" Noelle forced out.

"He was walking, so can't be too bad. Keyes and Reed were inside when it went off. Everyone else was back a bit."

Relief nearly made her legs give out. "Thank you."

Stevens appeared to be talking to the men grouped around him, so she turned toward the FBI's RV. Someone had driven it in from the staging area.

As she got closer, she saw a familiar profile.

Noelle blinked rapidly, forcing back tears.

An agent was slathering something on Max's face as he leaned against the RV.

What would I do if he'd been killed?

It would have left a giant hole in her soul. The man had slipped under her defenses and set up camp in her heart.

It happened so fast.

He spotted her and pushed the agent's hand from his face. He strode toward her through the snow, but she saw he was unsteady.

"Oh my God." She halted and stared at his face. Two-thirds of it was bright red, and a large part of his beard was gone. He was missing an eyebrow. And some lashes. Some of his hair had burned away, and the agent had slathered something on the back of his head, making more hair stick out.

"That bad?" he asked, lifting a hand to touch his hair.

"Don't touch!" She pulled his arm down and wrapped herself around him.

He's so lucky. I'm so lucky.

"Am I hurting you?" she asked.

"Not really."

She let go and lurched back.

"I'm kidding. Come here." He enveloped her with a hug, and she felt him shake. "I thought I was dead," he said in a rough voice.

"He's probably got a concussion," said the agent, who'd approached and was putting more goo on his neck. "He landed on his back and hit his head, but the snow may have softened that. He's lucky. SAC Stevens's head hit a rock under the snow. You're gonna hurt tomorrow," he told Max. "Bruises will pop up that you had no idea were coming."

"I'll take you to the hospital." Noelle tugged on him.

"No. I'm not leaving until everyone is taken care of," said Max. "I'm not the priority here." He glanced at the other agent. "Go help someone else. I'm okay."

Noelle held back her response that he was a priority to her; she understood what he felt.

"I wasn't far from the first bunker," Max told her. "Reed and Keyes had just gone inside. Either they triggered something, or it was on a delayed timer."

"To give a false sense of security and cause the most casualties. This was murder." Noelle looked Max in the eye. "Reed didn't make it. And it doesn't look good for Keyes. I'm sorry."

He closed his eyes and exhaled. "Shit."

"I know."

"No one will go near the second bunker," Max said. "They're bringing out more specialists tomorrow. They'll disarm it if needed." He grimaced. "The two ATF agents that blew the doors are blaming themselves, believing they missed a booby trap." He shook his head. "The bunkers were buried in snow. No one could blame them."

"Did we act too fast?" Noelle whispered.

"I don't know," said Max. "I requested that someone find Ricky Dowd. I need to know if we were deliberately sent into a trap."

"I didn't feel he was lying," said Noelle.

"Maybe he was used," said Max. "Someone knew we'd interview him after Chisholm was identified. Was he misled somehow?"

"By Hammaker?" asked Noelle. "Dowd said he hadn't seen the man in years—oh!" She told Max about the photos of him found in Hammaker's room.

"More evidence that he had it in for me." A stunned look crossed his red face. "Was I supposed to die here?"

"I can't see how Hammaker would have arranged that," said Noelle. "But we're back where we started, trying to figure out what big event is going to happen . . . or was this their plan all along? A federal agent is dead, and another probably won't make it. It could have been a lot more."

"You think this is what the chatter was leading up to?" asked Max.

Noelle thought for a long moment. "My gut tells me no."

37

The next morning, Noelle watched the coffee stream out of her machine and deeply inhaled the scent, trying to jump-start the caffeine. Max was still sleeping, which was understandable. It'd been a long night.

Once all the wounded had been removed from the scene at the bunkers, Max was finally willing to be driven to the ER. Under the bright hospital lights, he had looked as if he'd stood too close to the sun.

While they waited for the doctor, Max asked a nurse for a razor and shaved one side of his face so it would match the side where his beard had burned off. His hand shook, and after he made a second bleeding cut, Noelle took the razor away and finished it herself.

She jokingly offered to shave off his other eyebrow, but he suggested it be trimmed short. She found some scissors and did an awkward job of it. She also trimmed some of his hair. His coat had scorch marks, and he had no idea what had happened to his hat.

It probably disintegrated.

The doctor had pronounced that he didn't have a concussion.

Thank you, snow.

Max was given some ointment for his burns and turned down the prescription painkiller. The doctor's expression indicated that was a decision Max would later regret. Noelle told the doctor to send it to the pharmacy anyway.

They'd gotten home at four in the morning and Max had fallen asleep instantly. Noelle had lain awake, trying to put the sight of Keyes's and Reed's burned bodies out of her mind. Keyes had been pronounced dead at the hospital.

Then Noelle worried about Emma, wondering where she would turn up. If she turned up. After last night, Noelle didn't know what to think about Emma's relationship with Hammaker.

During Max's time at the hospital, reporters had swarmed the emergency room, full of questions about what had happened on Hammaker's property. Over and over, they were referred to the sheriff's public information officer, who Noelle suspected would purposefully ignore his phone until he'd been briefed later that morning.

The mission had been a mess.

Fingers would be pointed. Lawsuits would be filed.

But Max had survived.

Her phone vibrated on the counter. Her first instinct was to ignore it, considering she hadn't had any coffee, but she flipped it over to see who was calling.

Cory Johnson. Mercy's FBI informant.

Noelle immediately answered. "Cory? Are you okay?"

"Detective Marshall?" asked the woman. "I left a message for Agent Kilpatrick, but I don't know if she'll get back to me, and I need to talk to someone."

Noelle was suddenly as alert as if she'd been poked with a syringe of caffeine.

"I can help you. What's going on, Cory?"

"Is it true what they're saying? Did a bomb go off and kill some FBI agents? Is Agent Kilpatrick okay?" Her questions ran together.

"Agent Kilpatrick wasn't there," said Noelle. "She's fine." She hesitated, not wanting to release any other information.

"Oh, thank God." Relief was palpable in her voice. "I was so worried."

"How did you hear about it, Cory?"

"I saw it online."

Noelle had already checked online for news of the explosions. The available information was vague, referring to an explosion of unknown origin on private property, but it did say that two federal agents had been killed. "One was an ATF agent and the other was FBI," she told Cory.

"That's what I wanted to talk to Agent Kilpatrick about," she said after a long pause. "I talked to one of those men last night. You know, one from the group of three I saw in the bar a while back. Where Rachel . . ." She couldn't finish.

"You saw the man that went home with Rachel?" Noelle was stunned.

"No. One of the others."

Max padded into the kitchen, his face drawn with pain. Noelle pointed emphatically at the little orange pill bottle on the counter. He shook his head.

"Hang on a second, Cory." Noelle muted the conversation.

"Cory?" Max asked, his eyes narrowing. "Cory Johnson?"

"Yes. Take the medication, and I'll tell you why she's called."

Indecision warred on his face. He finally opened the bottle and grumpily dry-swallowed two.

I knew I'd have to bargain.

She unmuted the call. "Cory, I'm going to put you on speaker. Agent Rhodes is now here with me."

"You're at work already?"

"Well, a lot happened last night, as you know. We're busy," Noelle answered, not about to tell the woman that Max was standing in her kitchen. She touched her phone's screen and set it on the counter.

"Go ahead and tell us about the man you talked to last night," said Noelle, holding Max's gaze. "The one who was at the bar with the man who went home with Rachel."

Max's lopsided eyebrows shot up and he winced.

"I saw him come in and immediately recognized him," said Cory. "He took a seat—"

"Why didn't you call the police?" asked Max. "Or notify one of us?"

"You know how long it takes the police to respond there?" snapped Cory. "And this guy looked ready to bolt. He was looking over his shoulder and checking every shadow. I decided to just give him some attention. You know, drinks, conversation, flirt a bit. It always works."

"What happened, Cory?" asked Noelle, getting impatient.

"Well, I took his order and doubled the booze. Brought him some sliders that I told him had been made accidentally. He relaxed after a bit, but was still watching everyone who came in. He'd taken a seat at the end of the bar where he could see everything that was going on inside."

"Did you get a name?"

"Chet. Not sure how true that was. Anyway, on his second drink I finally say, 'Chet, you're looking around like you expect a lion to jump out and bite you.' He laughed and said, 'Something like that.' I turn up the sugar, and we chat for a while, but all I'm thinking about is that he might know who killed Rachel."

Max opened his mouth, and Noelle shook her head. "Don't," she whispered, knowing he was about to ask again why she hadn't called the police. Noelle knew Cory wasn't the type of person to trust most law enforcement. Mercy had said she was very flighty. The fact that she'd called Noelle was huge.

"Anyway, he sort of admitted that he was avoiding some people. And when I pointed out that he was in the wrong place to avoid anyone, he said they were all supposed to be out of town. And that he'd been lying low until tonight. 'Sounds like you need to celebrate,' I told him. By now I'm laying it on pretty thick, and I can tell he's getting interested."

She uses sex appeal to get what she wants.

Noelle was torn between feeling sorry for the woman and being impressed at how skillfully Cory could wield her tools.

"He told me I needed to watch the news the next few days. Stuff was going to happen. I pushed for more information, but he said he didn't know. He finally admitted he'd been about to do something with a group but backed out, and that was why he was lying low. He was afraid they'd be angry with him. I teased him and tried to draw out more information, but he wasn't giving it. I don't think he actually knew any details like when and where."

"What about names?" asked Noelle.

"Every time I steered the conversation that way, he shut down, so I backed off. But he did keep repeating that no one would get hurt. But I've got to tell you, Detective, I think he was trying to convince himself. I think he was hiding from this group because he believed whatever they had planned was going to hurt people."

Noelle could tell Max was biting his tongue.

"What else can you tell us?"

"As he got more drunk, he kept mumbling, 'It's too late. It's already on.' Then this morning I saw online what happened overnight, and I knew I needed to call. Do you think that's what he was talking about? Obviously people got hurt."

Noelle eyed Max's burned face. A bruise was starting to darken on his neck.

"Maybe," she said.

"He paid in cash, so I didn't get a full name. But I followed him out to the parking lot, and I got his license plate. I'll text you a photo."

Max's eyes widened. "That's fantastic, Cory."

"You'll find him, right?" begged Cory. "He'll tell you who killed Rachel?" Her voice cracked and she started to cry. "I knew I had to just keep stringing him along and let you guys catch up to him later. I was afraid that if I asked who he was with that other night I saw him, he'd vanish. Sounds like he knows who set off that bomb that killed those agents overnight."

"We'll see where the license plate leads us, Cory. You did really good," Noelle told her. "I'll let you know what we find out. Anything else?"

"I feel so bad about not calling anyone right away," Cory whispered. "Maybe those agents wouldn't be dead."

"What time did he come in?" asked Max.

"It was nearly eleven."

"We were already on scene by then," said Max. "I don't think you could have done anything to change what happened."

"You were there?" Cory whispered.

"Yes." His word was clipped.

"I'm so sorry." She sniffled loudly.

Noelle comforted her for a few more seconds, then ended the call. Max handed Noelle the ready cup of coffee and then pushed a few buttons to start another for himself. While he waited, he looked at the license plate photo on her phone and sent off a text.

"How are you feeling?" Noelle had noticed he was moving one of his arms very carefully.

"Sore. I've got pain in every limb." He scrolled on his phone, scowling. "Two more agents are in the hospital with breathing issues. Probably some sort of chemicals in the air after the explosion. I've got twenty texts and two dozen emails." He looked up. "Let's get showered and go in. It's going to be a busy day." His phone vibrated with another text, and his face fell. "The license plate Cory sent us was stolen."

"Shit," said Noelle. She'd had high hopes. "But maybe he'll return to the bar. Sounds like he might have a thing for Cory. I think she'll call right away next time."

His phone buzzed again. "What the—that's weird." Confusion shone in his eyes.

"What is it?"

"Garrison. My boss. He just sent a location to our office group text using the satellite option on his phone."

Noelle looked over his shoulder as a message from Mercy popped up in the group text.

Jeff, you ok? Mistake?

"Mercy thought it was odd too." The two of them stared at the screen, waiting for him to reply.

"The location he sent puts him in the middle of nowhere," said Noelle.

"I know he went out of town a day or two ago with some friends," said Max. His phone rang. It was Mercy, but she was calling the group.

"Mercy?" he answered on speaker. "What's going on?"

"I sent a bunch of texts on my own to Jeff," she said. "They're not going through. I tried to call too."

"He's in the boonies. He had to use satellite to send that location."

"And my texts should have been delivered to him that way. They weren't."

A beeping sound indicated that Melissa, the Bend FBI branch's office manager, had joined the call. "Anyone get a hold of Jeff?" she asked.

"I can't get through," said Mercy. "I know he's been scheduled off for part of this week. Where did he go?"

"He's on a retreat," said Melissa. "He went with a bunch of government officials and their families."

"That's right," said Mercy. "The location notification must have been a mistake."

"Wait," said Max, his voice sounding choked. He covered his eyes with one hand. "Who's he with?"

"Ummm. It's at the district attorney's cabin. Our mayor's there. The city manager—"

"Judges?" asked Max.

Alarm tightened Noelle's throat.

"I think two are judges," said Melissa. "And I believe the governor was going too."

Max's fierce gaze met Noelle's, and he took a deep breath. "Judge Holtz told me he was going to the district attorney's cabin for a getaway. His wife said she didn't feel like being social and wanted to get out of the state instead.

"I think this could be where the terrorism event is going to happen—or has happened. It makes sense with what Ricky Dowd said about creating a vacuum at the top. Dammit! Families and children are there! All Jeff managed to do was send us the location before . . ."

Max didn't know how to finish the sentence, Cory's words running through his head. "It's too late. It's already on," she'd claimed the man in the bar had said.

Are Jeff and the others still alive?

38

Emma jerked awake.

Boom. Boom-boom. Boom.

That's gunfire!

It kept going. She curled into a ball and pushed across the dirt floor into the corner farthest from the door. The shots weren't close, but they weren't far away either.

After what felt like an eternity, but was probably less than two minutes, they stopped. She waited, straining to hear more sounds. It was silent.

She exhaled and slumped back down on the ground, suddenly exhausted and wanting to go back to sleep, but her brain wouldn't slow down.

How long have I been here?

She suspected she'd spent two nights in the cell. Twice she had slept for what seemed like long periods. And once, someone had come in.

He'd yelled at her to get away from the door and stand against the far wall. Said he had a gun and would shoot her if she didn't obey. She'd stood where he said. The door slowly opened, and the tip of a pistol showed, then a face.

She didn't know him. He was probably in his mid-twenties. Short. Thin. Acne. His gaze was apprehensive, as if he expected her to lunge at him.

"Take one step and I'll shoot!"

"I won't move."

He'd tossed a small bag to one side and more protein bars spilled out. "Hand me the water," he'd said to someone still outside the door. Several gallon jugs of water followed the bars. He'd gestured at her nasty-smelling bucket. "Pick that up and put it in the middle of the room, then go back to your position." She'd done as he asked, and he'd carefully come forward to grab it, never taking his gaze from her.

"I'm not going—"

"Shut up!" He'd waved the gun and grabbed the plastic bucket, walking backward to the door. He'd set the bucket outside the door. "Give me the other one," he'd said, and another's handle had been placed in his hand. He'd thrown it across the room at her, and she'd jerked out of the way.

"Watch out!" she'd snapped at him.

A second man had suddenly appeared in the hall behind the first. He was older. Probably forty. He had a graying beard, and his shoulders seemed as wide as the doorway. He'd scowled and looked her up and down. "What'd you do?" he'd said to the first man.

"Nothing." His gaze had warned her not to say anything.

The man with the beard had looked to one side in the hall and jerked his head. "Come look."

Then Uncle Tommy appeared.

Emma couldn't breathe. Her eyes had locked with his, and he had a gash on one cheek.

"She's doing great," said the large man.

Uncle Tommy had said nothing. The first man had stepped out of the room and slammed the door shut. Locks slid and clanked.

Emma had launched herself across the room and beaten on the door with both hands. "Uncle Tommy!" she'd shrieked, yelling his name over and over.

No one ever came back.

The gunfire abruptly started again.

Boom! Boom! Boom-boom!

Emma plugged her ears but could still hear it. Then it stopped.

She waited for more, wondering if people were target shooting, but it'd sounded like a lot of weapons had started firing at once, over and over. The gunfire had been the first noise she'd heard since the man took her bucket and she'd seen Uncle Tommy.

She asked herself for the millionth time why he hadn't said anything, why he hadn't told them to let her go.

It doesn't make sense.

She'd pondered the cut on his cheek but had no answers. He could have gotten in a fight or walked into something. He'd looked fine other than that.

The sounds of locks sliding and clicking caught her attention. "Get against the far wall!" yelled someone. "Face the wall. If you don't, I will shoot you dead!"

The voice was different from that of the young man who'd taken her bucket. She did as he said and faced the wall. A second later the door squeaked as it opened. "Don't move!" he ordered.

She wanted to peek over her shoulder.

"Put your hands behind your back."

Emma paused. It sounded like something a police officer would say.

"Do it!"

She did it. He grabbed her hands. She felt something wrap around them and then heard the distinctive sounds of a zip tie. Then a strip of fabric came around and pressed against her mouth.

"Open up."

They're gagging me!

She opened, and the cloth went between her teeth. The man tied it at the back of her head. Her tongue touched and pushed it, and then bile rose in her throat. Emma breathed through her nose, trying to stay calm and pretend the gag wasn't about to make her throw up.

"Let's go." He grabbed one elbow and turned her around. The young man with the acne was at the door, his pistol aimed her way.

The man holding her elbow seemed about the same age but was taller. Both men wore heavy canvas coats, camo pants, and leather work boots.

Outside her cell, they walked down a short, dark hallway that smelled as musty as her room. At the end, one pushed open a door, and light streamed in. Emma winced and her lids screwed shut at the brightness of the snow and sun. The men pulled on her arms, and she stumbled forward, trying to force one eye open, then the other.

"She's a kid," muttered the taller man. "It's not right."

"He said no one would get hurt, Ezra," said Acne Man.

"There shouldn't be kids," Ezra mumbled under his breath.

Emma nearly corrected them by saying that she was eighteen. But something in their hushed tones kept her quiet.

The snow was well trampled. Lots of boot prints. She glanced over her shoulder and saw they'd come out from the bottom level of an old cabin built into a steep hill. She'd been right: Her cell's walls were against dirt. The cabin had a thick layer of moss on its roof, and the few windows she could see were dark with dust and dirt. The roof over the front porch sagged, and steps were missing. But a lot of vehicles were parked around it, so several people had to be inside. There were probably ten pickups and SUVs.

Acne Man jerked on her arm to make her face forward as they continued through the snow and between the tall pines.

"Where are we going?" she mumbled through her gag.

"None of your business," said Ezra.

"I think if you're making me go somewhere, then it is my business." The snarky, almost unintelligible words out of her mouth surprised her. She'd never been one for back talk.

"Shut up," said Acne Man, with a sharp jerk on her arm.

They fed me. They gave me water. Uncle Tommy is here somewhere.

She didn't think they would hurt her.

They plodded on for a few minutes. Emma kept her eye on the trail, wondering how many people had tromped through the snow.

The roofline of another cabin started to show through the trees. As they drew closer, Emma saw it was newer than the one they'd left and much bigger. In fact, it was huge. A covered porch wrapped around the two sides in her view, and rocking chairs and little tables dotted it, inviting people to relax and enjoy the outdoors. It had a green metal roof and windows that were gigantic and shiny and clean.

The trail they'd been following split. Some boot prints went toward the back of the home, but the men followed the footprints that went toward the front. They went up a bit of a hill and reached the cabin's driveway. The vehicles in the driveway were in a different class from the ones she'd seen at the old place. Mercedes, BMW, Land Rover. All SUVs.

No pickups here.

They took her up the steps to the front door, stomping their feet to shake off the snow. And then Emma noticed the man on the porch. He must have been watching them from the moment they'd come out of the woods. He wore a rifle slung over his shoulder and a pistol on his thigh.

He's a guard.

"Mark's waiting for her," Acne Man said to the guard. The guard looked her over and opened the double front doors. They stepped into a grand entry, its walls lined with pale wood and soaring to high ceilings and a huge chandelier.

Emma gawked. She'd never been inside such a nice place.

Ezra pulled on her arm, and she followed them down a wide hall. Ahead were tall windows with an amazing view. And she heard someone speaking loudly, as if lecturing a class. "Unchecked authority *should not* exist! That leads to unjust decisions! So many of us have been victims of this abuse of power!"

As they reached the end of the hall, Emma was suddenly in a huge room with big windows, where she stared at a half dozen men sitting on the floor, their arms tied behind them and gags in their mouths.

Their gazes were full of fear.

Then she realized more people were looking at her. A dozen or so more men stood in the room, all with a rifle or pistol or both.

The men on the floor are prisoners.

"There she is," said one of the standing men, whom she recognized as having been in the hall when Acne Man threw the bucket at her. His voice had been the one declaiming abuse of power. He was a large man, and his bulk gave the impression that there was muscle under his coat, not fat. "See, Mac?" He stroked his graying beard as he grinned.

Emma followed his gaze to where Uncle Tommy sat on a barstool at a gigantic kitchen island. He leaned on the island, a cup of coffee before him. Looking as if this were the most normal situation in the world. "I see her, Mark," he said in a monotone. And sipped his coffee.

What is happening?

"Sit her over there," said the large man.

"You don't want her with the others?" asked Acne Man.

"I said *over there*."

Emma was pushed into a large easy chair near the line of men sitting on the floor. She frowned at the debris of white chunks and powder all over the floor and her chair. She looked up and saw several holes in the ceiling. They were everywhere. Some of the men on the floor had white powder in their hair.

They shot at the ceiling to make them behave.

She shifted, trying to get her hands, still behind her back, into a better position in the chair. It was impossible. She scooted forward until she was perched on the end of its seat.

"Cut her hands," said Uncle Tommy. "She can't sit like that."

Acne Man looked to the man with the beard whom Tommy had called Mark. "Do it."

He took out a knife and sliced the zip tie behind her back. Her arms fell to her sides, and she sighed, rubbing her wrists. The gag was still in her mouth, and she looked from Uncle Tommy to the bearded man, hoping one of them would tell someone to remove it.

"The gag stays," said Mark. "Any movement from you and the zip ties go back on."

"In the front," added Uncle Tommy.

Mark glared at him but agreed, "In the front." He cleared his throat and continued his speech about abuse of power. "We're here to show that they can be reached! That they can be knocked down! That they are vulnerable." He paced through the big room, one hand on his rifle, staring at each of the men on the floor. "The weak will step down; the strong will rise." At times he'd turn to Uncle Tommy and say, "Right, Mac?" and Uncle Tommy would agree. *Uncle Tommy sounds as if he's lying, just pacifying Mark.*

Emma studied every person in the room. The men who were standing had weapons and held the power. But something very nervous lurked in their eyes. They shifted their feet and occasionally glanced at one another. Not one of them would meet her gaze.

On the kitchen island was a clear food storage container full of cell phones.

Two of the men sitting on the floor had split lips and dried blood on their chins.

Those have to be their phones.

Some were dressed in T-shirts and flannel pajama pants, as if they'd been pulled out of bed. Something about them was different.

They're city.

Those are their vehicles out front.

Emma had spent 90 percent of her life around people who lived in rural areas. She looked at the standing men and knew they belonged to the pickups at the old cabin.

A baby's wail sounded through the house.

Astonishment shot through her, and the men on the floor all shifted, concern emanating from them.

"Tell her to keep it quiet," said Mark, and he pointed at Ezra, who'd helped escort Emma to the house. Ezra turned and went through the kitchen, past Uncle Tommy, and opened a door on the other side.

Emma choked behind her gag.

When the door opened, she'd had a glimpse of three small children and two women. She knew instinctively that there were more locked in the room.

What is happening here?

39

“Here we go again,” Noelle said under her breath.

She stood in the back of the room with Max and Mercy Kilpatrick, listening as the SWAT commander spoke to his team. Earlier the Portland FBI SWAT team had sent two members ahead to recon the area from which Jeff Garrison had sent his location. The rest of the team members looked physically tired, but everyone had determination in their eyes. They wanted to go out there again, they wanted to find who'd killed their fellow agents.

“How do we prevent another fuckup like last night's?” Max asked softly.

“It won't happen again,” said Noelle with a certainty she didn't feel. At least it was daylight and the snow had stopped. FBI SWAT team leader Stevens was still in the hospital with a minor skull fracture and concussion. The second-in-command of the team had stepped up. Special Agent Pete Preston. Now the team leader.

From what Noelle had seen so far, the command transition was seamless. All attention was on Preston, and he spoke with confidence. He put up enlarged satellite photos showing two cabins among dense forest.

“Here's what we've got so far from recon,” said Preston. “The larger cabin is where we believe SAC Garrison sent out his location. It's owned by district attorney Julie Ferrandis. We'd hoped to stage at the smaller cabin two hundred yards away, but recon reports it has a dozen vehicles parked at it. They photographed all the license plates, and we're running them now. They cleared the cabin, finding evidence of recent habitation. Foodstuffs. Sleeping bags. They've currently moved on to the second cabin." Preston's phone buzzed and he touched the screen. "I've got a list of the vehicle owners. Looks like they're mostly from Deschutes County, and several of the names have been associated with militias in the past." Preston was rattling off names when Max visibly flinched at one.

"Agent Preston!" Max took a step forward. "Mark Bourdon was brought up as a possible suspect in the car bombing of Judge Howard Holtz. He was released from prison eight months ago, I believe. Holtz ID'd him as the most likely suspect based on his actions toward Holtz in the courtroom. It's very possible he's responsible for the murder of the man in the trunk. And two other murders we've been investigating."

"Thank you, Agent Rhodes. I'll move him to the top of the investigation list." Preston paused and squinted at Max. "Your recovery status?" Noelle wasn't surprised the agent had asked. Half of Max's face was still bright red, and he looked as if he'd been beaten. Colorful bruising had appeared on his cheekbone and neck.

"I'm fine. Just a little toasted."

A quiet ripple of grim amusement went through the room of agents.

An image of Special Agent Keyes's burned body flashed in Noelle's mind, and she fought back a wave of nausea.

That could have been Max.

Another agent approached Preston, a piece of paper in his hand, and they had a quiet discussion for a long moment. Preston took the paper and turned back to the room. "Our recon team has done some scouting of the second cabin. More vehicles are parked at this cabin, and recon reports a guard with a rifle at the front entrance and another on the rear deck."

Mutters rose in the room. Preston held up a hand for quiet.

"Our belief that county and state leaders are in that cabin has been confirmed by again running the license plates." He looked at the paper and started to read. A grumble went up as he read SAC Jeff Garrison's name and was quickly followed by a louder reaction at the name of Oregon's governor. DA Ferrandis, Bend's mayor Doug Ross, judges Howard Holtz and Cassandra Tedesco. "Several of these people have been close friends for years. It's believed that the families of all these officials are present in the cabin, and that the guards indicate a hostage situation has taken place." He nodded at three team members who had stood and gathered their things when he said "hostage." "I want our hostage negotiators on scene ASAP. I think we've got a fantastic team here, but I've also requested they activate HRT out of Quantico."

Hostage Rescue Team.

Noelle glanced at Mercy and Max. Both agents had their gazes locked on Preston, apparently not surprised at the request for help from the East Coast. The energy in the room was restless, and agents shifted in their seats.

"Has anyone laid eyes on the hostages?" asked an agent.

"[illegible] has not seen the hostages," said Preston.

There's a possibility they're already dead.

"Let's head out," said Preston. "We've got an hour drive."

What if we're too late?

A few minutes later, Max and Mercy were in Noelle's vehicle as she drove. The SWAT team led the way, and several vehicles of agents followed, spaced out a bit so it wouldn't appear that a large law enforcement action was underway. But there was no hiding the mobile command center RV or the BearCat. Noelle hoped word wouldn't travel ahead to the cabins that something big was about to happen.

"Information on Mark Bourdon was just sent out," said Mercy, looking at her phone. "He's stayed out of trouble since his release eight months ago, but he hasn't had a job."

"At least not a job on the books," added Noelle.

"Could be," Mercy continued. "His address is in Prineville, and he attended all check-ins with his parole officer until two weeks ago. The officer says he's been unable to reach him. And of course, under 'Associates' are Thomas Hammaker and a few of the same names that Agent Preston read off in the briefing."

"But Hammaker wasn't linked to any of the vehicles at the first cabin?" asked Noelle.

Mercy paused as she double-checked the list. "He's not. It's possible he's not there."

"I don't understand," said Noelle. "Maybe he rode with someone else."

"What was Bourdon doing during the two weeks his parole officer couldn't reach him?" asked Max. He rode in the passenger seat and was applying more salve to his burns.

"Probably planning a car bombing, a few murders, and whatever is happening up at the DA's cabin," said Noelle. "I think it's all tied to Hammaker too."

"Did you hear anything from Emma Chambers?" asked Mercy.

Noelle's heart contracted. "No. She's been silent." She wondered how long she'd carry guilt for not acting sooner to help the girl.

"I'm sorry, Noelle."

"She'll turn up," said Noelle, trying to convince herself.

"Information is coming in on the possible hostages," said Max, studying his phone. "They're gathering data on everyone's immediate families, trying to get an idea of who and how many could be in the cabin. Right now they're estimating eleven adults and six kids. Ages six months to nine years." He paused. "I met Judge Holtz's wife and twins. I have no doubt they are in there."

"At least Garrison isn't married," said Mercy. "He used to date Judge Tedesco, but now he's good friends with her husband."

"Everyone else is married," said Max. "They've been contacting their offices, trying to find out if coworkers knew if their families went."

Noelle gripped the steering wheel. After the disaster last night, she prayed today's operation would not be deadly.

An hour later a staging area had been set up near the first cabin, blocking the road that led to both cabins. Two special agents cleared the first cabin again and stayed on-site, keeping watch for any returning kidnappers. "There appears to be a cell under the cabin," said Preston as they grouped for a briefing outdoors. "Someone was held there. They found bottled water, protein bars, and a bathroom bucket. There's a well-broken path in the snow that leads from cabin one to cabin two."

The FBI SWAT team was fully geared up, listening intently. Another dozen law enforcement personnel, including Noelle, Max, and Mercy, wore ballistics vests and helmets. The additional personnel were there for support and to back up the SWAT team, and they would handle any arrests. Each had a shield, and several of them had AR-15s slung over their shoulders. Everyone wore an earpiece, a microphone, and a radio.

Preston had the large satellite photos and was marking them up, assigning his team. "Repeat, Blue-seven," he said into his mic, listening hard as he stepped back from the photos on the folding table. "Permission granted, Blue-seven and -eight."

Preston looked at the group. "The recon team is following one of the guards who left his position at the front door to take a leak."

"Catch him with his pants down," mumbled one of the team.

"We have the cabin's building plans from the city," said Preston. "But knowledge of what's happening inside would be priceless."

A woman appeared in the mobile command center's doorway. "Negotiators are ready, sir."

"I'll let you know when your speaker is in place," Preston told her. "I want more intel first."

Noelle knew the negotiators would start with a loudspeaker outside the cabin, essentially a long-distance bullhorn, requesting that the kidnappers use a provided radio for communication.

Preston touched his earpiece. "Copy, Blue-seven. Bring him in." He looked at the assembled team. "We've got him. Went off without a hitch."

Several of the team bumped fists, and Max grinned at Noelle and Mercy.

"The guard says that if anyone misses him at his position, they'll assume he split," said Preston. "Says the leader is already pissed about someone who left. Let's move his vehicle in case they come looking for him at the first cabin."

A few minutes later, the two SWAT team members appeared from the woods, escorting a very tall man in a heavy coat and hat.

Noelle gasped.

I know him.

"That's Trevor Baylor," she told Max and Mercy. "Evan and I interviewed him about being at the party location where Michael Munoz's body was found. This is the last place I'd expect to find someone like him." Noelle strode toward the commander as she studied the young man. His shoulders were slumped, and his cheeks were wet from tears. "I didn't want to do it. They made me. I really haven't done anything," he kept repeating.

Another connection to the Michael Munoz murder.

40

The door closed to the room where Emma had seen the children and women. Her gaze flew to Uncle Tommy, and finally some emotion showed as he looked her right in the eye and gave the smallest shake of his head.

He's not happy about what's happening.

Emma didn't understand why he didn't do something about it. Then she realised he was the only man—besides the hostages—who didn't have a weapon.

It didn't make sense.

The baby crying in the other room suddenly went quiet, and one of the men on the floor slumped his shoulders, shaking his head.

It must be his child.

Ezra came out of the room, a dark look on his face.

"What did you do?" The shout was barely understandable behind the man's gag. It was the one Emma thought was the father. He lurched forward, trying to get his legs and feet underneath him.

"If you ever want to see your family again, sit down!" ordered Mark. He pointed his pistol at the man on the floor. "What happened?" he asked Ezra.

"She's nursing the baby now. That shut it up." Ezra leered at the father. "She's got great boobs."

The father collapsed back to sitting and refused to look at Ezra.

A movement in the corner of her eye made Emma look out the large windows to the wraparound deck. A guard had paused outside, his rifle on his shoulder. He continued his stroll after watching through the glass for a few moments.

It's like a prison.

Mark strode over and kicked the knee of one hostage. "Holtz! Your judicial immunity doesn't exist here. You're at our level now. We will take the accountability we're owed."

The blond man looked up at Mark but didn't say anything.

Mark squatted in front of him, and Emma knew he was showing off for the other men in the room.

He's enjoying this.

"Now who's got the upper hand?" Mark whispered loudly, leaning toward the man Emma assumed was a judge. "How's that make you feel?" His voice made her skin crawl. "How would you like to be locked up at my whim?"

A large man in pajama bottoms next to Holtz shifted and coughed behind his gag.

He did that on purpose.

Mark turned his attention on him. "What's that, Guv'ner? You don't like the way I talk to one of your lackeys?" Mark spit on the man's bare feet, making him flinch. "You're no different than me. But you believe your power makes you better than me." He stood and glared at the six men. "Abuse of power," he shouted as more spit flew from his mouth. "I declare all of you guilty!" He raised his hands and turned to his men. "See how easy that was? Anyone can pass judgment. But first we need to get rid of the current abusers. We've all been waiting for that sign that it's time for a change." He looked at the six men. "And this is my sign."

What's he going to do?

"Get the other judge and the DA out here," he ordered Ezra, who headed back to the room where the baby had cried.

Mark stopped in front of one of the gagged men and shook his head. "Don't know what two of you were thinking by marrying women like that. They walk around with your balls in their purses, and you let them."

Ezra returned with two women, both gagged but with their hands zip-tied in front. One was in red flannel pajamas and the other in yoga pants and a long-sleeved T-shirt.

"On the floor!" ordered Mark.

The women awkwardly dropped down, exchanging looks with the male hostages. One woman eyed Emma with surprise and then concern in her gaze.

"Now you two without balls can go in with the other women and kids." Mark chuckled, his eyes sparkling as the men got to their feet.

"You too." He pointed at Emma. "Follow them. Zip-tie her," he told Acne Man.

"Leave her hands in front," added Uncle Tommy.

Acne Man roughly grabbed for her hands and then yanked the zip tie too tight, and Emma gasped. Uncle Tommy was immediately on his feet. "Do it right, you shithead!" he roared at Acne Man.

Acne Man looked at Mark, who nodded. He dug a knife out of his pocket, flicked the blade open, and sawed through the ties. Emma stood frozen, expecting to be cut. A second zip tie went on, and Mark shoved her in the back. She stumbled toward the door where Ezra waited.

He slammed the door behind her, and Emma found herself in a small room. Three women, two men, and six children. Everyone stared at her.

A woman holding a baby slipped her own gag out of her mouth. "Where did you come from, honey?" she whispered.

41

"According to Mr. Baylor," said Commander Preston, "there are eleven men inside, one guard outside—now that he's left—and seventeen hostages. Everyone is healthy except a few men who fought back and were punched in the face for it."

Max briefly closed his eyes.

So many lives at stake.

"He told us there was an early-morning raid to catch the occupants off guard, and they fired their weapons into the ceiling to bring people under control." He took a deep breath. "Everyone is armed. Most with more than one weapon."

"Why the fuck did they do this?" asked an agent.

"Mr. Baylor is a little unclear on the exact reason why," Preston said with a grimace. "Mark Bourdon brought this group of men together. At first it was just a political thing—get together and bitch and moan with like-minded folk. Discuss how they want the world to be changed. But then Bourdon talked about taking action, and things turned into more of a militia-type organization. Mr. Baylor states he was caught up in it but then he started to suspect that Bourdon had some personal vendettas he was using this group for."

"You mean Baylor and the rest are just a bunch of followers," said Max. "They don't think for themselves. Are the others in there starting to sour like Baylor did?"

"He's probably happy we got him out," muttered Noelle.

"He said there's been talk," said Preston. "Not a mutiny, but people who just want out. They don't like what they're seeing, and this isn't what they signed up for."

"They were fooled into coming out here with arms and taking families hostage?" asked Mercy. "That's a bunch of bull."

"Mr. Baylor was told it would be government officials. He was surprised to find families."

"So he was fine with killing a bunch of bureaucrats," said an agent.

"Mr. Baylor claims he was told this was just to threaten them, scare them. Enough to make them leave their jobs. But once he was on-site, it became clear that Bourdon had some personal axes to grind."

"Do the others feel this way about Bourdon?" asked Noelle. "Will they back down if offered the chance?"

"That's what the negotiators are about to find out," said Preston.

He pulled out the cabin plans and pointed. "Mr. Baylor says that six men are gagged and tied up on the floor in this main room. The children and women are shut in this room next to the kitchen. We've got entrances here, here, and here. Lots of windows too. Our snipers have confirmed that they can see people in this main room, but there are sheer curtains covering most of its windows and the entrance to the deck. They don't have visual access to the room with the children. In the meantime, we're going to get our perimeter in place and entry team ready."

Preston touched his earpiece. "The speaker's in place. Time for negotiations to start."

"Attention inside the cabin," came a man's amplified voice from outside, making Emma jump. "This is the FBI. We would like to speak with you. We are placing a radio at the bottom of the front steps for you to communicate."

Emma stared at the captives in the room. "The FBI is here?" she squeaked.

"Oh, thank God." One of the women buried her face in her son's shoulder and started to cry.

They'd all pulled out their gags. Emma and two of the other women had their hands tied in front and were able to work the gags out of the men's mouths. The children climbed onto their mothers' laps and ducked under their tied wrists to get as close as possible, their mothers' arms around them.

"Please pick up the radio," repeated the man on the loudspeaker. "We would like to discuss your situation."

One of the bound men went to the window and pushed aside the curtain with his face. "There's some sort of speaker out there. And I can see a box at the bottom of the steps."

"Do you think it's a trap?" asked the woman with the infant. Her name was Cassidy. "The FBI will shoot whoever picks it up?"

"No," said one of the other women. "They always try to negotiate first."

The door suddenly flew open, and Mark stood in the doorway. "You." He pointed at one of the small twin boys. "Come with me. We're playing a game."

"No! Jett!" His mother threw her tied hands over her son's head and pulled him close. The boy's twin burrowed his way under her arms and buried his face in her chest. "It's okay, boys," she said in low tones. "You're not going with him."

Mark scanned the room, and his gaze landed on Emma. "You'll do. Get up."

"Do what?" she whispered.

"Go get that radio."

"You were going to hide behind a five-year-old?" snapped the twins' mother. "Some big brave man you are. Disgusting."

Mark took a step toward her, anger in his eyes, and Emma jumped to her feet. "I'll do it." She headed for the door, making Mark lunge after her and grab her arm. He slammed the door behind them. He spun Emma around to look her in the eye.

"You'll go down the steps and bring the radio back. You try to run, and I'll shoot you in the back. Then I'll make one of those little boys go get it, and he'll have to step over your dead body."

He's like my dad.

A bully. An asshole.

Emma wasn't scared. She'd dealt with a man threatening her for most of her life. "I'll bring it back." She looked at her tied hands. "Can I pick it up like this?"

"Yes." Mark dragged her to the door, passing several of his men.

She caught some of their gazes. Anger, disgust, pity.

They don't like him sending me out.

Mark opened the front door, keeping himself hidden behind it. "Wait a minute. Where's Baylor?" He looked back at the others. "He was guarding the front, right?"

Nods.

"Fucking asshole split. Or the feds already got him."

He shoved Emma in the back, and she stepped outside, the wide wooden planks creaking under her feet

Freedom.

But I won't run.

Emma fully believed that Mark would shoot her in the back.

She moved to the top of the stairs and scanned the yard. It was silent, and she didn't see the loudspeaker. She moved down the snow-covered stairs and bent to pick up the box. It had a handle, making it easy even with her wrists bound together.

Uncle Tommy had insisted they tie her hands in front of her because she knew how to get out of them. He'd taught her, leaving her with sore wrists and arms for a week.

Not yet, though.

She looked around again, wondering if the FBI could see her.

"Hurry up!"

Emma ran back up the stairs.

◆ ◆ ◆

"Sniper-one reports they sent out a teenage girl wearing zip ties to get the box. Those assholes," said Preston.

Anger shot through Max, and Noelle grabbed his arm. "What'd she look like?" she asked the commander. He repeated her question into his mic.

"Orange coat. Blonde hair. Not very tall."

"That's got to be Emma," said Noelle, relief flooding her voice. "She's okay." She caught herself. "She's okay for now," she added slowly.

"Who is she?" asked Preston.

"She's an eighteen-year-old neighbor of Tom Hammaker, who she calls Uncle Tommy, but they aren't related. Her father's been missing, Gage Chambers. I wonder if he's inside too."

"If he's one of the kidnappers, why would her hands be tied?" asked Max. He looked around the staging area. All the FBI agents, including Mercy, were in position around the cabin. Preston had eyed Max's injuries again and asked him to stick around. Only a few county deputies, ready to transport any arrests, and Noelle were left.

"I don't like all these children on the scene," said Preston.

Max nodded. The FBI carried the scars of incidents like Ruby Ridge and Waco where operations had gone to hell and children had died. He'd thought about it a dozen times already. No doubt it was weighing on Preston even more.

"Let's see if they've answered yet," said Preston. He led them inside the mobile command. Two agents were in front of the monitors, and there were three negotiators at a table with an old-fashioned-looking phone and a handheld radio. Each had a yellow notepad already covered with notes.

Max now had eyes on the scene. Sort of. The monitors only showed what the SWAT team could see, and they were far back from the cabin.

One perk to being injured.

"This is Hank Plessinger with the FBI. Who am I speaking with?" said one of the negotiators.

Hank's voice was mellow but focused. He would try to establish a rapport with Bourdon. If he was unsuccessful, the other man in the group would try. Given everything the FBI now knew about Bourdon, it was decided that Agent Sophia Stearns would only speak if absolutely necessary. Bourdon's history indicated he would not react favorably to a woman.

"This is Hank Plessinger with the FBI. Who am I speaking with?" he repeated.

"You can call me Boogie, Mr. FBI," came a voice over the speakers.

From boogaloo*?*

"Okay, Boogie. How's the situation in there? Does anyone need medical attention?"

"Nope. Everything is great except for the feds in the woods."

"Sorry about that, Boogie, but we're concerned with the safety of the people in that cabin. We know you've got women and children in there."

"Yes, I do."

"What can we do to get them out safely?" asked Hank. Agent Stearns gave him a thumbs-up.

"You can't give me what I want."

"Okay. Then what do you think will work?"

Silence.

"I know there's a six-month-old baby in there. Little Peyton Ross. How about you let her and her mother go? And we can keep talking about what will work for you."

"No one is going anywhere at the moment."

The two other negotiators smiled at each other, and Max replayed Bourdon's words in his head, looking for what they'd liked.

He said "at the moment," implying that it could happen later.

It didn't feel like a big win to Max, but he wasn't a negotiator.

"Well, until then let's figure out what you need. How's the food supply in there? I know there were only supposed to be eleven adults for a few days, and now you've got what, twenty-three? Maybe more? What can we get for you?"

"Hey! What the hell!"

The connection broke, and all three negotiators sat back in their chairs.

"What happened?" asked Preston. "Why'd Bourdon yell?"

"Not sure," said Agent Stearns. "But—"

"This is Sniper-two," came over the speakers. "People have come out of the cabin."

Emma had stayed in the main room after bringing in the box, using her superpower of avoiding notice. Mark and Uncle Tommy had argued about what to say on the radio before answering. Tommy wanted him to let some hostages go for concessions. Mark refused. Mark was refusing everything Tommy suggested.

The men in the room continued to shift their postures and shoot furtive looks at each other, occasionally shaking their heads. "You okay?" one had asked her when she came in with the box. His gaze had been concerned.

They aren't happy with Mark.

Emma wasn't happy either after seeing the children in the next room. It was one thing to kidnap her and lock her in a cell, but to threaten to use one of the little twins the way Mark had showed his true character. She glared fiercely at the other men with guns in the room, causing looks of surprise. All of them had proved that they cared about no one but themselves.

Mark finally answered the radio.

Emma listened. The man on the other end seemed nice. He hadn't threatened or yelled at Mark as she'd expected. She thought he made a good point about not all the hostages needing to stay. Especially baby Peyton. But Mark wasn't giving an inch.

As Emma looked around the room, she noticed one man had slowly backed his way into a bedroom off the big room they were in. A few seconds later, she heard the faint sound of a window sliding open and then a thump as he landed outside.

Would they notice if I did that?

Another man took a step in the direction of the bedroom, casting a nervous glance around. He caught Emma's eye and froze. She jerked her head, telling him to go.

The second man finally eased into the bedroom, out of sight.

Mark suddenly spun around and realized people were missing. *"Hey! What the hell!"* He slammed down the radio and sprinted into the bedroom, yelling that he'd shoot anyone who left. Three of his men took advantage of his distraction and darted out the front door.

Boom. Boom-boom!

The gunfire was so much louder than in her cell.

Mark reappeared at the bedroom door. "The asshole tried to kill me!" He looked around, taking count. *"What the fuck!"*

Four men plus Mark and Tommy were left inside.

And all the hostages.

42

Everything happened at once, and Noelle didn't know where to look. Loud reports abruptly crackled through the command center's speakers.

"Sniper-two! A man crawled out a window on the first level. He is armed and running toward seven o'clock. The last outside guard is going with him."

"Copy. Blue-six has eyes on them. We've got them."

"Sniper-two! A second man came out the same window. He's firing back at the cabin. Now running toward nine o'clock."

"Copy. This is Blue-one. I've got him."

"Sniper-one! Three men just came out the front door. All are armed."

"Rest of blue team. Move in," ordered Preston.

Several camera views on the monitors suddenly jerked and bounced, indicating several members rushing forward. *"Put down your weapons! Put down your weapons! Hands where I can see them! On the ground! Now! Move! Move! On the ground!"*

The three men appeared on the monitor views. They'd already dropped their guns and were lowering themselves to the ground.

"Total of six in custody."

"Counting Baylor, that's seven," said Noelle. "Six more to go."

"And all the hostages," said Max.

"Things definitely went to hell inside," said the negotiator. "I hope no one's hurt. One of them fired back at the cabin." He looked at Preston. "I don't know if we can get him back on the radio."

"Try."

Emma held perfectly still, trying to avoid pulling attention to herself.

"Get those kids and women out of here!" Tommy yelled at Mark. "They're gonna come in shooting, and their deaths will be on your hands!"

"This is how it's supposed to happen!" shouted Mark, advancing on Tommy. "We need to take advantage of the chaos! If people die, they die!"

"Fuck you and your chaos goals. You're just trying to get people killed." Tommy pointed at the six hostages still sitting on the floor. "You just want payback for your time in prison! This isn't how to do it!"

The radio from the FBI started to buzz.

Mark ignored it and swung his pistol around at the four of his men who were left. *"Do you want to leave? Do you want to run away too?"*

All four men shook their heads. But Emma knew by the fear in their eyes that they lied.

"Let the children go!" shouted Tommy. "No one is going to respect you for getting kids killed!"

"What about Waco?" Mark yelled back. "The FBI never recovered from that scandal, and part of the reason was they were responsible for getting those kids killed! It will never be forgotten!" Mark's eyes glowed, making Emma take a step closer to the wall.

He wants to be remembered.

He doesn't care who dies.

"What happened to you, *old man*?" Mark got in Tommy's face, his pistol still in his hand. "You used to be a *leader*! Now you hide and kiss up to the FBI! You're a disgrace to the movement."

The radio kept buzzing.

"Movement?" Tommy practically spit the word. "There's no movement! All I see is a bunch of guys feeling sorry for themselves, so y'all get together for a circle jerk!" His gaze swept Mark's four remaining men. "I wouldn't be here if you hadn't grabbed Emma and threatened to cut her head off if I didn't come!"

Suddenly dizzy, Emma pressed into the wall and slid to the floor.

Mark will kill me without a second thought.

Every gaze in the room was on her. Sympathy from the hostages. Horror and anger from Mark's men. She tried to cover her eyes with her bound wrists, the weight of the people's stares crushing her.

"Mark." The kidnapper closest to Emma stepped forward, placing himself between Emma and the man. "This isn't—"

"Shut your fucking face!" Mark roared. "I'm in charge here! I say what happens! You!" He waved a gun at one of his other men. "Get the rest of those hostages out here! It's time we all had a come-to-Jesus moment!"

What's he going to do to us?

Emma cowered on her knees, curled up in the smallest ball possible, her cheek pressed to the floor.

Will he shoot all of us?

The man Mark had ordered paused and then marched across the room. He flung open the door to the hostage room and froze. He whirled around, his face white. *"They're gone!"*

Emma's eyes squeezed shut at Mark's roar.

"Sniper-one. We've got movement! People are climbing out a window on the other side of the cabin. It's the hostages! Kids are being handed out the window."

Max scanned the monitors. None of the SWAT helmet cameras were aimed at that window.

"How many, Sniper-one?" asked Preston.

"Two women, a baby, two children, another woman—maybe a teen—more kids being handed out."

"Teen?" Noelle whispered to Max.

"Maybe," he said.

"Sniper-one. We need backup to get these people to safety."

"Copy, Sniper-one." Preston looked at Max and Noelle. "I'll direct the rest of the county deputies to get over there. Go!"

Max grabbed their helmets, shoving one on his head and handing the other to Noelle as they dashed out the door. They still wore their vests and pistols. Max had his AR-15 and Noelle grabbed a lone shield left outside the command center. They sprinted around the RV and met up with three deputies responding to Preston's callout.

Max was puffing by the time they'd covered two hundred yards in a full-out sprint. Over the radio he heard that male hostages were trying to come out the window but were struggling because their hands were tied behind them. One member of the entry team got over there, cut their bindings, and hauled them out.

Max spotted the BearCat up ahead. The six men from the militia who'd abandoned the cabin were on their stomachs in the snow, two SWAT members watching over them. "Go!" Max told the two men, breathing heavily. "We'll watch the guys in custody." The two SWAT members ran back to join their team.

Max pointed at two of the deputies who'd come with him. "You two watch these six. Keep them on the ground. Noelle and you with me," he told her and the remaining deputy. They jogged around the perimeter and spotted the group of hostages being led by one SWAT team member.

The hostages were all barefoot.

Max took over, guiding the hostages away at a jog, and the SWAT team member darted back to his position.

No Emma or Garrison.

Noelle picked up and ran with a toddler who stared at her helmet. His feet were like ice. "Where's the teenager?" she asked the adults. "Blonde hair?"

"Don't know," said one of the men, running beside her. "Still inside somewhere. My wife's still in there!"

"Mine too!" said the other man. "All our spouses are."

Max had swept up one of the twins. "You Jett or Chase?" he asked the barefoot boy as he ran with him in his arms. The boy said nothing.

"Jett," said Tamara, who had her other boy.

"How'd you get out?" asked Noelle.

"Our hands were zip-tied in front, and I showed the others how to break them," said a woman, panting as they ran. "We'd discussed going out the window but knew there was a guard out there. Once we heard all the yelling inside, we decided to break them and go. But the men's wouldn't break since they were tied in back."

"I was willing to fall on my face out the window to get out of there," said one of the men. "The leader guy inside there is nuts."

Max led the group beyond the SWAT perimeter to the BearCat, and Jett started to shake with cold.

Or shock.

"Everyone in the BearCat. We'll get the heat going." He handed Jett off to one of the male hostages, who climbed into the back of the SWAT vehicle. Noelle yanked open the driver's door and turned on the engine. A few seconds later, the fans started blowing heat in the back and all the hostages were inside.

"This is Agent Rhodes," Max said into the radio. "Hostages are in the BearCat. Still six adult hostages and one teen hostage inside the cabin."

"Copy, Agent Rhodes," said Preston. "Our attempts to reestablish contact inside aren't being answered. Send the deputies back with the six militia. I want to talk to them."

The deputies heard and started gathering up the men who were in the snow.

"Send back any coats or boots you can find," Max told the deputies.

The hostages had little to wear. Noelle shucked off her vest and removed her coat, then wrapped up two of the children in it. Max did the same.

"Can you tell me what's happening inside?" Max asked the group as he strapped his vest back on.

"We were in that room the whole time," said Tamara, snuggling both her boys in Max's coat. "This morning that group broke into the house, shooting up the ceiling and yelling and splitting us away from the men. Then later they took two of the women and sent in their husbands."

"My wife's the county DA," said one of the men. "From what I gathered while in the main room, the leader's furious with the judicial branch. The governor and the FBI too. One of the guys is the head of the local FBI office. Jeff Garrison."

"That's my boss," said Max. "Anything helpful you noticed that I can pass on to the entry team?"

"They're going in?" asked the other man, fear in his eyes.

His wife's still there.

"Not yet," said Max. "But it may come to that."

"With their numbers down, I doubt the entrances are being guarded as thoroughly from the inside," said the DA's husband. "There's an outer door into the daylight basement, which has stairs inside up to the main level. That's worth investigating." He leaned his head against the wall of the BearCat, his eyes closed. "Please get them out safely." The other hostages murmured in agreement.

"That's their goal," said Max, meeting Noelle's worried gaze as he passed on the information to Preston.

We can only hope for the best.

Emma's gaze followed the angry leader inside the cabin.

He's going to kill us all.

Mark turned his fury on the man who'd reported the hostages were gone. Mark grabbed him by the shirt and shoved his gun into his jaw.

The radio buzzed again, pulling Mark's attention. He shoved the man toward the radio on the island. *"Get that thing out of here!"* The man's stomach slammed into the edge of the island, forcing air out of his lungs, and he tipped over toward Tommy, who steadied him, keeping him on his feet.

"I said *get it out*!" Mark yelled at him.

The man sucked in a loud, rattling breath, snatched up the radio, and ran down the hall toward the front door, flinging it open. He hurled the radio out the door and then looked back. Emma met his scared gaze.

She caught her breath as he tore out the door, sprinting down the steps, his arms in the air, screaming, "Don't shoot, don't shoot!"

Three guards left. Plus Mark and Uncle Tommy.

The front door hung open, letting in a rush of cold air. Emma cringed, expecting to hear gunfire. But she only heard far-off shouts.

Mark realized what had happened, and his face went red. "That fucking pussy chickenshit asshole!" He paced back and forth, muttering to himself, shooting angry looks at her and the hostages. Tommy still sat at the kitchen island, his hands clenched on its edge.

"Be ready," he mouthed silently at her.

Emma didn't know what to be ready for, but she nodded.

"Each of you!" Mark gestured at his three remaining men. "Grab two hostages each! Get them on their feet."

The men looked at each other, then each grabbed two hostages. "Front door, deck door, downstairs door," Mark said, as he pointed to each man and his hostages. "On my order, follow them out your door. Make them run. Shoot them in the back if they don't! Then run your ass off and hide in the woods. They can't watch all of us at once." Mark put on his heavy coat and slung his rifle over his shoulder as he spoke.

He strode to Emma and hooked a hand under her armpit, hauling her to her feet and pushing her toward the door to the deck.

I'm his hostage.

"Now! Everyone go!"

The man and two hostages in front of Emma ran out the door to the deck. Mark pushed her toward the same door.

Emma looked back to Tommy and slammed on her brakes. Tommy stood at the island with a gun pointed at Mark.

That's the gun from the man who grabbed the radio.

Mark bumped into her and then turned to see what she was looking at. *"Hammaker! Don't you fucking dare!"* He raised his gun toward Tommy.

Emma dropped to the ground as two gunshots sounded. Then Mark pulled her to her feet again. "Go!" He shoved her out the door, and she struggled against him to look back. Tommy was on the ground, not moving.

"Nooo!" she screamed.

43

"Blue-six! I've got three people running out the front."

"Sniper-two! Three people are coming out the basement door."

"—going in different directions!"

"—out the back door!"

Two gunshots sounded.

The shouting voices jumbled together over the radio as several more reports came in at once.

Max tried to make sense of them. "Is it the hostages?"

"Let's go," said Noelle, grabbing her shield and running toward the perimeter. Max took his AR off his shoulder and followed. Voices continued to shout through his radio.

"It sounds like a mass exit," he told Noelle as he followed her, weaving through the pines.

They reached the edge of the woods and stopped, each taking cover behind a tree. Max saw SWAT running between the vehicles in front of the cabin as they shouted, "Get down, get down, get down!"

"People to the east!" shouted Noelle.

Three more people were running toward the woods from the side of the cabin. Several SWAT peeled off and went after them, shouting orders.

Two are hostages.

Their hands were bound, making them stumble as they ran.

"On the right!" Max told Noelle as three more people on the other side of the house ran for the woods. One SWAT team member ran after them.

"I'll back him up." Noelle sprinted after the agent.

"Damn," muttered Max. Shouts were coming through the radio and echoing out of the woods.

There.

A man ran into the woods from the east side of the home, pushing a small figure in an orange coat. Max lifted his AR and looked through the scope.

Emma. And Bourdon.

Max was too far away. He sprinted at an angle, trying to get ahead of the duo. Emma was fighting back, slowing her pace and pushing against her captor. Bourdon grabbed her arm and hauled her through the snow with brute power. A gun in his other hand.

Max's chest heaved as he ran. The snow was a foot deep and hid every rock and crevice. He stumbled a dozen times.

I've got to get ahead of them.

Emma and Bourdon were having the same problem with the snow. Suddenly Emma stopped and raised her bound hands over her head. She whipped them down as if to touch her elbows to her shoulder blades. Her hands flew apart, the zip tie broken. She turned and slammed her palms into Bourdon's chest. Bourdon laughed and grabbed her hair, yanking up.

As he continued to run, Max saw Emma's feet leave the snow. He estimated he was twenty yards away. He came to a stop, tucked the butt of his gun into his shoulder, and looked through his scope.

"Bourdon! Put down the gun!" shouted Max.

The man swung his arm around Emma's neck, pulled her to his chest, and ground his gun into her skull. "I'll kill her!" Bourdon yelled back. "Let me pass!"

Emma's face filled Max's scope; her green eyes were wide with fear.

Green eyes.

Déjà vu swept through him. He'd been in this position before. His decision to shoot had taken a teenager's life and put Max's in a tailspin.

Max blinked rapidly as Emma's blonde hair and light eyes moved through his crosshairs and called up a face from his past. Another terrified girl being used as a human shield.

Eleanor. The twelve-year-old cousin of Jacob McHale.

The boy Max had shot and killed.

I'm breathing too hard.

I did the right thing. Jacob was ready to kill his cousin.

Max adjusted his aim up a fraction, and part of Bourdon's face came into view. He was ducking behind Emma's head.

I should've fired immediately at Bourdon. Not shouted at him.

It would have been justified.

Am I scared it'll create more life-altering consequences?

"Let her go!" shouted Max. "It's all over, Bourdon!"

"I'll kill her!" he shrieked back. "I'll do it! Doesn't matter that she's a woman! I've done it before!"

Max didn't doubt him.

He killed Rachel. I know he'll do it again. Right here, right now.

I must stop him.

"Let her go, Bourdon!" Noelle's voice sounded from far to Max's right.

Bourdon swerved to look in her direction.

Now.

Max fired.

Bourdon dropped to the ground in an explosion of blood and brains, landing on Emma as she screamed.

Max lowered his rifle, his heart pounding, her wails filling his ears, but he knew Emma was safe.

His shot had gone through Bourdon's right eye.

I did the right thing.

It's over.

◆ ◆ ◆

Screaming, Emma shoved Bourdon's arm off her chest and rolled away as fast as she could. She pushed up to her hands and knees, staring at the man who'd said he would kill her.

One eye was a red, bloody hole. The other looked blankly up at the falling snow. The white fluff around his head was covered with red, chunky spray.

He's dead.

"Emma!"

She blinked. Detective Marshall sprinted toward her, a pistol in her hand. To the right, a man with a rifle approached more slowly, his gaze fixed on Mark.

That man shot him. She scrambled unsteadily to her feet, fear slicing through her veins, as she scanned the cabin and woods, terrified of more danger.

I should run.

"Emma!" Detective Marshall halted a few yards away. She holstered her gun and held her hands out as if to stop her. "You're safe, honey. It's over. It's all over."

Emma held her gaze, every cell in her body screaming that nothing was over. She stumbled back two steps and spun in a circle, searching for more threats.

"Emma. It's okay. He's dead. Everyone else is in custody. It's *over*," the detective repeated, still holding out her hands as she slowly approached. The man who'd fired stood back, watching, somehow knowing he shouldn't come closer.

"You shot him," Emma said, her voice trembling as she met his gaze.

"I did. You're safe now." He didn't move.

"That's Max, Emma," said Detective Marshall. "He's a friend."

Emma looked at the motionless man in the snow, his gun a yard away.

He shot Uncle Tommy.

"Uncle Tommy!" Emma lurched away, stumbling until she caught her stride, and ran toward the cabin. *"Uncle Tommy!"*

"Emma, wait!" The detective ran behind her.

Is he dead?

Her brain wouldn't accept it. She tore up the steps to the cabin's back deck. The slider was still open, the sheer curtains waving through in the breeze. Emma darted through the door and slammed to a stop. Detective Marshall came through the door and halted beside her.

"Oh, Emma." She gripped Emma's shoulder.

Two men in SWAT gear were on their knees next to Uncle Tommy, who was spread out on the floor, blood pooling around him. "Can you apply pressure?" one yelled, looking at them. "We've called for the medic!"

The detective was at his side in a flash. Emma approached more slowly, taking in the blood, the anxiety on the faces.

He's not going to make it.

"Uncle Tommy?" she asked, kneeling at his head, tears burning down her cheeks.

He opened his eyes. "You okay?"

"I'm fine. You're going to be fine." She set a hand on his forehead.

Suddenly anger flooded his gaze as he looked past her. Emma glanced back. It was the man—Max—who'd saved her. He was staring at Uncle Tommy, his face blank.

"You—you!" Uncle Tommy spit out, blood wetting his lips, hatred in his eyes.

He's confused.

"That man saved me, Uncle Tommy. Mark had a gun to my head. He was going to kill me." Her voice shook. "That man shot before Mark could."

Some of the fire went out of the old man's gaze.

Max knelt behind Emma. "I know it was you who sent those things," he said quietly, looking at Uncle Tommy. "I understand why you did it, but I had no choice that day. Just like I had no choice today except to save Emma."

What is he talking about?

Uncle Tommy closed his eyes.

"No!" shrieked Emma.

"Where's the medic?" The men and Detective Marshall worked more frantically.

Uncle Tommy's eyes opened. The anger was gone, resignation left behind. "Thank you," he whispered, looking at Max. Then he met Emma's gaze. "Your daddy's dead, girl. Mark killed him months ago." He struggled to get the words out. "I didn't know until today. I'm sorry, baby."

Shock froze her lungs.

I don't know what to say.

"It's okay to hate him, Emma." Breathing hard, Uncle Tommy licked his lips, spreading more blood. "I love you, girl. Always have."

"I love you too," she said, her tongue tripping over the words, misery filling her. No one had said the words to her since her mother left.

Someone finally loves me, and he's gonna die.

"Max," said Detective Marshall. She motioned for the man to take her place, and she moved to Emma, wrapping an arm around her shoulders. "I'm so sorry," she whispered, pressing her cheek against Emma's hair.

Uncle Tommy's eyes were still open.

But he was no longer there.

Emma leaned into the detective and cried, her heart breaking again.

44

One week later

Noelle sat on her back patio, wrapped up in a fleece blanket, the gas firepit making cheery flames nearby. Nearly all the local snow had melted, but it'd left a thick white coat on the Cascades. The deep-blue sky and white mountains made a stunning view from her chair.

But her favorite view at the moment, way out by the stable, was of Emma leading the old horse Harley out to a pasture as Ina Smythe watched from close by. The older woman had stopped by three times in the past week to check on Emma. "She's our girl now," she'd told Noelle. "She needs looking after."

It was nice to have a horse in the stable. Noelle had doubted she'd ever use the facility, but now she wondered if Harley needed a companion. She didn't like the idea of the old gelding alone in the big stable at night.

How quickly I went from no horses to possibly multiple.

Or maybe a goat or donkey would be fun. She'd read somewhere they made good horse companions.

She'd brought Emma home with her the first night, promising she could stay as long as she wanted. The teenager had been distraught about Hammaker's death. He'd been the only person who'd been kind to her in a long time. Noelle had driven Emma to her old home to grab whatever she needed. To Noelle's shock, all she'd done was dig in her mattress to get a charm bracelet.

"It was my mother's," she'd told Noelle. "It's all I have left."

She had wanted nothing else from the house. Except Cornbread. She couldn't catch the cat, so they'd borrowed a cat trap. He'd been furious inside the trap, hissing and spitting, but he'd calmed down when he realized Emma was nearby.

Then they'd gone to get her clothing and check on Harley at Hammaker's farm, where Noelle had promised the tearful teenager that the gelding could live out his days in her stable.

A wild cat, a bracelet, and an old horse.

It wasn't a bad set of possessions.

Her father's body hadn't been found. Mark Bourdon's rented town house had been searched from top to bottom. Gage Chambers had probably been dumped somewhere like Michael Munoz.

After all the men involved had been interviewed, it appeared that Mark Bourdon simply got rid of people who disagreed with him or caused problems. When Gage Chambers hadn't returned to the meetings, Mark had told them he'd dropped out. The same had happened with Michael Munoz. But Eli Chisholm had seemed to be more deeply involved. The other men believed he'd helped with getting rid of Gage Chambers in return for his truck. But something had gone south, and Mark had had him killed.

No camera had covered him when he'd placed the body in the judge's trunk. But Noelle's money was on Monday evening, when the judge and his wife had gone to a restaurant and he'd parked down the street instead of in the lot to avoid door dings.

Mark's home had been a huge source of information on boogaloo, conspiracy theories, and white nationalism. He'd come out of prison with a new tattoo, indoctrinated and convinced that he could lead the group he'd belonged to years before, when Tommy Hammaker had been the leader.

But suddenly he was using his power for retribution against people who'd disagreed with him. As he'd done with Gage Chambers, who'd once been a close friend of Mark's. Now his body couldn't be found.

Noelle's phone chimed. Max had inputted the code to open her gate. She smiled, watching on her phone as his vehicle came up her long driveway. He'd been staying at her place as much as Emma.

Almost losing him in the bunker explosion had made her realize how important he was to her. Her life would have never been the same. In a short time, Max had made a huge impact, and she couldn't imagine being without him. This wasn't a time to be taking things slowly. Soon she'd ask him to move in.

I know he'll agree.

◆ ◆ ◆

Max paused outside Noelle's front door, then opened it and walked right in.

That was a first.

"Noelle?" She probably knew he was on the premises, but it seemed polite to announce himself. "Emma?" No answer to either name.

"Meowrrr."

The orange cat did a figure eight between Max's legs. "Hey, Cornbread." He bent over and scratched the cat's head. The outside cat had rapidly become an inside cat when he realized he had a heated bed and several cat condos to nap on and scratch and that his food bowl was always full.

Yeah, it's a good life here.

Max had brought a bag with more clothes. He'd taken a good-natured ribbing from Keira and TJ about his new sleeping situation. The couple had spent two nights in hiding and then had been shocked to hear what had occurred while they were gone.

Keira had canceled her sisters' weekend visit. She had told them what Max had gone through, including being forced to shoot to save a life, but nothing had changed on their end. Radio silence from both women and Max's mother continued.

There's nothing I can do. I've tried.

It was time to move on. If they had a change of heart, they could reach out to him. He'd always be ready to have them in his life again.

He dropped his bag in the primary bedroom and went looking for Noelle, soon spotting her wrapped up in a blanket on a lounger on the huge patio. The wall of windows framed her with the mountains in the background, sharp against the blue sky.

How is this my life?

He slid open the glass door, pulled up a chair next to her, and handed her *their* latte.

"Hey, beautiful," he said, leaning in for a kiss.

After a long moment she pushed him away and studied his face. "How can it be worse than this morning?"

"I know. I can't wait to get through this part." He was peeling. And peeling and peeling. No matter what he put on the burned area, it eventually flaked off and peeled some more. He found white flakes all over the front of his clothes every day.

Hammaker's second bunker hadn't been wired with a booby trap like the first. The consensus from the interviews with Bourdon's men was that Hammaker had cleaned out the weapons and explosives over the years but left the timed booby trap. Possibly it had been payback for anyone who attempted to steal from him—even if they'd discovered an empty bunker.

The men said Hammaker hadn't been around their group in years. They'd been surprised to see him show up at the cabins. Later they'd understood he was only there because Bourdon had threatened to kill Emma if he didn't cooperate. Bourdon had realized he was losing support; he'd thought Hammaker's presence would help rally his men behind him.

That plan had slowly crumbled in the cabin.

Max sat back in his chair and put up his feet, holding her hand. He couldn't wait for summer and warm breezes as they sat outside. A far-off movement caught his eye, and he spotted Emma out with the horse.

As usual.

If she wasn't cuddling Cornbread—who'd rapidly morphed into a lazy lap cat—she was out with Harley.

"Mercy told me she talked to Cory," said Noelle. "She decided it was the right thing to tell Cory that Rachel was pregnant when she died."

"How did she take it?"

"Not great, but better than Mercy had hoped. She's pulling together her sister's poems. She's planning to print them in a book."

"That's great," said Max. "It might be very healing."

"I hope so."

"Today Emma asked if I could look for her mother," Noelle said quietly. "I'd already done a little checking. It's been ten years, and I found nothing recent under her name."

"She might be dead," said Max. "I don't know if I would have ever trusted Gage Chambers."

"I wouldn't have," said Noelle. "The more stories Emma tells me, the more I hate him. It wouldn't surprise me one bit if he killed his wife."

"Do you think Emma has considered that?" asked Max.

"Yes. She told me her suspicions today."

"That poor girl," said Max. "She's had a tough life."

"I'm determined to change that," said Noelle. "I called my lawyer about setting up a trust for her. But I know she needs more than money. She needs friends. And a community. I'm going to try my hardest with that too."

"You're a very good person," said Max, surprised that he loved her more than ever after hearing her say that. He hadn't thought a deeper love was possible.

"You're a good person too," she said, sitting up in her lounger. "More than I deserve. That damned explosion nearly took you away before we'd really gotten started. I hated that I didn't know if you were dead or alive for several minutes. It tore me apart."

"I'm sorry," said Max. "I didn't intend to almost die."

"Not funny!" She glared at him. "But even with your poor sense of humor, I love you a lot. More than a lot."

"I love you too."

She's leading up to something.

"I know I've insisted that we take it slow," she said, gripping both his hands in hers. "But I'm over that."

"You are?" Something hopeful swelled inside him. He'd been sticking close since he nearly died, and he thought he'd felt a change in her, but he'd decided to not say anything, still worried that he might scare her off.

I've known since day one that she was the woman for me.

Keeping his mouth shut had been the ultimate exercise in patience.

"Absolutely. You could say I've had the ultimate wake-up call." She took a deep breath. "I want more of you in my life—no, I want it all if you're willing." She held his gaze, her blue eyes intense. But lurking behind her eyes, he saw a flicker of fear that he would turn her down.

Never in a million years.

"I've wanted to be with you since I first saw you," he told her as he pulled her onto his lap. "But I couldn't step over that professional line." He kissed her neck, leading up to her ear. "Once we got past that, I was willing to wait for you to come around. But you are so stubborn, and *damn*, it's been hard to wait."

She tipped her head back and narrowed her eyes at him. "Is that an insult?"

"Nope. That's the truth. I love you, and I can't wait to see what our life together will be like."

It'll be perfect.

ACKNOWLEDGMENTS

All my books have been published due to the hard work of the Montlake crew. I would still be cleaning teeth without them. Thank you especially to my editor Anh Schluep, who has guided my books through the publishers' channels for a decade. And as always a big thank-you to Charlotte Herscher, who has edited all my novels with a skilled and caring hand. I've learned so much from her. Meg Ruley is my agent and head cheerleader. She's always there when I need some help or to be talked off a ledge—a figurative writing ledge. I'm very lucky to have such a strong crew of women watching my back and lighting my way.

I hope my readers have enjoyed getting to know Noelle and her world a little more. I knew when she confidently strode onto the page in the Columbia River series that this was a character who deserved more than being a secondary character or being the primary character in just one novel. I don't plan ahead for my books. I never know what will happen in the next one until I sit down to write it. So I love it when I stumble across a character who informs me, "I've got this. I can carry a series." It's only happened a few times for me. Mercy Kilpatrick, of course, and before her Mason Callahan and Ava McLane.

More Noelle books are coming. I hope you enjoy the journey with me.

About the Author

Photo © 2016 Rebekah Jule Photography

Kendra Elliot is the *Wall Street Journal* and Amazon Charts bestselling author of the Mercy Kilpatrick novels, the Columbia River novels, the Bone Secrets series, and the Callahan & McLane series. She is a three-time winner of the Daphne du Maurier Award, an International Thriller Writers Award finalist, and an RT Award finalist. Kendra was born and raised in the rainy Pacific Northwest but now lives in flip-flops. For more information, visit www.kendraelliot.com.